Conwy Lloyd Morgan

The Springs of Conduct

Conwy Lloyd Morgan

The Springs of Conduct

ISBN/EAN: 9783337365875

Printed in Europe, USA, Canada, Australia, Japan

Cover: Foto ©Andreas Hilbeck / pixelio.de

More available books at **www.hansebooks.com**

THE

SPRINGS OF CONDUCT

BY

C. LLOYD MORGAN, F.G.S.

PRINCIPAL OF UNIVERSITY COLLEGE, BRISTOL

AUTHOR OF 'ANIMAL LIFE AND INTELLIGENCE,' ETC.

NEW EDITION

LONDON

EDWARD ARNOLD

Publisher to the India Office

1892

PREFACE TO THE CHEAPER EDITION.

When I consented to a cheaper re-issue of this volume I reserved to myself the right of distinctly stating that, though I am more than ever convinced of the truth of the views therein set forth, so far as their general drift and tendency is concerned, I am not now, after some years of further thought and study, prepared to maintain *all* the opinions therein expressed. In a word, I have to confess that my views have undergone some alteration in the course of their development. And I am not ashamed of the confession.

It is not my intention to burden this preface with any account of the changes that my opinions have undergone. I may, however, state that sundry developments may be found in my work on *Animal Life and Intelligence ;* that the tendency of my views on ethics may be partially gathered from an article on *The Morality of Animals* in *The National Review**; and that certain conclusions as to the nature of the connection of consciousness and neural energy will be found in *The Monist†*, etc.

* November, 1891.   † January, 1892.

Some of the questions herein discussed I propose to reconsider in a forthcoming volume on *Social Evolution.* The plan and scope of the two works are, however, so widely different that this does not appear to me an adequate reason why I should withhold my consent to the reissue of ' The Springs of Conduct.'

C. LLOYD MORGAN.

FEBRUARY, 1892.

CONTENTS.

PART I.
KNOWLEDGE.

PART II.
THE STUDY OF NATURE.

PART III.
THROUGH FEELING TO CONDUCT.

CHAPTER I.

CHAPTER II.

CHAPTER III.

ERRATA.

Page 103, lines 20 and 22, *for* "isomeric" *read* "metabolic."
,,   137, line 1, *for* "isomeric" *read* "metabolic."
,,   175, line 25, *for* "do" *read* "are."
,,   192, line 5, *for* "affectation" *read* "affection."

PART I.
KNOWLEDGE.

"First I shall inquire into the originals of those ideas, notions, or whatever else you please to call them, which a man observes and is conscious to himself he has in his mind; and the ways whereby the understanding comes to be furnished with them."—JOHN LOCKE.

THE

SPRINGS OF CONDUCT.

CHAPTER I.

GENERAL CONCEPTIONS.

"It is the thought of past humanity imbedded in our language which makes Nature to be what she is for us ; and the world in which we live is a world of general conceptions."—W. K. CLIFFORD.

LOOKING out over the ocean I see in the far distance a white speck, and tell my companion that it is a ship. ·

Nothing can well be simpler, at any rate at first sight, than the mental process which I describe in these few words. But simple as it is, it will serve as an introduction to the subject of this chapter. A little consideration, moreover, will show that it is not quite so simple as, at first sight, it appears to be. There would seem to be at least four definite stages in the process. In the first place I receive a stimulus or impression from without. Then I perceive that it is due to a white and distant object. Thence arises so complex a conception as that of a ship. Whereupon I make use of a word or symbol by means of which I may call up in my neighbour's mind a similar idea. Sensation, perception, conception, symbolization—these are the stages in the process.

I mark out these four stages, not with any idea of giving a complete analysis of the mental operation, but simply with the object of drawing attention to the fact that the ultimate *product* is the result of a *process*, and that it is not difficult to point out some of the steps of the process. For so complete is the fusion of the stages, so rapid is the evolution of the idea, that the very fact that there are stages, that it is an evolution, is apt to be lost sight of.

Let us now take the first two stages and see what is involved in them. When we get no higher than the perception that the external object, which gives rise to the process, is something white and distant, we find that much is involved beside the mere reception of an impression from without. For the impression is recognized ; that is to say, it is perceived to be like certain sensations previously received and unlike others. In addition to the impression of sensation originated from without, there arises an impression of relation originated from within. Nor is this by any means all : for recognition implies memory ; it involves a number of mental ideas or images of former sensations with which the new sensation may be compared. I say a number of mental ideas or images, because it is quite clear that it is impossible to recognize the similarity of a given sensation to other sensations previously received, unless there be a number of different sensations, represented in ideas, from among which the like may be chosen and the unlike rejected. So that the memory implied must be complex, must supply many remembered impressions.

And is this all ? By no means. The object is perceived, not only as white, but as distant. It is instinctively perceived in its relations in space. It is there and not here. In the mere recognition of it, moreover, as like certain sensations previously received, it is also recognized as differing from them in being now and not then. It is instinctively perceived in its relations in time. While the very fact of its being referred to something external, which is supposed to have given rise to it, implies an instinctive recognition of a yet further relationship, that of causation. Thus the simple perception of the impression, as due to a white and distant object, implies memory, implies recognition involving impressions of the relation of likeness and unlikeness, and is only possible under conditions of time and space and causation.

Let us here notice how we have already a basis for all science; for science is the outcome of knowledge, and knowledge consists in referring events and phenomena to their causes, and in ascertaining their resemblances and differences as manifested in space and time. Upon the perception of likeness and unlikeness, in fact, are based the sciences of observation and experiment; and when the perception of likeness develops into the perception of equality, the foundation-stone of the abstract science of mathematics is securely laid.

And now we may pass on to the third stage. We shall at once be struck with the enormous increase in complexity. For the comparatively simple perception of a white and distant object suggests so complex an idea as that of a ship. Now, suppose that, instead of standing by the sea-shore, I had been gazing across a wide stretch of American prairie-land; it is clear that the perception of a white and distant object would have suggested anything else rather than a ship. This is a commonplace. But from this commonplace it will be seen that, in forming an opinion as to the nature of the object, I was instinctively guided by the influence of surrounding conditions; and that the conception *ship* was a joint product of a special perception and a number of more general perceptions. So

that, indeed, it would seem that there was already a partial
connection or association between my ideas of a blue
stretch of ocean and of a ship, which it only wanted the
perception of a white speck to make complete.

Here, then, we come upon two important facts with
regard to the contents of my mind and the processes that
go on therein : first, that certain ideas are already more
or less completely associated together, the association of
internal ideas being moulded in correspondence with the
association of external things ; and secondly, that the
simple perception of a portion of an object can, under
appropriate conditions, cause the mind to *construct an idea*
of the object as a whole.

Were this volume a treatise on psychology instead of
just a talk with my readers on science and conduct, it
would be my duty to enter into the manner in which such
an ideal construction as that which I symbolize by the
word *ship* may have been formed. As it is, it is sufficient
to indicate that such a general conception is the result of a
process of gradual fusion and storage ; and that this process
of fusion and storage has been going on through generations and generations of ancestors. Our individual constructions take of course their colouring from our individual experience. But the rough sketches of the objects
we construct are a part of the heritage of our mental constitution. And these rough sketches, I say, are the outcome
of a long-continued process of fusion and storage. Certain
sensations enter into relations and are fused into perceptions ; and then a number of perceptions, thus formed,
themselves enter into relations, and are themselves fused
together into conceptions which, especially under the
influence of language, undergo a process of generalization,
so that the ideal construction comes to stand for a group of
more or less similar objects, symbolized in our speech by

such a group-word as *ship.* Such is the process of fusion. But accompanying and rendering possible these successive fusions is that all-important process of storage, not only storage in the individual memory, but storage in such a form as to render the power of reproducing the matter stored capable of being transmitted to offspring.

Truly wonderful, truly marvellous, is this double process of storage by memory and of the inheritance of mental constitution. Nor does the study of the organic processes which are the objective aspects of these mental processes remove one whit of the mystery. But, at the same time, we must remember that, mysterious as they are (if that current phrase be the appropriate one), they are only mysterious in the sense that every natural phenomenon is mysterious. They are neither more nor less mysterious than the fall of a stone to the ground. In such mystery all ultimate facts are shrouded; and the phenomena of mind and body do but participate in that mystery.

Let us, then, return to, and definitely grasp, the fact that an object as we know it is a thing *we construct for ourselves.* All that we receive from without is a bare suggestion; at the bidding of which suggestion we construct the object by the operation of that mental constitution which we received by inheritance and which has been modified by our personal experience. The rough sketch of the object thus embedded in our mental constitution is the result of a synthesis of certain of its qualities; and these qualities are the relations which the body is perceived to bear to other surrounding objects and to ourselves. A theoretically perfect idea of any object, a perfect portrait, would involve the perception of all the possible relations of that object to ourselves and to surrounding objects. Such a conception is, however, obviously impossible to beings of limited capacities. As a rule our synthesis is the merest sketch; it comprises a

very few of these possible relations—just those important
few which are suggested by immediate association. To a
child, for example, the sight of crystallized sugar-candy
suggests by association a certain taste, and smell, and an
idea of its size, shape, and " feel." The object he constructs
is built up of this group of associated qualities. But to
these qualities suggested by association a man of science
may add on reflection a great number of others. He builds
up a new and more complex object, which is the result of
his synthesis by reflection. Of this object, indeed, he cannot
get a clear-cut and definite image. But by letting his
mind's eye range backwards and forwards over it he builds
for himself a fuller and more complex ideal construction,
he reaches a richer general conception. But no man of
science, no human being, can grasp any object in the
entirety of its relations. Every synthesis must be incom-
plete, must be a sketch ; a perfect synthesis, a true portrait,
is impossible to a being of limited capacities. A perfect
knowledge of any single object would involve a perfect
knowledge of the universe.

·   We reach the conclusion, then, that, in my mind, there
are certain stores of memories more or less closely linked
together ; the association of ideas being mainly determined
by the association of things. And when I look out over
the sea, I receive a certain complex of impressions which
calls forth a still more massive complex of memories ; just
as the striking of a chord on a musical instrument calls
into being more or less rich harmonics. The complex of
sensations and the complex of memories, entering into
relations of likeness and unlikeness in space and time
under the influence of causation, then give rise to the
general conception that I have of a ship sailing upon
the sea.

Now, when I tell my companion that I see a ship, it is

quite obvious that I do not attempt in any way to describe the mental process, thus briefly sketched, by which I have myself reached this conclusion. All that I wish to do is to suggest a like idea to a mind which I have much reason for believing to be somewhat similar to my own. And I do so by means of the word *ship*, which I believe calls up, by association of ideas, in his mind a general conception more or less like that which has arisen in my mind. When we were both young the sound of the word *ship* fell on our ears at the same time as a certain image was formed on the retina of our eyes. In this way the two became intricately intertwined together, so that, in after life, the one inevitably suggested the other. Much of our education consists in the formation of such links. Complex as is the question of the origin of language, there is nothing at all complex in the association of the word *ship* with the conception it symbolizes.

Notice, then, the different ways in which a similar conception is called up in my mind and in that of my companion. To me it was suggested by a visual image formed on the retina of the eye ; to him it was suggested by the arbitrary sound-sign *ship* falling on the tympanum of the ear. Notice, too, that the general conception thus called up will depend very much upon the previous contents of our respective minds. I am from an inland town, he is from a seaport town. He has crossed the Atlantic, I have not. The result is that his general conception is much fuller and richer than mine, though I saw the white speck myself and he merely heard an arbitrary sign.

And now pass on to notice this still more important fact. General conceptions constitute our mental atmosphere. Conceptions, not sensations, form the medium in which our minds live and work, just as water, and not oxygen and hydrogen, forms the medium in which a fish habitually lives. The world is, in fact, to each of us a world of general conceptions, and it is so mainly because we are social beings and can communicate with our fellows in words which are the signs for general conceptions. The world is, indeed, to me somewhat different to what it is to my neighbours. For it is literally true that each of us lives in his own world and has it all to himself. We are like musical instruments upon which the same musician plays somewhat the same tune. In each case the quality of the music depends upon the nature of the instrument. The notes are not simple vibrations ; but each has its own special *timbre* depending on the subsidiary vibrations which the main series calls into being.

It is by means of language that I am able to some extent to call up in the minds of my neighbours the general conceptions that there are in my own mind, and in return can have my general conceptions moulded and modified by those suggested by my fellows. In this way language tends to produce a partial uniformity in our general conceptions. In this way my thoughts, your thoughts, and those of humanity in general are closely intertwined. In this way I live in and for humanity. But it must not be forgotten that the correspondence so produced is by no means exact. My ideal construction formed at the bidding of any word depends upon the accuracy of my memory and the extent of my knowledge, neither of which is exactly the same as that of my neighbour. The word *sun*, for example, is common to Mr. Norman Lockyer and the London street Arab. But the conception called up by this word in two so differently furnished minds must be wholly unlike. And what different ideas will be called up in different minds by the word *universe !* That word to some of us is the highest general conception we have reached, resulting from the synthesis of all other general conceptions. The impression it produces is the most massive and diffused impression we have. Bound up in it is the work of all thinkers, poets, artists, since thought began to crystallize into words. It is not a universe for us, but for all men. It is to some the manifestation of the Unknowable ; to others the visible garment of God ; but to yonder nursemaid the word, if it exist at all in her vocabulary, probably carries with it scarcely any definite meaning.

Let us now proceed to note that there are at least three ways in which such a general conception as that of a ship may be called up in my mind. In the first place it may be suggested, as before described, by a white speck across the sea. Here one of a cluster of related sensations suggests a recollection of the rest of the cluster which normally goes along with it. In the second place, the word *ship* may suggest a memory of the same cluster of possible sensations, no one of which is actually presented to consciousness. Thirdly, the sight of a book or photograph may suggest the thought of a distant relative whom I much wish to see. And in this way the idea of a voyage, and hence the idea of a ship, may be suggested. -So that this general conception may be suggested directly, or indirectly, or remotely—by an image, by a sign, or during a process of thought. But it seems very questionable whether such a complex conception as is symbolized by the word *universe* could be suggested directly. It could, indeed, only be suggested with any fulness during a train of abstract thought. Nor is it easy to imagine that such an idea could have been reached in the absence of language as a medium for thought. Such a word is essentially a condensed sentence ; nay, more, it is a condensed volume of thought. Analyze the idea, and it splits up into a vast aggregate of propositions, each of which might be decomposed into minor propositions, the ultimate terms of the analysis being (with an exception to be considered presently) sensations and the relations between sensations.

It should be noticed, however, that the word universe suggests an impression *as a whole*, just as the metal of a bronze penny produces an effect as a whole, though that effect is the result of the fusion of three metals. But as long as it continues to produce the true universe impression, as I may perhaps term it, that is, the impression of the universe as a whole, it is more or less vague and diffused, like the first effect of a distant landscape. This analogy is, I think, a helpful one. On looking out on a landscape I am conscious of a combination of separate objects which form what is practically a single and indivisible impression. But if now I continue to look, I see woods and lakes and fields, and perhaps a background of mountains. In doing so, however, I cease to have the individual impression of a landscape, and in its place have a series of separate impressions of the elements of which it is composed. In much the same way, as I continue to think of the universe the very complex general conception, in which there seemed to be, so to speak, so much background and so little foreground—this very complex general conception, I say, splits up into a number of propositions, the terms of which are general conceptions of a somewhat more simple character. But in doing so the general universe impression is lost ; and I am conscious of separate ideas of parts of the universe, which are probably more distinct than the original impression but are certainly less massive.

General conceptions, resulting from a process of ideal construction, form the key-note of this chapter. The fact which I wish to stand out clearly is this : that every im-

pression received from without has the property of con-
densing around itself a body of associated memories taken
from the stores of knowledge already laid up in the individual mind. The impression from without is like the
touch on the trigger of a fowling-piece, which sets free a
store of accumulated energy. Everything, in each case,
depends upon the store already accumulated. Or again,
the impression from without is like a simple sound entering
the mansion of the mind through one of the portals of
sense. As it rings through the sounding corridors it calls
forth other sounds, with which it enters into a series of fuller
and fuller combinations, until it rouses all the sleeping
music of the place into rich and rolling harmony. But the
music must be there, or, rather, the elements of which the
music is composed. The strings or reeds of a thousand
instruments are ready to be called into vibration by the
breath of the passing sound. If they be all tuned aright
there will be the harmony of *true* conceptions : if some of
them be not tuned aright we shall have the discord of *false*
conceptions.

Now, between the comparatively simple general conception symbolized by the word *ship* and the extremely
complex conception symbolized by the word *universe*, there
are many intermediate degrees of complexity. But merely
regarding them as cognitions (leaving the feelings and the
will entirely out of consideration), they may all, with the
exception to be ere long considered, be decomposed on
analysis into sensations and the relations between sensations.

Sensations and the relations between sensations are the
elements of all thought, the bricks of the house of knowledge. Sights, sounds, smells, tastes, touches from without;
the impression of their similarities and differences from
within—these are elements of knowledge. Not even does

an analysis of our general and abstract ideas yield us any other elements. A general idea is an idea that stands, not for any particular object, but for a group of objects. An abstract idea is a conception of an isolated quality or isolated relation. Our abstract nouns stand for the latter; all other common nouns symbolize the former. Take, for example, the noun *mountain* or *dog*. Each stands, not for this or that particular mountain or dog, but for any mountain or any dog. We understand at once what is meant by these words; but if we wish to image them they must be more or less particularized. At any rate, it is so in my own case. The word *mountain* invariably suggests to me the image of the Matterhorn : the word *dog* suggests two alternating mental pictures of two favourites. Other words standing for less familiar objects, however, call forth a generic image ; not a definite and clear-cut image, but an ill-defined image with blurred edges. And yet others suggest no image at all but merely a series of propositions. Still, whatever be the nature of the conception, it is formed in terms of sensations and their relations.

Abstract nouns stand for isolated qualities or relations. The ideas they symbolize are essentially the result of reflection, and are, as I believe, indissolubly associated with the use of language. We see a plum, and we find that it is round and blue and sweet, and offers resistance to gentle pressure. From these adjectives, by means of which we express certain qualities of the plum, we, in process of time, have formed abstract nouns, roundness, blueness, sweetness, resistance. We then, by an inevitable mental tendency, endow with a separate existence the qualities we have thus by the aid of language isolated ; and we call our conceptions of these isolated qualities abstract ideas. Our general conception of an object is a representation in thought of the group of qualities which, in practical experience, we find associated together; for example, the roundness, blueness, sweetness, and resistance of a plum. But by the process of abstraction we isolate a certain quality which is never found isolated in experience. It is the use of language, I believe, that has enabled us to do this. I do not say that the process is the result of language or that language is the result of the process. Both have gone on together, each rendering the other possible. Remembering this, then, we may say that the word enables us to isolate the special quality which it symbolizes. So, too, does the word enable us to isolate a relation apart from related things or events. We thus come to speak of abstract ideas of similarity, justice, causation, time, and space. Time, for example, is the abstract of all relations of sequence; space is the abstract of all relations of co-existence. There is no such thing as space; there is no such thing as time. And yet both space and time are the ineradicable outcome of all experience, individual and ancestral. And since every object, every event, must be known in its relations in space and time if it is to be known at all, the answering ideas are ineffaceable in consciousness, and may fairly be said to condition all our knowledge. Nevertheless, when we speak of space and time as separate existences apart from the experience in which these funda-mental relations are manifested, we are in the position of one who should maintain that whiteness, blueness, muski-ness, have separate existence apart from white, blue, or scented objects. When mathematicians discuss the pro-perties of space of negative curvature, they are dealing, not with a thing that has real and separate existence, but with relations different to those which practically obtain throughout the universe ; in other words, with experience differently conditioned to our own. But if abstract ideas are thus isolated qualities or isolated relations, they must surely trace their descent, through those conceptions from which they have been isolated, to the primary sensations and relations between sensations, out of which those conceptions have been elaborated.

These are the elementary cognitions. They always go together, but they are quite distinct. There is no conscious sensation without recognition ; without sensation recognition is impossible. Neither is independent of the other. For a relation to exist at all there must be related terms which are ultimately sensations. For a sensation to become a part of consciousness, it must enter through memory into relations with past sensations. The two, indeed, are quite distinct, but they are altogether inseparable.

But these elements—this warp and woof of the web of consciousness—are in the human mind woven into a meshwork of the most extraordinary complexity. "An eminent divine," writes W. K. Clifford, "once said to me that there were only two kinds of consciousness—to have a feeling, and to know that you have a feeling. It seems to me," he continues, "that there is only one kind of consciousness, and that is to have fifty thousand feelings at once, and to know them all in different degrees." Elsewhere Prof. Clifford likens the human consciousness to "a rope made up of a great number of occasionally interlacing strands." Of these strands, now one, now another, comes to the surface and sees the light. But the greater part of the rope lies in a deeper shadow of sub-consciousness. In that deeper shadow there seem to me to be three definite strands, which I may call the *social* sub-consciousness, the *personal* sub-consciousness, and the *organic* sub-consciousness. The first of these, the social sub-consciousness, is called into being by the existence of my fellow-men, among whom and for whom I live. It dominates almost every act of my waking life. The very objects which I see around me are objects not for me alone, but for my fellows too. And the fact that the object suggests at once a *word*, that is a sign for the object to my fellows, seems to imply this social sub-consciousness, from the influence of which I can never shake myself free, so long as I remain a social being. Nor is the personal sub-consciousness, that connected with my personal identity, ever absent. It is implied in every recollection that I can call my own. It interweaves itself with every thought and act and feeling, and forms part of them. But this part is not, under ordinary circumstances, definitely and distinctly present to consciousness. The same is true also of the organic sub-consciousness, which constantly underlies my consciousness, in the form of vague sights and sounds and pressures, and muscular contractions. All these sub-conscious states, social, personal, and organic, remain in the shadow of my mental life, present but unfelt, so long as they undergo no great change in their intensity. Their monotony prevents their coming to the light. But if the sights or sounds are vivid, the beating of the heart laborious, or the pressures in excess of their ordinary amounts, I become conscious of these facts. So, too, if I am anxious to convince my readers of any truth, I at once become definitely conscious of the social factor. And in the same way if an acquaintance tells one of my best stories as his own, my personal consciousness asserts itself, as I inwardly growl that I was the first to originate the story.

Thus as a broad and deep stream, to use another simile, with a surface of definite consciousness, and with undercurrents of indefinite sub-consciousness, flows on the tide of my mental life. At the surface of the stream are the states of mind of which I am fully conscious; then those of which I am half conscious, the absence of which would altogether alter the definite consciousness; lower are those

C

states of mind answering to the secondary automatic
actions, that is to say, those actions which once involved
voluntary consciousness, but are now performed involuntarily and unconsciously; lowest are those states of mind
which answer to such automatic actions as were connate,
the performance of which in the *individual* never involved
(under normal conditions) consciousness. These are submerged feelings. The whole stream of mental states constitutes my personality; and it is difficult to over-estimate
the effect which the emergence into consciousness of sub-
conscious states has upon the sense of personality. Or, in
other words, this stream of mental states constitutes my
mind. Hence the expression *contents of my mind*, which I
have occasionally used, is incorrect. What I have called
the contents of my mind are only portions of that continuous stream which *is* my mind. Apart from that stream
my mind has no more existence than a river from which
the water has been taken away. Stop that stream, and
mind ceases to exist. But if it be distinctly remembered
that the mind and its contents are one, that there is no
mind apart from its contents, there will be no harm done
by using such an expression as the contents of my mind.
Nay, rather, good will come. For in our words and forms
of speech there is not infrequently implied a false and
misleading metaphysical theory. But as we cannot summarily get rid of and sweep away our everyday speech, we
must learn so to interpret it as, so far as is possible, to
emancipate ourselves from such false conceptions as underlie it. We are terribly tyrannized over by our words, and
we should do our best to break through that tyranny. Run
away from it we cannot.

There is one little word in especial which we cannot
banish from our speech, and which in the hands of meta-
physicians becomes a most "masterful entity." I mean

the first personal pronoun. In this chapter, for example, I have used the expressions, "I have a sensation," or, "I am conscious of a perception;" and I must use such a form of words if I am to be understood at all. But what am I apart from the stream of my mental states? The sum of my states of mind at any moment constitutes *me*. I and my states of mind are one; and apart from my states of mind, I have no conscious existence. This, however, I do not here attempt to prove; if, indeed, it can be actually proved. I am utterly unable to see any grounds for believing in a separate entity *ego*, presiding over and separate from the series of perceptions which I am content to call me. But my neighbour may hold a different opinion; and I have no wish to quarrel with him for doing so. I am quite ready to listen to his arguments if he will but couch them in terms understanded of the people. All I wish to point out here is, that throughout this volume I disclaim this metaphysical theory, and that in using such a phrase as, "I am conscious of a feeling," I, in effect, merge myself in that consciousness.

And why should I so persistently speak of *my* feelings, *my* consciousness, *my* mind? For a very good reason. It is the only mind of which I have any direct knowledge. It may be a very poor criterion by which to judge of mind in general—my neighbours' minds and the great minds which look out at me from the past through printed pages— but it is the only criterion I have. Indeed, it would only be by a somewhat elaborate and roundabout process that I should arrive at the conclusion that my neighbour had a mind at all, had not the belief grown up with my race for many generations. In this matter, as in all other matters of common sense and of science, what I should do would be this: I should form an hypothesis on the firmest basis I could find, and then see how the hypothesis worked out.

By the comparison of my neighbour's actions with my actions I should think myself justified in supposing that his actions are accompanied by consciousness, just as mine are. And then, finding that this hypothesis worked well, I should most certainly adopt it, until I discovered a better. As it is, however, there has been no necessity for me to go through any such process. When I came into the world this hypothesis was in possession of the field. I had nothing to do but to enter into the fruits of the labours of others. For all this, however, when I think of other minds I am forced to think of them in terms of my own mind. I can never see my neighbour's mind, nor any part of it. I may see a man angry, but I cannot see the anger that I believe he feels. What I can see are actions which are like my actions when I am angry, and I therefore imagine that he who exhibits these actions has also those feelings which, under such circumstances, accompany my actions, and which I call anger. What I cannot see, feel, touch, or come in direct contact with in any way whatsoever, are those feelings. And suppose that I have never been angry ; then it may be said of me with literal truth that he does not know what anger is.

Thus my neighbour's mind can never be to me an object ; since an object is an ideal construction built out of the elements of sensation and relation. It is something that I can never come into direct contact with. It is something of which I can only gain a definite knowledge by a process of inference, individual or ancestral. I say *definite* knowledge, because I have long believed it to be not only possible but probable that each mind creates around itself a sort of mental atmosphere by means of which it may vaguely influence neighbouring minds. It seems to me quite conceivable that the molecular vibrations of one brain may radiate waves of influence through which like molecular vibrations may be called up in another brain ; or, in other words, and from the subjective aspect, that the thoughts of one mind may call up like thoughts in another mind. This would seem to be the essential truth of much that we hear about thought reading. Browning seems to have felt it when he says in one of his most beautiful poems ("By the Fireside"):

> "When if I think but deep enough,
> You are wont to answer prompt as rhyme."

And elsewhere in poetry may be seen the germs of the same idea. But I believe that it will some day become an acknowledged scientific doctrine, and one, be it noted, not without its influence on conduct. I do not mind confessing that this belief has for some years led me to keep a stricter guard on my thoughts, lest I might, unknown to him, be influencing a human soul for ill, and that I might possibly influence him for good. I commend this doctrine to those whose privilege it is to be teachers of the higher life, as giving an additional incentive to be pure and true in thought, as well as in word and deed.

Be this as it may, we have now come upon a truth which is of the utmost importance with regard to the contents of my mind. Here is a piece of knowledge which no amount of sensations entering into relations could develop. Here is an element, and to a social being one of the deepest import, altogether different in its nature from the other elements of which cognitions are composed. And yet there is nothing of which, practically speaking, I am more certain, than that my neighbour has a consciousness more or less similar to my own. I project a modified image of my consciousness into every human being that I meet, and feel assured that I am right in doing so.

And this is a purely legitimate process, and one altogether justifiable by the scientific method. The existence of Science as an organized body of doctrine presupposes the existence of other minds than my own. The legitimacy of the assumption is indeed so fully justified from hour to hour that it ceases to be regarded as an assumption. And it may well cease to be so regarded, for it interweaves itself with all our mental life; it makes social beings of us; it lies at the root of all æsthetics, science, and morality. For all that, the peculiar nature of the process must not be lost sight of. It is a process which has its centre and origin in each of us individually, and spreads from that centre on all sides. I am conscious; and all my knowledge of consciousness is a knowledge of my consciousness, or is built up upon the basis of that knowledge.

This "fundamental isolation of the individual mind" has long been recognized in the domain of psychology. "Such is the nature of *Spirit*, or that which acts," says Bishop Berkeley, "that it cannot be itself perceived, but only the effects which it produceth." "Thinking things as such," writes Kant, "can never occur among outward phenomena; we can have no outward perception of their thoughts, consciousness, desires; for all this is the domain of the inward sense." But it is only of late that we have had a convenient term by means of which to express the product of this so remarkable process. In a very striking and valuable essay, however, "On the Nature of Things in Themselves," Professor Clifford coined the word *eject*, which exactly meets the requirements of the case. My neighbour's mind is to me neither subject nor object; it is an eject thrown out from myself. Into every man that I meet I breathe an image of my own mind, and thenceforth he becomes for me a living soul.

A concluding paragraph by way of summary. During our waking hours our minds are chiefly occupied with more or less complex general conceptions. In us civilized folk these general conceptions are largely called forth by the words which fall from our neighbour's lips, or meet our eye in printed pages. The word *house*, for example, suggests a general conception which is characterized by vagueness and extreme generality. But suppose I actually see the house ; the general conception symbolized by the word is, so to speak, individualized. That which at the suggestion of a word floated formless in my mind, acquires definiteness on sight of the object. Or again, if I choose, I can individualize the conception by an act of imagination, by thinking of the house in which my childhood was passed. But whether existing in its vaguer form, or limited either on sight of an object, or by an act of vivid imagination, in either case the complex conception has this characteristic—that its main features are furnished by the mind on the suggestion of some impression received from without, or of some passing thought within. Moreover, so far as their genesis is concerned, these general conceptions, complex as they are, owe their origin to, and are elaborated out of, sensations which are ever entering into more and more intricate relations. But at the same time they are profoundly modified by a consciousness of personality, and by the ejects or images of his own consciousness with which each one of us instinctively endows his neighbours. Thus our conceptions deal not merely with the objects by which we are immediately surrounded, but with a past with which memory brings us in contact, and with a future of which anticipation, which is but inverted memory, gives us a dim prevision. Nor is the world around us a world for us alone, but for our neighbours also. And the great conception of the universe, growing daily in breadth and depth, is not for us, but for humanity.

CHAPTER II.

THE SOURCE AND LIMITS OF KNOWLEDGE.

"There are not a few problems in the natural sciences of which a man cannot speak justly without calling metaphysics to his aid."—GOETHE.

THOSE of our scientific men who are the most patient investigators and the deepest thinkers, fail not honestly to confess that there are great gaps that sever the continuity of our knowledge, and that there is a great blank beyond the limits of our knowledge. And the gaps are of two kinds— gaps of *ignorance* and gaps of *nescience*. Gaps of ignorance which may be, nay, will be, more or less completely filled in by patient research ; gaps of nescience which are inevitable, and result from the nature of our mental and physical constitution.

With the gaps of ignorance we have here no concern. Their boundaries are constantly changing with the steady onward conquest of Science. But with the gaps of nescience the case is different. Their boundaries, for man as he is at present constituted, are immovably fixed ; and to ascertain these boundaries is an important part of the business of philosophy. For the object of philosophy is, as it seems to me, to enable us to reach a coherent and consistent theory of thoughts and things ; just as it is the object of religion to afford us a centre of love and service. Such a philosophy should be termed, did not the phrase now carry with it a more limited meaning, "natural philosophy," since it is based on the study of Nature, including human nature. Thus Pythagoras, when he was asked what he meant by his statement, "I have no art; I am a philosopher," answered, "We quit our country, which is heaven, and come into the world, which is an assembly where many work for profit, many for gain, and where there are but few who, despising avarice and vanity, study Nature. It is these last whom I call philosophers." The term "natural philosophy," which would be the obvious antithesis to "supernatural philosophy," having at present a limited implication, the term "philosophy of science" may be used to denote a natural theory of thoughts and things, antithetical to which will stand "the philosophy of faith" which denotes a supernatural theory of thoughts and things. It is with the former alone that this chapter and this book pretend to deal.

The philosophy of science, then, with which alone we are here concerned, deals with two questions, to which it seeks to give highly generalized answers. These two questions are, What *can* we know? and What *do* we know? And it is on the consideration of the former of these two questions that we have now to enter.

What are the limits of our knowledge? Let us at the outset clearly grasp what is comprised in this question. What we have to consider is not what we at present know as opposed to what we do not know, but what we *can* know as opposed to what we cannot know. We have not to assign limits to our *actual* knowledge, but to define the sphere of *possible* knowledge. We have not to point out the admitted gaps of ignorance, which may be more or less completely filled in by future research or bridged over by future reasonings, but to set a definite boundary to the region in which scientific research and scientific reasonings hold good. For our faculties in all cases are conditional; in the dark the eagle's eye is blind; in a vacuum his wing is powerless. And beyond its sphere the reason of the philosopher is as helpless as the fancy of a little child.

Our first step, therefore, must be to ascertain what are the sources of our knowledge. We will then endeavour to become acquainted, if it be permissible so to say, with the region of nescience; after which we shall be in a position to apprehend, if not to comprehend, the sphere of our knowledge. It will thus be well to subdivide this chapter into three sections: (1) the sources of knowledge; (2) the region of nescience; (3) the sphere of knowledge;—it being clearly understood that it is *natural* knowledge and *human* knowledge with which we are dealing.

1. *The Sources of Knowledge.*

" Experience transcends the facts of individual feeling and includes those of the race. The experiences of millions of men co-operate in the determination of the thoughts and acts of the individual."—G. H. LEWES.

If I were to find on the shelves of the British Museum library a volume purporting to deal with the insects of the moon, or one pretending to treat of the conifers of Mars, I should feel assured that, whatever else they might be, these books were not scientific treatises. And I should feel certain of this without glancing at a single page. Now, on what should I base my opinion? And why should I hold a very different opinion with regard to a volume on the metals of the sun? Surely for this reason: that, in the first place, it is physically impossible for a man, organized as he is, to see, touch, or handle the organic products (if such exist) of our satellite or of our neighbour planet; that, in the second place, all our knowledge of plants and animals is obtained by more or less elaborate processes of seeing and handling; and that, therefore, it is physically impossible to have any knowledge of the animals or plants of the moon or of Mars. With regard to the metals of the sun, however, the case is very different. For, by the spectroscopic analysis of the light emitted by an incan-descent body, we can ascertain, within limits, the composition of that body, and it matters not, in the slightest degree, whether this body is near to or far away from the eye, the retina of which receives the etherial vibrations which constitute light. From which special facts and others of like nature, these general facts are suggested : that scientific knowledge is proximately or ultimately gained through the medium of the senses, and that all that lies beyond the direct or indirect reach of the senses is, to science, unknowable.

But here let us pause for a moment to make sure that we understand what we mean by this word " knowledge." We shall not, I think, find a better definition of the essential conditions of knowledge than that given by Locke. According to Locke, knowledge is the perception of the agreement or disagreement of two ideas. I hear a sound ; but the impression thus produced is not knowledge. Not till I, consciously or unconsciously, compare the idea produced by this impression, with the ideas I have of other similar or different impressions, does knowledge emerge. I see a coin ; but I only know it to be such on perceiving that the idea it has produced agrees with the ideas previously produced by similar objects. And so with the other special sensations. The direct action on the sensory organs, which Hume called an *impression*, is not knowledge. Only when the *idea*, or reproduction in memory, of such an impression is mentally seen to be like or unlike other ideas, have we any knowledge of the impression.

We think in relations; and the relation which lies the deepest of all, that which is the basis of all our knowledge, is the relation of likeness or unlikeness.

Thus, in addition to impressions of sensation, we have equally indecomposable impressions of relation. Take a familiar example. I hold in my hand a cedar pencil. From it I receive certain impressions of sensation through touch, sight, and smell. But it is not by mere sensation that I know anything about it. These sensations must be perceived in their relations before I can recognize the nature of the object. Sensation alone can tell me nothing of its size and shape, while its colour, smell, and solidity can only be known in their relations to other sensations of the same order. And the pencil as a whole can only be known to be what it is by perceiving its likeness or unlikeness to other familiar objects.

But although we may firmly believe that the impressions of relation, such as that of the likeness or unlikeness of two bodies, are as undecomposable elements of consciousness as are the impressions of sensation, we may perhaps still, without inconsistency, believe that all our knowledge is proximately or ultimately gained through the medium of the senses. Unless the senses provide the raw material, on what can our powers of reflection exercise their faculty? Unless the hydrogen and oxygen present the requisite elements, whence can we obtain our water? Unless successive air pulsations merge into a tone, how can music arise? For just as a succession of air-waves, beating against the tympanum of the ear, coalesce in sensation to form a musical note, the quality of which is modified by subsidiary systems of more rapid air-waves giving over-tones; and just as these musical notes are combined into chords by the cunning combination of which a symphony may be composed,—so too, not improbably, do units of consciousness coalesce to form sensations, sensations enter into relations and form knowledge of sensations, and these simple relations enter into compound relations of ever-increasing complexity.

Thus, as Leibnitz said, the senses though necessary for all actual knowledge, are not sufficient to give it all. If I may be allowed to use a chemical analogy, it is because sensations do not merely form mechanical mixtures, but enter into true chemical combination, that knowledge is possible. We may add oxygen to hydrogen and get nothing but a mixture of these two gases. But pass an electric spark through the mixture, and the gases, entering into true chemical combination, are transformed into water. So, too, we may add sensation to sensation, and nothing comes of the addition. But bring them under the influence of that organized product of evolution, a human mind, and they enter into true relational combination, and knowledge emerges. And "without this law of combination," as Mr. Herbert Spencer points out, "there could be nothing but a perpetual kaleidoscope change of feelings—an ever-transforming present without past or future."

Bearing in mind, then, this law of composition, may we say that the elements which enter into composition are in their ultimate analysis impressions of sensation ? Before we finally answer this question let us see what objections may be raised to this view.

How far, it may, for example, be asked, can *innate ideas* be said to be ultimately dependent on sensation ? The old-fashioned answer to this objection was simply to deny their existence. But this answer is in manifest antagonism to that experience in support of which it was brought forward. " In all seriousness," writes Professor Huxley, "if the existence of *instincts* be granted, the possibility of the existence of innate ideas must also be admitted. The

child who is impelled to draw as soon as it can hold a
pencil ; the Mozart who breaks out into music as early ;
the boy, Bidder, who worked out the most complicated
sums without learning arithmetic ; the boy, Pascal, who
evolved Euclid out of his own consciousness—all these
may be said to have been impelled by instinct as much as
the beaver and the bee.   And the man of genius is distinct
in kind from the man of cleverness, by reason of the working within him of strong innate tendencies, which cultiva-
tion may improve, but which it can no more create than
horticulture can make thistles bear figs.   The analogy
between a musical instrument and the mind—according to
which the organ of thought, prior to experience, may be
compared to an untouched piano, in which it may properly
be said that music is innate, insomuch as its mechanism
contains, potentially, so many octaves of musical notes—
holds good here also.   Art and industry may get much
music of a sort out of a penny whistle ; but, when all is
done, it has no chance against an organ.   The innate
musical potentialities of the two are infinitely different."

We cannot, then, answer the objection raised on the
score of innate ideas by summarily denying their existence.
We must apply to Biology for an answer, and that answer
we obtain in the word *inheritance.*

Locke, who argued strenuously against the existence of
innate ideas, likened the mind of an infant to fair white
paper, inscribed as yet with no characters, but ready to
receive impressions of sensation and reflection.   By an
apter simile, however, it may be compared to paper
inscribed with invisible ink, in which the warmth of a
fire develops characters hitherto unseen.   In our largely
developed brain, in fact, we inherit vast potentialities of
thought, potentialities to be rendered into actualities by
the varying play of sensation.   And though we are totally

unable to conceive how the vibration of brain-molecules can give rise to consciousness, we have, nevertheless, strong grounds for believing that such molecular vibrations are the invariable *accompaniments* of consciousness. And just as, in the adult, impressions of sensation or relation recall faint representations of other similar impressions, acquired during childhood, which we call memories, so also, in the child, impressions of sensation or relation recall faint representations of impressions, acquired during the childhood of the race, which we may call *inherited* memories. Innate ideas, and so-called *à priori* truths, are such inherited memories : and though it is probable that *in* the individual they are only developed by impressions gained ultimately through the senses, just as the characters written in invisible ink are only developed by the heat of a fire, it may be taken as certain that they are not acquired *by* the individual. But of what, it will now be asked, are these ancestrally acquired ideas the memories ? To this question, it seems to me, there is but one answer. They are the inherited memories of impressions, gained proximately or ultimately through the medium of sense.

Such being, in brief, the answer to the objection on the score of the existence of innate ideas, we may pass on to consider a second objection. How, it may be asked, could the knowledge we undoubtedly possess of such states as hunger and anger be gained proximately or ultimately by the senses ? The senses tell us of an outer world of things, not an inner world of feelings. Here is a fragment of knowledge which is constituted neither by impressions of sensation nor by impressions of relation, but is the product of pure feeling.

Containing though it does the germ of a hitherto unnoticed truth, this objection implies a misconception of what is meant by the expression " gained proximately or

ultimately through the medium of sense." For by sensation is meant something more than the testimony of the
five special senses—sight, hearing, smell, taste, and touch.
Under the general head of sensation are included all those
impressions of the so-called organic senses which result
from stimuli coming not from without, but from within the
body, and of which hunger, as a mere feeling, is a tolerably
little modified example, and hunger as a desire one that is
more complex. In the sequel we shall see that the desires
and some of the lower emotions result from the nascent
sensations which would normally accompany those *actions*
to which the impulse prompts, while some of the higher
emotions occupy the same position among feelings as
the highly general and abstract ideas occupy among cognitions. It is unnecessary to anticipate here what will be
said there. Suffice it to say that, if the view there advo-
cated be correct, not only hunger and anger, but the higher
emotional states have their origin, if not in sensation (since
that term is, perhaps, liable to misconception), at any rate
in *experience*. And just as innate ideas are to be regarded
as the result of ancestral experience transmitted to us by
inheritance, so, too, are innate emotions and desires the
result of ancestral experience transmitted to us by inheritance. In the one case, as in the other, the individual
education of experience *educes* or "draws out" those products of ancestral acquisition which were lying latent in
our organization and in our character.

This objection, however, brings into view hitherto unnoticed elements in the contents of mind which, if they do
not enter largely into the structure of knowledge, are none
the less important from their intimate association with
both the impressions of sensation and the impressions of
relation. These elements are pleasure and its opposite,
pain. Pleasure and pain would seem to be distinct and

undecomposable elements of consciousness. They are not impressions of sensation ; they are not impressions of relation. They are distinct from and yet arise out of both. They are separate elements which are *associated with* these impressions, or their faint representation in ideas. Out of association with these impressions or their ideas we know nothing of pleasure or pain. And it is hardly possible to doubt that experience, the common source of our knowledge of sensations and relations, is the source also of our knowledge of pleasure and of pain.

Another objection to the view that the elements which enter into the composition of our knowledge are ultimately derived from experience, might be urged in the following terms : " The very science in which you trust deals with objects *beyond the possible range of experience,*" so might an objector affirm, and truly affirm. "Atoms and molecules, the ether and its luminiferous undulations, the solar atmosphere, the nebular hypothesis, the origin of the plutonic rocks—all these are, and for ever must remain, extra-sensible. Listen to the words of one of the leaders of scientific thought. 'Indeed, the domain of the senses in Nature,' so writes Prof. Tyndall, 'is almost *infinitely small in comparison with the vast region accessible to thought which lies beyond them.* From a few observations of a comet when it comes within the range of his telescope, an astronomer can calculate its path in regions which no telescope can reach ; and in like manner, by means of data furnished in the narrow world of the senses, we make ourselves at home in other and wider worlds, *which can be traversed by the intellect alone.*' This extra-sensible world of science proves your assertion, that the elements of our knowledge are derived from sense, to be false and futile."

To which objection the answer is obvious. It is true that the astronomer can calculate the path of a comet in

regions which no telescope can reach ; it is true that we
can make ourselves at home in other and wider worlds
than that of sense. But how ? By means of the data
furnished in the narrow world of the senses (How came you,
my friend, to omit to italicize these words ?). Just as the
trigonometrical survey of a whole continent may be constructed from a single accurately measured base-line, so
may we construct the vast extra-sensible world of science
from the accurately measured base-line of sensible experience. And the value of our construction in science will
be strictly commensurate with the value of our measured
base-line.

Another objection, the last we need consider, may be
briefly stated thus : We have a conception of a perfect
circle ; but all circles in the world of sense are imperfect ;
therefore my conception is not derived from sense ; for no
amount of sensible experience of imperfect circles could
give rise to my conception of a perfect circle. To which it
may be answered, Why not ? In the circles which we draw
in the world of sense we perceive a certain *relation* of parts.
What we have in the geometrical circle is an abstract
conception of relation. It is not a general conception of
real circles. In such a conception the imperfections common to all could not be eliminated. But in the formation of an abstract conception such elimination is the
essence of the process. From the many approximately
similar objects in the world of sense we rise to the abstract
relation of likeness, which, as a relation, can know no im-
perfection, though it may be imperfectly exemplified in the
objects around us. So, too, from the many tangible, visible,
circles which we observe in the world of sense we rise to
an abstract idea of relation which we may define geometri-
cally. The circularity, as a relation, cannot be imperfect,
though it may be imperfectly exemplified in what we are

pleased to call real circles.   The abstract ideas of relation employed in geometry differ in no wise in kind from other abstract ideas, such as those of quality.   With them they stand or fall.   And there seems no reasonable ground for doubting that it is in and through our acquaintance with the real tangible objects of sense that human beings have been able to rise to abstract ideas of quality or relation which transcend sense.

Thus, if the views above sketched be correct, although we may not say that all our knowledge has found its way into our minds through the inlets of sense, for the impressions of relation have assuredly not gained entrance in this way, still we may say that all our knowledge has been elaborated out of the raw materials supplied by experience.

2. *The Region of Nescience.*

" Man is not born to solve the problem of the universe, but to find out where the problem begins and then to restrain himself within the limits of the comprehensible."—GOETHE.

Let us suppose that we form part of the audience of an imaginary lecturer who performs and describes the following ideal experiment :— *

" I have here, gentlemen," says this phantom professor, " a minute metallic spring.   Let me ask each one of you to examine it for himself.   You observe that it is solid, offering tangible resistance to the touch, and that it has a proper size and shape.   And when I set it vibrating thus, you perceive that it is capable of certain motions, either as a whole or in its parts.   Now, I have devised a method by which this spring may be set vibrating at

* Some such illustration as this has been used by G. H. Lewes, Croom Robertson, and others, and is, I believed, borrowed from the German.

a constantly increasing rate, and also a method by which
all subsidiary and disturbing vibrations may be eliminated.
I am anxious that you should experience for yourselves
the results of such vibration. I will, therefore, with your
permission, extinguish the light ; and now in darkness and
in silence we will await the results of my experiment. For
long, you perceive, the spring gives no sign of its existence.
But I can assure you .that it is still there, and is now
trembling at a rate of ten, twelve, fourteen vibrations per
second.   Now it reaches sixteen vibrations per second ;
and some of us begin to *hear a low hum.* Thus does the
spring give evidence of its presence.   As the rapidity
increases the musical note emitted by the spring rises in
pitch ; it is getting shriller and shriller : and now, at a rate
of 36,000 vibrations per second, the shrillness has for me,
and probably for most of us, passed into stillness.   Again
the spring gives no sign of its existence.   I can assure
you it is still vibrating, though I have caused the vibration
to be transferred from the spring as a whole to its constituent particles. You see, we have long to wait in patience.
The vibrations are as yet unable to awake sensation.   But
now that the rate has risen to 30 million million vibrations
per second we feel a new sensation, that of *warmth.* Heat is
now being radiated from our vibrating spring ; and just
as the sound ranges from 16 to 36,000 vibrations per
second, so will the heat range from 30 million million
through many octaves of heat.   There is, however, in the
feeling of warmth nothing .analogous to the rise in pitch
which we noticed in the sound.   But now you will perceive that, before the heat sensation dies out, our wonderful little spring finds a new way of informing us of its
existence.   There are at the present moment somewhat
over 400 million million vibrations per second ; and we
can now *see* the deep red glow that is emitted by the

trembling spring. The red grows to orange, yellow, green blue, indigo, violet ; thus passing through the seven rainbow colours. But now, at nearly 800 million million of vibrations per second, the violet fades away into darkness, just as the sound lapsed into stillness. All is now still darkness again. Nor will any further increase in the rapidity of the vibration of the spring bring it again directly within our cognizance, wait we never so long ; though we may through photography come indirectly within its influence up to nearly 1600 million million vibrations per second. The experiment is over, gentlemen, and my part is played. It is for you to draw your own conclusions, and to learn the teachings of the trembling spring."

And what conclusions shall we draw ? What teachings shall we extract from the trembling spring ? This to begin with : that only within certain limits is it able to give us any direct evidence of its existence. At the outset we assured ourselves of its tangible reality by means of touch. Then it was set vibrating ; and in the dark we waited to see what sensations it could call forth in us. Until the vibrations reached 16 in the second it could evoke no response. Then between 16 and 36,000 it called into play our sense of hearing. Between 36,000 and 30 million million there was a vast gap, during which we were absolutely dead to the influence of the rapid vibrations. Then arose the sensation of warmth ; and before that had died away, at somewhat more than 400 billion vibrations per second, there followed a sight sensation, which lasted until the number of vibrations reached somewhat less than 800 billion per second. Beyond that we were again dead to the direct influence of the spring. Below 16 ; between 36,000 and 30 billion ; beyond 800 billion ; we were insensible to the waves of air or ether which beat in upon us.

Our organism has no structures fitted to respond to these vibrations.

So much for the direct teaching of the spring. But has it not more general teachings ? Does it not stand for us as a type of the world of things around us ? May not, nay, must not, the world of things be pulsating with a thousand influences to which we are, and from our constitution for ever must remain, insensible ? Undoubtedly this must be so. Our knowledge may be likened to the habitable globe in which there are certain continents for our occupation. Touch, smell, taste, hearing, sight, and sundry detached islands of the so-called organic sensations, we may till and cultivate to the best of our ability. But around this habitable land of knowledge, with its many pools and lakes of ignorance, which may by patient care be drained and reclaimed and made to yield a fertile soil,—around this *terra firma* of knowledge there lie wide oceans of nescience which we must leave to be the dwelling-place of creatures, if such exist, of different constitution to our own.

Or, to change the illustration, each individual mind may be conceived as the centre of two concentric spheres, an inner and an outer sphere. The outer sphere is the external world shedding influence towards the centre from all points of its surface. The inner sphere is the bodily organism. For the most part this inner sphere is opaque, and cuts off from the central mind the influences which are shed by the outer sphere of the external world. But here and there are the stained-glass windows of sensation. Through them the central mind obtains glimpses of the external world. And fusing these together, inferring also somewhat about the unseen in terms of the seen, it constructs a continuous picture of the outer sphere. And this picture it calls the world of experience ; an imperfect picture, it is true, but one that amply suffices for practical needs.

Such an illustration as this, however, is a mere scaffolding by means of which we may reach a due conception of the necessary limitation of our powers. When we have reached the conception we must abandon the scaffolding. Let us not, then, be led by our illustration to forget that the organism is not separate from the external world, but is just a part of it specially differentiated off from the rest ; and that the mind is not distinct from the organism, but is just a highly specialized mode of its activity.

We have thus brought into view part of the vast region of nescience, namely, that part which is consequent on the limitation of our knowledge to objects which can in some way, directly or indirectly, affect our organization. But not only is our knowledge in this way limited to sensible objects ; our knowledge of those objects is also limited to the manner in which they affect our senses. Our knowledge of objects is a knowledge of the way in which they are manifested to us in experience. We can only know them in their relation to our organization : out of such relation we can know them not. Thus even our habitable land of knowledge floats on a vast underlying ocean of nescience. Let us now try and penetrate to this underlying ocean of nescience.

Locke, as is well known, accepted the two-fold division of the qualities of objects into those which are primary or real, and those which are secondary or subjective. "The particular bulk, number, figure, and motion of the parts of fire and snow," he says, "are really in them, whether any man's senses perceive them or no ; and, therefore, they may be called real properties, because they really exist in these bodies. But light, heat, whiteness, or coldness, are no more really in them than sickness or pain is in manna. Take away the sensation of them ; let not the eyes see light or colours, nor the ears hear sounds ; let the palate not taste, nor the nose smell ; and all colours, tastes, odours, and sounds, as they are such particular ideas, vanish and cease, and are reduced to their causes, *i.e.* bulk, figure, and motion of parts."

Let us be quite sure that we grasp Locke's point. His argument ·is that " light, heat, whiteness, or coldness," do not really exist *as such*—" as they are such particular ideas "—in the bodies that seem to possess them, but are merely modes in which those bodies affect our senses. And if we revert for a moment to the trembling spring we shall see that this must be so. As the trembling grew more rapid there came sound, but the sound did not exist as such in the spring, though there was something about the spring which caused in us the sensation of sound. After a period during which the trembling spring was unable to call up in us any fresh sensations, there came a sense of warmth. But the warmth, as such, was not in the spring, though there was something about the way in which the spring vibrated which called forth in us the sensation of warmth. And so, too, with the varying colour of the spring as the rate of vibration passed up from four to eight hundred billion in a second. The redness, the yellowness, the blueness did not exist as such in the vibrating spring ; but something ·about its rapidity and mode of vibration called up in us the sensations of colour. Thus the testimony of our vibrating spring is clearly in favour of Locke's contention. The sound, heat, colour, do not reside as such in the spring, which is only a piece of vibrating metal ; but are called up in us by the manner of its vibration. And thus, in the words of Locke, we " reduce these sensations to their causes, *i.e.* bulk, figure, and motions of parts." These are the real properties which truly and actually exist in the metal itself, " whether any man's senses perceive them or no."

Locke's intellectual successor was the subtle Berkeley, Bishop of Cloyne. Attacking, with a mind of marvellous acuteness, the "difficulties which have hitherto amused philosophers," he succeeded in completely breaking down the distinction between the primary and secondary qualities of matter. "In short," he says, "extension, figure, and motion, abstracted from all other qualities are inconceivable. Where, therefore, the other qualities are, there must these be also, to wit, in the mind and nowhere else."

Revert again to the vibrating spring. Locke, we will suppose, has explained to the attentive Berkeley that the colour which appeared to be a property of the spring does not exist as such in the vibrating metal, but is really a mode in which the rapid trembling of the spring affects his consciousness. To which Berkeley answers, "Your argument proves too much or too little—too much if I am to believe my senses ; too little if I am to doubt their testimony. My sense of sight tells me in the plainest and most unmistakable manner that the colour is in the spring and not in me. You teach me that this clear testimony of sense is false. You check the vibration of the particles of the metal, and the colour goes. You show me the metal and explain that in reality the only qualities that it possesses are solidity, extension, figure, and motion of the parts. But how can you ask me to believe the senses that you have taught me to doubt ? Only through sensation can I reach a knowledge of the solidity and extension of the spring. And the sensations through which I gain this knowledge are no whit more real, more vivid, more convincing, than the sense of sight which told me, in the plainest and most unmistakable manner, that the spring was coloured. You have taught me to doubt, and my faith in sense is gone. Nay, more ; you have convinced me that the colour sensation, as such, was merely an affection of the percipient mind, and it is now my turn to convince you that the same line of argument proves that the solidity, the extension, the figure, and motion of parts, are merely affections of the percipient mind. In and for that percipient mind they have their existence ; elsewhere *as such* they do not and cannot exist. But when I have thus taught you to be thorough in your doubts, and to see that *all* qualities are subjective, then I shall hope to lead you back to a new trust in your senses, and induce you to confess that though subjective they are none the less real—really existent in and for you, if not really existent in the external world."

To this argument it only remains for the champion of the external reality of matter to reply, " It is true that all the *qualities* of matter, primary as well as secondary, are only the modes under which the matter can affect the percipient mind. These qualities, however, are but the garment in which the true substance of matter clothes itself. Behind this vesture of *appearance* lies the true essence of *reality*. Does not our common speech admit as much when we talk of the qualities of matter ? "

Let us once more, and for the last time, appeal to our metallic spring. Our first tendency was to believe that the heat and colour which we felt or saw it to possess were real properties which the spring possessed, whether any man took notice of them or not. But Locke made it clear to us that the warmth and colour could not really exist as such in the spring, which did, however, possess certain real and independent qualities, such as bulk, figure, and motion of parts. Whereupon Berkeley pointed out that the argument that proved the dependence of the secondary qualities on our percipient organization proved also the similar dependence of these real qualities ; so that no single known quality of the object could be said to be independent of the mind of the percipient. It seemed, therefore, clear that all our knowledge of the spring was relative— dealt with the way in which the spring affected us. That neither bulk, figure, nor motion of parts, neither hardness, extension, nor colour, neither heat, sound, smell, nor any other conceivable quality existed *as such* in the spring, since these were only the modes in which the spring affected our consciousness. But now the realist (transformed or untransformed) steps in and says, " One thing alone is independent —the matter or substance itself which possesses these properties or which is manifested to us under these modes. It is true that of the nature of this ultimate substance we do not and cannot know anything. We can only know it as manifested to us under its qualities. But that it does exist, has real independent existence whether any man's senses take notice of it or not, is an inevitable inference which we cannot avoid without admitting that the manifestations may be manifestations of—nothing."

And what has the bishop to say in answer to this? He replies imperturbably, " I am unable to see how the testimony of sense can be alleged as a proof for the existence of anything which is not perceived by sense," though he forgets to add *or for its non-existence.* But this is a point to which we shall presently return.

We have now sufficiently brought into view the region of nescience which lies around and beyond our knowledge. Our knowledge being limited, in the first place, to such objects as can in some way affect our organization, and in the second place to the manner in which they affect that organization, it follows that in the region of nescience lie all those objects, if such exist, which can in no way affect our organization, and all those modes of existence, if such there be, by which the objects we know affect not us but beings, if such exist, of different constitution and organization to ourselves.

"And the upshot of it all comes, then, to this," so may exclaim some impatient objector, "that our knowledge is limited to what we can know, and that of what we cannot know we must remain for ever ignorant. Truly a most sapient conclusion!" But if the objector will kindly turn to the history of philosophy he will be able to judge for himself how far the questions therein discussed fall within the sphere of knowledge and how far they lie in the region of nescience. The business of philosophy, it has somewhere been said, is to ceaselessly attempt to explain the inexplicable. And "the only method of freeing learning at once from these abstruse questions is to inquire seriously into the nature of human understanding, and show, from an exact analysis of its powers and capacity, that it is by no means fitted for such remote and abstruse subjects. We must submit to this fatigue, in order to live at ease hereafter; and must cultivate true metaphysics with some care, in order to destroy the false and adulterated" (Hume).

3. *The Sphere of Knowledge.*

"Reason sees a full light which illuminates certain places; but that light borders upon the most profound darkness."—DAVID HUME.

The world of knowledge is the very world in which we live. Around it and beyond it there may lie the region of nescience, but herein is the realm of action; herein we must seek the springs of conduct.

And is it, then, a phantom world, a world of mere appearance?—a world of shadows, which to the unthinking may *seem* real, but through which the eye of reason pierces to the underlying bare existence—a colourless, intangible, unimaginable somewhat, of which we can only assert that it *is?* Does philosophy tell us that this *Inconceivable Is* alone

possesses reality? that of this golden sovereign I hold in my
hand the colour, the hardness, the figure, the size—every
quality that has a name—are dependent on me and my
perception, and that apart from me and others of my kind
they have no real existence? That all these but appear
to be, and only an unknowable something *is?* If so, we
are tempted to exclaim, Away with it, for its conclusions
are proved false by the plain and obvious teachings of
common sense.

Of which common sense the philosopher Kant somewhere remarks that it is the notable invention of modern
times, whereby the emptiest noodle can place himself on a
level with the profoundest thinker.

Now, the dicta of common sense in matters in which
it is properly instructed are simply invaluable; they are
neither more nor less than instinctive judgments, in which
we have the advantage, not merely of the experience of the
individual, but, to some extent, of that of the race. But
when the dicta of common sense concern matters in which
it is *not* properly instructed, they are often little better than
sheer nonsense. As Goethe has said, "the province of common sense is active life. In action it will not lightly go
wrong; but the higher regions of thought, speculation, and
large conclusions are altogether outside of its jurisdiction."
When common-sense Reid wondered why the idealist did
not run his head against a post, which, having no real
existence, could not injure him; and when common-sense
Johnson said to the disciple of Berkeley, "Pray, sir, don't
leave us; for we may perhaps forget to think of you, and
then you will cease to exist," they were indulging in witty
nonsense; and when the great doctor said to Boswell, "Sir,
we *know* our will is free, and there's an end of it," he
indulged in the nonsense without the wit.

The chemist affirms that he can cause the metal potassium to ignite by throwing it into water. Common sense exclaims, "Absurd!" and thereby proclaims its ignorance. The physiologist describes certain purposive acts performed by a brainless frog. Common sense murmurs, "Ridiculous!" but alters no whit the fact. The mathematician speaks of the ether. Common sense replies, "Impossible!" but the mathematician takes no heed of the remark. And long ago Galileo maintained that the apparent motion of the sun was due to the real motion of the earth; but then common sense, fitly embodied in certain dignitaries of the Roman Catholic Church, had the best of it, and clapped him into prison.

But why insist here upon the proper limitation of the sphere of common sense? For this reason. The question of the reality of the world around us has two sides—a practical side and a speculative side. The practical side falls within the province of common sense, and to any suggestions common sense has to offer in this region we should listen with thankful attention. The speculative side is assuredly "altogether outside of its jurisdiction," and any remarks on this head it may offer, in an off-hand way and without due instruction, must be regarded as simple impertinence. And now let us turn to the practical side.

In the first chapter two facts were intended to stand out clearly. First, that the objects we see around us are, to a very large extent, products of our own constructive skill, built up by our minds, at the bare suggestion of a sensation from without, out of the vast store of memories individually or ancestrally acquired. That was the first fact. The second was that the object is not an object for me alone, but for humanity. This arose, it will be remembered, out of the fact that I am a social being. "This belief," to quote the words of Prof. Clifford—"this belief in the existence of other men's consciousness, in the existence of ejects, dominates every thought and every action of our lives. In the first place, it profoundly modifies the object. This room, the tables, the chairs, your bodies, are all objects in my consciousness ; as simple objects, they are parts of me. But I somehow infer the existence of similar objects in your consciousness, and these are not objects to me, nor can they ever be made so ; they are ejects. This being so, I bind up with each object as it exists in my mind the thought of similar objects existing in other men's minds, and I thus form the complex conception—'this table, as an object in the minds of men ;' or, as Mr. Shadworth Hodgson puts it, an object of consciousness in general. This conception symbolizes an indefinite number of ejects, together with one object which the conception of each eject more or less resembles. Its character is, therefore, mainly ejective in respect of what it symbolizes, but mainly objective in respect of its nature. I shall call this complex conception the *social object ;* it is a symbol of one thing (the *individual object*, it may be called, for distinction's sake) which is in my consciousness, and of an indefinite number of other things which are ejects and out of my consciousness."

The object, then, is for me an ideal construction, and it is an ideal construction not only for me but for my fellows. And the physical world is a world of objects, and of objects not for me alone but for man. The question is, How far is it *real?* How far are the objects of which it is constituted really existent ?

I reply that in the practical and scientific sense of the word (though not in the philosophical) they are real ; that for knowledge and for feeling out of which arise the springs of conduct—for the springs of conduct are within us—they are so real as to constitute *the* realities of practical life. And if I be asked what is the test of their reality, I answer

verification; for verification is the test of practical reality,
just as prevision is the test of practical truth. My ideal
construction is real when it is a verifiable construction,
verifiable not only by me as an "individual object," but
verifiable also by my fellows as a "social object."

There lies before me a golden sovereign, and I am
convinced that as an object it is really existent. And, first,
what is the nature of the object? It is an ideal construction
I build up at the bidding of a certain visual impression;
and it is a social object, having value not only for me, but
for my fellows. And how can I test its reality? By
verifying my construction. If my construction has objective
reality, I shall find that the object, which at present I
merely see, will, when put to the test through the medium
of other senses, turn out to be hard, weighty, and roughened
at the edge; and that it is an object not for me alone, but
also for my fellows, will be shown by the fact that my
neighbour will not hesitate to give me twenty shillings in
silver in exchange for it.

And if now a "philosopher"—by which term I would
imply one who had imperfectly grasped the teachings of
philosophy on this head—steps in and says, "But, my dear
sir, do you not perceive that the yellowness cannot exist
as such in the sovereign; the colour depends upon the eye
that sees; in the absence of the seeing eye there is no such
thing as colour." To this I would reply, "Assuredly in the
absence of the seeing eye there would be no such thing as
colour, and in the absence of wings there would be no
such thing as flight. But, for all that, birds, having wings,
do fly; and mankind having sight, the yellowness *does*
exist as such in the sovereign. The yellowness forms part
of the ideal construction. A blind humanity would have
constructed a different object; but a seeing humanity has
constructed an object in which the yellowness most

assuredly does exist as such, and forms an integral part of the object as thus constructed."

"Your argument lands you in an absurdity," perhaps the "philosopher" may return. "It so happens that I am colour-blind. This rose which appears to you red, appears to me green. To the object you construct redness is essential; to the object I construct greenness is essential. But the real object cannot be both red and green, and I maintain that it is neither."

This objection, however, merely brings out the fact that in some cases the social object and the individual object do not coincide. As a social object, the rose is red; and, therefore, it may, I think, be fairly said to be *really* red. But for certain abnormally constituted individuals, characteristically called colour-blind, the object they construct is not red, but green. Their individual object clashes with the social object. As an individual object, their rose is undoubtedly really green; but as a social object, the rose is assuredly red. And since the social object—the object constructed by and for the normally constituted mass of mankind—is of far greater importance than the individual object constructed by this, that, or the other abnormally constituted cripple—if they will forgive the word—it would seem that common sense is justified in its assertion that the rose is really red, and that the cripples, whether "philosophers" or not, are really labouring under a delusion.

Once more our "philosopher" objects—and let us suppose that he is a so-called materialist, who reduces the phenomena of the world to the phenomena of matter and motion—once more this materialist "philosopher" objects that we are confounding essentials and non-essentials. He recalls our attention to the vibrating spring. He reminds us that the spring during its vibration gave rise to sound

of varying pitch, to warmth, and to light of different colour.
These, he maintains, are no part of the object proper, which
is really a minute metallic spring, but are merely accidents
of the manner of its vibration. They may exist or may
cease to exist without destroying the integrity of the spring
as a really existing object.

Of all fallacies connected with this subject this is, perhaps, the most insidious. It partly arises out of common
but misleading forms of speech. We are apt to say, for
example, that the same object may be hot or cold ; and
we therefore come to imagine that its temperature is not
essential to our conception of the object. But this is
merely a legacy of the false metaphysics of the primary and
secondary qualities, or rather, perhaps, a legacy of the
false way of looking at things to which that metaphysics
gave definite expression. Here is a teaspoon ; I may use
it to stir my tea, and it becomes a hot teaspoon ; or I may
use it to eat an ice, and it becomes a cold teaspoon. But
teaspoon, hot teaspoon, cold teaspoon are not one but
three objects. Let us suppose that the object teaspoon is
formed by the synthesis of certain qualities, which, without
particularizing, we may call *abc*. Then, in hot teaspoon,
we have a synthesis of these qualities with the addition of
hotness ; we may call it *abcx*. And, in cold teaspoon, we
have a synthesis of these qualities with the addition of
coldness instead of hotness ; we may call it *abcy*. Now, it
is clear that *abc*, *abcx*, and *abcy* do not stand for the same
object, but for three different objects. They are different
syntheses, different ideal constructions. And when we say,
in popular language, that it is the same object that is at
one time hot and at the other time cold, what we really
mean is that the elements *abc* are common to all three
constructions. We may say, then, that *abc* is our general
conception of a teaspoon, while *abcx* is our more particular

conception of a hot teaspoon, and *abcy* is our more particular conception of a cold teaspoon. And this, it seems to me, is all that common sense really means when it says that the same object may be either hot or cold.

There is always something valid and valuable in the criticisms of common sense in matters within its own proper sphere of the practical. And when it maintains that there are certain things which are essential to our idea of a teaspoon and certain other things which are unessential, it is on safe and solid ground. There are certain things which are essential to our *general* idea of a teaspoon ; it may be hot or cold, it may be clean or dirty, it may be silver or plated, it may be plain or fiddle-patterned, and still remain a teaspoon. The essential *abc* still remain. But take away its resistance to the touch, take away its proper form, alter its size beyond certain limits, and it ceases to be a real teaspoon and becomes something else—a phantom, a lump of metal, a dessert spoon.

Why, then, may not the materialist "philosopher" maintain that the sound, warmth, colour of the vibrating spring are no part of the object proper, but are mere accidents of the manner of its vibration? Wherein lies the fallacy? Here. That when the spring is giving rise to sound he wishes to persuade us that the sound is no part of the real nature of the object, but merely a temporary accident of its mode of vibration. But no hocus-pocus of this sort can alter the fact, that so long as I hear the spring emitting sound, so long is the sound part and parcel of the object. It is no use to tell me that if the vibrations grow more rapid or become less rapid the sound will cease. Because *under different conditions* there will be a coloured object and not a sounding object, he wants to persuade us that the sound is not an essential part of the object *under these conditions.* His argument somewhat resembles that of certain supporters of free-will. They act in a certain way under certain circumstances. On reflection they perceive that their action was unwise. Afterwards, on the recurrence of similar external circumstances, they act differently. And they point to this difference of action under similar external circumstances as proof of the freedom of the will. But they forget that, though the external circumstances remain the same, the internal circumstances have altered. Reflection has wrought a change in character, and the character having chànged the action is not likely to be the same. So too the spring under different conditions of vibration is not likely to remain the same. But under certain conditions the vibrating spring excites the sensation of sound, and under these conditions the sound is essential to the object—it is part of the synthesis. Under other conditions the vibrating spring is a centre of warmth, and under those conditions the warmth is essential to the object—is an integral part of the synthesis. Under yet other conditions the vibrating spring gives rise to colour sensations, and under those conditions the colour is essential to the object —it is a necessary part of the synthesis.

What, then, shall we say of that materialism which proclaims that nothing really exists but matter and motion? Shall we not say that it is neither philosophy nor common sense? It is certainly not common sense. For the world around us is full of scents and sights and sounds which, though analysis may resolve them into matter and motion, are really for us something more; just as a written word, though analysis may resolve it into a number of arbitrary signs, is really for us something more. And it is certainly not philosophy. For philosophy has long since disallowed the validity of any subdivision into real and subjective qualities, and teaches that all experience is of the phenomenal and relative. Matter and motion are no more

real, in a philosophical sense—that is, no more independent of the percipient organism—than colour or scent;
just as the letters we use as signs, and of which we build
up our written words, are no more independent of our
intelligence than the words themselves into which we
weave them.

The strange thing is that men should be found, I do not
say among the leaders of physical thought, but among
their more humble and yet less humble followers, who seem
firmly to believe that the ultimate elements reached by
analysis have a truer reality than the phenomena which are
submitted to analysis. The chemist, so far as I know, does
not assign to the sixty or seventy elements a greater reality
than is possessed by the countless compounds into which
they are built up. And yet the materialist would seem to
believe, or to talk as if he believed, that his elements,
matter and motion in space and time, have a transcendent
reality which is not possessed by the phenomena in which
they are manifested. Energy, we are told, is the one
true existence; and what we call the world is merely our
manner of regarding it.

Against this materialistic view I strongly protest. And
while deeply grateful to physics for its masterly analysis of
phenomena, I still, in the region of the practical, hold fast
by the good, honest, everyday testimony of experience,
and claim for the syntheses, which I call objects, a full,
perfect, and true reality—that is, a reality that is verifiable,
and verifiable not only by me, but by mankind.

In turning now from practical to speculative reality,
from the reality of everyday life to the reality of philosophic thought, we enter a totally different region, a region
in which to tread safely requires not only care but some
little preliminary training. The question here is, How far

has the world of things around us, not only a reality *for us*, but an *independent* reality?

The common-sense view of the question is that, of course, the reality is independent of us. Suppose the whole human race were annihilated to-morrow, the world of things would thereby be in no wise changed; the reality of their existence would be no whit altered. That is the offhand dictum of common sense. But question commonsense, and you will find its dictum mean just this: that if, after the annihilation of the human race, a single fortunate individual were allowed to revisit the world, just to peep and see how things were going on, he would find matters very much as they were, the real existence of earth and sea and sky not the least impaired by man's absence from the scene. And this no one denies. It is like the old question, whether a rose is still red in the dark. The man who maintains that it is, is certain that with keen sight *and just a ray of light* the rose would be seen to be red.

How, then, could we settle this question about the rose? Since the tiniest ray of light is inadmissible, and since no eye can see in the dark, the question seems an insoluble one. But it is not insoluble. Physics has solved it for us. How? By proving that colour is absolutely dependent on light, whence it follows that the complete absence of light must bring with it the complete absence of colour. Thus, reasoning based on experience solves the question in which, from the nature of the case, the direct testimony of experience is dumb.

And how can we settle the question of the independent reality of the world of things? Since no prying individual is permissible, this question too seems at first sight an insoluble one. But it is not insoluble. Philosophy has solved it for us. How? By proving that the practical reality of the world of things around us is absolutely dependent on the percipient organism—is, in a word, a reality *for us ;* whence it follows that in the absence of the percipient organism, *this* reality vanishes with that on which it depends.

Certain of the older philosophers, however, maintained, as we have already seen, that the true independent reality is the matter or substance itself which manifests itself to us under the form of this practical reality. Although it is, and must for ever remain, unknowable, still its existence, its real independent existence, is an inevitable inference which we cannot avoid without admitting that "the manifestations are manifestations of—nothing." To which argument, as we have seen, Berkeley replied, "I am unable to see how the testimony of sense can be alleged as proof for the existence (or, let us add, the non-existence) of anything which is not perceived by sense." Set forth more at length, the Berkeleian argument would seem to be this : that the "inevitable inference" of the independent existence of material substance is based on our conception of causation ; but of causation beyond the realm of experience we know and can know nothing, therefore we have no right to infer either that they are caused or that they are uncaused. It is right to add, however, that Berkeley himself believed that they were caused, the Eternal Spirit Himself being the direct cause, needing no hypothetical substance of matter as a go-between.

Locke maintained that we can know nothing whatever about substance of any kind ; Hume declared that it was something that we must take for granted in all our reasonings ; and modern Agnosticism looks up to it with a kind of mild enthusiasm as the Unknowable. All assume its existence. And yet it seems to me that the words of Berkeley ring true. How can the testimony of experience be alleged as proof of the existence or non-existence of that which lies beyond experience?

But does it lie wholly beyond experience and the inference that is based on experience? Let us see.

There is one thing of the reality of which it is impossible to doubt, and that is thought. Its real existence is implied in the very doubt of its reality, if, indeed, such doubt were ever seriously entertained. The objects which constitute the phenomenal world around us are syntheses of mental impressions. We live in the world of mind, a real world of ideas, the true and real existence of which it is simply impossible to doubt.

Now, suppose that a physiologist is discoursing of my brain and nervous system, the integrity of which depends on the integrity of my body as a whole. He speaks of something practically real, of an exceedingly complex material product in which there go on exceedingly complex modes of motion. That is what it seems to him as an object, as a complex synthesis by reflection. But I know, what he can never know directly, that the true reality of which my brain is only the practical or objective reality is *not matter but mind.*

And suppose that I in turn am discoursing of his brain as an exceedingly complex material product in which there go on exceedingly complex modes of motion. That is the objective reality. But as an inference from my own experience, I believe that behind this there is, though I never can get at it directly, an independent reality; that is, a reality in no sense dependent on me as a percipient. And that independent reality I call an *eject.* I believe that *mind* is the true reality that underlies the phenomenal mass of matter which I call a brain; and, practically, this is what most of us believe. The real man is not the material body of flesh and blood, but what we characteristically call the living soul within.

But if *mind* is the true reality that underlies the phenomenal mass of matter I call a brain, may I not, nay, must I not, believe that the true reality that underlies other forms of matter is similar in its essential nature? that, if not mind, it is, as Clifford calls it, mind-stuff?

To this view common sense will assuredly dissent. But we must remember that we are now in "the higher regions of thought, speculation, and large conclusions, which," as Goethe says, "are altogether beyond its jurisdiction." The chief objection it will raise will, no doubt, be, that on this view we attribute consciousness to a dining-table or a seed-cake. But common sense must be told that not even mind and consciousness, still less mind-stuff and consciousness, are identical. I shall in the chapter on Mind and Body contend that a continuity of mind underlies the discontinuity of consciousness. Here it is enough to state my belief, that mind-elements, which when they come into relation constitute consciousness, are themselves unconscious.

The reality that underlies the mass of grey matter within my neighbour's skull I believe to be mind-stuff, so grouped as to constitute mind, which is capable of rising into consciousness. But if, now, I trace backwards the history of that neighbour of mine, I find that some thirty years ago he was a minute ovum $\frac{1}{120}$ inch or so in diameter. From that ovum he has gradually developed by the assimilation of material from without. But when did mind come on the scene? For my own part, I find it utterly impossible to conceive so great a break in continuity as the arbitrary appearance at any one epoch of the mental element. I am constrained to believe that in the ovum and in the material assimilated, there lay the germs of mind-stuff from which the mind arose by a complex process of coalescence.

Nor can I stop here. Believing as I do that somewhere and somewhen the inorganic gave rise in process of evolution to the organic, I am constrained to believe further that, associated with every molecule of phenomenal matter, there is the underlying independent reality of noumenal mind-stuff. And if I be allowed to infuse into a dry and, to some minds, perhaps, repellent philosophical creed the warmth and glow of poetic emotion, then I will say, with good Bishop Berkeley, that the world of practical reality, in which I live, rests securely upon the bosom of the Eternal Spirit.

PART II.
THE STUDY OF NATURE.

—◆—

"The motive of science is the extension of man, on all sides, into Nature, till his hands shall touch the stars, his eyes shall see through the earth, his ears understand the language of beast and bird, and the sense of the wind ; and through his sympathy heaven and earth shall talk with him."—R. W. EMERSON.

CHAPTER I.

THE METHOD OF SCIENCE.

"Science arises from the discovery of Identity amidst Diversity."—
W. STANLEY JEVONS.

I PROPOSE in this part, which deals with the *Study of Nature*, to consider some of the more interesting and important questions which arise out of the science of our day. Beginning in this chapter with a few remarks—for this little volume neither claims nor deserves to be regarded as a treatise, nor, indeed, to be anything more than just a prolonged talk to my readers on matters in which I am deeply interested—beginning, I say, with a short consideration of the Method of Science, I shall then proceed to say somewhat on the nature and validity of scientific laws and the kind of accuracy they may reasonably claim. We will, then, see to what conclusion we are led by an ultimate analysis of phenomena ; after which, as a relief from this perhaps somewhat dry analysis, we will turn aside to consider whether the scientific mode of regarding Nature has of necessity a deadening influence on the poetic side of our human nature. The question of the evolution of scientific knowledge will, then, claim our attention. And after that I shall beg my readers to let me talk somewhat more at length on Body and Mind and the nature of their connection.

First, then, as to the method of science.* It is strange, in this age of science, to note how prevalent is a misconception of the very nature and essence of science. I suppose that four out of every five fairly educated persons that you meet will define science by its subject-matter. Expressed or unexpressed, their notion is that science deals with chemical, physical, astronomical, geological, biological facts. But it cannot be too often repeated that this is not so ; that science deals with no special and restricted class of facts, but claims as its domain the whole realm of fact as distinguished from the realms of fiction and of fancy, though it undoubtedly deals with these facts in a special way and by a method of its own.

If, then, the whole realm of fact is claimed by science as its wide domain, may we say that all knowledge of fact is science ? Assuredly not. A man may be cram-full of facts and have very little science in his composition. My neighbour may possess a million bricks, but that is a very different thing to possessing a house. So, too, a man may know a million facts ; but unless they are built into a definite system they do not constitute science. And yet we may not say that facts are the bricks of which the house of science is built ; for the house of science is a spiritual house, a house not made with hands. A closer analogy may, perhaps, be found in the aggregation of particles, which before had floated formless in solution, into a crystal of well-defined form ; for this analogy brings into view the condensation of knowledge previously diffused and the continuous growth of the resulting science. But a far happier and more complete analogy is to be found in the similarity of science to an organism, which grows, not as does the crystal by mere accretion or the addition of

* This chapter is based on the opening lecture for the session 1884-5 of the University College, Bristol.

new external layers, but by assimilation or the incorporation of new matter into its living substance. Every new fact it has well been said must be digested by the organism of the sciences. We cannot, I think, better define science than by means of this analogy. Science as a product, then, I would define as organized knowledge. Science as a process is the organization and extension of our knowledge. And the business of the man of science, as such, is to organize and extend our knowledge.

To organize and extend our knowledge, not (as such) to apply that knowledge to practical material ends. That is the function, not of science, but of the technic arts, which utilize the *prevision*, made possible by science, in *provision* for our material welfare. The distinction between science and the technic arts is the distinction between discovery and invention, the distinction between the making of knowledge and its application. Scientific discovery and technic invention are twin sisters, born at the same hour, but of entirely different individuality. And so long as they walk through the world together hand in hand, so long will they be happy and prosperous. Let us not forget, however, that twin sisters though they be, each has a separate individuality and her own special work to perform. Or, to put the matter more practically, let us not forget that the chemist, the physicist, the geologist, the biologist, are men of science ; while the metallurgist, the engineer, the miner, the medical practitioner, are professional men. The aim and object of the science of chemistry, to take one example, is to form a body of doctrine concerning the combinations and recombinations of the various substances which enter into the composition of the earth's crust. But it is possible that the chemist may come to the conclusion that pure science does not pay. The charge of having come to this conclusion has, indeed, been recently laid at the doors of certain leading English chemists. He may, therefore, utilize his knowledge in the assay office, in glass works, in a brewery, in bleaching works, as a metallurgist, and so forth. But in so doing he becomes, so far, a professional man, and not a man of science. And the charge against certain English chemists to-day is that they are devoting themselves too much to professional and too little to professorial work. In the same way the navigator, the land surveyor, the engineer, the medical practitioner are men who study science for the sake of their professional work. But unless they are extending the boundaries of our knowledge, or contributing to the organization of our knowledge, they are not men of science in the true sense of that term.

At the same time, it is absolutely essential, if they would do good and original work in the field of technics, that they should proceed on the method of science. The *process* must be scientific, though the *product* be technical. And what is that method? *To proceed by observation and experiment, by guarded hypothesis and careful verification, from the known to the unknown, on the well-founded assumption of the uniformity of Nature.*

In illustration of this method, let us take two examples, one in the field of science, the other in the field of technics. And first in technics. The lead obtained from certain English and other ores contains a varying quantity of silver, often several ounces to the ton. Up to 1833, however, no method was known by which lead, containing less than eight ounces to the ton, could be desilverized. Thus not only was a large quantity of valuable metal lost, but the lead itself was rendered by the silver harder, and therefore, for certain purposes, less valuable. In 1833 Mr. H. L. Pattinson, among others, was endeavouring to solve the problem of the separation of these two metals, and it is reported that he chanced to drop a crucible containing molten lead rich in silver. Such an accident might happen a hundred times and nothing come of it. But Mr. Pattinson's keen eye detected crystalline grains in the spilt metal, and he carefully picked some of them out for separate examination. What passed through his mind it is impossible to say, but he may not improbably have said to himself something of this sort: "When sea-water freezes, the ice formed is comparatively free from salt, while the water remaining is comparatively rich in salt; it may be that these solid grains are similarly comparatively free from silver, while the lead remaining is comparatively rich in silver." If he argued thus, he framed an hypothesis as the result of observation. At all events, he set to work, and carefully analyzed the crystals, and found as a practical fact that they *were* nearly pure lead. Taking for granted, then, the uniformity of nature, Pattinson saw that what had taken place by an accident in his laboratory could be reproduced of set purpose on a larger scale in a metallurgical process; and by the process which he thus devised, which is called after him Pattinson's process, thousands of tons of lead are now being treated every year. This discovery of Pattinson's affords us a good example of the scientific method in technics, the scientific knowledge gained being in this case, so to speak, a by-product.

In the field of science, let us take Darwin's discovery of the law of Natural Selection. In a letter to Haeckel, in 1864, he wrote as follows:—"In South America three classes of facts were brought strongly before my mind. *Firstly*, the manner in which closely allied species replace species in going southward. *Secondly*, the close affinity of the species inhabiting the islands near South America to those proper to the continent. This struck me profoundly, especially the difference of the species in the adjoining

F

islets of the Galapagos archipelago. *Thirdly*, the relation of the living Edentata and Rodentia to the extinct species. I shall never forget my astonishment when I dug out a gigantic piece of armour like that of a living armadillo.

"Reflecting on these facts, and collecting analogous ones, it seemed to me probable that allied species were descended from a common parent. But for some years I could not conceive how each form became so excellently adapted to its habits of life. I then began systematically to study domestic productions, and after a time saw clearly that man's selective power was the most important agent. I was prepared, from having studied the habits of animals to appreciate the struggle for existence, and my work in geology gave me some idea of the lapse of past time. Therefore, when I happened to read 'Malthus on Population,' the idea of natural selection flashed upon me."

Thus Darwin prepared the way for his subsequent advance by careful observation; the Essay on "Population" gave rise to the hypothesis of Natural Selection ; and the careful verification of this hypothesis became the main work of the remainder of his long and honourable life. And what was the idea in Mr. Malthus' book which was the seed of so noble a tree as the "Origin of Species"? That the rate of increase of the population is in excess of the rate of increase of food, and that there is, therefore, a struggle for existence, through which only the fittest survive. This is the idea which, germinating in the mind of Darwin, and applied not only to mankind but to the whole realm of existence, has revolutionized not only biological but the whole of philosophic thought. If any man in the world proceeded on the scientific method, that man was Darwin. He, if any, proceeded by observation and experiment, by guarded hypothesis and careful verifi-

·cation, from the known to the unknown, on the well-founded hypothesis of the uniformity of Nature.

It is not that Darwin was the first to formulate a theory of organic evolution ; by no means. It is not, even, that he was the first to throw out the hypothesis of Natural Selection ; for Wells and Malthus were before him, and Wallace was at his side. It is that Darwin—and his fellow-labourer Wallace, also, to whom all honour—proceeded on the method of science, amassing and classifying observations, calling in the aid of experiment, and applying, wherever possible, the indispensable test of verification. This it is that places Darwin beside Newton.

CHAPTER II.

THE FACTS OF NATURE AND THE LAWS OF SCIENCE.

"What we call the Laws of Nature are not objective existences, but subjective abstractions—formulæ in which the multitudinous phenomena are stripped of their variety and reduced to unity."—G. H. LEWES.

SOME time ago a little fellow came to me with a very simple question, to which he hoped to get an equally simple answer. The question was, What makes a stone fall to the ground? And he seemed not a little disappointed when I told him that I could not answer his question, for the very sufficient reason that I did not know. Two or three days afterwards I met my little friend, and asked him whether he had found out about the stone. He said that his father had told him that the stone *must* fall to the ground through the action of the law of gravitation. With this answer, as perhaps befitted a dutiful son, he seemed abundantly satisfied. But satisfaction gave way to disappointment when I showed him that he had merely hidden his ignorance, or rather his nescience, under a high-sounding phrase.

The fall of a heavy body to the earth is one of the simplest and commonest of natural phenomena. And the study of natural phenomena, or more briefly the study of Nature, consists mainly in classifying the phenomena, reducing them to order and then giving to the groups of facts thus ordered their simplest expression in what are termed laws of Nature. The law of gravitation is such a law of Nature ; and the fall of a stone to the earth is one of the phenomena which fall under the group of facts thus summarized. To the man who is acquainted with the laws of Nature, the explanation of a fact is, first, the reference of the fact to this or that group of facts more or less definitely summarized in a natural law, and, secondly, the demonstration that it is the inevitable outcome of certain other facts thus summarized. But to a person ignorant of the laws of Nature, such a reference affords no explanation, but merely a cloak under which his ignorance may be hidden. To such a person, the only way in which a phenomenon can be explained is by referring it to some simpler and better known phenomenon in the same category. The motion of the earth in space may, for example, be to some extent explained to one ignorant of its nature by throwing a stone, pointing out the curvature of its course under the joint action of the impulse given by the thrower and the earth's attraction, and referring the curvature of the earth's course to the joint action of *its* onward motion in space and the attraction of the sun. But when a boy asks the explanation of so simple and ordinary a fact as the fall of a stone to the earth, there being no simpler phenomenon by means of which it can be explained, all we can say is, " My dear boy, I cannot tell you *why* the stone falls in the way in which you and I see it fall, but I can tell you something about *how* it falls, and I can make that fall illustrate a great many other facts of Nature."

My little friend's father, however, was probably quite satisfied with the answer he gave his son—that the stone must fall to the ground through the operation of the law of gravitation. But if I had had the opportunities of

cross-examining the father that I had of cross-examining
the son, I should have been tempted to inquire, Why *must*,
my friend ?   To which question he would, I conceive, have
been unable to give a scientific answer.   And yet it is
strange how many people of average education and
intelligence import this metaphysical idea of necessity
into the laws of Nature.   It cannot be too frequently
reiterated that what we call laws of Nature are simply well-
proven and oft-verified inferences from known facts, and
also, as we believe, generalized statements of *all* the facts
of like nature, whether we have observed them and verified
the law in their case or not.   There is neither any idea of
necessity nor any attempt to show why the facts are as
they are.   That the stone must fall to the ground is only
true in the same sense as it is true that the stone must be
a stone.   And it is surely much simpler and less misleading
to say that the stone *is* a stone and that it does, as a matter
of fact, fall to the ground.

That a stone is a stone is an identical proposition.   It
remains true so long as the external object and the conception it calls forth in our own minds remain unchanged.   If
we like, we may say that it must be true under these
conditions.   That a stone if unsupported does fall to the
ground is a verbal proposition.   Weight or a tendency
to fall to the earth is an ineradicable part of our ideal
construction of the object.   And when we state in the
form of a proposition that a stone if unsupported does fall
to the ground, we merely give expression to what was
already latent in our conception of a stone.   It too remains
true so long as the external object and the conception it
calls forth remain unchanged.   And, if we like, we may say
that it must be true under these conditions.

But if there is no mysterious metaphysical necessity
about the facts, whence comes it in the law, which is just

a well-verified generalization from the facts? We may say, if we like, that a law of Nature must be true, because if untrue it is not a law of Nature. But this truth (or truism) has no higher value than the proposition that a stone must be a stone, because if it is not a stone it is something else. And yet there is a prevalent notion that there is a mysterious necessity about the laws of Nature which casts its shadow over the facts and enchains them with a mystic constraint. Here, again, as in so many other cases, our common forms of speech are greatly to blame. We speak of facts as determined by law ; we say that the universe is rigidly law-bound ; we write treatises on the Reign of Law. And then we are told that laws imply a law-giver ; therefore there exists a Supreme Law-giver, our current forms of speech being adduced as " abiding witnesses " of the truth of this conclusion (Argyll). Now, against the conclusion itself, I do not desire to say one word ; but against the manner of reaching it and the alleged proof of its truth, I wish strongly to protest. From the point of view of science and the philosophy that is based upon science, with which alone this volume deals, the word *law* stands for a definite conception concerning the order of nature, to which an attentive study of the facts has led us. The facts are not determined by law, but the law is rather determined by the facts. And instead of speaking of the reign of law we should rather speak of the tyranny of facts, a tyranny bitterly galling to some minds. We have no right whatever to import into the conception symbolized by the word *law* in its scientific sense, ideas which are proper to the word *law* in its legal sense. And our current forms of speech in this case no more prove the truth of the conclusion that a Supreme Law-giver exists, than our current forms of speech in another case prove that the sun sinks down into the ocean.

It may be that the laws to which we rise by the successive inductions of science are but imperfect expressions of the immutable edicts which have issued from the council chambers of the Eternal Spirit ; that the laws of science are also the fiats of the Omnipotent. But this is a question which is beyond science, which transcends the philosophy which is based thereon, and which must be referred to the philosophy of Faith, which has other canons and other methods.

But if there is so strong a tendency in our words to carry with them misleading implications, we must be all the more careful to acquire clear conceptions of the meaning of the words we employ. To attempt to alter current forms of speech would be as unwise as it would be hopeless. Were we to issue to-morrow a fresh coinage, the clear-cut image and superscription would soon be blurred by the careless handling of a thousand hazy thinkers. Our only chance is to carefully eliminate the sources of error. I would have it understood, then, that when in this chapter I speak of a law of Nature, I mean thereby a law of science concerning the facts of Nature. For Nature presents us with facts, not laws. *We* make the laws and test their truth by their accordance with the facts.

If, then, to return to our main theme, the laws of Nature be not necessarily true, except with such necessity as is the outcome of the tyranny of facts, upon what evidence do we believe them to be true ? By what canon do we extend those generalizations which we have erected on the basis of a limited number of instances to all instances of like nature ? What right have we to say that a law which has been proved to be true within the limits of experimental error holds good beyond those limits ? To this question I can see but one answer. We believe in the correctness of our interpretation of Nature *as an hypothesis*—as an assumption, if you will. We find that whenever we test our hypothesis it turns out to be correct. . We find that increased experimental accuracy only justifies increased confidence in the truth of our hypothesis. And therefore, until that hypothesis is proved to be false, like practical, honest folk, we refuse to be shaken in our belief; and in matters which admit of proof or disproof this is really the only thing to do.

Here again, however, it will be well, perhaps, to distinguish between practical and speculative accuracy. Take, for example, the law of the indestructibility of matter. We believe in the truth of this law because, within the limits of experimental accuracy, we have always found it to hold good. We are carried forward by the inertia of our own inductive processes to the formulation of a law, which we believe to have an accuracy beyond our powers of experimental verification. But the accuracy we believe in is a practical accuracy. It is an accuracy beyond our powers of verification, but not an accuracy transcending verification. And if some one should say to me, " But do you not believe it to be *absolutely* accurate ? " I should reply, " My dear sir, I reserve my beliefs and disbeliefs in science for matters which are capable of proof or disproof. Absolute speculative accuracy has no place in the world of phenomena, with which science has to deal in a practical way by means of experiment and observation and reasoning based thereon."

But the laws of geometry—they, at any rate, are absolutely and not merely practically accurate. That the three angles of any plane triangle are equal to two right angles, is not only true within the limits of experimental accuracy, but is absolutely true without the possibility of error. Yes, absolutely true within the abstract realm of Euclidian geometry. But whether true or not, in this absolute sense, within the realm of phenomenal Nature, altogether depends upon the deeper question, whether the assumptions of geometry are to be regarded as absolutely or only as practically true. Now, within the last half century, the foundations of geometry have been critically examined by mathematicians of acknowledged power. " And the conclusion to which these investigations lead is that, although the assumptions which were very properly made by the ancient geometers are practically exact—that is to say, more exact than experiment can be—for such finite things as we have to deal with, and such portions of space as we can reach ; yet the truth of them for very much larger things, or very much smaller things, or parts of space which are at present beyond our reach, is a matter to be decided by experiment, when its powers are considerably increased " (Clifford). So that here again the accordance of the laws of science with the facts of Nature can only be said to be practically exact.

The case of the laws of geometry, however, shows us a sense in which the laws of science may be said to be absolutely true. The laws of geometry are absolutely true within the realm of geometry. The geometer starts with certain assumptions which he takes as facts. Never mind whether they are true in the external world or not ; they may be absolutely true, or practically true, or they may be false. " Grant me these as facts," he says, " within the realm of geometry, and the laws which I enunciate shall be absolutely true." Here, for example, are certain laws rigidly deduced on the assumption that the curvature of all space is nearly uniform and positive. These laws are absolutely true within the realm of geometry. Whether they are practically true, or even true at all, within the realm of Nature is a wholly different matter, and one to be determined by experimental research and practical observation.

And whether they are absolutely true within the realm of Nature is again a wholly different matter, one which is indeterminable by science, and may be left to ontologists and theologians.

In the same way the abstract laws of science may be said to be absolutely true within the realm of science. The man of science starts with certain assumptions which he takes as facts—perfect gases, rigid bars, organic types, the indestructibility of matter, the conservation of energy, . and so forth. Never mind for the present whether they are true in the external world or not. They may be absolutely true, or practically true, or they may be false. "Grant me these facts," he says, "within the realm of science, and the laws which I enunciate shall be absolutely true." Here, for example, are certain mechanical laws deduced on the assumption (among others) that we are dealing with perfectly rigid materials. These laws are absolutely true within the realm of mechanics. Whether they are practically true, or even true at all, within the realm of Nature is a wholly different matter, and one to the determination of which by experimental research we are devoting our best energies. We know, indeed, that the laws can only be approximately true, because the materials in Nature are *not* perfectly rigid. Still, we believe them to be also practically true—that is, true within the limits of experiment—as abstract laws wherein all disturbing causes are carefully eliminated. But whether they are absolutely true within the realm of Nature is again a wholly different matter, and one which we contentedly leave to the metaphysician to discuss and rediscuss for some few centuries with such profit as he can gain therefrom.

Admitting, therefore, that there is a sense, and a most important sense, in which the abstract laws of science are absolutely true—that is, absolutely true if certain funda-

mental assumptions be taken as granted—the fact still
remains that the *correspondence* between the laws of science
and the facts of Nature, although practically accurate,
cannot be known through science or the philosophy that is
based on science to be absolutely or speculatively exact.

CHAPTER III.

"The step from past experience to new circumstances (involved in all scientific thought) must be made in accordance with an observed uniformity in the order of events.

"Are we, then, to believe that Nature is absolutely and universally uniform? Certainly not ; we have no right to believe anything of this kind."—W. K. CLIFFORD.

IN every branch of science there are certain well-verified hypotheses which form the basis—the fundamental assumptions, if I may so say—of their several departments of knowledge. In physical astronomy, the law of universal gravitation is the fundamental assumption. In chemistry and physics, the indestructibility of matter and the conservation of energy are the fundamental assumptions. In the historical sciences, the law of evolution is regarded by an increasing number of our best thinkers as the fundamental assumption. In psychology, the fundamental assumption is to be found in the law of ejects, that my neighbour has a consciousness analogous to my own. In metaphysics, the law of substance, that there is a substance of being, is the fundamental assumption. In religion, the fundamental assumption is the existence of God. But in addition to all these, underlying them, uniting them, and binding them into a homogeneous whole, is the assumption which is the fundamental of fundamentals—that of the uniformity of Nature.

Now, when we speak of the uniformity of Nature, we mean that the observed order of Nature is constant, and constant in the following respects :—First, that laws proved to hold good (practically) for certain phenomena hold good also for all like phenomena ; secondly, that the order of Nature is practically constant in time ; and, thirdly, that the order of Nature is practically constant in space. Let us take the last of these propositions first.

That the order of Nature is constant in space is assumed by the astronomer at every step of his reasoning ; and the marvellous accuracy of the results reached, the wonderful precision of the prevision, testify to the legitimacy of the assumption. When the astronomer observes with a spectroscope the light which reaches his eye from a distant star, he finds that the band of rainbow colours is cut by fine dark lines. What, then, does he do ? He ascertains by experimental work in his laboratory what terrestrial substances will have this effect upon the spectrum (as such a band of rainbow colours is called), and then infers that the same substances exist in the distant star. And by what right does he draw this inference ? In his experiments he finds that on the earth distance has no effect whatever in modifying the results he obtains with his spectroscope. From these particular instances he rises to the general conclusion that distance is no factor in any such results ; and he assumes that what holds good for terrestrial distances holds good also for astronomical distances. And he considers the fact that by this assumption he is enabled to draw conclusions which are in perfect harmony with the general body of scientific doctrine, to be sufficient justification for this extension of the constancy of the order of Nature in space.

So, too, in the case of the measurement of angles. It is found that if any three points be taken on the earth's surface, and be joined by straight lines—such as the lines formed by rays of light passing from one to the other—that in the triangle so formed the three angles are equal to two right angles. The astronomer makes use of this fact in his measurements. He assumes that the rays of light always and throughout all measurable space proceed in straight lines, and that the three angles of all triangles formed by such lines are equal to two right angles. And the accuracy of his results proves the legitimacy of his assumption. But, as we have already seen, the known accuracy is practical, not absolute—within the limits of experiment and observation, not transcending those limits. And now we must note that it is practically accurate only for such portions of space as we have explored or can explore. Whether it is even practically accurate for all space whatever we cannot say. The space that we know is practically homaloidal. It is possible that it may not be theoretically homaloidal—that is to say, it is possible that the shortest path between two points may not be an absolutely straight line, but a very, very little curved. And for parts of space at an infinite distance we do not know what conditions hold good. Were it possible for me to proceed for an infinite distance in what we call a straight line,* it is just possible that I might find myself back again here ; but it is equally possible that I might find myself in a region of space, the conditions of which I am unable to conceive.

The order of Nature, then, is constant in space, *practically* and for *finite* distances.

That the order of Nature is constant in time is assumed both in astronomical and geological reasonings. When Sir Charles Lyell found in the ancient rocks of Nova Scotia pittings which resembled the rainprints recently

---

* According to Leibnitz's definition.

made on the mud of the shores of the Bay of Fundy, he
assumed the constancy of the order of Nature in time, and
concluded that the marks in the ancient rocks were also
made by rain. And geologists, so long as they are true to
their science, invariably follow the same course. Finding
out by careful observation how rocks are formed to-day,
they maintain that similar rocks were formed by similar
agencies in times past. So, too, in the matter of scenery.
They note the varying play of the agents of denudation on
rocks of differing powers of resistance; and then applying
the knowledge thus gained to pre-historic times, they maintain that the horizontal contours—bays and promontories,
headlands and inlets—and the vertical contours—hill and
dale, mountain and valley—result from the differential
action of the sculpturing forces on land surfaces of varying
resistance. Throughout their science they apply their
knowledge of the present as a key by means of which they
may read the riddle of the past. And this method of procedure they base on a firm belief in the constancy of the
order of Nature in time. But the geologists of a few generations ago carried this too far. They maintained that,
pry as far as you will into the past, you will find a state
of things resembling in a general way the state of things
which you find at present. And why were they wrong?
Not because their method was fallacious; but because they
did not take into consideration *all* the facts; and this fact
in especial—that the earth is cooling. Extend into the
past the order of Nature as it is now, and the earth must
once have been liquid, and not improbably at a period
antecedent to that vaporous. Work back from the
present to the past on the hypothesis of the constancy of
Nature, and you reach the state of things which the
nebular hypothesis assumes as a starting-point. And we
may fairly accept such conclusions for what they are

worth ; never forgetting how great is the chance of there being other factors which we are leaving out of consideration. But when men of science go further and say that such physical reasonings hold good for *all* past time—or, at any rate, until we reach the first catastrophe of creation —must we not cry, " Hold ? " Must we not remind them that the order of Nature is only known to be practically constant, and for a time finite? Infinitesimal errors may in infinite time make too big a hole in our physical reasonings for them to remain afloat. Let us, then, keep within our province of the practical and the finite.

So, too, when we consider time future instead of time past. Geologists tell us that the present state of things will in all probability continue for an indefinite time ; but they tell us, too, that the time is finite. They believe that, through long ages to come, fresh land will continue to be upheaved by the gradual process of earth-cooling, for rain and rivers, glaciers and ocean waves, to gnaw away and carve into scenic beauty; but they believe also, that this state of things will surely come to an end. For they maintain that the earth will at last become so far cooled that upheavals will cease, and that, this being so, if the carving action still continue, all the solid land then above the waters of the ocean will slowly but surely be reduced to the level of the sea. And they tell us, moreover, that even if this be not so, the time will inevitably come when the sun shall be so far cooled that the conditions essential to life will no longer obtain on the earth's surface ; and that in any case the eventual fate of the earth is to fall into the sun, and be lost in his greater mass. Now, when men of science tell us all this, we may, I think, admit that their speculations are of a legitimate order, though we may, perhaps, deem that the problem is of too complicated a nature to warrant more than such qualified assent as is

G

implied in a "maybe." And when Sir William Thomson draws our attention to the fact that all forms of energy tend to run down to one form ; when he shows that the motion of masses, chemical attraction, electrical energy, and so on, tend to become degraded to uniformly diffused heat, and that the tendency is for all the matter of the universe to collect into one dead mass, while all the energy is at one dead level of lifeless stagnation—even so far we may go with the man of science, and may say, "We admit such a tendency." But when we are told by smaller folk that this, then, is the doom of the universe, this is the end of all things, must we not again say that this is an unwarrantable extension of the assumption that the order of Nature is constant in time? Must we not again insist that the constancy in time is practically true for finite periods, but beyond these limits may be true or may be false ?

That laws proved to hold good practically for certain phenomena hold good also for all like phenomena, is assumed in every field of scientific research. It is the fundamental axiom of causation ; an axiom so fundamental that it may well be regarded, like time and space, as a form of thought, one of the conditions of experience. The whole fabric of our science depends upon this fact—that no natural event is isolated, that every phenomenon depends on certain preceding phenomena by which it is conditioned, and which we call its cause, and gives origin to certain succeeding phenomena which it helps to condition, and which we call its effects. Every fact is a link in the chain of causation, an integral fibre in the warp and woof of the web of existence. Upon this, I say, the whole fabric of our scientific knowledge depends, that no fact is isolated ; just as the whole fabric of our morality depends upon the similar truth, that no human being is isolated.

We have already seen how a single impression upon

one of the organs of sense gives rise in our minds to the synthesis of a complex object. Even so, by a process of more elaborate construction, does the contemplation of a single fact or object give rise, through the associations of causation, to a complex mental picture of far-reaching operations of Nature. I have sometimes, for example, during one of the delightful halts in the ascent of a Swiss snow-peak, taken up a single snowflake and yielded up my mind to the reverie which it suggested. And then that single snowflake has told me an eventful story of its free existence in the ocean as a minute droplet, of its yet freer aerial life as the winds bore it mountain-wards, of its crystalization amid the fury of an Alpine storm, of its coming to rest where I found it ; and then of its future, its constrained motion in the glacier, its freedom in the mountain torrent, its participation in the stately flow of a great river, and its final arrival in its ocean home. All this was suggested with a fulness which it would take pages to describe. And yet, in truth, the picture was but the barest sketch ; and I have sometimes wished that the snowflake itself could find words in which to tell me all its story. Vain and foolish wish ! Vain and foolish, for it was that idlest of all wishes, the wish for an impossibility. Vain and foolish, inasmuch as, could it have been granted, the whole history of even the minutest snowflake would be far beyond human comprehension. For so closely inter-woven are the strands of causation, that a perfect know-ledge of the snowflake's history would involve nothing less than a knowledge of the universe. Vain and foolish wish, once more, because, could my comprehension have been so enlarged as to receive the whole truth, that truth would be little worth without the bracing labour through which it must be obtained. We sometimes complain of our slow advance in knowledge ; but, depend upon it, our knowledge increases as fast as our capacity for knowing enlarges.

Let us not forget that the smallest insect that we pet-tishly brush away into annihilation has, stored up in its tiny frame, the results of all modifying causes which have conspired to bring about its evolution through long ages. Who could tell, on examination of the germinal matter which constitutes that insect's egg, that this almost struc-tureless unit of living matter contained the impress of forces which had acted through untold ages ? It is true that you and I are not competent to trace the converging threads of causation which combine and meet in that minute speck of unstable life-matter. We cannot even trace the complex of causes which determines the course of the dead leaf which flutters down from the tall treetop, or the form of the pebble that lies in the river-bed. But the more intimately we are acquainted with Nature, the more firmly do we believe in the continuity of causation ; the more we advance in the study of Nature, the more clearly do we perceive, not only that every event is related to events which have gone before and to events which follow after, but that there is a quantitative equivalence between the events thus related. And so we come to believe that there is no such thing as chance ; that the word "chance" is but a cloak for ignorance ; and that the whole of Nature is one great, beautiful, complicated network, the interlacing threads and fibres of which are connected trains of events.

Projected on to the plane of moral life, this fact of the continuity of causation becomes a fact of deep solemnity ; and after all, if our science is not to influence conduct, of what avail is it ? Just as in the physical world the influ-ence of the smallest molecular wave-action is undying, so too in the moral world the influence of the simplest action is undying. The thoughts of every true thinker and seer

that the world has seen are living and germinating now.
"We can trace this truth best," writes Mr. Frederick
Harrison, "in the case of great men ; but it is not confined
to the great.   Not a single act of thought or character ends
with itself ; nay, more, not a single nature in its entirety
but leaves its influence for good or for evil.   As a fact the
good prevail ; but all act, all continue to act indefinitely
often in ever-widening circles.   And, in some infinitesimal
degree, the humblest life that ever turned a sod sends a wave
—no, more than a wave, a life—through the ever-growing
harmony of human society.   Not a soldier died at Marathon
or Salamis but did a stroke by which our thought is
enlarged and our standard of duty formed at this day.   As
we live for others in life, so we live in others after death ;
as others have lived in us and all for the common race.
For our lives live when we are most forgotten ; and not a
cup of water that we have given to an unknown sufferer, or
a wise word spoken in season, but has added (whether we
remember it, whether others remember it or not) a streak of
happiness and strength to the world."   These, to my mind,
are soul-stirring words.   Not a single thought or word
or deed, but is a link in the chain of moral causation with
effects, good or evil, sweeping forwards into all futurity.
Would that we could all remember this when we speak
and think and act.

And this is no modern doctrine, the outcome of Western
science, though Western science gives it full support.   From
the unscientific East we hear, "Not in the sky, not in the
midst of the sea, not if we enter into the clefts of the mountains, is there known a spot in the whole world where a
man might be freed from an evil deed."   And again, "In a
region of black cold wandered a soul which had departed
from the earth, and there stood before him a hideous
woman, profligate and deformed.   'Who art thou?' he

cried. To him she answered, 'I am thine own actions.'"
Spinoza, who lived before, though he anticipated, modern
science, saw clearly the same truth. "The wise man will
know," he says, "that each action brings with it its inevitable consequences, which even God cannot change." And
Mr. Ruskin, who is antagonistic to modern science, insists
on the ineffaceable consequences of an accomplished deed.
"And that is, indeed," he says, "the sorrowfullest fact
we have to know about our several lives. Wisdom never
forgives. Whatever resistance we have offered to her law,
she avenges for ever; the lost hour can never be redeemed,
and the accomplished wrong never atoned for. The best
that can be done afterwards, but for that had been better."

But although this view has been held by the precursors
of modern science, and is maintained by some who regard
modern science with disfavour, still modern science sets its
seal upon this doctrine, and points to its foundation in the
axiom of causation.

And what, then, shall we say concerning this axiom?
Let us hear Professor Huxley. "It is commonly urged," he
writes, "that the axiom of causation cannot be derived
from experience, because experience only proves that many
things have causes, whereas the axiom declares that all
things have causes. The syllogism 'many things which
come into existence have causes; *A* has come into existence; therefore *A* had a cause,' is obviously fallacious, if *A*
is not previously shown to be one of the 'many things.'
And this objection is perfectly sound so far as it goes. The
axiom of causation cannot possibly be deduced from any
general proposition which simply embodies experience.
But it does not follow that the belief, or expectation,
expressed by the axiom is not a product of experience
generated antecedently to, and altogether independently of,
the logically unjustifiable language in which it is expressed.

" In fact," he continues, "the axiom of causation resembles all other beliefs of expectation in being the verbal symbol of a purely automatic act of the mind, which is altogether extra-logical, and would be illogical, if it were not constantly verified by experience." So far, good. But what if the axiom of causation be carried into regions where verification by experience is impossible?

Let us suppose, for the sake of argument, that the phenomena of the universe may be ultimately explained in terms of matter and motion ; and let us suppose that all changes of matter and motion are caused, that is to say, flow out of, antecedent changes of matter and motion. Now, what answer are we to give, from a scientific point of view, to the question, What caused the existence of matter, and what first set that matter in motion? Surely this : That we are going altogether beyond our knowledge in saying that they were caused at all. All that we are justified in assuming is that the axiom of causation is practically true of such finite portions of space, and such finite periods of time as come or can come within human ken. Whether matter and motion were originally caused or uncaused, is a question that we cannot answer, or can only answer by a philosophy that transcends science.

The basis of that philosophy is the fundamental assumption that God exists. Against that assumption or in its favour I have here and now nothing to say. It is sufficient to indicate, in concluding this imperfect consideration of that conception of the uniformity of Nature which is in our time so largely influencing, and will in time to come more and more deeply influence the conduct of life—it is, I say, sufficient to indicate, in conclusion, that for those who admit the validity of this assumption, scientific beliefs are supplemented by beliefs which transcend science ; for them scientific laws are something more than condensed statements of fact; for them the order of Nature is more than practically exact, more than practically invariable; for them is Nature the reflection of the Absolute Perfection which can never be seen by the unaided eye of science; for them is this world what it is named by the Earth-Spirit in "Faust," the visible garment of God.

CHAPTER IV.

MATTER AND MOTION.

"The philosophers even seem universally to have observed this, that all the variety of matter, the diversity of its forms, depends on motion; for they said that Nature was the principle of motion and rest, and by Nature they understood that by which all corporeal things become such as they are found in experience."—DESCARTES.

IT is beginning to be generally recognized that science can give but proximate answers to our questions concerning the nature and origin of things. Explain and explain as we will, ere long we reach a point at which we must, if we be honest, confess our impotence. The growth of science has, indeed, brought a multitude of phenomena within the reach of something like true knowledge; but at the same time it has brought into clearer light the fact that there are stern limits to our knowledge, limits which we can no more transcend than, to borrow a simile from Sir William Hamilton, the eagle can soar above the atmosphere in which he floats.

Standing in the midst of rugged mountain peaks, and looking down on fertile valleys and deep ravines, the geologist is impressed at once with a sense of power and of weakness, of richness and of poverty. As he contrasts the knowledge which he possesses of the manner in which this scenic grandeur has been elaborated, with the information which was within the reach even of the wisest a century ago, he feels that his science has power to solve some at least of the problems of Nature. But as he traces back the streams of thought to their source, he becomes conscious that there are limits to his mental vision as there are limits to his physical powers of sight. Such, too, are the feelings of every true student of science as he pauses in his work to review his knowledge and his ignorance; and such are the feelings of the philosopher who tries to weave into one web the strands of knowledge worked out by the students of science in their several departments.

Much of the work of science consists in a searching analysis, by which may be effected the resolution of phenomena into their elements. From the intricate complexity of the web of the phenomenal we have to extract the warp and woof, the interlacing strands that have been inwoven in the loom of Time. And in each branch of science certain units are reached which are for the students of that branch, as such, elementary. The analysis of the physical geologist stops short at wind and wave, rain and frost, glacier and river, and other such agents of denudation, which exerting their denuding influence on clay and sand, limestone and slate, granite and solid lava, and other rock-elements, have given rise by their differential action to manifold diversities of scenery. The petrologist takes these rock-elements and pushes his analysis of them a step further, resolving them into their component minerals, quartz and calcite, and silicates without number. And then the chemist takes up the question where the petrologist leaves it, and analyses these mineral-elements into the yet more ultimate chemical elements. So, too, the anatomist analyses the body into a number of organs, the functions of which it is the province of the physiologist to study; then follows the histologist, who analyses the organs into their component tissues; while the student of organic chemistry resolves these tissues and their products into the chemical elements of which they are ultimately composed. Thus throughout the whole range of the phenomenal is this process carried on until the ultimate physical units, matter and motion in space and time, are reached. And then the metaphysician—not without some grumbling from his fellow-workers the physicists, who refuse to recognize his true place in Nature—then, I say, the metaphysician, in the person of Mr. Herbert Spencer, carries the analysis yet further, and resolves the units of the physicist into a unit yet more ultimate, namely Force. We have to consider the validity of this ultimate piece of metaphysical analysis. But before doing so, let us first glance briefly at the resolution of phenomena into matter and motion.

When the astronomer points his telescope towards the planet Mars, what does he see or infer? A mass of matter in constant motion through space. And if he recalls to mind the gradual advances in our knowledge of that planet, what does he find to be the essential nature of those advances? He finds that there has been a continually increasing definiteness in our knowledge of the changes of position which the planet undergoes, and of the nature and mode of aggregation of the matter of which it is composed. As the result of these advances he can, for example, point to the fact that the planet rotates on its axis once in about twenty-four hours and a half, and that it travels round the sun in an orbit of considerable ellipticity at a mean rate of about sixteen miles a second ; he can tell us that the figure of the planet is that of a spheroid of rotation, and that its density is slightly less than that of the earth, while its mass is rather more than one-eighth of the terrestrial mass ; he can show us continents and oceans, clouds, and a polar ice-cap. All the knowledge of the planet that he can give us concerns, in

fact, the matter of which it is composed and the motions of
that matter through space. And if we regard the earth
as an astronomical object, the same remark holds good for it
also. While, if we turn to the genesis of Mars, of the earth,
and of the solar system in general, we find, in the nebular
hypothesis an answer given in terms of matter and motion.

When the geologist seeks to discover the fundamental
facts which underlie his science, he too is driven back to
ultimate laws expressed in terms of matter and motion.
The sand-grains which make up the hill, the strata of which
he is mapping, were deposited in an estuary, whither they
were carried by the flow of water. The motion which
enables water to bear seawards the sand and mud particles
results from the molecular motion of sun-heat ; for not only
does this sun-heat raise the water particles from the ocean
in the form of vapour, but it gives rise also to the winds
which convey that vapour to distant continents, there to be
condensed as rain. The upward motion of the earth's
crust which gave the strata their present position is due
to the cooling of the earth ; is due, therefore, to loss of
molecular motion. The denuding forces, atmospheric and
aqueous, which have given to the hill its present form are
again due to motions of various kinds, deriving their origin
from the molecular motion of sun-heat. All geological
actions, ultimately describable as they are as the results of
the escape of earth-heat, the influence of sun-heat, and the
movement of tidal waters, are, therefore, ultimately explicable, so far as they are explicable at all, in terms of
matter and motion.

Ask the physiologist what is the ultimate aim of the
science he studies, and he will not improbably answer that
the aim of physiology is fully to explain the chemistry and
physics of the living organism, as displayed under the
complex conditions of vitality ; that is, in other words, to

explain the changes which an organism undergoes in terms of matter and motion. For it is the province of chemistry and physics, as branches of molecular mechanics, to elucidate the modes of aggregation of elementary matter, and the nature and changes of the motion of its molecules and atoms.

Merely regarding, then, the instances just given as examples of the fact, not by any means as proofs of the fact, we may say that the ultimate and most abstract explanations reached by all branches of objective science are expressed in terms of matter and motion ; that every phenomenon is in its essence a change in the arrangement of matter and motion.

The ultimate nature of the changes of the distribution of matter and motion has been summed up by Mr. Herbert Spencer in his " Law of Evolution." According to that law, there is, in every material system undergoing evolution, a tendency for the matter to aggregate into definite individual forms and groups of forms, and for its various parts, thus rendered definite, to become more and more closely interdependent upon each other, and thus to be linked into a more and more definite system. Accompanying these changes there is also a constant tendency for much of the energy originally possessed by the material system to be dissipated and lost to that system, and a further tendency for the energy that remains to assume more and more definite modes, among which may be traced a growing interdependence, analogous to and inextricably involved in that interdependence which is traceable in the material units. Such, in brief, is Mr. Herbert Spencer's law of evolution, which, however, I have now no intention of criticizing, and which, indeed, only concerns us here in so far as it is avowedly an interpretation of phenomena in terms of matter and motion.

Let us now pass on to consider whether there are any other conceptions which naturally and inevitably accompany these of matter and motion. We shall see that there are at least two.

In the first place let us note, however, how closely associated are these two, matter and motion, so that it is impossible to think of one without involving the other in the same thought. It is, at any rate, clear that the conception of motion involves the conception of matter.* We cannot think of motion without thinking of something moved. The idea of motion cannot by any effort of thought be divorced from the idea of a thing which exhibits that motion. So much is clear; but can we not think of matter without motion, can we not imagine matter absolutely still? I think not. It is now a matter of common knowledge that heat is due to or *is* the rapid vibration of the molecules of matter. So that matter *absolutely still* is matter *absolutely cold.* And of such absolutely cold matter we have no knowledge. From this, and from sundry other physical considerations, it follows that our conception of matter—such matter as we are acquainted with in the world around us—involves (at all events to those who have received some training in physical science) a conception of motion. The two cannot be mentally represented as separate, though for purposes of analysis they may be talked about and written about and argued about as separate.

But the conception of motion involves something more than matter moved. It involves space passed through and time occupied in the passage. So that accompanying a conception of what we call *motion*, there is also a conception of *matter* moved, of *space* moved through, and of *time* occupied in the transit.

* I speak for myself. Prof. Johnstone Stoney tells us that the study of nature has extricated some minds from this " supposed law of human minds."

And is there nothing else? Are these four the only physical ultimates? Is there no other conception as necessary to our conception of motion as matter, space, or time? There is, we are often told. Inextricably involved in our conception of motion is our conception of *force*, the cause of motion. Nay, more; we are told that in this force we find the conception out of which the others have arisen. In it we reach the ultimate of ultimates. As this view forms an essential feature in Mr. Herbert Spencer's system of philosophy, we will devote some little space to its consideration.

There can be little doubt that in physics the idea is confusing and misleading; confusing because the term "force" has of late acquired a special meaning, namely, the rate of change of velocity, or the change of momentum of a body considered as depending upon its position relative to other bodies; misleading because it almost invariably, in the minds of beginners, becomes confounded with a very different conception, that of energy. But is it necessary? This question I will not trust myself as a layman to answer, but will call in a specialist to my aid. "All we know as to force and motion," writes Prof. Clifford, "is that a certain arrangement of surrounding bodies produces a certain alteration in the motion of a body. It has been usual to say that this arrangement of surrounding bodies produces a certain force, and that it is the action of this force that produces the alteration of the motion. Why have this intermediate term at all? Why should we not go at once from the surrounding circumstances to the alteration of motion which follows? . The intermediate term is only a mental inference, either from the existence of the surrounding circumstances or from the occurrence of the alteration in the motion; and if we only accustom ourselves to pass from one to the other without its

assistance it will cease to be necessary, and like other
useless mental conceptions, be gradually forgotten. And
with it will pass all tendency to give to this useless
mental phantom any such real and material qualities as
indestructibility."

To this the champion of force will probably answer, in
the words of Mr. Spencer, that, "while this mode of con-
ceiving the phenomena suffices for physical inquiries, it
does not suffice for the purposes of philosophy." In metaphysics and psychology the idea of force is not a useless
mental phantom ; so far from it that, on the contrary, the
analysis to which the psychologist feels bound to subject
the physical ideas of matter and motion in space and time,
leads him inevitably to a conception of force as an ultima-
tum. "To formulate phenomena in the proximate terms
Body, Space, Motion, while discharging from the concepts
the consciousness of Force, is to acknowledge the superstructure while ignoring the foundation."

Let us, then, see what we may learn about this foundation. I propose, first, to state Mr. Herbert Spencer's contention as clearly and with as much cogency as I can ; *
and then to consider its validity.

Few will hesitate to admit that what we call matter,
motion, space, and time, are highly abstract ideas. When
we speak of matter we do not necessarily mean any
particular form of matter, such as granite or chalk or
woody fibre ; nor when we speak of time do we mean any
particular period of time. Let us consider, then, what we
actually mean when we speak of matter, to take one case,
in this general and abstract sense. The point to be ascer-

---

* I quote the next few passages, with slight alterations, from a manuscript
of my own, written some years ago, when I was a disciple of Mr. Spencer's, in
this matter of ultimate force.

tained is what is essential to our conception of matter, what is unessential. Looking around us we perceive numerous bodies which we call material. Some are red, some green, and some violet, while others are of intermediate shades of colour. We, therefore, see that colour is not essential to our conception of matter. Some, again, are symmetrical, some asymmetrical, there being various phases of symmetry and asymmetry. We, therefore, see that form is not essential to our conception of matter. Some, once more, are large and some small; so that we exclude size also. In the same way we exclude smell, taste, resonance, solidity and its opposite, hardness and softness, roughness and smoothness, etc., since these qualities vary in different kinds of matter. Whether solid or fluid, whether hard or soft, the matter is still matter. What, then, are the invariable qualities which matter possesses and without which it would cease to be matter. There are two. They are extension and resistance. We cannot think of matter at all except as something extended; nor can we think of it at all except as something offering resistance. But how do we get our notions of extension and resistance?

One of our simplest elements of consciousness is the sense of the power to move and of effort in moving. It is scarcely possible to conceive sensation to exist at all without a co-existing consciousness of muscular strains and tensions going on within the body. And what do these muscular strains and tensions effect? They effect changes of position in the limbs, and thereby bring about, not infrequently, changes of position in surrounding bodies. If, therefore, we agree to call that which produces motion, force (and this may be granted for the sake of argument), we are conscious of a power within ourselves of exerting force, or, in other words, we have a subjective sense of effort which accompanies our exercise of force. We must

H

not, however, construe this into an assertion that, since we can, or imagine we can, by what we call effort of will, set matter in motion, we are therefore originators of force. What we are conscious of is a series of muscular tensions which accompany the production of motion in certain parts of our body, and through them in external objects. How these tensions are produced is not a point under consideration. Assuredly they are not produced by any separate entity, the *ego*. Now, psychologically considered, we are bound to think of *all* manifestations of force as correlatives of our own muscular efforts. " Let any one hold a piece of iron near a strong magnet, and the feeling that the magnet endeavours to pull the iron one way in the same manner as he endeavours to pull it in the opposite direction is very strong." His conception of the external force is akin to his conception of muscular effort. Or let him press against a powerful spring. He is obliged to regard the opposing resistance as the objective correlate of that which, subjectively, he is conscious of as muscular effort. What objective force is in itself, apart from all relation to ourselves, we can never know. We must content ourselves with such conceptions as are possible to the human mind. But while we are obliged to think of the active resistance of force as an objective correlate of our muscular effort, we are obliged also to think of the passive resistance of matter in a similar way. If instead of pressing against a spring we press against a block of granite, we have, in place of what may perhaps be termed a sense of lively resistance, a sense of dead resistance. But the subjective element of which our conception is composed is, in this case also, a consciousness of effort. Something resists our own exercise of force ; and if we think of this resistance at all, we must think of it in terms of force.

So much for the element of resistance in matter. Let

us now turn to the element of extension. What do we
mean by saying that matter is extended? We mean surely
this : that in any mass of matter there are a number of
coexisting points which offer resistance. But it is only by
careful exploration, so to speak, of the mass, not actually
made, indeed, in each individual case, but inferred on the
strength of previous experiences, that we can say that there
are a number of coexisting points which offer resistance.
And such exploration can only be made with the aid of
continual muscular adjustments and readjustments. Even
in the case of vision, when we seem to "see the hardness
and softness which we do but infer," it must be remembered
that, for each separate position and each several distance,
there is a special adjustment of the muscles which regulate
sight. So that the sense of muscular effort here again
enters into the conception ; and thus our ideas of extension,
no less than our ideas of resistance, must be thought of in
terms of force, or not thought of at all.

Stated in other words, extension is occupancy of space.
But such a definition implies a pre-existing idea of space.
The idea of space, however, is an abstraction from our idea
of matter. Matter is that which has resistance and extension ; and in this extension we already have the idea of
occupied space. Take away from the conception of matter
the idea of resistance, and instead of having a number of
coexisting points which offer resistance, we have a number
of coexisting positions which offer no resistance ; and this
is a definition of space. Space is, in fact, an abstract of
all relations of coexistence. Its essence is relativity. For
Absolute Being space and time are annihilated. God
dwells in His heaven of the infinite here and the everlasting
now. But since the conception of space grew up out of
the idea of extended matter, since if we had no conception
of matter we could have no conception of space, it is clear

that, strange as it may at first seem, our conception of space arises from our experiences of force.

From a similar source springs our conception of time. Pass the finger lightly across the table, and there follows a sequence of sensations. From morning to night throughout our lives we have numberless experiences of sequences ; and we doubtless inherit generalized conceptions of sequences ancestrally acquired. But just as in course of time from countless experiences of coexistences there has been evolved an abstract idea of space, so from countless experiences of sequences there has been evolved an abstract idea of time. And since our conceptions of sequence arise from experiences of sequent sensations, which sensations are thought of in terms of force, and since in the absence of such sensations we could have no conception of sequence, it is clear that time, the abstract of all relations of sequence, arises from our experiences of force.

Only motion now remains to be considered. Now, motion is change of position of matter in space effected in time. Abolish, therefore, the conceptions of matter, space, and time, and the conception of motion vanishes. But since our conceptions of matter, space, and time originate in conceptions of force, it is obvious that conceptions of force are those from which our conception of motion also has been elaborated. So that motion, too, falls under the category of compound conceptions ultimately derived from experiences of force.

Let us now, before proceeding to view the question from another standpoint, note clearly the conclusion we have arrived at on this hypothesis of force, the ultimate of ultimates. The physicist, dealing with the factors of phenomena, reduces our knowledge of these factors to laws expressed in terms of matter, motion, space, and time ; adding to these conceptions the idea of force if he has to consider the cause of motion. These ultimate mechanical ideas the psychologist seeks to analyze. Taking our sense of muscular effort as that which subjectively answers to that which out of ourselves we call force, he endeavours to show that our conceptions of matter, motion, space, and time, have originated in our experiences of force. Deducting from the impressions caused by matter all those that are variable, he finds as a residuum two invariables, resistance and extension, which in combination make up our abstract conception of matter. Of these, the idea of resistance must be thought of directly as akin to our idea of muscular effort ; while the idea of extension is gained, as we have seen, through sensations of muscular adjustments. But the idea of the extension of an individual mass of matter, from which the abstract idea of extension is generalized, is only gained by an exploration of its surface ; and in this exploration a *series* of sensations is obtained. Hence arises an idea of sequence, from which by abstraction a conception of time is evolved ; hence, also— as it is found that during the exploration the same series of sensations is obtained, first in one order, then in another (as a row of figures may be read now forwards and now backwards)—hence, also, I say, arises an idea of coexistence, from which by abstraction a conception of space is evolved. Finally, by combining together a conception of matter, a conception of space, and a conception of a sequence of positions in space occupied by that matter, there arises a conception of motion, the cause of which motion we call force, and think of in terms of muscular effort.

Let us now look at the question in a somewhat different light, still on the ultimate force hypothesis. It is now generally admitted that all our knowledge of phenomena is ultimately acquired through the inlets of sense. But it is no less generally acknowledged that, besides impressions of sensation, there are equally important impressions of relation. Without these impressions of relation we could have no such thing as knowledge. For knowledge implies at least three things ; first, sensory impressions ; secondly, memory of former impressions ; and, thirdly, a perception of the relation which subsists between sensory impressions just received and sensory impressions previously received. Now, it is clear that, without sensory impressions, there could have grown up no conception of the relations between such impressions : hence there could have arisen no conception of time, the abstract of relations of sequence ; no conception of space, the abstract of relations of coexistence ; and therefore no conception of motion, which involves both time and space. We come down, then, to matter and force, the causes of our sensory impressions, as the elementary conceptions, without which our other conceptions fade into nonentity. And these two conceptions, distinct as they seem, are different phases of one conception : in the one case, an inert passive resistance to our efforts ; in the other case, an active and energetic resistance to our efforts. In either case it is a reaction to the force we exert ; and we are bound to think of it in terms of the force against which it reacts. Our conception of space, matter, and force seem, in fact, to be related in this way :—Matter is thought of as passive resistance *plus* extension ; space is thought of as extension *minus* resistance ; force is thought of as active resistance *minus* extension. But the idea of extension, or occupancy of space, involves a complex idea of relation ; it is, therefore, less ultimate than the simple conception of resistance ; hence it is evident that resistance, active or passive, is the ultimate which analysis discloses, and this resistance is thought of as force opposing the force we are conscious of exercising.

There is yet another point of view to which attention

may be drawn as further illustrative of the same contention. We say that all our scientific knowledge is elaborated out of sensations or has been obtained through the inlets of sense ; that is to say, looking at the question objectively, through the instrumentality of certain affections of our nerve fibres has been, in the course of long ages, built up our knowledge of the world around us. What, then, let us inquire, is the nature of the nerve fibres which are thus affected? They are composed of a delicate product of animal life, the molecules of which have an exceedingly complex structure, and are composed of great numbers of atoms. More than this, the atoms are arranged in a state of unstable equilibrium, and are ready on the slightest provocation to tumble over into a condition of more stable equilibrium. Now, when the termination of a nerve fibre is affected, ever so slightly, some of the molecules have the arrangement of their atoms changed in this way. The atoms tumble over into new groupings. Each molecule in which this change goes on affects its neighbour, causing a similar metabolic change, as it is called, in it ; and the neighbour promptly passes on the impulse. Thus a wave of metabolic change passes along the whole length of the nerve to the brain, and there sets up similar changes among the brain molecules. Viewed objectively, such are the nerve changes which accompany consciousness. And what is the ultimate nature of these changes? Motions impressed upon the material atoms of which the nerve substance is composed. But that which sets matter in motion is force. So that here, again, we come down to force as the ultimate cause.

Finally, it may be urged by the advocate of force that even in physics it is of value, since the persistence of force is a wider generalization than either the conservation of energy or the indestructibility of matter, including as it does both these laws, embracing also the laws of motion, and being the foundation of the doctrine of the uniformity of Nature. According to the principle of the conservation of energy, the whole amount of the energy in the universe remains unaltered. When analyzed this conception comes to this; that the sum of the actual and possible motion of a constant quantity of matter is itself constant. But this actual or possible motion is not itself an existence, but only the sign of an existence. And the existence of which it is a sign is force; that is to say, the amount of motion being constant, the amount of force which produces that motion must also be constant, for it is not conceivable that, the effects being constant, the cause should be in any degree variable.

I have endeavoured to put clearly and in a favourable light what may be said in support of the ultimate force hypothesis, for we cannot afford to treat lightly any contention of Mr. Herbert Spencer's. Let us now consider its validity; and, first, from the point of view of physics. The persistence of force claims to be a wider generalization than the conservation of energy, since it includes also the indestructibility of matter. But to this the physicist will reply, that the conservation of energy, though it does not explicitly include, implicitly assumes the truth of the indestructibility of matter. He will ask what advantage in physics is to accrue from the introduction of this wider generalization. What problems before insoluble hereby become soluble? Until this question is satisfactorily answered, the persistence of force will be rejected by physicists as an unnecessary concatenation of words. For if we accept the definition of force as that which produces a change of position, and its measure as being the amount of change of position produced, the doctrine of the persistence of force—that the amount of active and latent force which produces motion *plus* the amount of active and latent force which resists motion is a constant quantity—would seem to be a tolerably obvious truism, namely, that such changes of position in the molecules of a system as *have* already been produced, together with those which *can* still be produced, are the total possible changes of position among the molecules of that system. There is nothing here to outweigh the inevitable confusion that must arise in the mind of the young student on the introduction of such a doctrine as the persistence of force. To this ultimate force the physicist will continue to say, Matter I know, and energy I know; but who are you? The introduction of this doctrine into physics, however, has not been and is not likely to be effected; nor, indeed, I imagine, would Mr. Herbert Spencer (who formulated his persistence of force before the law of the conservation of energy had assumed its present position) contend that it has the same value in physics that he claimed for it in metaphysics.

What, then, shall we say of the metaphysical and psychological aspect of this analysis of phenomena into ultimate abstract force? May we unreservedly accept it? I think not, and for reasons somewhat similar to those which lead to its rejection in physics; namely, that it is unnecessary if not misleading, and tends to confusion rather than to clearness. And why unnecessary? Because, as it seems to me, it makes no advance upon the doctrine that all our knowledge of phenomena is built up out of impressions of sensations and impressions of relation. These impressions of sensation and impressions of relation between sensations, together with pleasure and pain, are the ultimates of psychological analysis. This is a clear-cut, tolerably comprehensible doctrine. To resolve these into a metaphysical conception of abstract force seems to me as retrogressive a step in psychology as the replacement of the conservation of energy, with its clear-cut definiteness, by a vague truism, the persistence of force, would be in physics. More than this, it is misleading. If we think of force as the objective correlate of that which we know in ourselves as muscular effort, it is difficult not to make this force an eject, and to impart into it some small share of that consciousness, in and through which we know anything about muscular effort. And even if this objection be waived, since it is expressly guarded against by Mr. Herbert Spencer, the doctrine seems to be misleading in giving an altogether unwarrantable predominance to the muscular sense, or sense of effort. That this is an important element among the impressions of sensation no physiological psychologist will for one moment doubt ; but that it is the sole element, or even the most important, he is not likely to admit.

The fundamental objection both from the physical and psychological standpoint has, however, still to be stated. It is this : that the force that is persistent is unknowable and inscrutable. "While it is impossible to form any idea of force in itself," writes Mr. Spencer, "it is equally impossible to comprehend its mode of exercise." But let us take from Mr. Spencer's chapter on the Persistence of Force a somewhat more extended statement. "Though on raising an object from the ground," he says, "we are obliged to think of its downward pull as equal and opposite to our upward pull ; and though it is impossible to represent these as equal without representing them as like in kind ; yet, since their likeness in kind would imply in the object a sensation of muscular tension, which cannot be ascribed to it, we are compelled to admit that force, as it exists out of our consciousness, is not force as we know it. Hence, the force of which we assert persistence is that

Absolute Force of which we are indefinitely conscious as the necessary correlate of the force we know. By the Persistence of Force we really mean the persistence of some Cause which transcends our knowledge and conception. In asserting it we assert an Unconditioned Reality, without beginning or end."

Thus the ultimate force which a complete analysis discloses as fundamental is unknowable. And such being the case, it will, I think, be wise to halt in our analysis just a little before we reach this stage of nescience. We have seen that the analysis of matter, motion, space, and time bring us down at once to ultimate force. But ultimate force is unknowable. Whence it follows that matter, motion, space, and time are the true ultimates so far as the knowable is concerned. In other words, we cannot practically get beyond them. Force, then, being unknowable, it is, I repeat, of this unknowable Force that Persistence (we must use capital letters lest these fade into nonentity) is predicated. On the question how the unknowable is *known* to be persistent, Mr. Spencer does not enlighten us. If we know it to be persistent from the persistence of its knowable effects, why not be content with stating the persistence of these known effects? Here we are on safe ground. But I presume that it is possible that the Unknowable may produce other effects, knowable to beings differently constituted to ourselves, concerning the persistence or non-persistence of which we are utterly in the dark. How the unknowable is known to be persistent in *all* its modes, then, Mr. Spencer does not inform us. Nor does he explain how we may safely take the step from the doctrine of the Absolute Persistence of the Unconditioned Reality to such practical generalizations as the laws of motion, the conservation of energy, and the uniformity of Nature. It would seem to be only by a bit of verbal legerdemain that Mr. Spencer can conjure his Force into the centre of the Chinese puzzle box of the universe. In a word, Mr. Spencer's Force, like other phantoms, is a somewhat slippery customer, who sometimes does duty in the realm of consciousness as a sense of effort; sometimes appears in the world of phenomena as energy; and sometimes makes himself invisible as an Unconditional Reality, without beginning or end.

In any case, however, whatever may be said for or against Mr. Spencer's doctrine in the realm of the speculative, to which as we now see it truly belongs, it is, I think, clear that in the realm of the practical, in physics and psychology, it has no place. And we shall do wisely, I think, to carefully avoid introducing into the sphere of the practical the forms of expression and form of thought which characterize another sphere of thought.

Material particles, then, having varying relations in space and time, whence arises our conception of motion, would seem to be the physical ultimates. Sensations—with which pleasure and pain are more or less closely associated—entering into various relations, whence arise our conceptions of matter, motion, space, time, causation, and so forth, would seem to be the psychological ultimates. Here we reach the limits of practical analysis. By that analysis we can reach a knowledge of phenomena. But we must not forget that by no process of practical analysis can we get behind the phenomenal, unless we are content with Mr. Spencer to capitalize our nescience and bow down before the Unknowable. Matter and motion we only know as they appear to us, as they are symbolized in our consciousness. And for practical purposes this is surely all we want. So long as we find practically that we can adjust our actions so as to correspond with the representations of the external world in our consciousness, we may rest content. So long as we can adjust those internal relations we call thoughts to those external relations we call things, thereby reaching what we call truth, there is no cause for repining. And the fact that we cannot practically reach a knowledge of things as they are, but only of things as they appear, will not cause the man of science to desist from his task. That task is to explain the world as it appears to us, the world that is practically real. This is the highest knowledge he can reach, and it is the only knowledge that practically concerns him.

Between physics and metaphysics there is chronic antagonism. But both have played an important part in the elaboration of our knowledge. Without metaphysics we might have fallen a prey to a dogmatic materialism ; without physics we might be the victims of a misty idealism. " The reconciliation of physics and metaphysics," says Professor Huxley, "lies in the acknowledgment of faults upon both sides ; in the confession by physics that all the phenomena of Nature are, in their ultimate analysis, known to us only as facts of consciousness ; in the admission by metaphysics that the facts of consciousness are practically interpretable only by the methods and formulæ of physics." " We can think of matter only in terms of mind," writes Mr. Herbert Spencer. " We can think of mind only in terms of matter. When we have pushed our explorations of the first to the uttermost, we are referred to the second for a final answer ; and when we have got the final answer of the second, we are referred back to the first for an interpretation of it."

But the human mind is prone to speculation. It is endued with an inevitable tendency to attempt an explanation even of the inexplicable. It frets at the limitations of the phenomenal which is only practically real, and longs with a passionate longing for the absolutely and speculatively real. Nor is it content with the one reality (in this sense) it can reach, the reality of thought as such. Guided by analogy, it strives to see in this thought, or in the elements of which it is compounded, the one reality which underlies the whole universe of phenomena. It sees in the structure and physiology of the human body how wonderful a piece of mechanism can be wrought out of the elements of matter by their combinations and recombinations into a complex system of mutually dependent parts. And guided by this analogy in the realm of the phenomenal, it imports the same conception into the realm of the real —the realm of thought. Since the human body is so complex a product of simple material elements, of elementary matter-stuff, may not the mind be, in a similar fashion, a complex product of simple mental elements, of elementary mind-stuff; and may not these elements answer point for point in the world of the mental and the real, to the material elements in the world of the physical and the phenomenal? So argues the speculative reason. It feels that the mind is the true reality which lies behind the phenomenal body; and it is impelled to believe that mind-stuff is the true reality that lies behind phenomenal matter-stuff. For just as the matter of which the body is composed is just a sample of the matter we see throughout the whole realm of the phenomenal, so may the mind-stuff of which the mind is composed be just a sample of the true reality which underlies and supports and is the essential being of the universe in which we live.

This is no new speculation. It may be seen more or less clearly or dimly in the thoughts and aspirations of the East and of the West. It may be true. It may be false. But whether true or false, it is worth the effort which is required to grapple with it and to grasp it. It is, at any rate, preferable to blank Unknowable Force.

CHAPTER V.

THE RHYTHM OF NATURE.[*]

"The vestments and ritual of Nature may take up all the attention and use up all the energies of her votaries; these superficial observers fail, however, to find the real religion of Nature—the beautiful but awful omnipresence which every flower and every insect reveals."—W. K. PARKER.

WE may regard Nature in two ways. We may either look searchingly into her secrets with the steady eye of the man of science, or we may dwell lovingly on her beauty with the sympathetic gaze of the poet. Our object in the one case is to organize and extend our knowledge of the laws of her mechanism; our object in the other case is to yield ourselves wholly to her refining and ennobling influence and to surrender ourselves heart and soul to her ceaseless teaching.

The outcomes of these so opposite processes are as different as the methods of procedure. The outcome of the former, the method of science, is a conception of the world as a rigidly law-bound piece of mechanism. The outcome of the latter, the method of poetic insight, is a conception of this earth of ours as the beautiful home of man, instinct with life and with a thousand spiritual influences.

[*] This chapter formed the substance of a lecture delivered in Cape Town, and printed in the *Cape Quarterly Magazine*. The lecture form has been to a large extent retained.

These are very different conceptions. But different as they are, we must remember that they are both essentially human products. On everything that we view we project the image of our minds ; and in those minds there are two distinct elements—thought and love. Neither of these elements, we may hope, can exist entirely without the other. But in some minds thought, in other minds love, preponderates. And, in the same mind, at one season thought and at another season love has the mastery. Science is the product of our thought ; poetry and religion are the outpourings of our love. And the world of Nature and of man is the raw material upon which both our thought and our love have to be exercised.

The outcome of science, I repeat, is a conception of the world as a rigidly law-bound piece of mechanism—everywhere the stern reign of law ; everywhere unalterable sequence, unwearied ebb and flow of events, ceaseless change, irreversible onward progress. All this science formulates, condenses, reduces to its simplest expression.

And the outcome of poetic insight, I repeat, is a conception of the world as instinct with life and beauty. To every mood of Nature the poet

> " is as sensitive as waters are
> To the sky's influence in a kindred mood
> Of passion ; and obedient as the lute
> That waits upon the touches of the wind."

Of the poet we may say with the poet (Wordsworth)—

> " The earth
> And common face of Nature speak to him
> Rememberable things."

And again—

> " From Nature and her overflowing soul
> He has received so much that all his thoughts
> Are steeped in feeling."

He has, too, an eye which is ever restless in its search for beauty—

> " an eye
> Which, from a tree, a stone, a withered leaf,
> To the broad ocean, and the azure heavens
> Spangled with kindred multitudes of stars,
> Could find no surface where its power might sleep."

And in, and through, and around, and beyond all the ever-varying aspects of Nature's beauty he is conscious of

> " a spirit that impels
> All thinking things, all objects of all thought,
> And rolls through all things."

Such, then, are the widely different products of these widely different modes of regarding Nature. What, I wish now to ask, is the influence of the one on the other? Are they mutually exclusive of each other? Are they indifferent to each other? Or do they to some extent mutually foster each other? I do not wish here and now to enter upon the wider and deeper question as to what is their relative influence on philosophy and religion. Both the man of science and the poet, as human beings, must fuse together the net results of all experience into a philosophy which shall be, as far as possible, a consistent and coherent theory of things, and a religion which shall form a centre of love and service. But upon these deeper questions concerning religion and philosophy, I do not wish here and now to enter. The question I do wish to raise is this : *whether the scientific method of studying Nature has of necessity the effect, as some would have us believe, of dulling our poetic appreciation of her beauty.* We live at a time when science is making enormous strides, when science teaching is becoming an important factor in education, when the scientific method and the scientific spirit enter into all earnest study. To-day, we may fairly say, science leavens all civilized thought. The influence of Newton and Darwin is scarcely

I

less felt than that of Shakespeare and of Wordsworth. Are we, then, in and through our study of science becoming *less* readily influenced by the charms of Nature, *less* inclined to regard her from the standpoint of the poet? Are we, in fact, losing our love of Nature in our constant thought about her? Or, on the other hand, are we through science becoming *more* readily influenced, *more* susceptible to her beauty?

This question I wish rather to raise than to discuss. I have myself no doubt whatever as to the answer. Analogy, philosophy, and experience all point, as it seems to me, in the same direction. Take, for example, the analogy of music. Would it not be somewhat ridiculous to maintain that the accurate and scientific study of music dulls our appreciation of the beauties of melody and harmony? Is it not rather true that intellectual mastery is a necessary accompaniment of thorough emotional enjoyment? And surely this is not less true of the study of Nature than of the study of music. Surely of the study of Nature also we may say, that the intellectual mastery is a necessary accompaniment of full emotional appreciation. At any rate, analogy suggests that this may be so. And the suggestion of analogy is reinforced by the more general teaching of philosophy. Philosophy—I am making a lax use of this term—philosophy tells us that any subject to which we strenuously direct our thought becomes enriched by an unusual share of our love. We grow to take delight in the subject that engrosses our earnest study. And if this be so, then Nature-study must beget Nature-love. This, moreover, I find to be my own experience. The more I study and endeavour to learn her ways the more frequently do I experience that feeling which Wordsworth has perfectly expressed in the lines—

" My *heart leaps up* when I behold
A rainbow in the sky."

For my own part, then, I do not only disbelieve what I sometimes hear confidently stated, that the march of science will do much to crush out of the human heart its innate tendency to love and reverence Nature, but I firmly believe that the more deeply we study, in the scientific spirit, Nature's harmony, the richer will be the answering harmony in our own hearts. For there is a harmony of Nature. There is a rhythm of natural events. And it is at the same time the business and the delight of the man of science to disentangle from the multitudinous vibrations of Nature's music the tonic sequences by which that music is produced. The harmony and rhythm must be disclosed by the patient investigation of science. New perceptions will be evoked. But they will not stand alone. They will be accompanied and enriched by the new emotions which are their natural counterparts.

Let me, however, deal with the question in a practical way. Let me make this rhythm of Nature my subject. Let me through it illustrate some of the disclosures of science. And let me, then, ask whether an environment of the facts thus disclosed is likely to be especially deadening to the emotional side of our human nature.

All motion is rhythmical ; it is by a constant *pulsation* of events that the life of the world is maintained. A hundred daily occurrences remind us of this fact. Our bodily life involves a complex series of rhythms, the rhythm of blood circulation, the rhythm of respiration, the rhythm of alternate wakefulness and sleep. Our organism varies in rhythmical response to the rhythm of Nature without us. Day and night, summer and winter, the waxing and the waning moon, the rise and fall of the tides, the alternation of the winds, recurring periods of drought and rainfall,—all these remind us that we live in the midst of a rich and complex harmony of natural events.

Fully to comprehend that harmony is beyond our power. All that we can do is to try and trace now one and now another of the series of tones which blend together to form this rich music.

Let us begin, then, by tracing in some detail a definite series. There is one closely connected with the rhythm of respiration which will answer our purpose. A moment's consideration will make it evident that to enable the rhythm of respiration to continue a wider rhythm is necessary. We are all well aware that the air we breathe out differs in quality from the air we breathe in. It has been robbed of its oxygen, as we say, and in place of this vitalizing oxygen it has brought out with it the poisonous carbonic acid. By every breath we breathe we poison the air around us, and not only we but every animal on the face of the earth is adding its quantum to this atmospheric poison, while every fire that burns contributes its due supply of carbonic acid. It is no exaggeration, I suppose, to say that millions of tons of this poisonous carbonic acid are constantly being poured forth into the air. And yet the air remains sweet and pure and fresh and invigorating. The air our Shakespeare breathed was not more impure than that inspired by Homer of old. What becomes, then, of all this load of atmospheric poison ?

There is an old proverb which says " What is one man's meat is another man's poison." We have here a somewhat extended application of that proverb. For "What is poison to the animal is food to the plant ! " Look out upon the field of green corn waving in the wind and glancing in the sunshine. In that green field the plant is by its subtle vital chemistry converting poison into food. Yes, it is doing even more than that ; it is pouring forth into the air a copious supply of vitalizing oxygen. The green blades spring, it is true, out of the earth, and from the earth they absorb certain materials necessary for their healthy growth; but the main part of their nourishment they receive from the carbonic acid of the air. The mass of green vegetation. that bends before the wind is itself to a very large extent formed out of that wind by the genial influence of sunshine. The carbonic acid that the animal breathes out is just as essential to the plant as is to the animal the oxygen, returned to the air by the plant. This is the wider rhythm on which the rhythm of respiration depends.

We will not leave it yet ; we will look at it a little more closely. Our life rests upon a basis of food. We must eat that we may continue to live. But whence do we obtain our supply of food ? Ultimately entirely or almost entirely from the vegetable world. It is true that we, in common with other carnivorous animals, have acquired through our ancestors a rooted dislike to the trouble and inconvenience of carrying about with us the somewhat cumbrous digestive apparatus necessary for directly extracting the goodness from vegetable fibre ; and that we therefore employ oxen or sheep to do the harder part of the work for us, knocking them thereafter on the head and enjoying the fruits of their labours. But when we eat mutton or beef, we are but enjoying grass at second hand.

Thus, then, directly or indirectly the animal feeds upon the plant, and by delicate chemical and vital processes the food so absorbed is made a living part of his living body; for the life of the organism is the sum of the lives of its constituent particles. But it is only through constant death that continued life is possible. The constituent particles of the body undergo continual change and decay and their place is supplied by a constant succession of fresh particles ultimately derived from the products of the vegetable kingdom. Our very life depends on this rhythmical succession of particles.

To the life of these constituent particles—as to the life of the whole of which they are constituent—vitalizing oxygen is essential. They, too, like the organism they compose, must breathe that they may live. And therefore the animal's body is provided with a means by which oxygen may be supplied to every particle, and by which also the poisonous carbonic acid they exhale may be taken away. Such a means is the blood circulation. The blood contains thousands on thousands of busy little carriers— the red corpuscles—which in the lungs are laden with life-giving oxygen ; which convey this oxygen to the remotest parts of the animal's frame ; and which come back to the lungs empty, while the stream in which they float is foul with the poisonous carbonic acid. In the lungs this poisonous gas is discharged and the stream is rendered pure again ; and at the same time the empty little carrier corpuscles are reladen with vitalizing oxygen for distribution throughout the system. Every time we draw breath, millions of carrier corpuscles bear off to the tissues of our bodily frame a fresh supply of oxygen ; and every time we draw breath, the blood stream, fouled with the carbonic acid which results from the waste of our tissues, is purified by the escape of that product of their waste. And this carbonic acid, thus breathed forth, goes out into the air and is soon greedily absorbed by the green leaves of plants, which extract from it the carbon without which they are unable to manufacture their tissues, setting free once more the oxygen which revitalizes the air and makes it fresh and pure for the animals to breathe.

To plant life, therefore, we owe the two prime neces-saries of our existence—the food we eat and the oxygen we breathe. But at the same time we are not less neces-sary to the plants than they to us. They supply us with the food and oxygen upon which our life depends ; we, on the other hand, supply them with the carbonic acid which is their daily food. In the animal, the carbon derived *from* the plant is brought into contact with the oxygen set free *by* the plant; carbonic acid, a compound of carbon and oxygen, is formed. In the plant, the carbon and oxygen thus united are torn asunder; the carbon passing into the tissues of the plant, the oxygen passing into the air. Then once more the animal eats the plant and so absorbs the carbon, breathes the air and so absorbs the oxygen, elaborates these again into carbonic acid which goes forth into the air—its constituents soon to be separated by other plants for the use of other animals. Thus is the rhythm of composition and decomposition maintained.

Now if this rhythm could continue without external aid we should have a practical solution of a problem dear to theoretical dreamers. For if the carbonic acid were formed in the animal, decomposed in the plant, reformed in the animal, redecomposed in the plant, and so on in unaided sequence—what would this be but the long-sought-for perpetual motion? But there is no such unaided sequence. To the mind trained in science the supposition that alternate composition and decomposition could continue on this earth without external aid is not less improbable than the supposition that a miller could work two mills side by side, one by the flow of water down from his mill-pond, the other by its upward flow into the mill-pond again. The formation of carbonic acid is like the downward flow of water. Its decomposition is like lifting the water once more into the mill-pond above the miller's wheel. Neither can the water be lifted nor the decomposition of carbonic acid by plants be effected without the aid of an external power.

What is this power that constantly comes to the aid of the plant? It is the genial sunshine in which the plants seem to revel, and which is in truth their very life—and not theirs only but that of the animals too, inasmuch as animals, as we have seen, depend upon plants for food and fresh air. "Life is bottled sunshine," runs a pithy epigram, "and Death the silent-footed butler who draws the cork."

We find that sunshine, then—I repeat the fact, for I wish to lay especial stress upon it—we find that sunshine is that which supports this as it supports so many other Nature-rhythms. The sun is the musician who strikes some of the richest chords in that Nature-music which may be heard and enjoyed by all who have willing ears and hearts not dead to love. Sunshine is the very essence of this rhythm of composition and decomposition ; and every noble tree in the forest has, condensed in the woody heart of it, the virtue of many summer suns. The woodman comes and fells the tree. He delivers it to us as fuel. And as we sit before the blazing logs, we feel somewhat of the warmth of those summer suns. The carbon meanwhile which through the power of sunshine was separated from its companion oxygen and fixed in the woody fibre, once more, as the log burns and blazes, unites with oxygen gas and goes forth into the air as carbonic acid—plant-food for new generations of plants.

Wood, we may therefore say, is condensed sunshine, and every little twig contains an entrapped sunbeam ; and coal—the coal that we burn in our grates and that becomes in the steam engine our source of power—what is that, too, but condensed sunlight, stored up sun-power? For the coal is of vegetable origin. The plants of which it is formed flourished long ages ago, and drank in the virtue of the sunshine of those remote days. Through many generations of plant life it has been lying quietly in the earth, protected by layer upon layer of rock from the action of atmospheric oxygen. But man by his industry exhumes the blackened remains of this ancient vegetation, and in his coal-fire feels in effect the warmth of the sunshine of those remote days. In this case, moreover, as in that of the burning wood or the breathing animal, carbonic acid is again formed. The carbon and the oxygen, which have been kept separate through these long periods of time, at length re-unite and pass forth into the air, only for plants again to decompose.

Such, then, is the rhythm of the composition and decomposition of carbonic acid upon which all life—animal life and plant life—depends. It is possible that this rhythm of composition and decomposition, wide as it is, may ultimately rest on a yet wider rhythm of composition and decomposition. For it has been suggested that sun-heat itself may be maintained by such a wider rhythm. Leaving that, however, on one side as merely a possibility, let us direct our attention to another and different Nature-rhythm. I know of none more suitable than the rhythm of the circulation of water, a rhythm which, as we shall see, is particularly rich in undertones.

First, let us regard the circulation of water in its broadest outlines. That sunshine which, as we have already seen, is doing good work wherever a blade of grass springs up from the ground or a tree puts forth its leaves when the winter is past—that sunshine has also good work to do over ocean tracts far from the land with its green vegetation. But its work here is of a different character. There it aided the plant to decompose carbonic acid ; here it aids the air, kept in restless motion by sunshine itself, to absorb from the ocean surface a rich store of water-vapour. Once absorbed into the air, this water-vapour is conveyed in an invisible form to distant mountain ranges. There the water once more assumes a visible form ; there it descends again to earth as rain or snow ; and there it begins that downward journey—first, perhaps, as a glacier, then as a mountain torrent, afterwards as a broadening stream, and eventually as a noble river, which brings it back once more to the parent ocean whence it originally proceeded and whence it will again proceed. Thus the circulation of water continues; the outward-bound particles sailing invisibly in the upper air, the homeward-bound particles pursuing their course over the surface of the land.

And here let us pause for a moment to notice the grand way Nature has of producing great results by very simple means. Take that circulation of air, for example, in and through which the circulation of water is made possible. What can be more simple? Warm air rises; cold air creeps along the surface to take its place, and thus leaves a vacant space into which the warm air, which has meanwhile been flowing thither through higher regions of the atmosphere, may descend and may thus complete the continuity of the circulation. What, I say again, can be simpler than the means? What can be grander than the result? For it is not too much to say that it is by virtue of this rhythmic circulation that our globe becomes a habitable earth. And then the complexity of the circulation is not less wonderful than its simplicity. This may seem paradoxical, but it is no less true. For though an isolated example of atmospheric circulation is simple— though the principle of all atmospheric circulation is simple —still the air circulation as it actually presents itself to our study is by no means simple. Phenomena as they are explained by science are always simpler than they are in their native freedom. And they must be so. How else could science pretend to be some sort of explanation of them?

This complexity of atmospheric circulation, we may here remark, is due not a little to the fact that there are so many systems of circulation going on at once, started at so

many independent centres. There is the great intra-
tropical circulation of the trade winds. This is perma-
nently felt over vast ocean areas. There are the monsoon
winds produced by the alternately heated plains of Asia
and northern Africa. These are subject to a half-yearly
reversal of direction, caused by the alternation of summer
and winter. There are the land and sea breezes along
coast-lines, whose period of reversal is due to the alternation of day and night. There are unnumbered local
winds and breezes, whose period is altogether uncertain—
all of these are subject to many variations partly due to,
partly giving rise to, the varying climatical conditions.
And they are all liable to overlap and to interfere with
each other's action.

Returning now from this digression, concerning the air-
circulation upon which the water-circulation depends, we
have next to consider that water-circulation in greater
detail.

Every pond, every streamlet, every lake, every broad
river, every inland sea, and the great ocean itself is constantly giving up from its surface some of its water substance to swell the amount of aqueous vapour in the air.
All over the surface of the earth this evaporation is constantly going on. The process is unceasing. And in the
Persian it is made the subject of a very beautiful thought.
"The sun sinks down in the ocean, and azure-hued vapours
arise, it is Nature's incense of devotion perfuming the
heavens." Considered in a more prosaic way, however, the
process is a wonderful one. I have somewhere seen it
stated—in Mrs. Somerville's delightful Physical Geography
or elsewhere—that more than 180,000 cubic miles of water
annually pass into the atmosphere in a vaporous condition.
I do not give the statement as conveying anything very
definite. Personally I gain very little by such figures. I

have only a somewhat bewildered sense of bigness. It will, no doubt, have its due effect on minds of greater grasp than my own. To others it may convey a more definite idea if I say that from every square yard of the surface of the Indian ocean there rises in twenty-four hours sufficient water-vapour to fill a room ten feet high, ten feet long, and ten feet broad.

Once entrusted to the restless air, this vapour of water is borne away perhaps hundreds perhaps thousands of miles from its parent ocean or lake. For long it remains in an invisible condition, but even then is not without its beneficial effects, for it checks the escape of heat from the sun-warmed earth. Then, not improbably in some mountain region, it once more becomes visible, and floats in the air for a while as cloud. I have often in Switzerland watched the process of cloud formation in progress. At first the only sign in the clear sky is the filmy cloudlet clinging to the summits of the higher mountains. Presently the cloudlet has grown, until every Alpine peak flings out proudly a sweeping cloud banner. Within that cloud banner, as mountaineers know well, the storm has already begun to rage, with thunder and lightning, and eddying gusts of icy wind laden with snow and hail. Meanwhile cloud has gathered over the whole mountain region, and the hidden snowfields are receiving fresh supplies of their crystalline burden.

But no sooner has the snow fallen on the Alpine mountains than it begins its long journey to regain its former home in the ocean. Even the broad white glistening snowfields have a slow but constant motion. They are creeping downwards towards the valleys. But it is especially in the valley depressions themselves that the steady onward flow is observable. Here the snow particles, compacted by the pressure of their neighbour particles into the more solid condition of glacier ice, are slowly but surely making their way downwards from higher to lower levels, from the mountains to the sea.

If we question a Swiss guide concerning this motion, he will probably be able to point to this or that huge moraine block which, a year or two ago, was higher up the glacier than it is at present. He may also be able to supplement his personal knowledge with recorded experience or experience which has been handed on to him and his fellow-guides by their predecessors. He may tell us, for example, how in 1788 De Saussure, while descending from the Col du Geant, lost a ladder, and how the remains of that ladder were found forty-four years afterwards, not at the spot where it was lost, but thirteen thousand feet further down the glacier.

Such might be the testimony of a Swiss guide. But we may obtain more accurate information than the Swiss guides are able to give us. On the Mer de Glace, Principal Forbes and afterwards Professor Tyndall made careful observations on the rate and manner of flow of the glacier. I can but barely mention the chief results of these observations. In the first place, they put beyond question the fact that the motion was not spasmodic, but continuous. In the second place, they showed that the motion was more rapid near the middle than at the sides, just as the motion of a river is most rapid near mid-stream. In the third place they established a further resemblance between glacier-flow and river-flow, in the fact that where a bend in the course of the ice-stream occurs, the line of maximum flow is thrown nearer to the concave bank. And, lastly, they made the analogy still closer by showing that, just as the flow of water in a river is more rapid at the surface than near the bottom, so, too, the flow of ice in a glacier is more rapid at the surface than near the bottom.

Thus, then, does the solid ice of a glacier flow onwards and downwards like an almost arrested river. But ere long it reaches a lower level, where, owing to the increased warmth of the air, it melts, and, no longer hampered and constrained in its motion, assumes the form of a glacier stream, which leaps and rushes through valley gorges until it reaches a lake or joins some mighty river flowing sea-wards. Many scenes does that river reflect in the mirror of its broad surface ere the waters regain the ocean home from which they proceeded. The cottage and the hamlet are not less faithfully reflected than the castle and the populous city; the sheep in the upland meadows are as clearly imaged as the deer in the broad-stretching park; sloping fields of corn and flax are mirrored as truly as ancient trees of stately growth. But in the upper reaches the reflections are only disturbed by the splash of the ferry-man's oars, while nearer the ocean the screw-blades of the ocean steamer leave a longer and more troubled track on the waters.

Having now traced in some detail the main rhythm of the circulation of water, I have next to draw your attention to some of the undertones, if I may so call them, which accompany and enrich this rhythm. For the water in its circulation has work to do; the rhythm of circulation is enriched by the undertones of work.

I have already mentioned incidentally that the presence of vapour of water in the air enables the atmosphere to check the escape of heat from the sun-warmed earth; and we shall presently see how the vapour of water becomes a bearer of heat from the warmer region of evaporation to the colder region of condensation. This is the more special work which is done by the vapour of water.

To the glacier work of quite another order is assigned. To it is assigned the double work of earth-sculpture, and of

the carriage of detritus. Take the latter first. We have
seen how the glacier bears on its surface long trains of
moraine matter. The amount of rocky matter thus borne
slowly downwards by the larger Swiss glaciers must be
very great ; but I am not aware that any one has been at
the pains of calculating, even approximately, its amount.
It may be safely estimated at many thousands of tons.
And of what does all this moraine matter consist ? Of
the chips and flakes which are struck from the surrounding
mountains as they are slowly carved into their rugged outlines by the untiring chisel of giant Frost. All these
fragments are carried downwards by the glacier from higher
to lower levels—from the mountain precipices above to the
grass-clad valleys below. And constant as is the supply
of material from above, the glacier is equal to and more
than equal to the task of its transport. Such is the work
of carriage or transport. The work of sculpture is no less
important. Nothing can be more striking and characteristic
than the appearance of a district that has been subjected
to the action of glacier ice. The rocks have a rounded,
dome-shaped appearance which at once strikes the eye and
arrests the attention. Even the lower hills may have been
impressed with this dome-like form. The moving mass of
ice has, in fact, worn off all angular asperities and smoothed
all irregularities of outline. Close inspection will show,
too, that it has scored the rock with characteristic grooves
and scratches and fine striations, while every glacier stream
tells of the work in actual progress by the amount of fine
rock-powder with which it is laden, all of which is ground
off the rock surfaces over which the glacier ice forces its
way.

If, now, we turn to those regions where the water is
precipitated, not in the form of snow but in that of rain, we
shall find that here, too, the undertone of work is less con-

spicuous perhaps, but not less noteworthy. If we go out
into the fields on any rainy day we may see this work in
progress. We shall quickly notice that, though much of
the rain rapidly sinks into the ground, it generally trickles
a foot or two over the surface before it disappears. Even
if it only runs for a few inches, it bears with it a few grains
of soil for this distance. Then, if the rainfall continue, these
few grains will presently be carried a few inches farther,
and ere long a few inches yet further, always travelling
from higher to lower levels. At the bottom of the field
there may perhaps run a little rill, which may communicate
with a streamlet, which in turn falls into a river. We shall
find that some of the soil is carried by every heavy shower
of rain into the rill, and thence into the streamlet and the
river. And after a wet day we cannot fail to notice that
all the tiny rills, the little rivulets, the streams, and the
great rivers themselves are laden with a rich supply of the
soil which the raindrops have removed from the fields.
Thus the land is very literally always flowing downwards
to the sea; not a particle can get up again when once it
has been carried even a few feet on its downward course;
and this action is going on wherever rain falls upon the
surface of the land.

Such, then, is the effect of rain. We must not imagine,
however, that when the rain has collected into a streamlet,
or when the glacier ice has melted to form a mountain
torrent, and streamlet and torrent have united into a river
—that then the work of water is done. By no means.
The work of earth-sculpture and transport is only begun.
Here the river, winding from side to side and eating steadily
into its concave banks, carves out a broad and beautiful
valley with sloping sides. *There* in a country of less yielding
rock it cuts its way downwards and produces a grand ravine,
like the Cañon of the Colorado, more than three hundred

miles long, with precipitous walls of rock in places more than a mile in perpendicular height. *There again* the river cuts its way backwards at some giant waterfall, like that of the Niagara, which has in this way cut out for itself a ravine seven miles long and 160 feet or more in depth. And we must remember that the ravines of the Colorado and the Niagara are only giant examples of the kind of work which every river on a larger or smaller scale has to do and *does*.

Add to this power of sculpturing the earth's surface, the power of transport exercised by rivers. Sir C. Lyell calculated "that if a fleet of more than eighty Indiamen, each freighted with about 1,400 tons weight of mud, were to sail down the Ganges every hour of every day and night for four months continuously, they would only transport from the higher country to the sea a mass of solid matter equal to that borne down by the Ganges in the four months of flood season." Out of the materials thus transported are formed such great deltas as that of the Ganges-Brahmapootra system, which is 60,000 square miles in area, and has been proved to be in the neighbourhood of Calcutta more than 481 feet in depth.

But I will not weary you with details. And indeed, I must hasten on to the conclusion of what I have to say concerning these undertones of the rhythm of water circulation. One more secondary rhythm in connection with the primary rhythm I have yet to describe.

Besides the solid matter which rivers carry down to the sea in suspension, that is, in a visible form, there is much that they carry down in an invisible form in solution. A little of this is common salt, and this remains in the sea-water and goes to increase its saltness. Most of it, however, is limestone, which the river has derived from the chalk or other calcareous rocks over which it has flowed or

K

from which it has received tributary streams. What, then, becomes of all this limestone thus borne down to the sea? It does not remain in the sea-water, but is extracted by sea-shells and other minute marine organisms. Living in multitudes near the surface of the warm ocean there are minute creatures, which are busy elaborating this limestone into their beautiful internal or external skeletons, forming of it shells of exquisite workmanship. When these little creatures die, the shells they have constructed sink to the bottom, and there form layers of a material which in many important respects closely resembles chalk. For chalk has been shown to have been formed in the past in some such way as this ooze, as it is called, is being formed to-day. Other creatures, too, such as the corals and ordinary shell-fish, are also busy extracting the limestone from sea-water; but we may restrict our attention to this ooze. See, then, the nature of this secondary rhythm.

Ancient rivers carried down prehistoric limestone to the sea. There, in those remote ages, the calcareous matter was extracted by minute creatures, and was by them, in the course of many succeeding generations, built up into chalk. For long periods this chalk remained in the ocean depths. But at length it was, by the stress of the internal fire-forces, raised above the sea-level to become a portion of a continental area. But no sooner did it form an integral part of the dry land than rivers began to dissolve it and raindrops to erode its surface. That solution and erosion is still in progress. The old-world chalk is being dissolved and carried out to sea by the rivers of to-day. And in the sea of our own times the modern descendants of the chalk-building creatures are busy, as their forefathers were once busy, extracting once more the limestone and forming a new chalk, which may some day itself in turn be raised above the surface of the sea, and may itself form an integral part of a new continental area. Then, perhaps, the rivers of the future may dissolve this new-world chalk and carry it particle by particle out to sea, only for the minute organisms of that future to convert into the chalk of a future yet more remote. Solution, transport by rivers to the ocean, elaboration by minute organisms into chalky ooze, elevation above the sea-level ; re-solution, re-transport, re-elaboration, and re-elevation ; thus this beautiful rhythm continues, the periods of time in which it is accomplished almost baffling human comprehension.

Such, then, are some of the undertones, as I have called them, in the rhythm of the circulation of water. To this main rhythm I now return merely for the purpose of recapitulation. Mark the phases in the rhythm. Evaporation from the ocean, transport by the winds, condensation into cloud, precipitation from the cloud as snow or rain, collection into water streams or glacier streams, downward flow toward the ocean as a great river, union once more with the ocean ; re-evaporation, re-transport, re-condensation, re-precipitation, and so on in rhythmic succession. And then, as the result of this circulation, the retention of the heat acquired by the earth from the sun, the various phases of earth-sculpture, the transport of rocky matter from higher to lower levels, the supply of limestone afforded to the minute marine organisms, and the gift to mankind of rivers, the highways of civilization. And then, once more, as a source and support of this circulation, the genial warmth of our sun.

Is there, I now ask, in the study of all this anything especially calculated to dull the poetic faculty of the student? I cannot believe that there is. On the contrary, I believe that it opens up fresh fields for poetic thought and reverie. It is true that we must open heart as well as eye to the influence of Nature's teaching in this as in all

other cases. It is true that we must be as ready to expand
the mind that we may take a broad and comprehensive
view of the facts, as we have before been to contract its
view in the examination of minutiæ. It is true, too, that
we must view the facts from a different standpoint. Still
I believe that the reverent study of science does much to
strengthen the poetic side of our human nature.

I am anxious here not to be misunderstood. I do not
for one moment suppose that the scientific study of Nature
will induce a love of Nature in a mind in which, if it be
possible, no faculty for such love already exists. Nor do
I for one moment suppose that the *exclusive* study of
science can in any way develop the poetic faculty left, as
it must thus be, in utter idleness. You must grant the
possession of the faculty ; you must grant its moderate use.
These things being granted, I strongly believe that the
wider knowledge of Nature opened up by the study of
science will carry in its train the development of this
faculty, and thus will draw after it a wider love of Nature.
The man of science should above all others be ready to
echo the words of the poet (Browning)—

> " This world's no blot for us
> Nor blank—it means intensely, and means good :
> To find its meaning is my meat and drink."—(*Fra Lippo Lippi.*)

And again—

> " O World, as God has made it ! all is beauty :
> And knowing this is love, and love is duty."—(*Guardian Angel.*)

Our study of the rhythms which I have chosen for
illustration might well be carried further. Attention might
be drawn to the rhythmic changes of energy, which
accompany the composition and decomposition of carbonic
acid gas, and the evaporation and precipitation of water.
And somewhat might be said concerning Sir William
Siemens' fascinating hypothesis, that the maintenance of

sun-heat is itself due to a wider and more far-reaching
Nature-rhythm. But space forbids.

Let us not, however, in any case forget how much we
owe to the sun as the centre of so many of those rich
rhythms which make up the harmony of Nature. So much
do we owe to the sun that we are tempted to ask, What do
we not owe to his power? To him we owe the circulation
of water, to him the motions of the winds; he it is that
enables the plant to put forth its shoots; he that gives life
to the animal; but for him we should have no grand process of earth-sculpture; but for him no available sources of
energy. All Nature rejoices in his rays; he is the very life
of the world.

> "Oh, for a voice to sing this Sun of ours
>   That floods the earth with his glad brilliancy,
>   That shines alike on giant forest tree
> And all the little trembling delicate flowers!
> Our golden Sun, that bathes yon rocky towers
>   And mountain bastions with his radiancy,
>   That glints o'er ocean wavelets till with glee
> They leap and dance throughout the daylight hours.
>
> "Magic musician he of rarest art,
>   He strikes his full rich chords through earth and air
> Till Nature rings with his glad minstrelsy.
>   Soft echoes answer in the deepest heart
>   Of souls whose strings are tuned to poesy—
> Heaven holds its breath to hear the music rare."

I earnestly hope and believe that with all our advances
in science we shall always keep our hearts open to the
beauty and tenderness of the simplest and commonest
daily occurrences. "The daily light, fresh as a young
child every morning, and dignified as the mellowness of
age at even"—I quote a favourite passage of mine from
the writings of James Martineau—"the yearly changes less
fair and clear to our infancy than to our maturity, the
weariness of Nature as she drops her leaves, the glee with

which she hangs them out again, the silver mists of autumn, the slanting rains of spring, the sweeping lines of drifted snow, all are as the natural language of God—the turns of His Almighty thought—*to the spirit that lies open to their wonder;* to others they are but a spinning of the earth, an evaporation of the waters, an equilibrium of the winds." Listen again : " The modest flower, nestling in the meadow grass ; the happy tree, as it laughs and riots in the wind ; the moody cloud, knitting its brow in solemn thought ; the river, that has been flowing all night long (what a beautiful expression of continuity that is !—the river, *that has been flowing all night long*) ; the sound of the thirsty earth, as it drinks and relishes the rain ;—these things are as a full hymn when they flow from the melody of Nature, but an empty rhythm when scanned by the finger of Art ! "

Let us all so live our life that our spirits may " lie open to the wonder" of these things ; then will the " empty rhythm " form an integral part of the " melody of Nature." Then, indeed, shall we be able to feel that " beneath the dome of this universe we cannot stand where the musings of the Eternal Mind do not murmur round us, and the visions of His loving thought appear."

CHAPTER VI.

THE EVOLUTION OF SCIENTIFIC KNOWLEDGE.*

"That law is universal will become an irresistible conclusion when it is perceived that the progress in the discovery of laws itself conforms to law."— HERBERT SPENCER.

THE traits which characterize the progress of science are the traits which characterize the progress of organic life, the progress of society, the progress of the universe—the' traits of evolution. And what are these traits? The processes of evolution are processes of *differentiation* and *integration ;* that is to say, they are processes by which the parts of that which is being evolved become more *different*, and by which those parts, at the same time, become more *dependent* upon each other, and are bound together into a more *definite complex whole.* Where, as in most cases, evolution is accompanied by growth, the differentiation and integration are not confined to those parts which originally existed in the system, but are extended to the material which is gradually incorporated with the original matter. And where, as is always more or less the case, the parts of the evolving system are in motion, this motion also is subject to the processes of differentiation and integration.

Imagine, for the sake of example, a tribe of savages in

* This chapter is partly based on an article in the *Quarterly Journal of Science*, for July, 1880.

a pre-social stage. Each individual does for himself all that he wants done : he cuts his own bow, makes his own arrows, and shoots for himself the wild creatures from which he has himself to prepare food, and perhaps clothing. Now, let evolution come into play. Differentiation sets in. There is an incipient division of labour. One individual devotes himself to the making of bows and arrows on the understanding that they whom he supplies shall procure him food and clothing ; another dresses the food or the skins on similar terms ; and so on. It is needless to elaborate this example ; for without elaboration it is clear that the individuals of a tribe so far evolved have become more different, and at the same time more dependent on each other ; while the tribe itself has been converted into a more definite, complex whole.

Such being, therefore, the law of evolution, let us note how the advance in complexity, definiteness, and integration, which constitutes evolution, is seen not less clearly in our *knowledge of phenomena* than in the phenomena themselves. It matters not, I believe, to which branch of science we turn our attention ; all tell the same tale. Definiteness of observation, complexity of subject-matter, interdependence of phenomena, comprehensiveness of generalization—all these advance hand in hand. The history of science is the history of an evolution, and the law of evolution is the outcome of that evolution.

At the outset, however, an objection may be raised to this application of a physical law to the products and processes of the mind. And to those who see no connection between consciousness and the vibration of brain-molecules, who recognize no physical basis of mind, the objection is probably insuperable. But while the fact cannot be too frequently insisted upon, that we are utterly and completely unable to conceive *how* the vibrations, decompositions, or ~~isomeric~~ metabolic changes of grey, nitrogenous matter, have become associated with the phenomena of conscious thought, or *why* the noumenal mind-staff should become an object of sense as phenomenal brain-stuff; while we must honestly, but without parade, confess that this is an ultimate fact behind which we are unable to pry, still we seem forced by the balance of scientific evidence to infer that there does exist a definite connection between what we characteristically call brain-power and thought. And if this be so, then it is evident that the evolution of scientific knowledge is but the sign of the evolution of one portion of the individual and social organism. For, just as the varying sound of the voice from feeble treble to resonant bass testifies to the gradual development of the vocal organs, so does the evolution of scientific knowledge testify to the evolution of the brain-power and brain-complexity of which that knowledge is one of the products.

Before we proceed to the consideration of some special instance of this evolution, it will be well to devote a short space to the broader question, From what has science in general been evolved? To this question the answer is not far to seek. For, since science is the organization of our knowledge of fact, it would seem to follow that science arises out of that unorganized knowledge of fact which forms the vague mass of general information possessed by the unscientific or the pre-scientific. This vague and indefinite knowledge of fact forms the solution from which definite and accurate science crystallizes out. Or to follow the better analogy, general information is the surrounding medium from which the organism of science has been differentiated. From that medium evolving science assimilates such facts as are necessary to its growth. And as it passes from lower to higher grades of scientific life, it exercises more and more selective discrimination of the fit and proper food-stuff for its continued growth and evolution ; and eventually it devotes a large share of its attention (as does man the highest organism) to the preparation and manufacture of fresh materials for its nutrition and growth.

The first step towards knowledge of any kind is classification, and classification is based on the recognition of likeness and unlikeness. We only know an object when we recognize that it is like something we have before met with. If it be like nothing that we have before seen or heard of, we say that we do not know what it is. And just as classification is the grouping together of like things, so is reasoning the grouping together of like relations among things. Now it is by the extension of these processes of grouping together like things and like relations among things that science arises. But so far the science is only *qualitative*. It is only when the recognition of *likeness* grows into the recognition of *equality* that science becomes quantitative ; for equality—equality between things and equality between relations—is the fundamental conception which underlies all mathematics and logic. Out of this conception of equality, therefore, springs *exact science*, endowed with the power of such quantitative prevision as is pre-eminently seen in the science of astronomy. Let us take this science of astronomy as our special example of the evolution of scientific knowledge.

Among the early Greeks the phenomena of the heavens were, according to Whewell, from whose writings I draw largely for my facts, explained on the supposition that the sky is a concave sphere or dome, to which the stars are fixed, and that the celestial sphere revolves perpetually and uniformly about the pole or fixed point. Here, then, we have an explanation in some sort physical, but one of extreme simplicity and generality, and one, therefore, which exemplifies an early stage in evolution. But ere long this simplicity gave way to incipient complexity. To account for the way in which the appearances of different nights succeed each other, the sun also was supposed to move round among the stars on the surface of the concave sphere ; and, if we are to believe Pliny, Anaximander was the first to point 'out that the circle in which the sun moves is oblique to the circles in which the stars move about the poles. Other irregularities were in process of time discovered, and the celestial mechanism by which they were explained grew proportionally in complexity. The wandering planets changed their course, moving now forwards and now backwards ; and to account for this motion each was supposed to be placed on the rim of an invisible wheel, which revolves on its centre while it moves around the sphere. Such a wheel was called an epicycle. Then it was discovered that the motions of the sun and moon also were irregular, so that they too were placed on the rims of imaginary epicycles ; while it was found that, for purposes of calculation, the same results were reached if—abandoning the epicycle—the sun were supposed to revolve in a circular orbit in which the earth does not occupy a central position, but is placed rather nearer to one side. Such an orbit was called an eccentric. Finally, as further anomalies and irregularities were discovered in the motions of the sun, moon, and planets, further extensions of the hypothesis of eccentrics and epicycles were rendered necessary until the master-mind of Hipparchus formulated and organized this system, the essence of which consists in the resolution of the apparently irregular motions of the heavenly bodies into an assemblage of circular and uniform motions.

In those days, it must be remembered, circular motions were the only motions admissible ; the idea of "such dis-

order among divine and eternal things as that they should
sometimes move quicker, and sometimes slower, and sometimes stand still," was considered impious, " for no one," it
was said, " would tolerate such anomaly in the movements
even of a man who was decent and orderly." And thus
there sprang up that complex system which gave rise to
the celebrated cynical saying of Alphonso X., of Castille,
that " if God had consulted him at the creation, the universe
should have been on a better and simpler plan."

That the history of early astronomic thought above
sketched exhibits an advance from the vague to the definite,
and from the simple to the complex, while it shows also an
increase in integration and dependence of parts, cannot, I
think, be for a moment doubted. And the views of Hipparchus, as developed by Ptolemy, may perhaps be looked upon
as the culmination of the evolution of the geocentric idea,
while the later history of astronomy exhibits the evolution
of the heliocentric idea.

A scientific theory in some respects resembles an organism, and especially in this—that it must harmonize with its
environment or die. The environment of theory is fact.
So long as a theory is in harmony with the known facts of
Nature it can exist, the development of a theory being its
modification in accordance with newly discovered facts.
But when the plasticity of a theory ceases, when it refuses
to accommodate itself to fact, its days are numbered, and
it must give place to a more fortunate rival in the struggle
for existence. In this way the earth-centre theory of our
system, organized by Hipparchus and developed by Ptolemy,
had to give place to the sun-centre theory, foreshadowed by
Pythagoras and worked out by Copernicus. As Whewell
truly remarks, so long as the *positions* only of the heavenly
bodies were considered, the hypothesis of Hipparchus is a
close representation of the truth ; but when once the pro-

cesses of measurement. gave sufficiently accurate results with respect to the *distances* of these bodies, the theory and the environing facts were out of harmony, and the theory was doomed. And when Galileo discovered, with the newly invented telescope, in the system of Jupiter and his moons, a model of the solar system; when he found that Venus, in the course of her revolution, assumes the same succession of phases which the moon exhibits in the course of a month;' and when Kepler observed the transit of Mercury, and Horrox the transit of Venus; then the fate of the old hypothesis was sealed, and the success of the new theory was secured.

Copernicus, however, retained the conception of circular motion, and the consequent existence of epicycles. But the idea of epicycles, like the geocentric idea, ere long ceased to be in harmony with the environment of fact. Kepler, we are told, attempted to reconcile the theory of Mars to the theory of eccentrics and epicycles, the event of which was the complete overthrow of that hypothesis, and the proposition in its stead of the theory the central truth of which has long since been abundantly established, that the planets move in ellipses. And this, be it noted, was a substitution of a more complex and integrated kind of motion for a combination of more simple kinds of motion.

As we now know, indeed, the motion substituted is even more complicated than Kepler supposed. For not only does the ellipse itself revolve slowly round the sun, but its shape undergoes change, being sometimes more nearly circular than at others, while, at the same time, the plane of the planet's motion oscillates about a mean position. Thus it comes about that the ellipse which accurately represents the planet's motion at one part of its course does not accurately represent that motion at another part of its course.

But the indefatigable industry of Kepler, besides establishing the elliptical theory, led him to the discovery of two other fundamental laws of formal astronomy: that the line drawn from sun to planet sweeps over equal areas in equal times; and that the square of the time taken to describe a planet's orbit, divided by the cube of its mean distance from the sun, is a fraction which is the same for every planet of the system. These laws are grand generalizations, though when the idea of force entered into these considerations the last had to be modified or amended thus: the cubes of the distance are as the squares of the times multiplied by the sum of the masses of the sun and planets. This modification, however, is the outcome of the splendid generalization which was inevitably to follow on the laws of Kepler which formed its basis.

For the next great step in astronomy was Newton's splendid induction. So gigantic was the onward stride then made—a stride without parallel in the history of science—that it seems at first sight impossible to reconcile it with the gradual advance implied in a development by evolution.

But a closer study of history makes evident the parallel but imperfect generalizations which were simultaneous with this more perfect and exact generalization. While Newton at Oxford was pondering on cosmical gravitation, Borelli in Florence was publishing his theory of the "balancing of the planets," arising, as he conjectured, from the equality of an "appetite for uniting themselves with the globe round which they revolve," and the "tendency to recede from the centre of revolution." While Newton was preparing his "Principia," Huyghens, Wren, Halley, and others seem to have possessed a general idea that the attractive force exercised by the sun varies inversely as the square of the distance from the centre. Hooke even went so far as to claim priority in publication to Newton himself. And it is undoubtedly true, as Whewell points out, that Hooke's *assertion* was prior to Newton's demonstration. Francis Bacon, again, had not only speculated on the mutual attraction of the particles of matter, but devised an experiment to ascertain "whether the gravity of bodies to the earth arose from an attraction of the parts of matter towards each other, or was a tendency towards the centre of the earth." But these were but foreshadowings of the truth. It remained for Newton to demonstrate that the same law—that the attraction is directly as the joint mass of the attracting and attracted bodies, and inversely as the square of their distance asunder—holds good for the sun's attractive influence on different planets and on the same planet in different parts of its orbit ; for the earth's attractive influence on the moon, and on bodies near the earth's surface ; for the mutual attraction of sun, moon, earth, planets, and satellites on each other ; and for the attractions of the individual particles of which these masses are composed.

The bearing of these well-known facts on the theory of evolution will now be evident. Not only does the conception of universal gravitation exhibit a great advance in the ideas of the inter-dependence of the members of the solar system—not only does it show an onward stride in the integration of our knowledge, but it displays also a vast increase in the orderly complexity of our views of that system by introducing definite conceptions of matter and force in addition to those of motion and distance. And here we might well leave the history of astronomy, satisfied that it has afforded ample illustration of the law under consideration. But, for the sake of rounding off the argument, attention may be drawn to the advance in the traits which characterize evolution implied in the nebular hypothesis of Kant and Laplace, which affords a not improbable conception of the mode of development of our system ; and implied also in the results of modern spectroscopic researches, which teach us that the chemistry of the sun and stars is not dissimilar to the chemistry of the earth, and which have raised the physics of the sun to the rank of an independent science. When we take into consideration, too, the conceptions concerning stellar distribution, started by Wright, developed by William Herschel, and subsequently criticised and opposed by Proctor, and add to these the results concerning the motion of the sun through space, the velocities of motion of certain stars determined by Huggins, and the " drifting " of star groups inferred by Proctor, we shall not lack instances of advance in definiteness of knowledge, in inter-dependence of ideas, and in complexity of our total conception of the phenomena of the heavens ; while the labours of Schiaporelli, Huggins, Donati, Lockyer, and Sir William Thomson, the results of which point to an intimate connection between nebulæ, comets, meteorites, and falling stars, bring into view a proportionate advance in the integration of that knowledge.

We have been obliged, from lack of space and for the sake of clearness, to confine our attention to the evolution of one branch of scientific knowledge. It must not be forgotten, however, that in no case is the evolution of one branch of such knowledge independent of the evolution of other branches. The term *branch*, indeed, suggests the conception of a general tree of knowledge of which they are the offshoots. But the special sciences might perhaps be more profitably likened to the organs of the animal organism. For not only do the several organs progress together with the progress of the whole of which they are the parts, but each organ ministers in its own fashion to the welfare of the whole and of the other organs. Mr. Herbert

Spencer has given many examples of the dependence of the advance of one branch of science upon the advance of other branches. It is, therefore, unnecessary here to do more than indicate the nature of the evidence. Where would astronomy be now, it may be asked, without the advance in optics implied in achromatic telescopes ; without the discoveries in mechanics of the laws of motion, and of the isochronism of the pendulum ; without the determination of the specific gravity of the earth, and the measurement of a degree on the earth's surface? There is, indeed, scarcely a branch of science upon which astronomy does not call for aid. In addition to those just mentioned, she relies on atmospheric physics for tables of atmospheric refraction ; upon chemistry for photographic processes ; upon electricity for various recording instruments ; and upon psychology for the personal equation—the time which elapses between seeing and registering which varies in different individuals. These facts are sufficient to exemplify the inter-dependence of the sciences, and they form not a tithe of the number which could be adduced. We have only to trace the interaction of terrestrial and astronomical physics on mathematics, to watch how new problems in physics called forth new mathematical processes, which processes enabled further physical advance, and thus led to fresh problems ; we have only to consider how chemistry has aided electrical science, and been aided in turn by that science ; we have only to observe how geology has profited by the advance of biology, and at the same time has aided in solving important biological problems ; we have only, in a word, to study the history of science in a scientific spirit, to see how completely the organs of the body scientific are dependent on each other, and are bound together into a definite complex whole.

- It only remains to illustrate a little more fully the differ-

L

entiations which are going on within the sciences. We will take the differentiation in the field of " Natural History " as our example.

" The register of knowledge of fact," says Hobbes, " is called history. Whereof there be two sorts, one called natural history ; which is the history of such facts or effects of nature as have no dependence on man's will ; such as are the histories of metals, plants, animals, regions, and the like. The other is civil history; which is the history of the voluntary actions of men in commonwealths." Professor Huxley, who quotes this from " The Leviathan," traces the gradual specialization of the term Natural History, and its final abandonment for the more happy term Biology. First, there separated off from it those sciences which were susceptible of mathematical or experimental treatment, or both, namely astronomy, natural philosophy (a term since abandoned in favour of physics), and chemistry. There were then left, as included under the term Natural History, physical geography, geology, mineralogy, the history of plants, and the history of animals. But as time went on the inorganic branches in turn separated off from the organic, and natural history came to mean simply the history of animals and of plants.

The introduction of the term biology in place of natural history dates from the beginning of this century, and has been generally accepted for some quarter of a century. Within this field the differentiation into botany and zoology is of much earlier date, as is also the separation of psychology and sociology, which are by rights branches of biology, and the latter of which takes the place of the civil history of Bacon or of Hobbes. Confining our attention, however, to zoology, we find that it splits up into four main divisions : morphology, which deals with form ; physiology, which deals with function ; ætiology, which deals with origin ; and distribution. Within these, again, differentiation has gone on. In morphology, for example, there is a division of labour into anatomy, which deals with macroscopic structure ; histology, which deals with microscopic structure ; taxonomy, which deals with classification; and development ;—within which last, again, there is a differentiation into ontogeny or embryology, which deals with the development of the individual ; and phylogeny, which deals with the development of the race. Once more distribution is differentiated into chronology, or distribution in time ; and chorology, or distribution in space.

Let us put these facts in tabular form. (*See* p. 148.)

Such a table exhibits at a glance the differentiation which has gone on in one field of scientific research. In it we can readily trace the line along which embryology, for example, has differentiated from the general body of natural history ; just as, in an analogous table of races, we could trace the line along which the English have differentiated from the Aryan stock ; or, in a table of the vertebrata, the line along which the horse has differentiated from the mammalian type. The very fact of our being able to represent the differentiation in such a table seems to testify to the truth of the evolution of scientific knowledge.

Let it, then, be clearly noted that the advance in scientific knowledge is not merely, as some suppose, an increase in the mass of accumulated facts. It is this ; but it is much more besides. Just as the more extended view which the mountaineer obtains as he rises above the valley does not charm so much by the multiplicity of objects as by the connection which is disclosed among them, so, too, the more extended view which the philosopher obtains, as he climbs the hill of science, does not owe its value so much to the number of facts as to their definite organization.

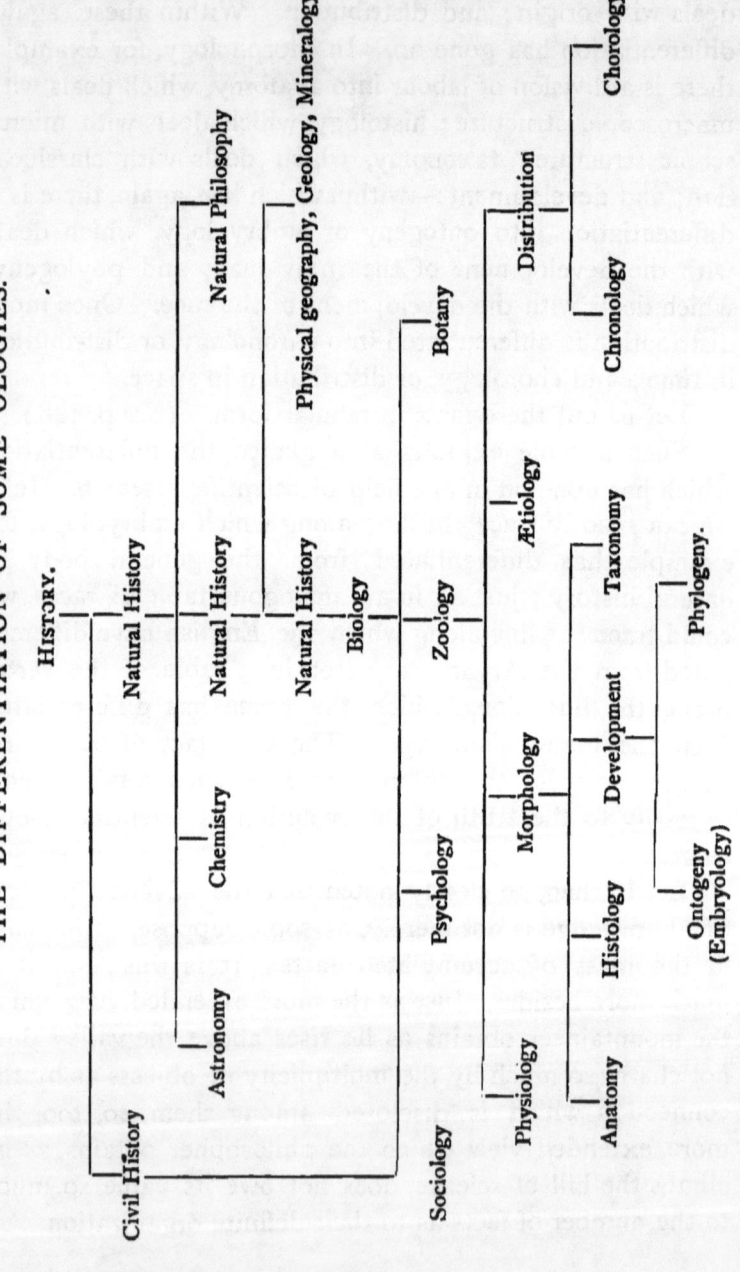

THE DIFFERENTIATION OF SOME 'OLOGIES.

In conclusion, one or two general facts may be pointed out. There is no more striking trait in the evolution of knowledge than the fact that not unfrequently the same discovery is made almost simultaneously by different workers labouring altogether independently of each other. Instance the theory of natural selection elaborated simultaneously by Darwin and Wallace ; instance, again, the independent liquefaction of oxygen by MM. Pictet and Cailletet ; instance once more the theory that the floras of the world originated in the northern hemisphere and migrated thence to the south, which seems to have been brought forward independently by Thiselton Dyer, Count Saporta, and Wallace. Or, again, perhaps we find that the same law or theory is advanced by several men as a speculation, and by one master mind as a demonstration. This may be said to have been the case in the discovery of the law of universal gravitation. Now, these facts are in full accordance with the theory that the development of our knowledge is an evolution. When the environment of ascertained fact has reached a certain stage, its influence inevitably calls forth the development of a new theory which shall be in harmony with all the conditions. In the minds of Newton's contemporaries the environment of accumulated facts called forth general conceptions more or less in harmony with these facts ; but in the master mind of Newton not only was the environment of fact more extended from his powerful grasp of intellect, not only was that environment more pressing from his constant habit of earnest thought, but the conceptions were more definite from the extraordinary depth of his mathematical insight. The result was the production of a law and a book which have been the wonder of all after-time. Newton's contemporaries were at a high enough level of thought to accept his generalization, which thereupon became part of the environment which induced subsequent though minor generalizations. But this has not always been so. Sometimes the conception of a master mind has fallen amid conceptions having so little in common with it, that its influence has not been felt until the subsequent advances of knowledge have caused its re-development, and called the attention of the world to a genius who lived before his time. Such was the case with some of the generalizations of Archimedes, and of Roger Bacon, to mention no other names.

Finally, we may notice the fact that, just as in the organic world we have the highly organized human being existing side by side with the lowly organized *entozoon*, so too we have, in the world of thought, conceptions in some sort in harmony with the grandeur of the Cosmos side by side with conceptions moulded to the meanest and most trivial facts. But there is nothing here at variance with the theory of evolution. The human being and the entozoon are each more or less in harmony with their several environments, and any advance in the development of each is such as to bring it more closely in harmony with all the conditions. So, too, the conceptions of the philosopher and the clown are each more or less in harmony with the environing facts by which they are respectively surrounded; and here too, in each case, any advance in development is such as to bring the conceptions more closely in harmony with the surrounding facts.

To this parallel between the organic world and the world of thought we may add another. It is now generally admitted that the evolution of the individual is a condensed epitome of the evolution of the species to which that individual belongs. The evolution, for example, of an individual frog from the undifferentiated egg to the complex adult, epitomizes, with much abbreviation or even the suppression of some stages, the evolution, through long ages, of frogs from simpler forms of life. So, too, does the evolution of the conceptions of the individual philosopher epitomize, with much abbreviation or even the suppression of some stages, the evolution of philosophic thought in general. Both in the individual and in the race the discovery of law is itself subject to law ; and, if there be any truth in the views above set forth, the law to which it is subject is the law of evolution.

APPENDIX.

THE EVOLUTION OF MACHINES.

"Look abroad and contemplate the infinite achievement of steam-power."
—KENNEDY.

THE end and object of the attainment of knowledge by human folk is the *conduct of life*. And that knowledge is of most value which bears most closely upon our moral and our physical well-being. As the sworn enemy and unflinching foe of superstition, Science has done much, and is destined to do more, for our moral welfare. As the fountain and source of mechanical inventions, Science has added enormously to our physical comfort.

It is this material aspect of the question to which I would now direct attention. And to what has been said concerning the evolution of scientific knowledge, I propose here to add a few remarks by way of Appendix on the evolution of machines.* Taking the history of the steam-engine as a concrete example, we will endeavour to ascertain whether the traits which characterize the growth of the steam-engine are the traits which characterize evolution.

It is interesting to notice that the earliest practical attempts to make use of the expansive force of steam, and the vacuum which it creates when it again condenses to water, was for *pumping;* and it was long before the use of steam separated itself from the almost exclusive application to the raising, from mines or in waterworks, of the fluid from which it was itself

---

* My friend and colleague, Prof. H. S. Hele Shaw, made this the subject of a valuable and interesting paper before the Society of Arts, March 4th, 1885.

generated. Little is known of the "water-commanding engine" which the second Marquis of Worcester erected (c. 1650) at Raglan Castle and at Vauxhall. This, however, would seem to be certain, that the steam was allowed to exert its influence *directly* on the surface of the water which it was alternately to suck up from below by its condensation (through the instrumentality of atmospheric pressure), and to force upwards to a greater height by its expansion.

In the engine of Thomas Savery (1698), which was evoked by the pressing need of freeing the Cornish mines of water, the same system of direct action was employed ; but the engine was made more efficient, and at the same time more complex, by the addition of " a system of surface condensation, by which he was enabled to charge his vessels when it became necessary to refill them ; and a secondary boiler, which enabled him to supply the working-boiler with water without interrupting its work" (Thurston).

So far the steam was allowed to act directly upon the water to be raised. But in the Newcomen engine we find a marked advance in efficiency and in complexity by the introduction of an intermediate mechanism between the steam-action and the water-raising. This consisted of a piston—a device employed in 1680 by Huyghens in a piece of apparatus in which gunpowder was used for the displacement and rarefaction of air, and used by Papin with steam, but subsequently abandoned by him in favour of a floating piston, which merely acted as a "cushion to prevent the steam from sudden condensation in contact with the water." In Newcomen's engine the piston was distinct, on the one hand, from the boiler where the steam was generated, and on the other from the water which was to be raised. More than this : not only was the steam made to act through the intervention of a piston, but an oscillatory beam was interposed between the piston and the pump-rods.

Further advances followed. In place of the surface condensation of Savery, a jet of water was thrown directly *into* the cylinder, by which process condensation was more rapid, and the engine became more efficient. By the introduction of a system by which the valves were opened mechanically, the engine became automatic. At first "they used to work with a buoy to the cylinder enclosed in a pipe, which buoy rose when the steam was strong, and opened the injection and made a stroke, thereby they were only capable of giving six, eight, or ten strokes in a minute, till a boy, named Humphrey Potter, in 1713, who attended the engine, added (what he called a *scoggan*) a catch, that the beam always opened, and then it would go fifteen or sixteen strokes a minute. But this being perplexed with catches and strings, Mr. Henry Beighton, in an engine he had built at Newcastle-on-Tyne in 1718, took them all away but the beam itself, and supplied them in a much better manner."

Beighton's apparatus was thus more simple than Potter's. And perhaps it may be objected that this is not evolution, for evolution proceeds *from* the simple *to* the complex. But it must be remembered that in many cases the simplification of parts is absolutely necessary for the further evolution of the whole. When in astronomy the system of epicycles and eccentrics was abandoned in favour of a simpler theory of celestial motion, this simplification was a necessary step, without which the further evolution of astronomical knowledge was impossible. Again and again has the same thing taken place in the history of machines ; but such simplifications have been steps which have eventually aided in the evolution of a more self-contained complex whole.

Thus in the hands of Newcomen and his fellow-workers the steam-engine became more efficient, more economical, and more complex. Then Smeaton took it in hand ; and though he did not introduce any new principles of construction, he added not a little to the efficiency of the machine by marked improvements in the proportions of parts ; that is to say, he contributed towards the evolution of the steam-engine, not by increasing the complexity of the mechanism, but by skilfully guiding it in the path (equally essential in evolution) from the indefinite to the definite. And thus he paved the way for the epoch-making improvements of Watt.

Of this great man it may truly be said that he occupies a similar position in the field of invention to that which Newton and Darwin occupy in the field of science. All three were characterized by an intense love of verification, by a resolute and unflinching appeal to fact, by the constant application of the criterion of truth. There have appeared in the ranks of men of science and inventors, speculators as great as they, men of insight not less penetrating. But it is not insight alone which conquers ignorance and commands the material world. That which is revealed to the eye of genius must be felt and handled and proved to be real by the sense of touch trained by science. Newton withheld his theory of gravitation until a remeasurement of an arc of the earth's surface proved that this conception was in harmony with fact; Darwin brooded over the theory of natural selection until his accumulated observations and experiments had afforded sufficient verification; and Watt spent many of the best and most valuable years of his life in experimental researches, which should form a firm and lasting basis for his superstructure of invention.

In each case, too, the work of these master minds was the outcome of the work done by their predecessors. Kepler paved the way for Newton; Malthus gave to Darwin the seed from which sprung the "Origin of Species;" and Watt made some of his earliest experiments on the model of a Newcomen engine which was entrusted to him for repairs. Enormous as was the stride in astronomy under Newton, in biology under Darwin, and in invention under Watt, it was in each case a stride which is not incomprehensible as a growth by evolution. Each of these three commanding intellects absorbed all that learning and research had previously done in their special provinces, and then pushed on the evolution, stamped with the ineffaceable stamp of his genius.

A mere enumeration of the improvements effected by Watt, will show the enormous advance which was made in his time.

1. The condensation of the steam was effected in a separate vessel, the "condenser."

2. The top of the cylinder was closed, and the piston-rod allowed to play through a stuffing-box; the cylinder, moreover, was encased in a steam jacket, which prevented loss of heat and obviated the ill effects of leakage.

3. This improvement was but a step towards a further advance. The steam was alternately admitted above and below the cylinder, so that the engine became double-acting.

4. And this necessitated a further advance; for the piston-rod now not only acted by a pull on the beam, but during its upstroke delivered a thrust. The old chain-connection between piston-rod and beam would no longer suffice, and Watt devised his celebrated " parallel motion " to meet the difficulty.

5. The steam was cut off from the cylinder ere the stroke of the piston was completed, so that the expansion of the steam already admitted might be utilized. In this way the work done by a pound of steam was more than doubled.

6. By the introduction of a "governor" the engine was made automatically to regulate and render uniform its own rate of work.

7. By the addition of an "indicator" the engine was made to give information of the exact manner in which the steam was acting within the cylinder.

Add to these the introduction of the " throttle-valve," the invention of a water-gauge to show the height of the water in the boiler, and a steam-gauge to indicate the pressure of steam in the boiler, the suggestion of a second cylinder acting in concert with the first—add these and other minor or temporary improvements, and the Watt engine stands out a vastly more economical, efficient, complex, definite, self-contained piece of mechanism than anything which preceded it.

But Watt did not stand alone as an inventor. He introduced into his engine the improvements effected by his contemporaries. His own master-stroke of utilizing the expansion of steam by an early cut-off would have been impossible without the use of some such improvement as the double-D slide-valve of Murdoch. Nor could this expansion have been satisfactorily employed without some method of equalizing the irregular effect of the steam. Hence the employment of Fitzgerald's fly-wheel, as introduced by Matthew Wasborough, at first with Murdoch's "sun and planet" wheels, but eventually, on the expiration of Wasborough's patent, with the more familiar crank. And perhaps it may be said that Watt's governor and Wasborough's fly-wheel, by giving regularity of motion, rendered possible the extensive use of the steam-engine as a motor for extensive trains of machinery. Thus, though Watt, standing out as the great inventive genius of his time, throws the minor inventors into the shade, we must not suppose that other inventors were not busy with brain and hand. Hornblower claimed for his compound engine priority to Watt; Bull devised a pumping engine in which the overhead beam was done away with, the piston-rod being directly connected with the pump-rods; Murdoch patented an oscillating engine, the principle of which was afterwards largely applied to steam navigation; and Cartwright perfected a system of surface condensation, and introduced metallic packing in the piston.

To trace the further growth of the steam-engine would require more space than I can spare, and more knowledge than I possess. This, however, may be noted: that by the time of Watt the pumping engine of the old type had more or less completely reached the limits of its evolution. In no essential features are the pumping engines found in many of our Cornish mines to-day different from those of three-quarters of a century ago. New types of engine may, indeed, have superseded them for certain classes of work; but they are the results of evolution along fresh lines. They are like new organisms entering into competition with old-established forms of life. The old-established pumping engine may be said to have, like certain forms of life, early reached the limits of its evolution, and to have passed into the condition of a persistent type. The same is, to a certain extent, true of the stationary engine. But here the competitors are more numerous, and the struggle for existence is waged more fiercely. Still, amid younger machines developing along other lines, the old persistent type is still to be met with, and has not been entirely supplanted.

The chief modern developments of the steam-engine are for purposes of transit, in the locomotive on land and the marine engine by sea. These are machines which have taken to a new mode of life, and have been impressed with many modifications, called forth by the change in the environment. At first, both the locomotive and the marine engine showed, in the overhead beam, traces of their pump-engine ancestry. But this has long been discarded in the locomotive and in the marine engine of our large sea-going ships, though the powerful Mississippi steamboats still show a survival of the old rocking beam. In the locomotive, built as it is for speed, the suppression of the condenser has been rendered necessary by the conditions of existence, just as in the horse the suppression of unnecessary toes has been effected with a similar object. This suppression is, again, a case of simplification essential to the further evolution of the locomotive as such. So, too, in the marine engine the conditions of existence have made it imperative to abandon the internal jet-condenser, and to revert to surface condensation.

A good illustration of evolution is seen in the introduction of feathering paddles. In the ordinary paddle much power is lost by the inclination of the floats downwards when they strike, and upwards when they leave the water. In the feathering paddle this is obviated by causing the floats to enter, pass through, and leave the water in a nearly vertical position. "The usual arrangement is such that the feathering wheel has the same action on the water as a radial wheel of double diameter." Here, then, is increased efficiency accompanied by increased complexity and diminished bulk. But with this invention the limits of the evolution of the paddle-wheel would seem to be well-nigh reached —but not the evolution of steam navigation. In the screw-propeller we have evolution along a different line, and in that line, too, we have the traits of evolution. For the simple curve at first given to the screw blades has given place to a more complex but more efficient form. "The most efficient screws," we learn, "have a slightly greater pitch at the periphery than at the hub, and an increasing pitch from the forward to the rear part of the screw." So that here, again, we have increased complexity, increased efficiency, and diminished bulk, going hand in hand. The whole organization of the engines had, moreover, to be altered to meet the new requirements. "The introduction of the rapidly revolving screw in place of the slow-moving paddle-wheel, necessitated a complete change in the design of the steam-engine ; and the unavoidable change from the heavy, long-stroked, low-speed engines previously in use, to the light engines, with small cylinders and high-piston speed, was one which necessarily occurred slowly. It also became necessary to train up a body of engine-drivers who should be capable of managing these new engines, for they required the exercise of a then unprecedented amount of care and skill. Thus it happens that it is only after a considerable time that the screw attained its proper place as an instrument of propulsion, and finally drove the paddle-wheel quite out of use except in shoal waters " (Thurston). It is the old principle of the survival of the fittest. The screw propeller has well-nigh ousted the paddle-wheel from the ocean highways; but in shoal water the paddle-wheel is more completely in harmony with the environment, and there it holds its own.

And now compáre the engines of a modern ocean steamer with even the highest achievement of the age of Watt. Prof. Shaw, in his paper on this subject, gives a table to show the number of parts in the engines and boilers of a first-class Atlantic liner. In that table we see that no less than twenty-three auxiliary engines minister to the efficiency of the main engine, all being definitely connected together into one complex system. There are no less than 37 separate levers, and 147 distinct valves. And the total number of parts in the main and auxiliary engines, including nuts, pins, bolts, studs, and so forth, all of them necessary for efficiency, durability, and security, is something like 100,000! Such is the complexity of the modern marine engine.

At the close of Prof. Shaw's paper some remarks were made by Prof. Perry, which forcibly illustrate the nature of the evolution involved. In the course of these remarks, Prof. Perry, in playful banter, alluded to the evolution of machines in Erewhon, where the inhabitants, alarmed at the advance of machine-power, and seeing that they were more and more getting the slaves of machines which were becoming more and more automatic, and more and more capable of self-production—the inhabitants of Erewhon, I say, fearful lest there should be no room left on earth for human beings except as parasites, broke up the machines, and reverted to the most primitive tools. " All this evil," said the professor, " proceeded from their having a notion that they knew a great deal about the evolution of machines." From which it would appear that Prof. Perry regards Mr. Butler's romance as a sober record of fact. But if this was mere playful banter, let us hope that his earlier remarks on the marine engine were of the same harmless nature. "To consider the culminating example," said Prof. Perry, "of the engines of the Atlantic liner giving, say, 10,000 horse-power to the propeller shaft. Now, consider how Watt, one hundred years ago, would have given this horse-power to a shaft. If he had been asked to do this, he could have done it ; and he would probably have put in one hundred of his engines, filling the ship with machinery. It was also within his powers to have arrangements which would enable all his one hundred engines to stop or to reverse at the same time, and instead of the 100,000 parts of existing engines and boilers, he would probably have used in all his engines ten times the total number of rivets, and nuts, and other pieces. In fact, to give 10,000 horse-power to a shaft in Watt's days would have needed machinery much more complicated than the machinery in use at the present day."

If spoken in seriousness these remarks betray a total misconception of what evolution means, and at the same time afford a telling piece of testimony in favour of the evolution of machines. For evolution is not the multiplication of similar structures, but the production of one more complex structure which shall do the work of many. If it be true that the engines of the Atlantic liner are equivalent to one hundred of Watt's engines, how marked is the evolution ! Increase of efficiency, increase of complexity, and increase of economy of space, fuel, and material, have all gone hand in hand. Prof. Perry is to be thanked for bringing out clearly and prominently this aspect of the question.

Finally, let it be clearly remembered that the evolution of machines is but the sign and outward manifestation of the evolution of certain activities of that highest known product of organic evolution, man. From the subjective or ejective point of view, it testifies to the evolution of mind ; from the physiological point of view, it testifies to the evolution of those multitudinous muscular adjustments which enable man to gain the mastery over the materials at his command, not only directly, but yet more indirectly through tools and mechanical appliances ; from the morphological point of view, it testifies to the evolution of certain invisible structures within that most complex product of evolution, the human brain. Thus the evolution of machines is but a part of that general and far-reaching process of evolution to which not only man, his structure and activities, not only the whole organic world, but the entire realm of Nature, bears abundant and unimpeachable testimony.

CHAPTER VII.

BODY AND MIND.

" The object of the idea constituting the human mind is the body ; in other words, a certain mode of extension which actually exists, and nothing more." —SPINOZA.

1. *The Physiological Basis.*

"We thus comprehend, not only that the human mind is united to the body, but also the nature of the union between mind and body. However, no one will be able to grasp this adequately or distinctly, unless he first has adequate knowledge of the nature of our body."—SPINOZA.

THE crowning effort of the study of Nature is the adequate comprehension of human nature. To this great theme poets and philosophers, historians and men of science, have devoted centuries of observation and thought and imagination. And the results of all this labour are summed up in our civilization, our literature, our psychology, our physiology. Of man's bodily structure, of his mental qualities, of his moral attributes, we have, through this accumulation of experience, gradually acquired sufficient, and sufficiently exact, knowledge to form the basis of wide generalizations. But it is only of late that all this knowledge has stood forth in a new light—the light of the theory of evolution. In this light old questions assume a new aspect, and new solutions, before undreamed of or deemed impious, are seen dimly as possibilities, or stand

M

out more clearly as probabilities, admitting of a certain amount of verification.

One main result of the spread of the doctrine of evolution has been to lead men of science to seek in physiology a basis for psychology. Few psychologists of the present day are so bold as to ignore altogether the study of the structure and functions of the nervous system ; and many have been at the pains to acquire some sound practical acquaintance with the principles of animal biology. Convinced that there is, at any rate, some connection between neurosis and psychosis, they wisely deem that a knowledge of the former will materially aid in the comprehension of the latter, and that an inquiry into the question of the evolution of the one will throw light on the question of the evolution of the other.

It is no part of my present purpose, however, to attempt to give any description of the mode in which a nervous system may have originated. My limits force me to leave biological evolution altogether on one side, save in so far as a belief in such evolution may be from time to time implied or tacitly assumed. Suffice it to say, that when the organization of animals had reached a certain stage, there became necessary two all-important physiological systems—a vascular system and a nervous system—a system of irrigation and a system of telegraphy. With the advance of the evolution of these systems, indeed, the concomitant evolutions of other systems—alimentary, respiratory, excretory, and so forth—must have proceeded *pari passu*. But these two form the main linking or communicating systems, rendering growth and further advance possible. The vascular system—with its arteries, capillaries, and veins, ramifying throughout all parts of the body—makes possible the conveyance of food from the alimentary system to the various tissues for their nourishment ; the conveyance of oxygen from the respiratory organs to the various tissues for the efficient performance of their functions ; and the conveyance of the waste products of their activity—carbonic acid gas and urea—from the various tissues to the organs set apart for their excretion. The nervous system, on the other hand—with its strands and delicate fibres ramifying throughout all parts of the body—makes possible the conveyance of messages, so to speak, from one part of the organism to another ; and eventually as the evolution of the organism advances, the conveyance of information, from without, of occurrences in the external world which are likely to be beneficial or prejudicial to the well-being of that organism. But of what avail would be the passage to and fro of messages, or the conveyance of information from without, unless there were some centre or centres where messages and information could be so definitely co-ordinated as to enable them to minister to the welfare of the organism as a whole? And so, in addition to nerve-fibres for the conveyance of impressions, there have grown up nerve-centres, where those impressions may be brought into relation, combined, and co-ordinated.

And whereabouts in this process does consciousness emerge? When first do psychoses begin to run parallel to neuroses ? I, for one, do not know, and have no hesitation in confessing my ignorance. Were I fond of imposing phrases, I would say this is an inscrutable mystery. But I am content with saying simply, I do not know, and am unable at present to see how I can ever know. For I do not believe that any observations on the lower animals—invaluable as I hold such observations to be—can ever provide us with an answer to this question. Our knowledge of the mental endowments of animals is, and for ever must be, wholly inferential from a study of their actions.

Our conception of *their* mind is, and must remain, a distorted picture of *our* mind. We must steadily remember that our knowledge of even our human neighbour's mind is wholly *ejective;* that it is a modified image of our mind with which we endow him. And it is an image that is again and again proved incorrect in its blurred outline. And if our conception of our neighbour's mind is again and again liable to error, how much more our conception of the mind of even our favourite dog; and how infinitely more our conception of the mind of one of the lower vertebrata?

I have elsewhere stated my opinion that no science of comparative psychology from the ejective standpoint is possible. And I see no cause to change that opinion. In subjective psychology there is but one method, the method of introspection. By introspection I learn something of the working of my own mind; but it is tolerably obvious that, were I an isolated unit, shut off from all communication with my fellows, no science even of human psychology would be possible for me. I might, by the analysis of my own mental processes, arrive at certain conclusions with regard to my own states of consciousness. But this would not be a science of mind. A science of mind only becomes possible when I am able to compare my own conclusions with those which my neighbours have reached by a similar process of introspection. By means of language human beings can communicate to each other the results which each has obtained; and each human being is able to submit these results to the test of subjective verification. A science of ejecto-subjective human psychology is therefore possible, because you and I and all who are capable of introspection can compare and *verify*—each for himself in his own experience—the results obtained by psychologists. But my faithful dog, if he be capable of introspection, cannot convey to me the results at which he has arrived. In the psychology of animals no such verification is possible, and verification is that which makes science science. Therefore, I say, no science of ejective comparative psychology is possible.

Let it not, however, be for one moment imagined that I am assuming so absurd a position as the denial of intelligence in animals. On the contrary, I have a very high opinion of the intelligence of animals. That they have many intellectual faculties foreshadowing our own ; that they have passions as strong or stronger than ours ; that they may have the germs of moral sense,—I am not only convinced, but am logically bound to believe on the principles of evolution. What I do maintain is that out of these vague and unverifiable elements, it is impossible to build up a science of ejective animal psychology. We are, it seems to me, inevitably thrown back upon the science of objective psychology, which deals with "that perpetual adjustment of special inner actions to special outer actions which accompanies the increasing evolution of the nervous system." This study of the comparative physiology of the nervous system *plus* a comparative study of the corresponding adjustive actions, has every right to be termed a science, because the results admit of *verification.* And in the study of animal intelligence the more steadily we stick to the objective standpoint—the study of habit—the more sure, in my opinion, will be our advance.

Direct evidence of mental evolution in animals is therefore, if the views above briefly indicated be correct, unattainable. Wherefore it becomes all the more necessary to study in every possible way, and with all possible care and attention, (1) the structure and function of that nervous system the evolution of which has run parallel to or underlain the evolution of mind, and (2) the evolution of those external activities, habits, and customs which are external manifestations of the internal working of that nervous system. Thus we are led to see how important to the psychologist, who accepts the evolution hypothesis, is the establishment of a firm *physiological basis*.

To a necessarily brief consideration of this physiological basis let us now turn.

2. *The Structure of the Nervous System.*

" It is the great discovery of Descartes that the nervous system is that part of the body which is related directly to the mind."—W. K. CLIFFORD.

Very early in the development of any vertebrate animal, a groove, known as the medullary groove, is formed along the mid-line of that part of the organism which will form the back. In the neighbourhood of this groove the external layer of cells is somewhat thickened, and on either side of the groove there grows up a fold or ridge. Gradually, by the deepening of the groove and the upgrowth and over-arching of the folds, this structure comes to lie deeper in the body of the embryo ; and ere long, when the over-arching ridges have met, the groove becomes a canal, or tube, buried in the mid-region of the back. Out of this buried tube the central nervous system, the brain and the spinal cord, is developed.

At its anterior end (for we will suppose the central nervous axis to be *horizontal*) the tube gives rise to three successive bulbous enlargements, constituting the fore-brain, the mid-brain, and the hind-brain. In these parts complicated changes go on during development, by which are brought out that highly complex structure, the adult human brain. It will be sufficient here to note the following facts :—1. The floor and sides of the posterior part of the hind-brain become somewhat thickened, and constitute the part of the brain known as the medulla oblongata. 2. The roof of the anterior part of the hind-brain gives rise to a large and important structure known as the cerebellum. 3. The roof of the mid-brain gives rise to the optic lobes. 4. The floor and sides of the posterior part of the fore-brain give rise to the structures called the optic thalami. 5. From the anterior part of the fore-brain there grow out on either side the relatively enormous cerebral hemispheres which form the main mass of the brain, and which, lying pressed against each other side by side, form the crowning part of the nervous system.

Thus is formed the brain, protected by the bony brain-case of the skull. The rest of the medullary tube becomes the spinal cord which lies within, and is protected by, the bony arches of the vertebræ which constitute the somewhat flexible back-bone.

From this central nervous system there pass out, to be distributed throughout the body, a number of nerves, twelve pair making their exit through the walls of the skull, and thirty-one pair issuing from the spinal cord through the interspaces between the vertebræ. If we follow these nerves to their destination, we find that a great number of them enter into close connection with the muscles ; some of them go to glands ; many of them are distributed to the skin and to the organs of special sensation—sight, hearing, smell, and taste ; while some form channels of communication with a secondary nervous system—the sympathetic—from which nerves are largely distributed to the viscera and blood-vessels. The terminations of all these nerve-fibres may be more or less specially modified, so as to enable them more readily to distribute nerve impulses from within or to receive impressions from without, complex intensifying or modifying structures being developed in connection with the recipients, so as to make communication with the external world more definite and exact.

If we examine more closely an ordinary nerve, say a spinal nerve at a short distance from its origin in the spinal cord, we shall find that the whole nerve-trunk is composed of several bundles of nerve-fibres, each bundle being ensheathed in a fibrous coat, while more delicate fibrous tissue forms an internal support of the contained nerve-fibres. Examined yet more closely, each several nerve-fibre is found to consist of a central thread, the neuraxis ; a white substance, the medulla, surrounding this, but not continuously, being interrupted here and there by nodes ; and outside this medulla a sheath, the neurotheca. Some of these fibres are sensory, bringing in impressions from without, and some are motor, carrying out messages from within ; but there is nothing in appearance or structure by which the one may be distinguished from the other.

There seems to be very little reason for doubting that the neuraxis of the fibre is the really essential structure. The medulla or neurotheca may be lost before the nerve reaches its destination ; but this central thread forms a direct and absolutely continuous line of communication from a sensory or motor cell at one end to a cell in or near the central nervous system at the other end. The neurotheca and medulla are merely accessory structures for insulating the essential neuraxis.

It is a curious fact that the sensory fibres enter the spinal cord as a separate bundle, distinct from that by which the motor fibres emerge. These two bundles, or roots, fuse together at a little distance from the spinal cord, and the sensory and motor fibres become intermingled. Before they reach the spinal cord, however, the sensory fibres enter an enlargement, or ganglion, in the sensory bundle, and there it would seem that each fibre passes into a nerve-cell, whence it or another similar nerve-fibre passes out and on into the spinal cord. In the motor bundle or root there is no such ganglion ; but if the fibre be traced inwards into the spinal cord, it is found there to emerge from a nerve-cell, shaped something like a starfish. The fibre passes into one ray of the starfish, while each of the other rays breaks up into a number of the finest possible filaments. It is quite possible that the neuraxis, delicate as it is, is composed of a great number of minute fibrillæ ; that the nerve-cell is largely made up of an interlacement of these fibrillæ ; and that these then pass out as the very fine filaments at the end of the raylike processes.

In its minute structure the central nervous system, the brain and the spinal cord, is found to consist of two substances—the white matter and the grey matter. Of these the white matter is composed of a multitude of nerve-fibres, arranged somewhat in the same way as they are in a nerve-trunk, except that they are not bound up in separate bundles and have no neurotheca, or sheath, this structure being replaced by a network of transparent supporting tissue, called the neuroglia. The grey matter, in addition to nerve-fibres, which have here little or no medulla, contains as an essential constituent nerve-cells. White matter and grey matter are differently arranged in different parts of the brain and spinal cord, but their essential characteristics remain the same throughout. The white matter has, in all probability, for its function the establishment of communication between different parts of the central nervous system ; and with regard to this communication it is a curious fact that a sensory impression entering the spinal cord, say by a sensory root of the *left* side, at once crosses over to the opposite side, and proceeds to the higher brain-centres up the *right* side of the spinal cord (which is divided by anterior and posterior fissures into two semi-cylinders closely applied together and united by bridges of nervous matter on either side of the minute central canal, which represents the original medullary tube). From the higher brain-centres the motor impulse proceeds downwards, still on the *right* side of the brain ; but in the medulla oblongata crosses over to the *left* side of the spinal column, and, proceeding down the semi-cylinder of that side, makes its exit by the motor root which corresponds to the sensory root by which the original impression entered. Such communication, then, between various parts of the nervous system would seem to be the function of the white matter. The function of the grey matter, on the other hand, would seem to be the establishment of intercommunication between the various strands of communication, and thus to form centres wherein the incoming messages may be brought into relation, combined, sorted and co-ordinated, and eventually passed on, not without augmentation of strength, as outgoing motor impulses.

Before passing on, however, to consider the functions of the nervous system it will perhaps be well to sum up briefly the few facts concerning its structure which have here been brought forward.

1. The central nervous system consists of brain and spinal cord.

2. The brain may for our present purpose be divided into—

(i.) Hind-brain, with medulla oblongata below and cerebellum above.

(ii.) Mid-brain, with the optic lobes.

(iii.) Fore-brain, with the thalamus below and the enormous cerebral hemispheres above.

3. With the central nervous system there are connected nerves which are of two kinds—sensory, to bring in impressions from without ; motor, to carry out impulses from . within.

4. Connected by special nerves with the central nervous system there is a secondary nervous system, called the sympathetic.

5. Nerve-fibres consist of a central, absolutely continuous, nervous thread, surrounded and insulated by medulla and a sheath.

6. In the central nervous system the nerve-fibres have no sheath, but are supported and perhaps insulated by the neuroglia. The aggregation of nerve-fibres here is called white matter.

7. Besides the white matter there is grey matter, which contains, besides nerve-fibres, nerve-cells. A group of nerve-cells is called a ganglion.

8. Grey matter is not restricted to the central nervous system. There are ganglia on the sensory roots of the spinal nerves; and there are many ganglia in the sympathetic system.

9. The essential function of the nerve-fibres is to form channels of communication.

10. The essential function of the nerve-cells of the ganglia is to form centres of intercommunication and co-ordination.

3. *The Functions of the Nervous System.*

"The motion of the matter of a sensory nerve may be transmitted through the brain to a motor nerve, and thereby give rise to the contraction of the muscles to which these motor nerves are distributed; and this reflection of motion from a sensory to a motor nerve may take place without volition, or even contrary to it."—T. H. HUXLEY.

Let us begin with a simple case of reflex action. Touch lightly the hand of a sleeping child. The hand will be withdrawn. Or place your fingers within the palm. The little fingers will close on yours. There is no conscious action here. What takes place is purely automatic. The nerve-fibres which terminate just beneath the skin of the hand are stimulated by the touch. A wave of impulse passes along the sensory nerve to the spinal cord; reaches the ganglia there, or perhaps is passed on to higher ganglia; is there reinforced; and is thence reflected, and passes down the motor nerves to the muscles whereby the hand is moved or the fingers closed. Such is a tolerably simple case of reflex action. The parts concerned constitute what is sometimes known as a nervous arc, into the composition of which there enter three elements—a sensory nerve, a ganglion, and a motor nerve. Note that the resulting action is purposive—that is, performed for a definite end, but unconscious—that is, quite independent of feeling, intelligence, or will.

It is not only during sleep that such reflex actions are effected. A thousand acts of our daily waking life are the result of reflex action—that is, automatic, and maybe unconscious. Many of these automatic reflex acts are protective in their nature. Dr. Carpenter gives a case in point. An eminent chemist was holding up to the light and examining intently a bottle containing an explosive compound. Suddenly the compound exploded, and shattered the bottle, driving the fragments in every direction. But so sure and rapid was the protective reflex action, giving rise to the closure of the eyelids, that no particle reached the observer's eyes, though the lids were much cut. The message had been sent along the sensory nerves, had been reflected from the ganglia, and had travelled down the motor nerves to the muscles of the eyelids, and all with such rapidity that the lids had closed in time to save the eyes from injury.

Much of the normal working of the body is effected by means of reflex actions, some of them not a little complicated. The working of the viscera, the secretions of the liver and other glands, the prevailing tone of the muscular system, the rhythmic contractions of the alimentary canal— all these are regulated by unconscious reflex actions, some of them effected by the sympathetic system, few, if any, of them proceeding higher than the spinal cord, not troubling the brain at all.

For the performance of other reflex actions the lower nerve centres of the brain have to be called into play. Such are the reflex actions connected with breathing, with the regulation of the beating of the heart, with the contraction and dilatation of the blood-vessels, with the insensible perspiration of the skin, with the complex movements of swallowing—all these are under the guidance, not of the centres of the spinal cord, but of the medulla oblongata, which lies at the base of the brain.

Of the regulative action of this medulla oblongata, there is, perhaps, no more beautiful instance than that of the so-called vascular centre which has command of the irrigation of the tissues by the blood stream. The blood is pumped from the heart into the main delivery tubes, or arteries, which, branching again and again, diminish proportionally in size, and thus pass into the arterioles, minute tubes with muscular contractile walls. The arterioles then break up into a delicate meshwork of very fine vessels termed capillaries, through the walls of which exusion goes on, for the nourishment of the surrounding tissues. The meshwork of capillaries unite again into minute tubes, the venules, which are also provided with muscular walls ; and these venules, uniting together, combine to form thin walled veins which carry the blood back again to the heart. Now, suppose in any part of the body the arterioles contract while the venules are left widely open. There will be a diminished blood-supply to that part, and such blood as is supplied will run off rapidly through the open venules. There will be little exusion of nutritive fluid, and little nourishment of that particular organ. But now suppose, on the other hand, that the arterioles are left widely open, while the venules are contracted. Blood will be freely supplied to the part, and will not readily run off. Nutritive fluid will exude in quantity from the capillaries, and the part in question will be nourished. The contraction or relaxation of the muscular walls of these arterioles and venules, is placed under the control of certain vascular nerves.

"The influence which these transmit is here relaxing, there constricting, according (1) to the function which the organ is called upon to discharge ; and (2) to the degree of its activity at the time. In no single organ of the body is the supply of blood required always the same. The brain is during one hour hard at work, during the next hour asleep. The muscles are at one moment in severe exercise, the next in complete repose ; the liver, which before a meal is inactive, during the process of digestion is turgid with blood and busily engaged in the chemical work which belongs to it. For all these vicissitudes the tract of grey substance which we call the *vascular centre* has to provide. Like a skilful steward of the animal household, it has, so to speak, to exercise perfect and unfailing foresight, in order that the nutritive material which serves as the oil of life for the maintenance of each vital process may not be wanting. And so cognizant is this vascular centre of the chemical condition of the blood which flows through it, that if too much carbonic acid gas is contained in it, the centre acts on information of the fact, so as to increase the velocity of the blood stream. Still more strikingly is this adaptation seen in the arrangement by which the balance and pressure of resistance in the blood-vessels is regulated. The heart, that wonderful machine by which the circulation is maintained, is connected with. the centre, as if by two telegraph wires—one of which is a channel of influence, the other of information. By the latter the engineer who has charge of that machine sends information to head-quarters whenever the strain on his machine is excessive, the certain response to which is relaxation of the arteries and diminution of pressure. By the former he is enabled to adapt its rate of working to the work it has to do " (Burden Sanderson).

This medulla oblongata, therefore, may be regarded as the centre of the lower animal life. Serious injury to it causes instantaneous death. But in the lower animals, at least, so long as this remains intact, life continues. But the life is mere existence. The creature—frog, for example—must be artificially fed, and only exhibits the simplest forms of reflex action, though some of these are performed with unusual vigour. Even among human beings cases have been reported of children being born with no higher nerve-centres than the medulla oblongata. Such children have lived for a short time, breathing, sucking, and even uttering cries by reflex action. Whether such children, or the frog deprived of its fore and mid brain, are conscious of such reflexes as take place, it is exceedingly difficult to say, though the almost universal opinion is that they are not. Certainly when the medulla oblongata is destroyed in the frog, and when therefore life is extinct, one cannot suppose that there is anything like feeling. And yet in such a frog which has just been killed by the extirpation of the whole brain, if the side be touched with a drop of acid the leg of that side will be drawn up, and will wipe aside the acid. More than this : if that leg be held and prevented from reaching the side, the other leg will be brought round so as to try and reach the irritated spot. No actions could be more typically purposive ; and yet they are distinctly and unequivocally automatic.

So much, then, for the medulla oblongata, the chief centre for the lower vital reflexes. Above it, in the anterior part of the hind-brain, is the cerebellum. Gall, the founder of phrenology, believed that here were localized the sexual instincts. Modern investigation and research, however, render it more probable that this organ is to be regarded as a centre, perhaps the main centre, by means of which movements, especially automatic and semi-automatic movements, are co-ordinated. By it the balance of the body is maintained. We little think how complex is the adjustment needed for comparatively simple actions. Suppose a boy, as he listlessly trudges to school, sees a sparrow perched in a tempting position within range. An ingrained English instinct impels him to seize the nearest stone and throw it at the bird. His sole conscious object is to annihilate that sparrow. But with this object in view he has to hold the stone in a certain way, to go through the complex process of throwing, to let go of the stone at the right moment ; besides all this he has to balance his body in a certain manner, to modify the process of breathing, and so on. The nicest adjustment of the contraction or relaxation of a great number of muscles is requisite ; and all or most of this is done for him automatically by the cerebellum. According to Flourens, alcohol has a special action on the cerebellum. And the sign of drunkenness is ineffectual correlation of muscular actions. The man reels and totters, and with all his efforts of will cannot walk steadily. So, too, when in an animal the cerebellum is destroyed or injured, it reels and tumbles about as if it were drunk. It has, indeed, been suggested that these effects are more readily explicable on the supposition that the cerebellum is the organ of the muscular sense, the derangement being due rather to defective or destroyed sensibility in this respect, than to the absence of mere automatic correlation ; but this view, though difficult or impossible of disproof, does not find so many supporters as that of Flourens.

The optic lobes—of which there are four in man, two on each side, and' which are, therefore, more frequently termed the corpora quadrigemina—these optic lobes, as their name implies, seem to be intimately associated with vision. When they are wholly destroyed the power of sight would seem wholly lost ; when those on one side are destroyed, the sight of the opposite eye only is lost. It would seem, moreover, not only to be or to contain a centre of sight ; it also contains a centre for the complicated movements of the eyes necessary for the efficient use of those organs, as well as a centre for the contraction and dilatation of the pupil, and hence for the regulation of the amount of light which enters the eye. In a word it would seem to contain both a centre of sight and a centre of adjustment of the organs of sight.

Passing now to the fore-brain, we have in the thalamus an intermediate centre placed between the cerebral hemispheres, on the one hand, and the lower brain centres on the other. It would seem that injury to or destruction of the thalamus of one side gives rise to the impairment or total loss of sensation on the opposite side of the body. In which case, if we may not say with some that we have in the thalami the centre of sensation, it is at least probable that their integrity is essential to sensation. Their injury does not seem to impair the motor functions, the floor of the cerebral hemispheres themselves being supplied with structures—the corpora striata—which would seem in this respect to be intermediate between the higher and lower brain centres, injury or destruction of which gives rise to

N

the impairment or total loss of the power of moving the limbs of the opposite side of the body.

We come now to the highest brain-centres of all, the crowning part of the nervous system, the cerebral hemispheres. If in the frog, instead of removing all the parts of the brain above the medulla oblongata, only the cerebral hemispheres be removed, the creature is reduced to a curious state. It will eat if you feed it ; it will jump if you give it a suggestive prick ; it will swim if you put it in water ; if you place it upon a book and then gradually tilt the book, it will slowly climb and balance itself on the edge; if you put it on its back it will turn over again and sit up ; it will croak if you stroke it. It is thus capable of a great number of *responsive* actions—that is, actions in answer to definite stimuli. But all internal spring of action is gone. With the removal of the higher brain-centres, all the higher frog powers have ceased. It is utterly incapable of initiating any action, even the simplest, and if left to itself will remain motionless in one position until it dies.

There can be very little doubt that, not only in the frog but also in man, and in the multitude of intermediates to these extremes, the cerebral hemispheres are the brain structures which have allotted to them the most complex functions. And as we rise in the scale of the mammalia, these hemispheres increase enormously in size and are connected by a great special bridge of nervous matter, a bridge that is absent in the lower vertebrates, the so-called corpus callosum. This crowning cerebrum would seem to be the centre of all emotional, rational, and voluntary, and, in a word, *original* action. It is the organ of individuality, the locus of spontaneity, the seat of character. In it lie the springs of human action. In man it constitutes the main mass of the brain. It has an exterior layer, or cortex, of grey matter, rich in nerve-cells. This layer would seem to be the essential part; and by means of the many folds or convolutions into which the brain is involved, an area of some three hundred square feet of grey matter may be packed safely away within the marvellously and beautifully wrought ivory casket of the skull.

This cortical layer has been of late years the subject of much careful experimental investigation on the part of Prof. Ferrier and others. The outcome of these researches on the lower animals is that the stimulation of certain so-called "centres," localized on this or that cerebral convolution, causes the performance of certain actions; while the destruction of these "centres" brings with it inability to perform these actions, or inability to receive certain impressions from without. They clearly form parts of certain definite nervous circuits. There is, for example, a "centre of smell," the stimulation of which causes sniffing as if an odour were perceived, the destruction of which causes utter deadness to the influence of all odoriferous substances. There is, too, hard by, a "centre of hearing," the electrical stimulation of which causes the animal to prick up his ears and assume the attitude of listening attention, or even to leap aside as if to avoid some danger of which an unusual noise would be regarded as the signal. If this part be destroyed by cauterization, the animal is apparently unable to hear, or, at any rate, takes no notice of sounds which would ordinarily cause alarm. This kind of investigation has, moreover, been supplemented by observation of the results of brain disease in man. And such observation tends to confirm the result of experiment on the lower animals, and justifies our drawing conclusions from the latter mode of research which may be, are, and, still more, will be, of immense value to the pathologist and the surgeon. Experiment, for example, shows that the destruction of the anterior portion of the brain causes in monkeys loss of interest in everything into which before they pried with keen curiosity, dulness, apathy, and a tendency to doze or wander about listlessly and without apparent object. So, too, there is a case on record of a workman, a peculiarly clever and steady fellow, who after an injury to the anterior lobes became "capricious, vacillating, fitful, impatient, obstinate, and, as far as intellectual capacity was concerned, appeared to be a child, which, however, had the animal passions of a strong man."

Quite recently, in a celebrated brain-surgery case, the presence of a tumour in the cerebral hemispheres was indicated and localized through Dr. Ferrier's experiments on the lower mammalia, the conclusions derived from which were strengthened by the lessons taught by clinical observation; and by skilful surgical manipulation the tumour was removed. And though the subsequent death of the patient was hailed with something like a shout of irrepressible delight by the antivivisectionists, the future promise of good to man from this mode of research is clear and unmistakable. Would that the antivivisectionists would tell us clearly whether the legislation they advocate is for the prevention of pain to our dumb relations, or for the prevention of the moral degradation of man, or both. At present they shift their ground from the one to the other. If the former, the answer is obvious, that our duty to man is higher than our duty to beast. If the latter, the answer is a firm denial of the alleged charge that vivisection blunts the moral instinct. This charge is absolutely incapable of proof; for if it be shown that this or that vivisector, A. or B., is heartless and cruel, how can it be shown that had he not been a vivisector he would have been sympathetic and humane? How can it be proved that his blunted moral instincts are the result of his vivisection experiments? And even were this impossible proof provided, the question still remains whether Government may fairly step in and stop A. or B. from unintentionally degrading his moral nature. With so much good work to be done in the world, it is a subject for unfeigned regret that well-meaning men and women, of average culture and education, should not find better work than this. That they have every right to their opinions I for one would not for one moment deny; but that they should agitate to have their opinions enforced by Act of Parliament I cannot but regard as piteous. May we not hear next of an agitation for the suppression of agnosticism by Act of Parliament, and a rigid enforcement of an outward conformity to the Christian Faith, on the ground that by the former the moral character of man is inevitably degraded?

Let us now sum up with regard to the functions of the various parts of the nervous system.

1. Nerve-fibres transmit impressions.

2. Nerve-centres correlate these transmitted impressions.

3. The spinal cord contains many centres of reflex action for the performance of actions connected with normal life.

4. The medulla oblongata contains centres for such vital reflex actions as are connected with the regulation of the heart-beat, with breathing, the distribution of the blood supply, and so forth.

5. The cerebellum is largely occupied with the co-ordination of muscular movements.

6. The optic lobes are centres for vision and the adjustment of the visual apparatus.

7. The thalami are centres by which sensory impressions are transmitted; just as the corpora striata are centres by which motor impulses are transmitted. It is possible that purely responsive non-original acts require no higher centres than these.

8. "The cortex of the cerebral hemispheres is to be regarded as a continuous aggregation of interlaced 'centres,' towards which ingoing impressions of all kinds converge from various parts of the body : here they come into relation with one another in various ways, and conjointly give rise to nerve actions which have for their subjective correlatives all the perceptions, all the intellectual, and all the emotional processes which the individual is capable of experiencing" (Bastian).

9. Man, as an organism possessing so well-developed a nervous system, is capable of various actions, reflex, vital, responsive, and original. In all these actions the nervous mechanism, or some part of it, is essential.

10. He is also under certain circumstances a conscious organism. Unconsciousness is especially connected with the injury of certain parts of the nervous mechanism. Therefore consciousness is probably connected in some way with some part or parts of this nervous mechanism.

4. *The Mechanism at Work.*

"The human brain is an organized register of infinitely numerous experiences received during the evolution of that series of organisms through which the human organism has been reached."—HERBERT SPENCER.

Let us now follow up a little more closely the working of the nervous mechanism as a whole. As soon as the child is born, a great number of reflex actions are already going on, at once take place, or are thereupon possible under appropriate conditions of stimulation. Breathing commences, and does not cease till death. The heart is rhythmically beating. The complicated processes of sucking and swallowing are performed under the necessary conditions. We express pretty clearly the nature of these reflex actions when we say that they are altogether mechanical. How mechanical? In this way, that the appropriate stimulus is followed at once by prompt and unhesitating response. And why? Because the child inherits an organization adapted to these ends. Afferent nerves, ganglia, efferent nerves are all ready for unfailing action. The chick on emerging from the egg can walk at once. Why? Because the chick inherits an organization adapted to these ends, and already perfectly developed. The child cannot walk at once, has even to *learn* to walk when its limbs have acquired the requisite strength. Once more, Why? Because the requisite nerve connections have not yet been fully developed. But it learns to walk, stand, and maintain its equilibrium, in a wonderfully short space of time. Yet again, Why? Because during this time the inherited mechanism rapidly develops, and only requires a few preparatory trials to bring it into working order. It is even possible that the mechanism might develop into efficiency without any such preparatory trials. A case is quoted of a girl who, up to the age of two years, had not walked a step, or even tried to walk. One day the father put her down in a standing position, and to his great surprise she walked from one side of the room to the other (Bastian); a remarkable instance, which one would like to see confirmed by others of a similar nature.

Thus, there are some reflexes, such as those which are connected with the vital functions, which are performed at birth, and with unerring certainty; and there are others, such as walking, speaking, and the normal use of the muscular system, which are learnt with comparative ease. For the former, the nervous mechanism is ready developed; for the latter, the requisite nerve connections develop rapidly, and with but little assistance from the individual child.

Pass now a stage higher. Presently, when the child is somewhat older, it learns, perhaps, to play the piano. Here there is, in most cases, but little inherited mechanism, though in civilized races, and especially in some individuals, there is sufficient to constitute an aptitude or innate tendency. It is only after some years of steady application that the instrument is mastered. But when such mastery is acquired, the nerve connections have become so thoroughly organized that the performer can play a difficult sonata while his attention is busily occupied in tracing the details of the pictured landscape on the opposite side of the room. The nervous mechanism has become so adapted, after long education, that it will continue to work almost of itself. Somnambulists have been known to play long and difficult pieces.

Eventually, perhaps, the child, now a man, has developed into a mathematician. By careful training he has established in his brain very complex nerve connections. Of these connections as a civilized man he inherits, at least, the potentiality. Teach young negroes and young Europeans side by side and for awhile they will progress equally, or even the negro may outstrip the white ; but only for awhile. Ere long the white will shoot ahead, and breathe freely in an intellectual atmosphere in which the black boy can only gasp helplessly. The white inherits a potentiality of this higher development ; the black does not. At first our young mathematician has to give his utmost attention to the working out of even a very simple problem. But when he has mastered his science, he can solve a tolerably difficult problem while he is delivering an astronomical lecture to his students. In accustomed grooves the trained mind will work automatically. I have heard it said of a great lawyer, that he could give a better opinion in his sleep than any of his contemporaries could when they were wide awake. And a certain great orator of the past could make a better speech when he was drunk than any other living man when he was sober. Such things are quite conceivable. Abercrombie, in his " Intellectual Powers," gives the case of a lawyer who wrote out an important opinion in his sleep. Complex processes may go on in the brain without giving rise to definite consciousness. Common-sense judgments are the outcome of an almost automatic act of cerebration, and the voice of conscience pronounces similar judgments in matter of right and wrong. Such processes are the outcome of the whole previous discipline and training of the mind, grafted upon an inherited aptitude. Their value depends upon the aptitude, the training, and the discipline.

The more frequently an action is performed, the more perfectly automatic does it become, the more does it tend to pass into stereotyped reflex action. Those actions which have been performed not only by the individual but by a long line of ancestors, whose organization he inherits, are, or very soon become, completely, or in a very high degree, automatic. On the other hand, those actions which the individual has performed but seldom are effected with difficulty, owing to the imperfect connections established in the nervous mechanism. And if new connections are to be established, they must be established early. After the middle period of life, the nervous mechanism in most individuals begins to lose its plasticity. It becomes a matter of great difficulty to establish wholly new connections ; and these new connections, even when formed, have comparatively little stability.

Comparing now perfectly automatic action with imperfectly automatic action, we find that the former is characterized by promptness, accuracy, and absence of hesitation. A given stimulus is followed at once and without mistake by the appropriate response. On the other hand, those actions which are furthest removed from the automatic class are performed with deliberation, and are liable to error. Such are the higher intellectual operations. The well-known cares of office, resulting from the difficulty of seeing the right course, and the liability of even great statesmen to error, exemplify this fact from the subjective point of view. One of the main differences between the simple impulsive life of savages and the complex life of civilized men lies in the fact that the former live and work in and for the present, while the latter look forward and work to-day for results in the future. In responsive action the response follows close upon the stimulus. In the higher original action, as I have above called it, there are a number of intermediate actions lying between the stimulus and the response. Hence arises the fact that civilized man is so essentially contemplative. He is for ever storing up observations which may enable him to act more efficiently in the future. Much of his time is, therefore, spent in education.

This education, physiologically speaking, is the establishment of definite connections in the nerve mechanism, answering subjectively to definite association of ideas. Throughout the whole growth of the child's intelligence we must suppose the same process to go on. And during the all-important process of education everything depends upon whether the nerve connections are formed in correspondence with fact, or in correspondence with falsity. Action can only be true when the connections are in correspondence with fact. Answering, too, to the condensation and organization of knowledge, there goes on in the brain, in all probability, a concentration, organization, and centralization of nerve connections. As disconnected facts in knowledge are grouped under generalizations, and generalizations co-ordinated and condensed into scientific laws, so, we must imagine, do separate nerve connections become connected and groups of nerve connections become co-ordinated. "The whole process of the evolution of reason," Prof. Clifford aptly remarks, "is an attempt to pack into an exceedingly small box, the human brain, a picture of the enormous universe that is outside of it." Such a process is impossible without signs. The mathematician packs into a little group of algebraic signs an expression which can only be adequately explained in fifty closely printed pages. In each of those pages nearly every word stands for a more or less complex group of perceptions. Every perception is a co-ordination of sensations related in special ways. So, too, in the mathematician's brain do sign-nerve-connections come to stand for groups of word-nerve-connections, word-nerve-connections for groups of perception-nerve-connections, and these for groups of the connections answering to sensation. The actions, meanwhile, which normally follow on all sensations, are repressed and indefinitely postponed. The repression and postponement of actions is an all-important law of our being, and it is definitely connected with the physiological doctrine that the function of the highest nerve-centres is inhibitory.

If I were asked to name two of the most important general functions of the highest brain centres, I should name this inhibitory power, which we call, in the field of human action, self-restraint, as one. And the other would be spontaneity, or the readiness of the nerve-centres to answer on occasion to the slightest and most indirect stimulus. This we call, in the field of human action, orginality. By these two qualities the highest and noblest human activities are most widely separated from the automatic reflex action with which we started ; by them the philosopher is most completely differentiated from the savage and the clown.

5. *The Organ of Mind.*

"Every mental phenomenon has its corresponding neural phenomenon (the two being as the convex and concave surfaces of the same sphere, distinguishable yet identical), and every mental phenomenon involves the whole body."—G. H. LEWES.

Before we can answer the question, What is the organ of mind? we have to settle the surely not unimportant preliminary question, What is the mind?

To the world-old question, What is matter? Berkeley, completing the work which Locke had begun, triumphantly answered, "Matter is an abstraction. What we have to deal with is concrete tangible objects. If you ask me what is an object, I reply, an object is a synthesis of its qualities, and exists as such only in the percipient mind." In this, Berkeley's successor, Hume, fully agreed. But he went further in that he applied the principles of his predecessor to the solution of the equally world-old question, What is mind? "Mind," he said, "is also an abstraction. And just as the object is a synthesis of its qualities, so, too, is the subject a synthesis of our perceptions of these qualities. Take away the qualities, and no knowable matter remains ; take away the perceptions, and no knowable mind remains. Mind is like a river. And just as a river without the flowing water is an abstraction, so is the mind without its flow of impressions and ideas an empty abstraction."

Are we then to regard the world as a shifting and inconstant phantasmagoria of impressions and ideas, out of which we construct an imaginary external series of objects, and an imaginary internal continuously existing subject? Is it true that matter does not exist or persist, that there is no continuity of mind? Let us hear Hume on the former question. "We may well ask," he says, "what causes induce us to believe in the existence of body? but 'tis in vain to ask whether there be body or not ;—that is a point which we must take for granted in all our reasonings." So, too, in the latter question, it is true that all we directly know of mind is a series of impressions, a stream of conscious states. But we are inevitably forced to take for granted a continuously existing mind, of which these impressions, these states of consciousness, are activities. How else can we account for the conception of personality ? If by mind we mean merely the series of conscious states, then the river analogy is a false analogy. False in this : that in the river there is a continuity of flow, whereas in the stream of conscious impressions there is discontinuity. Between any two states of consciousness there is a break. In deep and tranquil sleep there is a prolonged cessation of conscious-ness. And if, in the midst of discontinuity, there is still an underlying unity (and who can doubt it ?), this must surely be because the mind is not merely a succession of states of consciousness, but something which includes and underlies them. The states of consciousness are rather, to modify the river analogy, like the ripples and wavelets on the river's surface. In the ripples there is discontinuity, but in the flow of the river there is no discontinuity. So, too, in the states of consciousness there is discontinuity, but in mind there is no discontinuity.

What, then, is this mind which is continuous ? It is that which corresponds on the subjective side to *all the nerve actions* which go on within the body. Prof. Huxley has introduced two valuable terms which will help us here. Nerve actions he calls *neuroses ;* and their subjective cor-relates, *psychoses.* Now we have seen that actions, which are at first performed with conscious deliberation, may pass into compound reflex actions, which are automatic and unaccompanied by consciousness. The element of feeling becomes, so to speak, submerged. Let us call all those submerged feelings which correspond on the subjective side to neuroses, but which do not see the light and emerge in consciousness, *hypopsychoses*, restricting the term psychoses to those mental states which do so emerge in consciousness. Then we may, I think, say that *mind is to be regarded as the sum total of psychoses and hypopsychoses.* "We must include under the word Mind," writes Dr. Bastian, in advocating this view, "all those well-known results of nerve action which are comprised under the general categories of (1) feeling, sensation, or emotion; (2) intelligence, instinct, or thought; and (3) attention, volition, or will; and we cannot exclude the multitudinous results of mere unconscious nerve actions, which constitute so many integral parts of our mental life, interpolating themselves from moment to moment, and having their origin in various parts of the nervous system."

Such, then, is the answer I would give to the question, What is mind? Let us now pass on to the further question, What is the organ of mind?

In the last section it was pointed out that certain reflex actions, such as that which governs the heart-beat, are already in full activity at birth; that others, such as that of taking the breast, can be performed by the child immediately after birth; that others, such as walking, are performed, almost without learning, when the nervous and muscular mechanism is sufficiently developed; and that yet others, such as playing the piano, require systematic learning. In the former, the nervous connections are more or less perfectly inherited ready made; in the latter, they have to be to a great extent individually formed. We saw, too, that, wherever definite nervous connections are established, the actions performed through their instrumentality tend to become automatic, and to partake of the nature of compound reflex actions. The right response follows on the proper stimulus without hesitation. The aim and object of education is to establish such nerve connections as shall lead to right action; and the process of education is, one may suppose, accompanied by the concentration and organization of nerve actions, answering to the condensation and organization of knowledge.

Now, for the performance of these various actions and activities, taken as a whole, the integrity, not of any one part of the nervous system, but of the whole nervous system, is essential. And since we have agreed to apply the term Mind to the sum total of all the psychoses and the hypopsychoses which correspond to the sum total of neuroses, it is obvious that, on this view, the whole nervous system is the organ of mind. But the nervous system ramifies throughout the entire body; there is scarcely a corner so remote as to escape the ultimate ramifications of the nerve-fibres. Whence it follows that we may justly say in answer to the question, What is the organ of mind? *the whole body is the organ of mind,* or, to express it in the old Latin phrase, *mens sana in corpore sano.*

Of the close inter-connection of mind and body, popularly but incorrectly described as the action of the mind on the body, or the body on the mind, instances abound. Well known and obvious as they are, it will be well to note, in the briefest possible manner, some of these correspondences between mental state and bodily organization. First, we have the correspondences now well known under the head of the expression of the emotions. Extreme anger is manifested by the clenched fist, the knit brow, the set teeth, the tightened state of the muscles. And it is, physiologically speaking, extremely probable that the invariable accompaniment of anger is a faint excitation of the nerves or nerve-centres involved in these actions. Perform these actions, and you call up a momentary feeling,

or ghost of a feeling, of anger.   Let the muscles relax and
put on a smile.   The feeling of anger departs and (at least
in my own case) cannot be recalled, so long as the face is
kept smiling.   Each emotion has its physical counterpart.
To have an emotion without a corresponding affection of
the bodily organization is, I believe, impossible.   And the
same is true of imagination.   As Mr. G. H. Lewes says,
" To imagine an act is to rehearse it mentally.   By such
mental rehearsal the motor organs are disposed to respond
in act.   Hence it is that the long meditated crime becomes
at last an irresistible criminal impulse."   Then, again, we
have the variation of intellectual power with the state of
the body.   The mind is fresh and acute in the early part of
the day and the early years of life ; it loses its activity
after the fatigues of the day and towards the close of life.
Do we not often say in the evening, when we cannot
recollect some fact or name, I shall remember it in the
morning ?   Do we not notice that in old age the memory
is impaired ?   Then there are those states of minds we
call desires or appetites.   No one can doubt their connection with the bodily organization.   When the system is
in want of food, for example, the nerves and nerve-centres
connected with the mastication and swallowing of food are
thrown into extreme readiness to respond to the appropriate stimuli.   Just as when we hear a sudden noise in the
night our attention is at once drawn (by means of an
increased supply of blood) to those nerves and nerve-
centres which are connected with the organ of hearing.
We are in a state of attention.   Soon other nerve-centres
are affected.   We are on the alert for action.   Owing to the
inhibitory power of the higher nerve-centres, however, we
do not act precipitately ; we repress action and remain on
the alert.   An increased supply of blood to the appropriate
centres makes us ready for immediate action, which the

inhibitory power of the higher centres enables us to repress. The effect of bodily condition on mental state is especially marked in some of the lower animals. "The sensational endowments," writes Dr. Bastian, "of the shark, of the python, or of the vulture, are, when these creatures are under the influence of hunger, exalted to the highest degree; so that at such time either of them may become keenly sensitive to odours, sounds, or sights, which, had they been in a state of satiety, might have passed wholly unheeded." In this state of satiety the blood is otherwise occupied. So, too, in ourselves. After a heavy meal it is useless to attempt hard study.

The physical aspect of alertness is, in all probability, an increased supply of blood. The state of the nerves depends very largely upon the supply of blood. When our hands are cold, the numbness is in part due to a deficient circulation of blood around the nerves. During intense mental exertion the supply of blood to the head is increased. The head becomes hot and throbs. Nerve-tissue, in fact, very readily becomes worn out, and it can only be renovated by the blood. When the blood is impure, we frequently notice unpleasant smells, which we seem unable to get rid of. This is what is termed a "subjective sensation," this term having been given to sensations which have no objective cause outside us. The nerves or nerve-centres are, however, affected just as if there were such an external cause. In delirium the blood throbs through the brain much more rapidly than usual. The nerve-centres are violently affected; and a disorderly sequence of terribly real sensations is the subjective counterpart of the affection of these nerve-centres.

A thousand instances of the correspondence between states of the body and states of the mind might be added. The influence of mental anxiety on the digestion and the

O

effects of indigestion on the temper are, unfortunately, but too well known. There is solid truth in that answer of Punch's to the question, Is life worth living?—that depends on the liver. And the converse of the old Latin adage holds true. That insanity is the result of disease, is but a corollary from *mens sana in corpore sano.*

6. *The Conditions of Consciousness.*

"It is clearly established, however, that the soul does not perceive in so far as it is in each member of the body, but only in so far as it is in the brain, where the nerves, by their movements, convey to it the diverse actions of the external objects that touch the parts of the body in which they are inserted."— DESCARTES.

If the body as a whole is to be regarded as the organ of mind, what part of the body, what centre or centres of the central nervous system are to be regarded as the organ of consciousness? And in this organ, what are the conditions of consciousness?

That nerve-motion is translated into sensation, to use a current phrase, somewhere in the brain, and that this takes place in the grey matter, that is, in the nerve-centres and not in the nerve-fibres, there can now be little reason to doubt. If the optic nerve,* running from the retina of the eye to the brain, be severed, irritations of the cut end of the portion, which is in connection with the brain, appear in consciousness as flashes of light. After an arm has been amputated, feelings of itchiness and discomfort are often felt in the absent members; that is to say, changes of the nerve-centres take place in the same way as they would do under ordinary circumstances, when there was some

* The optic nerve is shown by development to be really a part of the brain. But this only strengthens the inference that consciousness emerges in the higher brain-centres.

·discomfort in the hand. The man may even have the sensation of moving the fingers ; that is to say, changes of the nerve-centres take place in the same way as they would under ordinary circumstances when a message was sent down to the muscles, ordering them to contract. These facts, and others of like nature, the results of experimental and pathological observation, seem to show that in such cases, and therefore we must believe in all cases, the feeling is not in the eye, not in the limb, not in the sense ·organs or the muscles, but in the nerve-centres of the brain.

But how, it may be asked in passing, is it possible for nerve tremors in the brain, set up by nerve impulses passing down the nerve-fibres, to resemble, in the very slightest degree, the things outside of us which give rise to them ? They do not resemble them. They are only signs for them ; and it is only of the signs that we have, or can have, direct knowledge. Here we have, in fact, the physiological aspect of the philosophical doctrine, that objects as they appear to us do not and cannot resemble the things themselves. Our sensations are signs for external entities—they are symbols. And it is impossible to conceive that there' ·can be any resemblance between the symbol and the thing symbolized. As little can the symbol π be said to resemble the figures 3·14159, or the ratio of the circumference of a circle to its diameter for which they stand. Nor is there the slightest necessity, so far as our practical well-being is concerned, that there should be any resemblance between symbol and symbolized. A group of visual sensations tells us what group of tactual sensations we may expect. A group of auditory sensations predicts a group of visual sensations, and so on. Any one group of sensations gives us notice of other possible groups of sensations which we may seek or avoid, according as they give us pleasure or pain. What more can we want ?

Consciousness, then, is in some way connected with a change of state in certain grey centres of the brain. Whether this change of state, accompanied by consciousness, takes place in the thalamus, as some have maintained, or in the grey cortex of the cerebral hemispheres, as is now more generally held, is not for us a matter of great moment. Let us now inquire what are the conditions of consciousness.

This point is discussed in Mr. G. J. Romanes' valuable work on " Mental Evolution in Animals." To the question "What is the difference between the mode of operation of the cerebral hemispheres and that of the lower ganglia, which may be taken to correspond with the great subjective distinction between the consciousness which may attend the former and the no-consciousness which is invariably characteristic of the latter?"—to this question the answer there given is: "I think the only difference that can be pointed to is a difference of rate or time," and this "clearly implies that the nervous mechanism concerned has not been fully habituated to the performance of the response required." From which answer of Mr. Romanes it would seem to be fairly inferable that when the nervous mechanism *has* become fully habituated, as in the case of instinctive actions, to the performance of the response required, consciousness is absent. It is right, however, to state that Mr. Romanes does not draw this inference. Whatever may be inferred, or not inferred, with regard to its absence, Mr. Romanes clearly states his view that consciousness is present when, "instead of the stimulus merely needing to touch the trigger of a ready-formed apparatus of response (however complex this may be), it has to give rise in the nerve-centre to a play of stimuli before the appropriate response is yielded." " Reflex action," he aptly remarks, " may be regarded as the rapid movement of a well-oiled machine, consciousness as the heat evolved by the internal friction of some other machine, and psychical processes as the light which is given out when such heat rises to redness." And once more, " Consciousness is but an adjunct which arises when the physical process, owing to infrequency of repetition, complexity of operation, or other causes, involves what I have before called ganglionic friction."

The difference of rate or time, which constitutes the only difference that can be pointed to between those nerve actions which are accompanied by consciousness and those which are accompanied by no consciousness, is thus due to increased ganglionic friction; and this increased ganglionic friction is, in Mr. Romanes' estimation, the chief condition of consciousness. I should, however, feel disposed to add to this (following Dr. Bain) diffusion of the nerve-disturbance as a yet more important—to my mind the most important—condition of consciousness. Be this as it may, let us compare a little more fully automatic action and conscious action.

We have seen above that automatic action is especially characterized by promptness, absence of hesitation, and accuracy. Conscious action, being the antithesis to automatic action, would therefore seem to be characterized by delay, hesitation, and inaccuracy; or, let us rather say, postponement of action, deliberation, and acting for the best. Take a case in point. Shortly after I had written the last sentence, an acquaintance chanced to tell me the following: Two boys went to a farm in South Africa for a few days' shooting. One night the elder, by way of practical joke, dressed himself in white—they had been talking of ghosts—and stole into his companion's room. His friend, waking with a start, seized a pistol and shot him dead. " He did it almost unconsciously, poor fellow," added my informant. Yes, almost unconsciously. And what was the nature of his action? It was prompt, sure, and unpremeditated. Compare this with an act of deliberate choice, in which consciousness is especially prominent. Two courses are open to me at this moment. I may either continue writing beneath the shadow of this overhanging rock which shelters me from the South African summer sun, or I may bathe in the pool hard by. There goes on in my mind a conflict of motives, motives being a mild form of desires. Various considerations in favour of each course present themselves. Eventually one set of motives is victorious. I determine to continue writing for a certain time and then bathe. This determination is accompanied by a sense of choice. What is the nature of this act? It is deliberate; time was occupied during the consideration, and no one could, without an unattainable knowledge of my character, predict the result. I could not myself say which set of motives were the strongest, and would determine my choice. Here, then, in deliberation and postponement of action, we seem to have some of the subjective conditions of consciousness. What may we suppose these conditions to be in their neural aspect? Let us look, first, at their opposites.

Reflex action takes place when the adjustment of the nerve mechanism is practically perfect; that is, when the channels along which the "animal spirits" pass, are so well defined that there is, so to speak, no leakage. A given stimulus gives rise to a disturbance in certain nerve-endings; this disturbance is passed on down the afferent nerve to a ganglion. A change is set up there. The disturbance is at once transmitted down an efferent nerve to certain nerve-endings embedded in certain muscles, and the appropriate response follows. There is here no diffusion of the disturbance. Diffusion of the nervous disturbance would seem, then, by inference, to be one of the accompaniments of consciousness. Such diffusion, we may well imagine, was the concomitant of the act of choice above referred to. Involving as that act did a conflict of several motives, the nerve-currents must have diffused themselves over a tolerably wide area of nerve-centres.

But as I sit beneath this rock I am conscious of the sound of a rushing stream. Is there any diffusion of nerve disturbance in this case? Much diffusion: The moment I became conscious of the sound it became more than a mere sound; it became the sign for a somewhat complex conception. That is to say, by the diffusion of nerve disturbance there were called up in my mind ideas of water tumbling through a rocky channel. And this sound of rushing water called up a train of other ideas, which it is needless here to specify. A simple, undiffused nerve disturbance is, I believe, unaccompanied by consciousness. Only when the nerve disturbance diffuses itself does consciousness emerge in the form of a perception.

This law of diffusion, as Dr. Bain terms it (to which he adds the law of relativity or varying intensity), seems to be closely associated with some marked characteristics of human conduct; (1) that which I have before described as postponement of action, (2) spontaneity, and (3) originality.

(1) Concerning the postponement of action I have already said somewhat, perhaps enough. Compare the careful man of business who can "bide his time" with his more impulsive junior partner. The same possible transaction suggests to the one a number of consequences of which the other foresees nothing. This greater mass of associated ideas is, we cannot doubt, the subjective correlate of a greater diffusion of nerve disturbance. Take, again, the case of the man who is blessed with the power of self-restraint, who refrains from the youthful excesses into

which his neighbour falls. He is conscious not only of ideas of immediate gratification, but of ideas of a blighted life in the future. This wider range of view is, we must suppose, a concomitant of a wider diffusion of nerve disturbance.

(2) Spontaneity has for its physical accompaniment "the overflow of vital power" in the nerve-system. During a holiday tour among the mountains we rise in the early morning, go out, and look around us. Every sight, every sound, the very freshness of the air, brings with it a mass of very pleasurable consciousness. We notice many points of beauty or interest which we failed to see when we came in, the night before, tired with healthy exercise. We whistle or hum a favourite air. Thoughts tumble in upon us unbidden. We spring up the hillside to reach a higher elevation, and race down again from very gladness of heart. Even the dullest of us brightens up and ventures on a joke, at which the rest, heedless of its antiquity, laugh again. All this tells of rapid and vigorous diffusion of nerve-currents in the brain.

(3) Closely connected with this is originality. The commonplace man acts like his forefathers and the generality of mankind. You can tell exactly what he will do under these circumstances or those. His resources of action are exceedingly limited. The original man, on the other hand, takes us by surprise. His views are altogether novel. He at once creates new conditions, so that the question under discussion stands in a new light. His actions are unexpected, and so far from ordinary that we are apt to call him eccentric. And what does all this mean? A wider range of nerve action, a greater variety of nerve connections corresponding to an increased breadth of possible thought or action; in a word, greater diffusion of brain disturbance.

A further indication of the connection between diffusion of nerve disturbance and consciousness here presents itself. We have before noticed how conscious action may pass into unconscious automatic action. This would, on the view here taken, be accompanied by a concentration of the nervous discharge. As an action is repeatedly performed, less and less diffusion takes place, until eventually, when the concentration is carried to the utmost, consciousness ceases, and the action is carried on automatically. And in this case, what is true of action is true also of thought. Processes of thought may be so concentrated in definite channels as to be automatic, as we have already seen in unconscious cerebration. Narrowness of mind, dogmatism, bigotry, result from undue concentration of thought-processes, in questions of opinion concerning which the mind should be kept open to receive fresh lights, from whatever source they come. Here we see the well-known connection between dogmatism and ignorance. Only ignorance can make possible dogmatism in matters of opinion. And ignorance is unconsciousness of all those associations which constitute knowledge. It is accompanied by limited diffusion of nerve disturbance.

Diffusion of disturbance among connected nerve-centres seems, then, to be one of the physiological accompaniments of consciousness. To me it seems the most important. There may be, no doubt are, other physiological conditions; but this of diffusion is, to my mind, the most essential. By it many centres are called into relational activity. And it would seem to be not impossible that consciousness may accompany such diffusion and relational activity wherever it may take place in the brain. But at the same time we may well believe that, since in the cerebral hemispheres there is the widest possibility of diffusion, there, too, is the greatest amount of concomitant consciousness; and it is quite possible that, in man, *there* only can take place that wide and varied diffusion which must be the physical accompaniment of the complex human consciousness.

7. What is the Connection between Mind and Body? a. *The practical answer. Materialistic.*

"All our perceptions are dependent on our organs and the disposition of our nerves and animal spirits."—DAVID HUME.

This question, that of the nature of the connection between mind and body, is one that is as old as philosophy. There are two opposing views on this subject, the one held by the majority, the other by an increasing minority. Other views have been held from time to time, but we may confine our attention to these two :

1. That held by the majority, that there are two separate and distinct existences or entities, belonging, so to speak, to each individual, a mind and a body.

Of this view there are two subdivisions.

a. The vulgar view, that the body-entity can act on the mind-entity, and the mind-entity on the body-entity, the state of the one affecting the state of the other.

b. The philosophic view, that the mind cannot act on the body nor the body on the mind, but that there is a pre-established harmony between the actions of the one and the activities of the other, and in general between the course of Nature and the succession of our ideas.

2. That held by the minority, that there is but a single entity. Of this view also there are two subdivisions.

a. The practical view. That there is one organism— the human being—possessed of various qualities, physical, vital, and mental.

b. The speculative view. That there is one being—the

body-mind or mind-body—of which mind and body are
but different aspects.

Now, I do not know that there is a single argument
(except, perhaps, that from the law of parsimony) by which
a man who holds to 1 *a*, the vulgar view, can be convinced
that it is not the most satisfactory. It accounts perfectly
for all the facts. It is true that we are quite unable to
understand *how* the mind can act on the body, or the body
on the mind. But are there not the animal spirits which,
as Dr. Martineau puts it, "live a kind of amphibious life in
the philosophy of the seventeenth century, now running
through the body, and now diving off into the soul, so as
to play the part of messenger between them"? And if
the animal spirits fail him, is there not the ultimate refuge
in an honest confession of ignorance, or the more resonant,
Inscrutable Mystery? It is true also that we have no
experience of mind apart from body. But neither have we
any experience of magnetism apart from matter mag-
netized, nor of heat apart from the body heated, nor of
gravity apart from attracting masses, nor of colour apart
from coloured bodies, nor of chemical action apart from
certain elements, nor of sound apart from some material
substance set in vibration. If my neighbour likes to
assume half a hundred entities, connected in various inexplicable ways with material bodies, I know no way of
showing him his error. I dare not even say he is in error.
The believer in the practical materialistic view can only
say, "That, my friend, is your view. Hold to it by all
means, if it gives you comfort. Mine, I think, is simpler.
You must allow me to hold to it, even if it be not so com-
fortable; for neither have you any arguments by which it
can be shown that my view is incorrect."

Concerning 1 *b*, the view that there is a pre-established
harmony between mind and body, we can only say that it

is also unassailable. It is like the view of certain excellent and estimable old ladies, who, when certain difficult problems of science are discussed, shake their heads solemnly, and say, "Ah, no! we should not inquire into these deep matters. God made it so. Surely that is answer enough for us poor frail mortals!" Now, such a remark is clearly not intended for those who do not believe in God. And for those who do, it is quite beside the mark; for they will answer, "Of course, madam, God made it so. Did not God make *everything?* The question is, *how?* Your answer (forgive my bluntness) is not only childish, but mischievous. Childish because it is no answer; mischievous because, by pretending to be an answer, it puts up a barrier to stop the passage of honest inquirers. You would be content with the answer, God makes the chick to grow within the egg. Of course He does. But, thanks to the progress of embryology, we now know a good deal about the manner of His marvellous workings. You would be content with the answer, God made man and beast out of the dust of the earth. Of course He did. But, thanks to the theory of evolution, we now know a good deal about His methods of creation." The pre-established harmony hypothesis is unassailable; but it is no answer to the question, What is the connection of mind and body?

Passing over this, therefore, let us now let the upholder of the practical materialistic view speak for himself.

"If you wish me to set down my reasons for the view I hold, here they are.". So might he say to the believer in the vulgar view. "Take any ordinary object, such as a stick of sealing-wax. It is long, and round, and red, and heavy, and has a slight smell. That object I believe to be, so far as I can know anything about it, just a group of these possible sensations I can receive from it. The sensations, of course, are states of consciousness; but to avoid a roundabout way of talking, I call them qualities of the sealing-wax. You will agree with me that this is a direct, simple, common-sense view of the thing. I do not say, nor do you in all probability in this case, there is an entity matter, in which dwell the entities hardness, roundness, redness, and so on. Well, then, you too, as a human being, are an object which I can study. And in addition to certain other qualities, I find that you have mental qualities. And just as a special smell goes along with the special substance, sealing-wax, so too does this special mental quality go along with your nerve-centres. You, my friend, call this mind an entity; I call it a quality. I call it a quality because I called the redness, hardness, and so on qualities. I don't know why you call it an entity. But since you do call it an entity, I see no reason why you should not call magnetism and gravity entities. Very possibly you do, like some others, regard force as an entity. In that you are consistent.

"But perhaps you will contend that mental qualities, rising as they do in their higher manifestations into consciousness, differ altogether from any other qualities. In this I agree. But what then? We must accept facts as we find them. Our experience testifies that the facts we call mental are connected with a certain organism, man. I say nothing here about the lower animals. Of mental facts disconnected from such an organism experience tells us and can tell us nothing. From which I infer that mind is a constituent part of human nature. I do not see what other conclusion I can arrive at, unless I altogether change my way of regarding Nature; for if I regard the mind of man as a separate entity, I must certainly regard life as a separate entity, and force as a separate entity. I shall then have to deal with four distinct entities, matter, force, life, and mind. Force associating itself with all forms of

matter, life with certain special forms of matter, mind
with special modification of this special form of matter ;
all of them capable of separate existence, *none of them
known in experience as separate existences.* But then, I shall
not know where to stop. Your mind, my mind, and our
neighbour's minds are, you say, distinct entities. Carrying
this view, then, to what seems to me its logical outcome, I
shall have to look upon the world as an indefinite number
of matter-entities, variably associated with an indefinite
number of force-entities, an indefinite number of vital-
entities, an indefinite number of mental-entities ; all of
these capable of separate existence, *none of them known in
experience as separate existences.* I cannot say this view is
incorrect ; I can only say that it is somewhat confusing.

"In place of this crowd of entities I believe in one
universal existence. I am not going to give it any grand
name ; I am content to say that it is practically known to
us as matter and motion. The universal existence is
manifested to me, through experience and inference from
experience, in various ways ; and by grouping these
manifestations I form my picture of the world. By a process of abstraction, and for the sake of convenience, I
group together certain of these manifestations and call the
group matter, another group I call energy, another group
life, another group mind. But I do not forget that these
are abstractions. I regard them as modes of the universal
existence, not as separate existences. And if I study a
particular object, such as a human being, I do not regard
him or any part of him as capable of separate existence
apart from the universal existence. I regard him as just
a part of that universal existence. It is true that he is a
conscious part, that he has the power of knowing and
feeling his own existence and the existence of the world
around him. This I accept as a fact, or rather an irresistible

inference from facts of observation. It is a wonderful fact ; true ; so are all facts. As a fact, we must simply accept it with such wonder and mystery as are inseparably attached to it.

"It must be remembered that it is only by a process of inference that I know that my neighbours have feelings similar to those ,of which I am myself conscious. To no one, however, but a pure idealist is this a difficulty. We all show practically by our actions how complete is our belief in the justice of this inference. Accepting, then, this inference, I say that the human being is an object possessing physical, vital, and mental qualities or properties. In ordinary language we say that, so long as life is in him, he is capable of using force. But we do not mean that life and force are separate things, however clearly our common forms of speech seem to imply such a view. In the same way we say that fear makes him turn pale, and that a dis-ordered liver entails dejection of spirits. And summing up a number of such connections we say, in every-day speech, that the mind acts on the body and the body on the mind. But here, too, practical materialists do not mean that mind and body are separate things, however clearly their common forms of speech seem to imply such a view. So long as we continue to use such expressions as 'the stone falling through the action of gravity,' 'a tree still having life in it,' 'a current of electricity,' and half a hundred more of a similar character, so long may we con-veniently use such expressions as 'the mind acts on the body,' and 'the bodily state affects the mind.' At the same time we must remember that as it is only by abstrac-tion that we can separate gravity from the attracting and attracted bodies, life from the living tree, magnetism from the loadstone, so it is only by abstraction that we can separate mind from the living organism.

" This is the materialistic faith. And if a man does not believe in it, let him. by all means believe in something else, in whatever seems to him, after honest inquiry, to be true."

7. *What is the Connection between Mind and Body?* b. *The speculative answer. Idealistic.*

" Man must always in some sense cling to the belief that the unknowable is knowable, otherwise speculation would cease."—GOETHE.

As a practical answer, that of the materialist may, I think, be accepted. It is an answer in terms of phenomena, and in those terms the best answer that we have. But, do what we will, we fret under the restraints of the phenomenal. We strive to get behind the practically real and to reach the speculative reality which lies behind.

But can we do so and yet keep in any sense within the bounds of experience? Only, as it seems to me, on the hypothesis of mind-stuff. Thought is the one absolute reality that we know. The elements out of which thought is built up we may call mind-stuff. And it is conceivable that just as the mind is the true reality which underlies that phenomenal mass of matter we call the human organism, so too is mind-stuff the true reality which underlies all phenomenal masses of matter. This is nothing but idealism ; but it is idealism in a new form.

To what I have before said on this head, I have nothing here to add. Suffice it to say that this view seems to have the practical value of knitting together physiology and psychology, and of rendering conceivable the concomitant evolution of mind and body. The parallelism between neurosis and psychosis is merged in identity. They are not parallel series which run side by side, but one series which we regard under different aspects. To use the old philosophical phraseology, there are not two substances, a substance of matter and a substance of mind, but one substance, the substance of being.

And here once more we reach the border-line between the region of science and the region that lies beyond science ; a region which I may not tread in this book, but in which, for some of us, the Substance of Being is clothed with our highest ideals, and becomes the centre of our loftiest aspirations.

PART III.

THROUGH FEELING TO CONDUCT.

"The social factor is the real cause of the elevation of animal psychology into human psychology, the sensible into the ideal world, knowledge into science, emotion into sentiment, appetite into morality."—G. H. LEWES.

CHAPTER I.

CHOICE.

" By liberty, then, we can only mean a power of acting or not acting according to the determination of the will : that is, if we choose to remain at rest we may ; if we choose to move we also may. Now, this hypothetical liberty is universally allowed to belong to every one who is not a prisoner or in chains."
—DAVID HUME.

I. *The Fundamental Importance of Action.*

"Science is the getting of knowledge from experience on the assumption of uniformity in nature, and the use of such knowledge to guide the actions of men."—W. K. CLIFFORD.

WE have now to push our inquiries in a new direction. We have to work our way upwards from knowledge, through choice and feeling, to conduct.

It will be remembered that, in the first chapter—that on general conceptions—it was pointed out how the elements of sensation, entering into relation, give rise to conscious perception ; and how the same elements, under more complex conditions of relationship, finally emerge as general conceptions.

What we have now to notice is that the end and object of the sensational elements is, not only to enter into relations, and thus to be perceived or known, but also to produce action. And after they have thus entered into relations they not only give rise to consciousness, but they also produce action. And after sensations and the relations between them have been built up into propositions, the end in view is not only to constitute intelligence, but to produce action. Once more ; after propositions have been compounded into general conceptions, and these again, in turn, compounded and recompounded with each other, their end and object is not only to educe abstract thought, but also to produce action. This great fact, perhaps only fully appreciated after some training in physiology, is, as it seems to me, one of the foundation-stones of the philosophy of mind. Only when this fact is adequately grasped, does the law of the suppression of action assume its true import.

A simple sensation is, indeed, a triple point, a point common to three intersecting planes. From the sensations start, in the first place, those perceptions, propositions, and general conceptions, which constitute the field of know-ledge. From the sensations start, in the second place, those simple pleasures and pains, and those more complex emotions, which constitute the field of feeling. And from the sensations start, in the third place, those simple responses, those more complex movements, and those yet more complex groups of co-ordinated movements, which constitute the field of action. Knowledge, feeling, action ; these are three great and wide fields, but the greatest and widest is action.

Aristotle saw this long ago. "The end of our study is not knowledge," he said, "but conduct." And it is no less true to-day than it was then, that the acquisition of know-ledge is the means, but the right conduct of life is the end. Leviathan Hobbes emphasized it, when he wrote, "The scope of all speculation is the performance of some action or thing to be done." Comte summed it up in an epigram : "We gain knowledge in order to predict, and we predict in order to provide ; " or, far more pithily in the original French, "*Savoir pour prévoir, afin de pourvoir.*" Our own great Huxley insists upon it. "Knowledge of every kind," he says, "is useful in proportion as it tends to give people right ideas, which are essential to the foundation of right practice, and to remove wrong ideas, which are no less essential foundations and fertile mothers of errors in practice." Even thought itself must be active, as Clifford maintained in the panegyric on Whewell of his Cambridge days. "Thought is powerless," he said, "except it make something outside of itself: the thought which conquers the world is not contemplative but active."

And yet of Clifford himself we learn, "The pursuit of knowledge for its own sake, and without even such regard to collateral interests as most people would think a matter of common prudence, was the leading character of his work throughout his life. The discovery of truth was for him an end in itself, and the proclamation of it, or of whatever seemed to lead to it, a duty of primary and paramount obligation." Is there not some contradiction here? Can knowledge be both an end in itself, and also at the same time a means to a higher end? It can. Hear Clifford himself. "Although the true end of all knowledge is action," he says, "and it is only for the sake of action that knowledge is sought by the human race, yet, in order that it may be gained in sufficient breadth and depth, it is necessary that the individual should seek knowledge for its own sake." This I hold to be profoundly true. Knowledge, though its acquirement is ultimately justified by its influence on conduct, must, like virtue, be sought in singleness of heart for its own sake, and must be its own reward.

Remembering this, we must still not forget that, in the end, action is paramount. These are days of great educational experiments: not only the schoolmaster, but the professor is abroad ; we venerate, we almost worship, knowledge. And yet, if all this resolute grappling with ignorance have not for its main object the bettering of conduct, I, for one, care not much whether it be successful or unsuccessful.

2. *The Sense of Choice.*

"No amount of experience of the sway of motives even tends to make me distrust my intuitive consciousness that, in resolving after deliberation, I exercise free choice as to which of the motives acting on me shall prevail."— H. SIDGWICK.

The primary end of sensation, taking this term in its widest significance, is action. The function of the desires and emotions, fear, hunger, love, and all that arise out of these, is to supply the motives for action. And the privilege of thought is to guide and to control, or to suppress, the actions so initiated. But the matter does not stop here. For not infrequently there is a conflict of motives ; there is more than one course of action suggested ; there is the hesitation of deliberation ; and there is the eventual yielding to the strongest motive, accompanied by a sense of choice.

It will be observed that nothing is here said of an intervening volition or act of will. This may, to some, seem strange, seeing how potent is this faculty for good and for ill. Let us therefore endeavour to determine its true place in Nature.

"The motion of our bodies," said Hume, "follows upon the command of our will. Of this we are every moment conscious. But the means by which this is effected—the energy by which the will performs so extraordinary an operation—of this we are so far from being immediately conscious, that it must ever escape our diligent inquiry."

But elsewhere in his writings we read, " I desire it may be observed that, by the *will*, I mean nothing but the internal impression we feel, and are conscious of, when we knowingly give rise to any new motion of our body, or new perception of our mind."

" This description of volition," writes Professor Huxley, " may be criticised on various grounds. More especially does it seem defective in restricting the term 'will' to that feeling which arises when we act, or appear to act, as causes ; for one may will to strike, without striking ; or to think of something which we have forgotten.

" Every volition," he continues, " is a complex idea composed of two elements : the one is the idea of an action ; the other is a desire for the occurrence of that action. If I will to strike, I have an idea of a certain movement, and a desire that that movement should take place ; if I will to think of any subject, or, in other words, to attend to that subject, I have an idea of the subject, and a strong desire that it should remain present to my consciousness. And, so far as I can discover, this combination of an idea of an object with an emotion, is everything that can be directly observed in an act of volition. So that Hume's definition may be amended thus : Volition is the impression which arises when the idea of a bodily or mental action is accompanied by the desire that the action should be accomplished."

If, then, this view, thus clearly stated by Professor Huxley, be correct, there is, in volition, nothing that will not find a place under one of the three heads—initiating motive ; guiding thought ; resulting action ; either as immediate impressions or as re-presentative ideas. The act of will is, in fact, merged in the determining motive ; which consists in a clear conception of an action, the association therewith of a conception of pleasure or of duty, and the fusion of these elements into a desire for the occurrence of the action. We fancy that it is by the exercise of will that we ourselves determine our actions : but, in sober truth, they are determined for us ; our actions taking the line of least resistance under the stern pressure of the strongest motive.

There is, however, somewhat to be said in favour of Hume's "internal impression we feel, and are conscious of, when we knowingly give rise to any new motion of our body, or new perception of our mind." At any rate, as it seems to me, such an impression is generated whenever a conflict of motives arises. When we are thus prompted to opposite courses of action by conflicting motives, we have an uneasy sense of discomfort, a more or less painful feeling of embarrassment and hesitation ; but when the stronger motive at length prevails, there is an accompanying and complementary feeling of pleasure, a consciousness of relief, which would seem to partake of the nature of a "sensation of an inner sense." This feeling of embarrassed hesitation, followed by a feeling of pleasurable relief, I venture to call the sense of choice. And since all actions which "we knowingly give rise to" are voluntary actions— that is, actions which it is open to us either to perform or not to perform—it may perhaps be fairly contended that all such actions so performed are accompanied by "the internal impression" of which Hume speaks, and which I have here termed a sense of choice.

In this process, be it noted, all that we have any right to affirm is that we have a sense of choice—that is, that we are conscious of a conflict of motives and a final prevalence of one set of motives. What a great many of us *do* affirm, however, is that *we choose*. And this seems to imply that we have an independent power over our choice ; that we have, in a word, free-will.

3. *Free-will and Determinism.*

"It is inconceivable that two men, being themselves of like temper and character, and having before them like objects of choice in like circumstances, should choose differently."—*Chasdai Creskas.*

With regard' to the question of free-will, let us first notice that such an idea as freedom, implying as it must an idea of its opposite, determinism, is only possible when the powers of reflection are developed, when it is possible to review past action and see that it might have been other than it actually was. On a certain occasion we acted in a certain way. We see, on reflection, that our action was not the best. On a similar occasion afterwards we act differently. And we then imagine that we could have acted differently in the first instance. But it is clear that the two cases are not alike : reflection has altered one of the determinants of action, the character. The character having changed, the resulting action is different.

The whole question of the freedom of the will may, however, be summed up in this inquiry: Would a complete knowledge of all mental phenomena enable us to generalize and express them in the form of laws? Or, to put the same question in a more familiar form, Is my mind subject to law, or is it not? Let us approach this inquiry in a scientific spirit. I have before pointed out that the procedure of science and of common sense is to frame hypotheses and then see how they work. What hypothesis, then, have I, what hypothesis have my fellow-men, framed on this subject ?

As I was reading this morning there came, apparently without cause, across my consciousness a mental image of the *cabane* on the Matterhorn, and that so vividly as to take off my attention from Professor Rolleston's general description of the Cœlenterata in his " Forms of Animal Life." I had, in fact, read on to the end of a paragraph before I discovered that my mind was in Switzerland. At once there rose the question, " What made me think of that?" And this question is an answer to the inquiry just put ; for it implies the belief that there was, if I could only find it out, as indeed I readily did, some reason for that mental picture of the Matterhorn *cabane ;* that neither it, nor any other idea, comes into my mind hap-hazard. After that little question—and I suppose such an experience is a pretty common one—there was no necessity for elaborate introspection to ascertain that my hypothesis is that my mind is subject to law. And the fact that the question arose almost instinctively, shows that it is an hypothesis normally developed, and not the result of subtle philosophizing.

That, then, is my hypothesis concerning my own mind ; and all that I can make out of the minds of others through their actions, seems to justify and strengthen my hypothesis. But is it my individual hypothesis, or is it shared by the majority of my fellows? I do not know what all this pressing question of education can mean if it be not their hypothesis. If a child's mind is not subject to law, I cannot see the use of trying to influence it for good or for ill, for wisdom or its opposite. It is because we believe that the physical world is subject to law that we till the earth, and build cities, and launch steamships. And it is because we believe that the mental world is subject to law that we educate our children, and punish those who sin against the State.

But if my mind is completely subject to law, I have no free-will ; and if I have free-will, my mind is, to that extent, not subject to law. Now everything here depends upon what I mean by free-will. If, by saying that I have no free-will, I mean that I cannot go on writing if I choose, or stop writing if I choose, I am talking sheer nonsense. But I mean nothing of the sort. What I do mean is, that I never act without a motive, that my choice is not indeterminate, but determined.

If it were not that we are so frequently ignorant of the reasons which influence our choice—if it were not, as Spinoza has said, that men "are conscious of their own actions and ignorant of the causes whereby they are determined"—we should not be so ready to boast of our free-will. The whole of the confusion on this subject has arisen from the ambiguity involved in the expression, *I can choose.* If I am the sum of my states of consciousness at any moment, if these states of mind constitute me, then, since these states of mind determine those which follow, these following states and the actions which accompany them are determined by me. But, at the same time, they are part of an orderly sequence subject to law. The moment I identify myself with my states of mind, all confusion disappears, and free-will, in the ordinary sense of the term —that is, a consciousness of individual choice—is perfectly compatible with the doctrine that my mind is completely subject to law. And if my mind is not completely subject to law, it seems to me an altogether childish thing to waste time in trying to understand its contents. These contents are, indeed, so varied, and change so rapidly, that we cannot hope, at present, fully to grasp all the conditions of their being. But this is almost as true of many branches of physical science. We cannot at present grasp the complex of causes which bring about an unusually hot atmosphere or a light westerly wind. So changeful, and uncertain, indeed, is the weather, that many people find it exceedingly difficult to grasp that it is as rigidly subject to law as the motions of the earth in space. To them the words of the Hebrew poet, "the wind bloweth where it listeth," seem literally true. And perhaps if the winds were self-conscious many of them would boast of free-will.

Still, they would have much less cause for doing so than human beings have. And for this reason: that every human being carries about with him a special something, peculiar to himself, which is a most important factor in determining his choice in any so-called act of volition. This special something is his *character*. Place two clouds or other inorganic bodies under similar circumstances, and they will both yield to the influences in a similar fashion. Place two men under similar circumstances, and they will *not* both yield to the influences in a similar fashion, but each will act in accordance with his peculiar character. And the freedom which every man is conscious of possessing, is freedom to act in accordance with his own character. "We fancy we are free," writes Mr. J. A. Froude; "we are conscious of what we do; we are not conscious of the causes which make us do it; and therefore we imagine that the cause is in ourselves." And to a certain extent we imagine rightly. For we are not like inorganic clouds at the mercy of external forces, but *contain the springs of action in ourselves.* The brain is not a mass of merely inert matter; the organism is a *variable* piece of mechanism; hence it at different times acts differently to the same stimulus: and it is this difference of reaction that has helped to fix the idea that the will is free. Kant's definition of freedom will now be understood. ."Freedom," he said, "is such a property of the will as enables living agents to originate events independently of foreign determining causes." This is the true freedom which no man can take from us—to act in accordance with our own nature and character.

Of this character I shall have something more to say presently. Here I content myself with observing that the existence of such things as reformatories and penitentiaries, and our whole line of conduct towards the young, show our belief in the modifiability of character, show our belief that character is under the reign of law. It will be seen, however, that this way of viewing the question is entirely based on the supposition that there is no "masterful entity," the *ego*, separate from and presiding over my mental acts. Those who believe in such an entity hold it, I presume, to be absolutely free, utterly unfettered by law. Their chief difficulty is, and it is no slight one, to explain how such an entity can influence bodily action. To this, perhaps, they will answer, "How, then, do *you* explain how choice, a mental quality, can influence bodily action?" I, for one, am sure I do not know. I am utterly unable to see how such influence is to be explained or even imagined. Professor Clifford suggested in this connection a somewhat similar problem. "It will be found," he writes, "excellent practice in mental operations required by this doctrine to imagine a train, the fore part of which is an engine and three carriages linked with iron couplings, and the hind part three other carriages linked with iron couplings, the bond between the two parts being made out of the sentiments of amity subsisting between the stoker and the guard." The fact is, that the answer I have supposed, shows a misconception of the view maintained. The mental series must not be confounded with the physical series. The two run parallel, but do not intermingle. They are, indeed, but different aspects of the same series. A feeling gives rise to choice, and is followed by a consciousness of action. That is the mental series. A nerve tremor gives rise to brain vibration, and is followed by muscular contraction. That is the physical series. Let it be clearly understood that the two are practically distinct. And if in this little volume there be any apparent intermingling of the two, let it be put down to an imperfect command of language and a wish to avoid pedantry.

To talk of the mind influencing the body or the body the mind is, as was pointed out in the last chapter, misleading. It is only by a process of abstraction that we separate mental processes from bodily processes and bodily from mental. The same human thought-process is cerebral or mental according as we look at it from one point of view or another. It is a cerebro-mental process. The question is sometimes asked, "If the mind were withdrawn, would the cerebral processes continue unchanged?" which is not unlike asking, "If we remove the centre of a circle will the properties of that circle remain unchanged?" Again, it is sometimes said, "If the mind cannot direct the motions of the body, then the human race could have arrived at its present position without the aid of consciousness. An unconscious Shakespeare would have written (under the influence of inexorable physical law) to an unconscious humanity." Than this, nothing could be more ridiculous. It is surely obvious that we must take the facts of human progress as we find them. It is equally clear that we find that progress accompanied by certain cerebro-mental processes. Consciousness has been an element in the facts, as they are given us for consideration. To ask, therefore, whether the facts would have been the same had consciousness been absent, is not unlike asking whether birds would have flown had they been wingless; or inquiring whether water would have had the same properties without the hydrogen. Determinism simply comes to this—that both on the objective side, and on the subjective side, our actions are determined by law. On the one hand, a perfect knowledge of the organism,

plus a perfect knowledge of any stimulus and the surrounding conditions, would enable us to say how the
organism will act under that stimulus : on the other hand,
a perfect knowledge of the character, plus a perfect knowledge of any motive and the circumstances of the case,
would enable us to say what *feelings* would result (the
actions being the objective side of the feelings). If by
free-will it is meant that our actions are the outcome of
our individual character-organism, then free-will and determinism are at one.

Some further explanation may, however, be demanded
of the statement that free-will, in the ordinary sense of
the term, is perfectly compatible with the doctrine that
my mind is completely subject to law. This, then, is what
I believe goes on in my mind when, out of two courses
of action open to me, I choose one. Two sets of motives,
each of them subject to law, prompt me to opposite actions.
For a time there is more or less equilibrium ; but in the
end one set of motives, proving stronger than the other
set of motives, prevails, and brings about its corresponding
action. Now, in this process everything is subject to law.
By which I mean this : that if I could know perfectly my
own character and all the circumstances, I could always
and infallibly predict what my choice would be. And,
under like conditions, I could predict also any choice which
my neighbour might make. As it is, I doubtless know
enough of his character to predict, in a great number of
cases, and with comparative certainty, what his line of
action will be. But if his mind be subject to law, I could,
by a *complete* knowledge of his character, and of *all* the influences at work, predict his line of conduct with as much
certainty as the astronomer can predict the course of the
planet Venus. For all that, however, he would have a
consciousness of choosing, since the sense of choice is

Q

generated by the mental hesitation due to the equilibrium of motives, and by the eventual prevalence of one set of motives over another set of motives.

4. *Intelligence.*

"Reason or intelligence is the faculty which is concerned in the intentional adaptation of means to ends."—G. J. ROMANES.

AND what is the essential nature of that mental process in which there is a temporary equilibrium of motives, followed by the prevalence of one set of motives ? Surely this : that it is an *intelligent* process. An intelligent act is an act chosen in preference to some other act. On the other hand, an act performed without any of that mental hesitation which gives rise to a sense of choice, is at the same time an involuntary, and an instinctive, or non-intelligent act. Intelligence and volition thus go hand in hand. A sense of choice accompanies every intelligent process, and no process is intelligent without this sense of choice.

Opposed to intelligence, in this sense, is instinct. An instinctive act is, therefore, an act performed without the sense of choice. If I hear a sudden noise I start, and I do so instinctively. I have no sense of choice in the matter. I start involuntarily. After long practice, habits acquired intelligently with a sense of choice, and often with diffi- culty, become instinctive, and pass into the secondary automatic class, being performed without a sense of choice. Instance the oft-quoted case of the soldier who dropped the pie he was carrying home for his Sunday's dinner, when a wag behind him shouted the word *attention.* The act of reading aloud, acquired in childhood with consider- able difficulty, may become so far instinctive as to be performed without even giving rise to any recollection of the matter read. In the Rev. Stephen Hawker's life we hear that, during his wife's blindness, he spent much of the day in reading to her. But "after he had diligently read through the three volumes of some popular novel, he was found to be ignorant of the plot, to know nothing of the characters, and to have no conception even of the names of the hero and heroine."

From this we may see how closely connected are intelligence, memory, the will, and consciousness. Truly involuntary acts—that is, acts performed altogether without a sense of choice—are indeed always unconscious. And I think it probable that all conscious acts are voluntary; that is, performed with a sense of choice. But acts performed with a sense of choice have above been defined as intelligent. Therefore all conscious acts are also intelligent. From this, then, we see that the germs of consciousness (which, as we have seen before, necessitates memory), intelligence, and the will, all take their origin together.

A piece of speculation may be thrown in here for what it is worth. The germs of consciousness, intelligence, the will, and, as we shall see hereafter, feeling, arise together. But during evolution, actions once performed intelligently, and with a conscious sense of choice, pass over into acts performed involuntarily and unconsciously. And when does this take place? When the adjustment of the organism to its environment, as regards the action in question, is perfect. The sense of choice, and acts intelligently and consciously performed are, indeed, the results of the imperfect adjustment of the organism to its surrounding conditions. And what if, in the far distant future, the adjustment become in all respects and at all periods of life perfect? Then would all intelligent action, all sense of choice, all consciousness cease. And if this be so, a perfect organism would be an *unconscious automaton.*

From this theoretical conclusion I can see no escape. But practically it does not affect *us* in the least degree. From what we know of evolution, advance of life has always been accompanied by an increase in the fulness of consciousness; and the higher an organism stands in the scale of life, the further does perfect adjustment to all the surrounding (and, within limits, *variable*) conditions seem pushed into the unattainable.

Let us, however, return to the view that the germs of consciousness, intelligence, and the will, all take their origin together. To this conclusion several objections are likely to be raised. Let us consider some of them. A man under mesmeric influence, it may be said, is forced to act involuntarily and yet is in possession of full consciousness. So that the statement that involuntary acts are also un-conscious is here negatived. But it must be remembered that, when I speak of involuntary acts, I mean acts per-formed *without a sense of choice.* This, however, is not the sense in which the subject of mesmeric influence is said to act involuntarily. He has full sense of choice, but is forced to act against his own wishes. So that his acts are rather contra-voluntary than involuntary: just as the act of falling after a slip is rather contra-voluntary than involuntary. Again, it may be said that many of our everyday waking acts are conscious acts, and are yet not performed with any definite sense of choice. Granted; but that is a very different thing from saying that they are performed without *any* sense of choice. Take even an extreme case. Suppose that, from over-exertion or some other cause, my heart begins to beat so violently that I am conscious of the fact. Here there would seem to be an act of which I am conscious, but one which involves no sense of choice. And yet, so far as I am concerned, I am never conscious of the action of my heart without an accompanying wish that it should beat less violently. The consciousness of excessive action, and the wish that it should cease, go together. But a wish involves a sense of choice in favour of the thing wished for; so that, even in this case, it seems to me that a sense of choice and consciousness are inextricably connected. The normal action of the heart is, in fact, involuntary and unconscious; the abnormal action is contra-voluntary and conscious. But it may be said, Take an ordinary sensation, such as a touch: surely here there is no sense of choice. If there be any truth in the view—that there is no consciousness without recognition—there *is* a sense of choice; for every recognition involves choice. So that here again, so long as the recognition is conscious and not instinctive, it will carry with it the essence of a volition, if I may so call the sense of choice.

Once more; it will be said that, on this view, any creature that possesses consciousness possesses also intelligence; and that we must therefore call the lobster an intelligent being. I have before defined what I mean by intelligence—a mental process accompanied by a sense of choice. From this definition, and what I have said in the last paragraph, it follows that the germs of consciousness are accompanied by the germs of intelligence. To my mind, there is nothing to prevent our believing that *if* the lobster possesses the germs of consciousness it also possesses the germs of intelligence. Into the mental characteristics of animals, however, I do not here enter; though I firmly believe that their actions may be divided into those which are voluntary, intelligent, and conscious, and those which are involuntary, instinctive, and unconscious.

This broad division of actions, into those which are intelligent, and those which are instinctive, is paralleled by a similar division of judgments. By judgments I here mean such mental processes as do not immediately lead to action. They arise out of that important law of our being, the suppression of action. Whenever I form an opinion on a subject, I exercise an intelligent judgment, accompanied by a distinct sense of choice. But when I recognize a white speck on the ocean horizon to be a ship, my judgment is almost if not quite instinctive. There is just so much sense of choice as there is consciousness of the process. And in the formation of judgments, as in the performance of acts, we may notice that habit constantly tends to convert those which are entirely voluntary and intelligent, into those which are more or less involuntary and instinctive.

Here, too, it may also be noticed that many of our acts and judgments have either been instinctive from the first, or have passed through the intelligent to the almost instinctive stage with extraordinary rapidity. We are not, indeed, like the newly hatched chick, able at once to perform acts which require nicely balanced muscular adjustments. But we are able, at five or six years old, to form judgments concerning the world around us, which we could never have reached by the action of our own individual unsupplemented experience in so short a time. It must, indeed, be admitted that we come into the world with ready-made aptitudes of mind. And it is through these aptitudes that we are able, in a very short time, to fill in the pictures which our sensations only give us in the roughest possible outline ; and to fill them in correctly, in more or less perfect fulfilment, as Professor Clifford pointed out, of the laws of space and motion, of things and their attributes, of uniformity, and of numbers and classes. This is an important point ; but there is no necessity for me to go over the ground covered by the lectures on the " Philosophy of the Pure Sciences." I will content myself, therefore, with adding a few words on the same subject in my own fashion.

5. *The Mental Supplement.*

" In every sensation there is, besides the actual message, something that we imagine and add to the message. And in general this filling in of experience is *right.*"—W. K. CLIFFORD.

At the beginning of the first chapter of this book I stated my belief that, when I see in the distance a white speck, and tell my companion that it is a ship, there are several tolerably distinct stages in the mental process. An impression is received from without : it is recognized as a sight sensation ; the external object is perceived to be white and distant ; and it suggests that conception which I symbolize to my neighbour by the word " ship." Now, if there is any truth in this description of what goes on in my mind—if it is anything like a true story of what actually takes place—the only thing received from without is the bare but suggestive impression. All the rest is supplied by my mind. And this mental supplement that I myself add occupies, so to speak, much more space in the mental process than the message actually received from without. The point, however, here to be noticed is that the mental supplement is not only filled in so as to fulfil all the requirements of the sciences, but is filled in more or less correctly. And both these things follow from the way in which the mental supplement has been generated. For this supplement has been formed out of previous sensations individually acquired and mentally registered, and out of long-ago sensations ancestrally acquired and physiologically trans-

mitted. It consists of individual memories of past sensations and perceptions ; the rapid acquirement and complex
grouping of these memories having been made possible by
inherited aptitudes.

Now, the general conceptions built up out of such
memories are the things with which the sciences, whether
of space, or of motion, or of numbers, or of Nature, or of
anything else, deal. And it is impossible that such memories should not participate in the laws of these sciences.
The laws of science are, in fact, laws of the mental supplement every whit as much as they are laws of the external
objects which provide the immediate impressions. Nay, we
may go further, and say that the laws of science are laws
of the mental supplement to a far greater degree than they
are laws of the immediate impressions. For science is
essentially generalized knowledge, and is therefore knowledge far removed from, and far more complex than, that
supplied by immediate impressions and their primary relations. And it is only because the mental supplement is
built up of memories of such immediate impressions and
their relations, that it is a fairly accurate representation in
consciousness of the external world. It is only if this be
so, that we may conclude from our generalizations concerning the mental supplement, the laws of the external world
as thus represented in our minds. Yes, as thus represented ;
for we must not forget that scientific doctrine is generalized
knowledge concerning the world *as we see it.* We can only
see the world as it is reflected in the mirror of consciousness. The laws of science are the laws of our cognitions
transferred to the objects of the external world which give
rise to our sensations.

It would be interesting to turn aside here, had we space,
to trace the growth of our conceptions of the external world
through the following stages :—

1. The vague sensations of the infant not yet localized.

2. Localization and extradition.

3. Hence youthful belief in the *independent* existence, in the external world, of the objects of which our ideas are faithful copies.

4. Reflection of early manhood. Especial reliance on newly acquired pówers of abstract thought and reasoning. Hence metaphysical idealistic belief.

5. Sober conceptions of manhood that the external world exists for us, and for us is practically real, as it actually appears, and that it exists we know not how for other beings totally unlike us.

6. Hypothesis of mind-stuff, held avowedly as a speculation, but a speculation based on practical analogies, and having its starting-point in experience.

The first three of these stages are, I suppose, common to most of us. The last three I merely fill in from my own experience.

The laws of science, then, being the laws of our cognitions and of our general conceptions concerning the universe in general and the world on which we live in particular, it will now, I think, be seen how it is that the mental supplement conforms to the laws of science ; and how it is that it must so conform. This conformity may, indeed, be said to be due to *instinctive science,* processes once intelligent and voluntary having become instinctive and automatic ; the intelligent processes in one generation having become instinctive in the next : for " it is the silent toil of the first generation that becomes the transmitted aptitude of the next " (Bagehot).

It only remains to notice that just as there is, in this mental supplement, abundance of submerged consciousness, so, too, there is abundance of submerged choice. And what is the nature of this choice thus preserved for us, embedded, so to speak, in the mental supplement? Is it free and indeterminate? or has it been determined by fixed and inexorable law? Does the answer that it gives favour the hypothesis of free-will, or the hypothesis of determinism? When we remember that it is not individual and special, but general and common to the race,—when we recollect that it is moulded in accordance with the reign of law (so-called) in the world of phenomena around us ; the nature of the answers to these questions can hardly be doubtful.

6. *The Test of Truth.*

"The touchstone of knowledge is prevision."—G. H. LEWES.

And now we must go on to ask what is meant by saying that the mental supplement is filled in more or less correctly. What, in other words, do we mean when we say that a perception or a conception is true? And what is the test of truth? To take the last question first (it really includes the others), it may, I think, be said that *prevision is the primary test of truth ;* that is, of course, of the truth of perceptions and conceptions which relate to the world of external objects. The fact that I feel cold is, for me, an ultimate fact, the truth of which needs and admits no test. Then, following in the same track, we may say that those perceptions are true which will, if need be, lead to *right action.* Whence it follows that, in saying that the mental supplement is filled in correctly, we must mean that it is so filled in as to enable us to guide our actions and our judgments aright.

That prevision is the test of truth, seems to be shown as well by the experience of everyday life as by the procedure of science. Suppose that I enter a friend's dining-room and see upon the mantel-piece a yellow object, which

I suppose to be an orange. How shall I test whether my supposition is correct? By touching, lifting, and perhaps smelling, the object. I say to myself, If that is an orange, it will feel thus, and smell thus. And the correctness of my prevision will show the correctness of my perception. But if I find that the object is hard, heavier than I expected, and smells slightly of paint, then I know that the object is only an imitation of· an orange in china. The incorrectness of my prevision proves the falseness of my perception. Now take a case in elementary science. I find on my shelves a bottle from which the label has gone. From the oily appearance of the liquid I judge it to be strong sulphuric acid; and I say to myself, If I am right, this liquid will burn a black stain on paper, will make the water with which I mix it hot, and will turn this other colourless liquid milky white. And here, again, the correctness of my prevision proves the correctness of my judgment. Or take the case of the discovery of Neptune by the calculations of Leverrier (simultaneous with those of Adams). When M. Galle saw the new planet in that part of the heavens to which he had been told by Leverrier to point his telescope, he proved at the same time the accuracy of the great Frenchman's prevision and the correctness of that astronomer's thought. There is no need to multiply examples. I think it will be admitted that in such matters prevision is the test of truth.

In accepting prevision as the test of truth we are following Auguste Comte. It may be worth while, however, to point out the connection between this view and that adopted by Descartes and by Spinoza. According to Descartes, clearness and distinctness is the ultimate criterion of truth; or, to state it in Descartes' own words, and in the negative form which has been adopted by Herbert Spencer, "absolute certainty arises when we judge that it

is impossible a thing can be otherwise than as we think it."
Spinoza's view is contained in the following extract, " Who
can know," he asks, "that he understands anything unless
he do first understand the thing? In other words, who
can know he is sure of anything unless he is first indeed
sure of that thing? Again, what can be found more clear
and certain than a true idea, which may be the test of
truth? Even as light makes manifest both itself and darkness, so is truth the measure of itself and of falsehood."
Now, it is clear that these two views—the inconceivableness of the negation of a fact as the test of its truth, and
the self-evidence of a fact as the test of its truth—are the
positive and negative sides of the same assertion. But how
is it that the self-evidence of a fact or the inconceivableness
of its negation comes to be the test of truth? Surely because throughout all experience, individual and ancestral,
there has been no contradiction of the fact, no negation of
its truth. Or, to put it in another way, surely it is simply
because *prevision* has been constantly verified? Self-
evidence and the inconceivableness of negation are simply
the organized outcome of experience constantly verified,
and only as such have they any value as the test of truth
for external facts.

For all practical purposes, I take it, prevision is the
most valuable test of truth. Professor Jevons, indeed,
prefers to say that agreement with fact is the sole and
sufficient test of a true hypothesis ; but as hypotheses are
for *future* guidance, this comes to much the same thing.
Practically our object is to be able to guide our actions
aright in the future. Any theory which enables us to do
this is practically a true theory; when it fails in any case,
it is not a true theory.

It may be objected, however, that prevision can only
be a test of truth for the future—it can never be applied as

a test of the truth of our knowledge of the past. I do not
think the objection a valid one ; for though we cannot
apply the test directly, we can and habitually do apply it
indirectly. Let us see how.

It is the business of science to build up a body of
doctrine concerning our conception of the universe in
general, and of this world and that which takes place
therein in particular. Such a body of doctrine, if it is to
be so compacted as to resist the solvent effects of the many
and powerful acids of criticism, must be in all its parts
rigidly subjected to the test of truth. Only on this condition can it be implicitly relied on. But when this has
been done, the scientific doctrine may be used, as a touchstone, by means of which events long ago enacted may be
brought indirectly under the test of truth. This is really
exactly what the man of common sense does. This or
that event is recorded in history. He asks himself instinctively, Is it possible ? And if he considers it impossible, or if he regards it as more probable that the
witnesses or reporters were mistaken, in their observation
or inference, than that an event contrary to the usual
course of Nature should have occurred, he quietly disbe-
lieves it ; unless he is taught to accept it on grounds other
than natural. Now, what is the meaning of his instinctive
question, Is it possible ? Surely it comes to this. In asking the question he instinctively applies the particular
instance to the touchstone of general doctrine of which he
is possessed. And the value of his answer to the question
entirely depends upon the value of his touchstone. If this
has repeatedly stood the test of truth, his answer will have
as high a value as is possible under the conditions ; for it,
too, will have been subjected indirectly to the test of truth.

Here, again, let us take an instance in science. Let us
see whether the doctrine of evolution can be submitted to

the test of truth. It deals largely with the past. It contends that the state of things inorganic and organic that prevails on this earth to-day is just the natural outcome of the state of things that prevailed yesterday, and that it will give rise in natural sequence to the state of things that will prevail to-morrow. And looking back into any particular period of the past, it maintains that the state of things during that period arose naturally out of the preceding state of things, and gave rise naturally to the condition of affairs that followed. And it further contends that, throughout this natural sequence of events, carried on without external interference, there is traceable an ever-growing complexity, and an ever-increasing mutual inter-. dependence.

Evolution in the organic world goes by the name of the theory of descent ; to account for the *modus operandi* of which, our great Darwin brought forward his theory of natural selection. "I much question," writes Professor W. K. Parker, himself no mean labourer in this field, " whether there is a single modern work of any worth on any subject whatever, on mind or matter, that is not the better for what Charles Darwin, and his helpers and interpreters, have done." It must be remembered, however, that Darwinism is not the same as evolution, but is a definite hypothesis to account for the mode of organic evolution. According to this hypothesis, there are two opposing tendencies in the organism : the tendency for the offspring to resemble the parent, and the tendency for each individual to vary. The first tendency, regarded merely as an observed fact, is obvious to all. The second is less obvious. It is due to the fact that every organism is inherently active (by which it is differentiated from the inorganic world), and contains certain springs of action in itself. Or, to put the matter in a more ultimate form, every cell (and the organism is compounded of cells) has a tendency to resemble the parent cell, of which it is merely a separated part; but it has also an innate tendency to vary, such variations being restrained and guided by surrounding conditions. Now, given these two facts of organic nature, variation and inheritance, Mr. Darwin showed that the direction of variation is guided by a natural selection analogous to man's selection in the matter of varieties of pigeons or breeds of pigs; and that this natural selection arises out of the constant struggle of organisms with each other, and with surrounding conditions; first to obtain a sufficiency of food for themselves, and secondly to avoid becoming a source of food to others. Some are weeded out by surrounding conditions—that is, by the direct action of the environment; others are weeded out by other organisms which prey upon them or successfully compete with them. In any case the weakest are those that are doomed to extinction; while the strong and the clever possess the earth. There is also a sexual selection, a competition for wives, by which the lamentably imbecile are forced to remain bachelors, so that only the better sort become fathers. Such, in brief, is Darwinism. But if Darwinism were proved false to-morrow,—which is not very likely, since it would seem to be fairly established as embodying some of the factors of evolution,—but even if it were, the doctrine of evolution would not thereby be disproved, though its position would undoubtedly be profoundly altered.

Evolution, then, deals with the *fact* of progress, and with the *nature* of progress, and leaves the *how* to her well-loved children to investigate. Now, suppose the doctrine is laid before a young student of biology. How will he test its truth? He will accept it as a provisional hypothetical principle, and proceed to the work of deduction.

He will draw conclusions from the principle, and then proceed to compare them with facts. But these deductive conclusions, what are they but *predictions* of what ought to take place if the doctrine be true? If, therefore, our young student finds that his deductions are borne out by the facts of Nature, he will maintain that his predictions have been *verified.* And he will accept the doctrine itself just so far as it has proved to be true gold by the touch-stone of the test of truth.

Let us now set down certain fairly obvious deductions from the doctrine of descent, and then note briefly how far they may be said to have been verified in particular instances.

1. There should be direct evidence of descent in animal pedigrees ; and the classification of animals should be genealogical.

2. Related animals should share their fundamental features in common ; just as the related families of men and women which form a nation have a common type of countenance.

3. Animal families should be distributed around certain centres, and hemmed in by natural barriers ; just as, for example, Polynesian tribes are found in restricted groups of islands.

4. There should be a progression of life-forms from the older to the more recent geological times ; just as in the history of England we read a progressive improvement from the earliest times to the present.

5. There should be a shading of one species into another ; just as in England there are gradations from the dustman to the duke.

6. Fossil organisms should be less specialized than modern organisms ; just as the artisan of old England was less specialized (more jack-of-all-trades) than his modern

descendant. And there should be, among these fossil organisms, intermediate forms between existing groups, possessing characteristics now more isolated ; just as the ecclesiastic of old was priest, and lawyer, and warrior.

7. The evolution of the individual should be a short summary of the evolution of the species to which he belongs ; just as the progress of the child to some extent epitomizes the progress of the human race.

8. Species which have diverged from a common ancestor should have a common embryonic condition ; just as the childhood of the bishop, the poet, the lawyer, and the man of science has many features in common.

9. In any group of animals there should be lowly forms which have remained stationary while their fellows were becoming the winners in life's race ; just as we see the poor, the weak, the unenlightened, and the unsuccessful living on beside the rich, the strong, the highly cultivated, and the successful. And these lowly forms should retain features which are embryonic in the more highly developed forms ; just as the less favoured individuals among us are apt to be childish and undeveloped.

10. Lastly, there should be, lurking in out-of-the-way corners, degenerate descendants of ancestors more noble than they, as is too often seen in human affairs ; and degenerate rudiments of structures no longer of direct use ; just as our tail-coats have two meaningless buttons behind —meaningless now, because their function is lost.

In verification of every one of these deductions there is abundant evidence. Only a few instances out of many can in each case be given. And first with regard to direct evidence of descent. Such evidence is now before the world, and, through Professor Huxley, in the hands of the general reader, with regard to the horse-type. After describing, in his "American Addresses," the steps through

R

which the highly specialized horse, with only one complete digit in the fore limb, and complex teeth, may be traced back to a more generalized ancestor, with four complete digits in the fore limb, and relatively simple teeth, Professor Huxley says, " Thus, thanks to these important researches, it has become evident that, so far as our present knowledge extends, the history of the horse-type is exactly and precisely that which could have been *predicted* from a knowledge of the principles of evolution." One more special instance may be cited. In the fresh-water chalk of Steinheim, in Würtemburg, there are found the abundant remains of a fresh-water shell, Planorbis multiformis. " In the whole series of strata," we learn, "the varieties of this shell are distributed in such a manner that individual layers are characterized as successive strata, by the exclusive occurrence or by the predominance of single or several varieties which, within the layer, remain constant or slightly variable, but towards the limits of the next layer, lead by transitions to succeeding forms. The intermediate layers furnish evidence that the other forms originated by gradual metamorphosis from the earlier ones ; they, moreover, render it possible to range form to form, and to trace the evolution backwards ; hence it becomes manifest that what above seems distinctly divided meets below. Thus arises a pedigree richly endowed with main and side branches." (Hilgendorf, quoted by Oscar Schmidt.) Such special evidence as this may be supplemented by the more general evidence of the development of the existing or recent European mammalia from those which inhabited Europe in Tertiary times; of the development of South American mammals from those found entombed in the Brazilian caves ; of the development of New Holland carnivores, the ancestors of which were similarly preserved for us in caves ; and of the development of antlered deer, so carefully worked out by Mr. Boyd Dawkins.

But our whole system of classification is based upon the relationship of animals. It is essentially a system according to which animals are thrown into families, clans, tribes, and races. The mammalia, for example, form a great race, like the Aryan race among the peoples of the earth. From this great race have sprung, by process of differentiation, many families—the ungulates, the rodents, the carnivores, and so forth ; just as from the Aryan race have sprung, among others, the Teutonic, Romanic, and Keltic families. From the Ungulates, again, have arisen two great branches, the odd-toed and the even-toed ; just as from the Teutonic family have sprung the Low Germans, the High Germans, and the Scandinavians. And from the odd-toed group have sprung the horses, the tapirs, and the rhinoceroses ; just as from the Low German stock have sprung the English, the Dutch, and the Flemish. The analogy might be carried further ; for just as the English nation is split up into clans and families, so may the horse-family be split up into genera and species. But enough has been said to show the nature of the analogy. Now, is it conceivable that this analogy is practically meaningless ? Is it likely that, being able as we are to represent the present and past species of animals that suckle their young, as the twigs that spring from the branchlets and branches of the great mammalian stem—is it likely, I say, that, such a genealogical classification being not only possible but forced upon us, the animals so classified have no genetic relationship. To the older anatomists the "natural system," which with so much pains and labour they worked out, was a mystery. But the mystery disappears in the light of the doctrine of descent.

2. That related animals share their fundamental features in common is so well-known as to need but little illustration. Throughout the vertebrata from the

amphibians to man, the limbs are built on a common plan. The wing of the bird, the paddle of the dolphin, the fore leg of the horse, the wing of the bat, the paw of the bear, and the hand of man, all show a fundamental unity of structure, modified by suppression of parts, by coalescence of parts, or by unessential changes in the form of parts. Nor is this only shown in the great backboned family. All the appendages of the crayfish or the lobster—eye-stalks, antennæ, jaws, foot-jaws, forceps, legs, swimmerets, tail-flap—all are built on a common plan, and owe their diversity to suppression, coalescence or metamorphosis. And when we come to compare the organization of closely related families, such as apes and men, we find the similarity of structure to extend to the minutiæ of muscles, nerves, and blood-vessels.

3. That animal families are distributed around certain centres, and hemmed in by natural barriers, is perhaps most clearly exemplified in the Australian region. Here we have a special area of the world's surface which is tenanted by a very special, and in most respects peculiar and lowly set of mammals, namely those known as marsupials. To this group belong the kangaroos, wombats, and opossums. Why this group and no other should occupy Australia, New Guinea, etc., where the climate is as favourable to higher forms as that of South Africa or Southern Asia, is inexplicable on any theory save that of descent. "In birds it is almost as peculiar. It has no wood-peckers and no pheasants, families which exist in every other part of the world; but instead of them it has the mound-making brush-turkeys, the honey-suckers, the cockatoos, and brush-tongued birds which are found nowhere else in the world." (Wallace.)

4. The progression of life-forms from the older to the more recent geological times becomes more and more

evident with the increase of our knowledge of fossil remains. To confine our attention to backboned creatures, the earliest group to occur in the geological series is that of the fishes : and these are the lowliest of the vertebrates. The earliest fishes, moreover, belong to the less specialized of the sub-groups of that order ; the true bony fishes, to which our highest and most' specialized forms belong, not making their appearance till the epoch of the chalk. After the fishes the amphibians are the next to put in an appearance, and of them the less differentiated forms first. Reptiles are found later, and birds later still. The early mammals do not appear till Secondary times, and then of lowly types. Not till the Tertiary period do the modern highly developed mammals make a show in the world ; and they are dis-tinctly less specialized at the beginning of that period than at its close. Last of the mammalia appears man, the heir of all the ages.

5. The shading of one species into another, and of groups of species into other groups, is seen both in existing and in fossil forms of life. It was proved for the sponges by Oscar Schmidt and by Haeckel ; it was shown in the foraminifera by Carpenter, Rupert Jones, and Parker ; it is made apparent in the cilio-flagelata by the labours of Bergh. The ammonites of the Secondary epoch exemplify it, and the planorbes before mentioned offer a striking case in point. It is more or less obvious in every group of animals ; and it would be more obvious still, were it not to the interest of the species-maker to look out rather for points of difference than for points of resemblance.

6. The more generalized character of fossil organisms, as compared with their modern representatives, has been already incidently pointed out. A few instances of inter-mediate forms, or of intercalary types as they have been termed, may now be given. The great unwieldy Laby-

rinthodonts, with amphibian skulls and the scale-armour
of a reptile, are in so far possessed of characters now
restricted to separate groups and not found combined.
The Ichthyosaurus and Plesiosaurus, with reptile heads
and fish-like vertebræ, show also an intermediate condition. In America there are fossil birds, possessing teeth,
which are intercalary between the birds and the reptiles;
as are also the huge Deinosaurians of the Secondary epoch.
The Anoplotherium tends to connect the swine on the
one hand and the ruminants on the other; and the
Palæotherium shares some of the characters of the horse,
the rhinoceros, and the tapir. Instances might be multiplied, but enough has been said. I cannot omit to mention,
however, how vividly I was impressed, as a student,
by two diagrams employed by Professor Flower in one
of his Hunterian lectures. Of these only one was visible
at first. It showed the existing mammalian families as
scattered patches, separated by wide interspaces, and at
variable distances from a common centre. On the
removal of this diagram the second was displayed. It
showed the fossil forms in addition to those now existing.
The interspaces were largely filled in : the patches were
less scattered : the existence of intercalary types was made
strikingly obvious to the eye.

7. Passing on to the next deduction, we have ample
evidence that the evolution of the individual from the egg
epitomizes the evolution of its species. Much of it, however, rests on technical grounds ; but the well-known
development of the frog is comparatively free from this
objection. The frog belongs to the highest, tail-less, group
of the amphibians. In its adult form it is a complete air-
breather, forcing air into its lungs somewhat after the same
fashion that a fish forces water through its gill-clefts. The
common eft, or newt, belongs to a lower group of the amphi-

bians, and differs from the frog in that it never loses its long tail. It too, in the adult state, is an air-breather. Lower still are certain amphibians which are tailed and, even in the adult state, possess gill-plumes, though they have also lungs. Now the tail-less amphibia are not found so early in the geological series as the tailed amphibia. And on the theory of descent, the ancestors of the frog would be tailed but would lose their gills, owing to taking more completely to aerial life and to the more perfect development of the lung, which is, however, in the amphibians, always a comparatively simple structure. The ancestors of these, if we traced them far enough back, would be fish-like creatures, an intermediate stage being an amphibian with persistent gills. And these are just the stages through which every frog passes from the egg, through the tadpole, to the adult frog. In its early stages the respiration is exclusively aquatic, the heart and circulation are distinctly fish-like ; later it becomes a four-limbed, tailed amphibian, breathing by means of gills, though lung respiration is commencing ; later still the gills are lost and the frog is remarkably eft-like. At last the tail is absorbed, and the organism becomes a veritable frog. In the higher animals, such as the mammalia, the stages of development in the embryo are necessarily much shortened or even suppressed. But every mammalian embryo has the gill-clefts to point to its remote and fishy ancestor. Man himself bears distinctly, when he is yet but a minute embryo, awkward gill scars, the unmistakable marks of the beast.

8. Closely connected with this aspect of the question, and perhaps hardly separable from it, is the obvious deduction, that species which have diverged from a common ancestor should have a common embryonic condition. We have seen that mammals have, in their embryonic state, the marks of the fish ; so have birds, reptiles, and amphibians.

Let us take a different case. The difference between a starfish, a sea-urchin, a sea-cucumber, and a feather-star is considerable. But they all belong to the same great group, and, on the theory of descent, should have a common ancestry. They should, therefore, in the larval state resemble each other much more closely than in their adult condition. And what do we find ? That the resemblance is so close that they may be said to leave the egg " in a state almost identical." So, too, crustaceans so different as the cyclops (a minute water-flea), the barnacle, and the shrimp-like penæus, all pass through a common embryonic stage, known as the nauplius stage.

9. But there are also, in each group, lowly forms which are to some extent persistent embryos. From the standpoint of the tail-less frog, the tailed newt is in some sort a persistent embryo, a poor relation who has never risen in the world to the proud estate of a fully developed frog ; and the poor Mexican devil-fish is in a yet lower condition—a permanent child, who as a rule lives his life out as a child, but may once in a way develop into something a little better ; for the axolotl occasionally loses his gills, and passes into a higher stage of amphibian life, but more usually remains as a persistent embryo, propagating his species as such. The little lancelet, or amphioxus, is the poor relation of all the vertebrates. Every vertebrate, before he gets a back-bone, passes through a stage in which the central axial support of the body is a rod of gristly nature, known as the notochord. In the little lancelet, a vertebrate only by courtesy, the notochord is persistent, and the backbone is never developed. It is a persistent vertebrate embryo, a form of life that has been content with humble circumstances, and has refused the labour of a higher culture. So, too, the peripatus, a caterpillar-like, many-legged creature, found at the Cape and elsewhere, would seem to be in

some respects a poor relation of the Arthropods (insects, crustaceans, spiders, etc.), with a very decided trace of the worm as well.

10. Finally, saddest spectacle of all, we have those organisms which have not only not progressed, but have actually degenerated. There are, for example, certain crustaceans which, having taken to parasitic habits, become mere egg-bags attached to a simple digestive apparatus. In their youth, in their nauplius stage, they gave promise of better things, but instead of bravely fighting their way through the world and becoming daily better, and braver, and stronger, and cleverer, they have been content to "sponge" upon an unwilling host, and degenerate into inert, senseless lumps. Less reprehensible, but no less remarkable, is the case of the sea-squirts, which would seem to be, if we can trust the evidence afforded by the development of one at least of the group, degenerate vertebrates, who once possessed at least one eye and a powerful tail, but instead of making the best of the opportunities thus afforded them, fix themselves to a rock or stone, clothe themselves in a leathery coat, and live a life of a strictly vegetative character. So, too, does the barnacle, or the acorn shell, give up all attempt to vie with his active and clever cousins, the crayfish and the crabs, and, fixing himself for life, spends the rest of his time in "standing upon his head and kicking food into his mouth."

Similar, and yet very different, is the degeneration of structures or organs : similar, in being so far degeneration ; very different, as being a means to higher progress. What we have here specially to note about these rudimentary structures is that they are inevitable on the theory of descent, and utterly inexplicable on any other theory. They speak plainly of less specialized ancestors, in whom these rudimentary structures were serviceable organs. As examples, one may mention the fœtal teeth of whales, teeth which never cut the gum ; the eye-stalks of blind crusta- ceans ; the functionless eyes of some amphibians and fish ; the rudimentary hind limbs in whales and pythons ; the shoulder-girdle of the slow-worm, for the support of non- existent fore legs ; and our own minute ear muscles, some of which a few of us can, by practice, bring into feeble use, while others are utterly useless.

Such, then, are some of the facts which answer to the expectations which are inevitably called up in our minds by the doctrine of descent. As before mentioned, they may be fairly regarded as *fulfilled predictions ;* and in this fulfil- ment of prediction the doctrine of descent stands justified by the test of truth.

Let it not be for one moment imagined that this is equivalent to saying that the mode of descent of modern creatures from ancient creatures is now fully explained. Fully explained ! The work done by naturalists in this field is not one thousandth, not one ten thousandth, of that which remains to be done. But, whatever the general public may think in the matter, they know they are on the right track. And they earnestly beg all those who wish to offer an opinion on the subject, first to follow Professor Huxley's advice and get a little sound, thorough, practical, elementary instruction in biology, and then, each for him- self, to submit the doctrine of descent to the test of truth.

We have now seen how the test of truth may be applied to questions in which, since they are *historical,* prevision at first sight seems inapplicable. An apparent exception to the general principle, that prevision is the test of truth, may here be brought forward as an additional example of its mode of application. It is well known that the early astronomers explained the motions of the heavenly bodies on the hypothesis of a complicated machinery of circular motions in epicycles. This hypothesis enabled them to predict the positions of the planets. Here, then, the test of prevision was applied, and led to a false conclusion. For, in the hands of Kepler, the theory of epicycles gave place to a truer view. But how? What led Kepler to believe the theory of epicycles to be false? This; that the position of Mars, calculated on this hypothesis, differed from the position observed by eight minutes. "And since," says Kepler, "the Divine goodness has given us in Tycho an observer so exact that this error of eight minutes is impossible, we must be thankful to God for this, and turn it to account. And these eight minutes will, of themselves, enable us to reconstruct the whole of Astronomy." So that it turns out, after all, that by the very test of truth, by which it had hitherto seemed to be justified, the epicycle hypothesis was proved to be false. Increased accuracy of observation showed that, on the current hypothesis, prevision *was not exact.* And the hypothesis was doomed.

Take one more instance of the failure of prevision necessitating the remodelling of an hypothesis. According to the nebular hypothesis, worked out by Laplace, the solar system has been evolved by the gradual cooling of a rotating nebula; while according to an important modification of that theory the solar system has resulted from long-continued meteoric aggregation. In favour of such an hypothesis there is much evidence. There are in the heavens nebulæ in various stages of condensation. The spectroscope has shown that the elements in the sun are chemical elements with which we are acquainted on the earth. The orbits of the planets do not differ very widely from a series of concentric circles. These orbits lie approximately in the same plane, the plane of the sun's equator. The direction of revolution round the sun is the same in the case of all the planets and is the same as that of the rotation of the sun. The form of the planets is that which should be assumed by rotating bodies which had gradually cooled from a gaseous to a liquid or a solid condition. And in the satellites we have secondary systems which reproduce in miniature the primary system. All this was true of the solar system as it was known in Laplace's day; and is equally true to-day. But now we come to a point of difference. In the solar system as known to Laplace, the direction of rotation of each planet, and that of the revolution of the satellites round their planets, was the same. All were direct; there was no single instance of retrograde motion. And Laplace calculated that the chances were tens of thousands to one that, if a new planet or satellite was discovered, the revolution of the satellite and the rotation of the planet would be direct. That was his prevision. Has it been verified? No. "In the secondary worlds of the two planets furthest off—those of Uranus and Neptune—the rotations and revolutions of the satellites are in the opposite direction, that is to say, retrograde."

Thus the nebular hypothesis in its old form has not stood the test of truth. But it has quite recently been shown by M. Faye that this difference of direction of rotation does but tell us an additional fact with regard to the manner of condensation of the primitive nebulous mass. Those planets which separated off from the parent nebula *before* the formation of the central sun, would, on mathematical and physical principles, have a direct rotation, and their satellites a direct revolution; but those planets which separated off from the parent nebula *after* the formation of the central sun, would, on the same principles, have a retrograde rotation, and their satellites a retrograde revolution. This well illustrates how valuable are unexpected anomalies for further advance in science.

The hypothesis in its old form was proved incorrect by the application of the test of truth. It was not in harmony with the environment of fact; but in its new form, as modified in this respect by M. Faye, it would seem to be more stable than ever. Further researches may lead to further modifications, but in its main outlines the hypothesis stands the test of truth.

To the instances above given many more might without difficulty be added. All would, I think, show, as these show, that prevision is the test of truth; and all would, I think, show, too, by implication, that the mental supplement, involving many complex inferences suggested by messages received from without, is always filled in more or less correctly; that is, it is so filled in as to enable us to guide our actions and our judgments aright.

And how is it that the mental supplement has come, not indeed in matters far removed from the ordinary affairs of life, but in matters of everyday experience, to be filled in so correctly? I know not how the advocate of another theory will answer that question, whether by an appeal to direct intervention, to pre-established harmony, or how. But to the believer in evolution the answer is obvious. It is because those individuals, in whom the supplement has been so filled in as to enable them to guide their actions aright, have survived; while those in whom the supplement was incorrect have succumbed. Whatever may be said for a freedom of choice between truth and error in the individual; in the race, so far as matters of practical importance is concerned, truth is forced upon us, and determined by inexorable law.

CHAPTER II.

FEELING.

"After all has been said that can be said about the widening influence of ideas, it remains true that they would hardly be such strong agents unless they were taken in a solvent of feeling."—GEORGE ELIOT.

BROADLY speaking mental operations fall under two heads, *knowing* and *feeling*. To the former we devoted some attention in the opening chapter of this work. We there saw that for each of us the world is built up of general conceptions, which result from the combining and recombining of sensations, and their relations, into more and more intricate relations. But the matter does not end there; for, in the first place, as we saw in the last chapter, these general conceptions give rise to action; and in the second place, they carry with them feelings. Accompanying nearly all, if not all, our perceptions there is a feeling of pleasure or pain. Accompanying most of our general conceptions there are or may be complex emotional states. Each co-ordinated group of sensations has, indeed, two aspects—the aspect under which we recognize the group of sensations as giving rise to knowledge, and the aspect under which we regard it as something felt. The two are quite different, but they have a common origin; for cognitions and emotions are both built up upon the common basis of sensation. In the one case "we are occupied with the relations that subsist among our feelings"; in the other case, "we are occupied with the sentient states themselves" (H. Spencer). The meaning here attached to the word *feeling* will now be clear. Feelings are those states of consciousness arising out of sensation into which are inwoven the emotional elements pleasure and pain. In knowledge as such these emotional elements are disregarded. Let us take one or two examples which may illustrate this double aspect of mental operations.

Walking along the high road I suddenly feel a sharp blow on my wrist, and at the same time a stone falls to the ground. Knowing well that stones do not of themselves jump up and wound honest folk, I push my way through the hedge, and see a small boy making vigorous use of his legs. I give chase, catch, and chastise the urchin. Then, as I return to the high road I am conscious of the numb pain in my bruised wrist.

Thus, in this instance, one impression from without gives rise to two inner processes—first, to cognitions, localizing the spot struck by the stone, and tracing how and whence it came; secondly, to feelings entirely personal and not connected, as such, in any way with cognitions. I say, not connected *as such*, for the localization of the pain comes under the head of cognitions. It is to be observed, too, that so long as I occupy myself with the cognitions and the actions which arise from them, I am unconscious of the feeling of pain. Cognition and feeling, in fact, tend to exclude each other; and I suppose that there are few who have not experienced pain so acute as to paralyse the power of thinking: while the opposite experience is equally common, that active thought numbs—makes us forget, as we say—some forms of pain, especially such as are rather dull than acute.

The sight of a distant landscape, again, gives rise both to cognitions and emotions—cognitions, as we trace the relations of the observed objects to each other and to similar objects, differently grouped, in other remembered scenes; emotions, as we abandon ourselves to a calm receptivity, in what Wordsworth has called "the hour of feeling," when

"Thought is not; in enjoyment it expires."

Kingsley saw this when he put into the mouth of Alton Locke, "Indeed, the whole scene was so novel to me, that I had no time to analyse; I could only enjoy." And many of us, no doubt, have cause to remember how completely an argumentative friend, or a plain, matter-of-fact companion who inquires the name of each church-spire and each farm-stead, can break the enchantment of the most lovely scene. But a small thing is needed to dissolve the charm of the grandest panorama. Some years ago I had ascended the Corcovado to see the sun rise over the Bay of Rio. The scene was of the grandest: the calm bay with its narrow entrance, and the green islands on its broad expanse; the level sea on the one hand, and the peaks of the Organ mountains on the other; all around the vegetation of the tropics. I was fairly lost in admiration. But a rude gust of wind lifted my broad-brimmed hat from my head and bore it gently towards the Avenue of Palms, far below me. At once cognitions took the place of emotions. I thought of the hot sun, the long walk, and a ridiculous figure in a knotted handkerchief-cap passing along the streets of Rio. The question, How shall I get down without some risk of a sun-stroke? pressed for an answer. Disgusted, I turned away; nor could I again lose myself in enthusiasm. The view was the same; but matter-of-fact cognitions usurped the place of the higher emotions.

That the full play of the emotions cannot be enjoyed until the labour of cognition is overcome seems to me an everyday experience. Why is it that the well-thumbed page of our favourite poet gives us to-day a hundredfold the pleasure that it did on first acquaintance? Why is it that it is impossible to enjoy Chaucer until one has been at some pains to render his style and his quaint language familiar? Why is it that the best songs "grow upon us," and that we hear the same oratorio or opera with ever-increasing pleasure? Is it not that the labour of knowing is overcome, and that we are reaping the rich harvest of feeling? Every day we hear common-place folk wonder what pleasure this or that acquaintance of theirs can get out of the dry science, or the musty volumes, to which he for ever devotes himself. But they who have not sowed in knowledge cannot reap in feeling; and so long as they are ignorant, so long will they wonder. The heart of the ice-world must be toilfully gained, before glacier and snow-peak can stir the soul with emotions. Knowledge must be painfully acquired before the panorama which knowledge opens to our view can appeal to our inmost feelings. The schoolboy who drearily prepares the, to him, dry page of Virgil, does not know that he is laying the foundations of part of the pleasure of his after life. But it is true nevertheless, though, like some older folk, he cannot yet see that in the end duty is in the long run very often the highest self-interest.

The sensations, then, are the starting-points of the cognitions on the one hand, and of the emotions on the other. Sometimes the one, sometimes the other predominate. In certain individuals the one, and in other individuals the other, have a tendency to come uppermost in the mind. And in the same individual there are periods of cognition and periods of feeling.

The first and broadest division of these feelings is into those which are pleasurable, those which are painful, and those which are indifferent. It may be, indeed, as many

S

contend, that there is no feeling, properly so called, which gives neither pleasure nor pain. Certain sensations there are, no doubt, it may be said, which seem to give rise neither to pleasure nor pain. But this is either when such sensations are regarded merely as the bases of cognitions, or when, by rapid alternation, pleasure and pain tend to neutralize each other in feeling. If this be so we must speak of the pleasurable, the painful, and the apparently indifferent. However this may be, nothing can be clearer than that the same sensation may be accompanied either by a feeling of pleasure or by one of pain ; and that a feeling of pleasure may shade almost insensibly into one of pain. Coming in from a brisk walk, I feel hungry; and this healthy feeling of incipient hunger is decidedly pleasurable. But if I am kept waiting a couple of hours for my dinner, the pleasure will have given place to its opposite. Vigorous exercise gives pleasure ; but if the exercise be too severe or too prolonged, it ceases to give pleasure, and ere long gives, if not pain, at least that discomfort which is mild and diffused pain. To those who have active brains, brainwork gives keen pleasure ; but this changes into pain if the brain be over-taxed. Once again, and more generally, if body and mind be well exercised, but not over exercised, that diffused and massive pleasure we call happiness results ; if not, the reverse. To which examples many more might be added ; but these will, I think, be enough to show that pleasure accompanies the *healthy* and *normal* exercise of the bodily functions and mental faculties, while pain results from such exercise of them as is not healthy and normal.

A word or two of qualification, however, is necessary here ; for there are considerable limits within which the bodily functions and mental faculties may be healthily and normally exercised. Beneath and above these limits positive pain may result, or at least extreme discomfort; between these limits we experience happiness or unhappiness, enjoyment or weariness, with the continued rise and fall of our life-tide. For, as Spinoza says, "we live in perpetual mutation, and are called happy or unhappy according as we change for the better or the worse." This constant mutation is a necessary condition of conscious life. And since, within the required limits, there cannot be a constant rise, a life of continuous happiness, unalloyed by unhappiness, is impossible. Happiness cannot exist without its correlative unhappiness. A dead level of happiness would not be happiness but unconsciousness, since change is the condition of both consciousness and happiness. And when we consider how closely connected are, on the one hand, happiness and good, and, on the other hand, misery and evil, we shall, perhaps, be ready to admit that good cannot exist without its correlative evil, and thus shall perceive the germs of a sufficiently satisfactory solution of the world-old question concerning the existence of evil.

There can be no doubt, as Mr. Darwin clearly shows, that the satisfaction of any instinctive emotion carries with it a subdued form of pleasure, while, on the other hand, if those instinctive emotions be not satisfied, there results a still more marked feeling of uneasiness, which is a subdued form of pain. This is quite in harmony with the conclusion just reached. And it is an important conclusion. Constituted as we are, we consciously and unconsciously seek pleasure in our actions. And if this conclusion be a true one, in seeking pleasure we are gaining health. Pleasure, therefore, as a motive for action, is an important factor in the evolution of a healthy race. And how pleasure has thus come to be associated with healthy action is not difficult to see on the hypothesis of evolution. They in whom pleasure was, and is, joined with abnormal action and "excess," are led on to their own destruction; while they in whom pleasure was, and is, wedded to health are preserved in the struggle for existence. Many there are now, alas, in whom pleasure is not associated with the most healthy personal and moral action; they are like the herd of swine running down a steep place into the sea; they must assuredly be choked in the waters of ignorance and vice.

It must not be forgotten that, according to the view here adopted, all our instincts and all the more permanent traits of human character have been formed under the guidance of natural, individual, and social selection; such habits as were for the good of the species crystallizing, or rather organizing, into instincts or permanent traits of character; such as were detrimental quietly dying out. Or, again, we may say that these instincts and traits of character have been formed under the more general influence of the uniformity of Nature. Let me not be misunderstood here. The *conception* of the uniformity of Nature is one of late development; but the *influence* of the uniformity of Nature is dominant in every mental as it is in every physical process, mind being throughout its development moulded in conformity with an orderly external sequence of events. And in this moulding process, at all events in its later phases, the feelings have been largely called into play; for pleasure and pain are the normal incentives to action. And the whole complex process of evolution has been accompanied by the association of pleasure with such actions as tended to the preservation of the individual and the race, and the association of pain with such actions as were harmful to the individual or the race. It is only in this way that evolution could be furthered by individual action. Without the association of pleasure with right action, and of pain with wrong action, the natural selection of conscious creatures would be impossible. There is a natural selection of *structures*, and a natural selection of *actions*. The two must proceed in harmony ; and they must be studied side by side. Every structure is, or has been, *of use*. It has been developed for the furtherance of right action. But right action, if it is to be persisted in by a conscious creature, must be associated directly or indirectly with pleasurable feelings ; nay, more, if it is to be persistently persevered in, its non-performance must be associated with that dull form of pain which we call dissatisfaction. Only under these conditions can that form of conduct which tends to the survival of the individual and the race, be evolved. The principle of greatest happiness has its roots firmly embedded in the evolution of conduct throughout the whole realm of conscious existence.

The first division of feelings is thus into those which are pleasurable, on the one hand ; those which are painful, on the other ; and those which are intermediate or indifferent. So far there is no difficulty ; but this carries us a very little way. And when we go further we find, in grouping these emotions, more difficulties in our way than we encounter in classifying our cognitions. Still, we shall, I think, find it advisable to follow a somewhat similar kind of grouping. In the first place, then, we may set down the simple pleasure or pain accompanying a simple sensation. Of this the pleasure produced by a sweet smell may be taken as an example, so far as an example of so simple a process can be found in that most complex product of evolution, a human consciousness. Secondly, we may take those more complex feelings, answering to perceptions among cognitions, where a simple sensation calls up, by association, a number of feelings consolidated into an emotion. Instance the feelings experienced by some people on sight of a toad. In a third class we may place those feelings which are not directly suggested as in the last case, but are indirectly suggested by words or come into the mind during a train of thought. They answer to general conceptions among cognitions ; for just as the word *ship*, for example, will suggest a general conception which is less vivid than the actual sight of a vessel, so will the word *love* suggest to the maiden's heart an emotion which is only less vivid than the actual sight of the favoured individual. Fourthly, we may set down those higher and still more complex emotions that are abstract in their nature, such as the love of truth or of justice.

Let us note clearly the difference between these four classes. In the first class, the pleasure or pain accompanies or forms part of the sensation received : there is nothing further in the way of feeling suggested to the mind. In the second class, one of a group of feelings suggests the other feelings which normally go with it to make up the group, and which become with it consolidated into an emotion. In the third class, an arbitrary sign suggests a concrete group of feelings, no one of which is actually presented to the mind in sensation. In the fourth class, an arbitrary sign suggests an abstract group of feelings, an emotion called forth in favour of or against a *quality*, abstracted from the things of which it is a quality.

Taking, therefore, sensations as a starting-point, we may regard them as two-sided. On the one hand, they give us information ; on the other, they give us pleasure or pain. From each side there grow out branches. From the first are developed the directly suggested perceptions, the indirectly suggested conceptions, and abstract ideas ; from the second are developed the directly suggested emotions, the indirectly suggested emotions, and abstract emotions. But the cognitions always have also an emotional aspect, and the emotions may carry with them knowledge. The two can indeed no more be separated than the inner and outer aspect of a curve.

It must, however, be remembered that "throughout the whole range of sensations, perceptions, and emotions which we do not class as *æsthetic*, the states of consciousness serve simply as aids and stimuli to guidance and action. They are transitory, or if they persist in consciousness some time, they do not monopolize the attention ; that which monopolizes the attention is something ulterior, to the effecting of which they are instrumental. But in the states of mind we class as æsthetic the opposite attitude is maintained towards the sensations, perceptions, and emotions. These are no longer links in the chain of states which prompt and guide conduct. Instead of being allowed to disappear with merely passing recognition, they are kept in consciousness and dwelt upon, their natures being such that their continued presence in consciousness is agreeable " (Herbert Spencer).

Let us here note how this arises out of that fundamental law of our being, and not only of our being but of our well-being, the suppression of action. Not only knowledge but æsthetics, not only our love of the true but our love of the beautiful, is fostered by self-restraint. The action which is the normal consequent on sensation is postponed or suppressed ; and thus we are enabled to make knowledge, or beauty, an end to be sought for its own sake ; and thus, too, we are able to make progress, otherwise impossible, in science and in art. Sensations are the roots from which spring the sturdy trunk of action, the expanded leaves of knowledge, and the fair blossoms of art. The leaves and the flowers are the terminal products along certain lines of development ; but the function of the leaves is to minister to the growth of the wood, and the function of the flowers is to minister to the continuance and well-being of the race. So, too, in human affairs. Knowledge and art are justified by their influence on conduct; truth and beauty must ever guide us towards right-living; and æsthetics are true or false according as they lead towards a higher or a lower standard of moral life.

Passing by this question of æsthetics, however, as a side issue, it may now be pointed out that, with regard to our emotions, the view here adopted is that they have been unfolded by a continuous growth, and have been evolved· by successive complications; that just as all the higher cognitions have been evolved from sensations entering into relations, so have all the higher emotions been evolved from the same sensations, regarded in the light of pleasures and pains; which pleasures and pains, in their simplest conceivable form, may therefore be regarded as the emotional elements.

No attempt is here made to treat of the emotions systematically. My object is merely to consider of what nature are the contents of my mind, especially in their bearing on conduct, and to point out how, according to my belief, they have come to be as they are. I shall content myself, therefore, with taking one or two emotional states which have suggested themselves to me as somewhat typical, and with indicating, in barest outline, how they may have arisen. But before I do this I wish to indicate yet another point of view, from which the emotions may be regarded so as to suggest useful and instructive lines of thought.

The pleasures and pains of a little child are, I think, entirely personal. The little self is the sole emotional centre; but with increasing years, or rather, I should say increasing months, there arises the first germ of sympathy.

The sorrow or pain of the mother touches the little heart with a vague or dim reflection of that pain or sorrow ; and gradually this sympathy widens, embracing father, sisters, brothers, and, perhaps even earlier, the four-footed playmates. For some time, however, the home, with its immediate surroundings and branches, forms the utmost extent of the widened sphere of the emotions. There is as yet no room in the heart for more extended sympathies. But ere long the time comes when the school, the parish or town, and eventually the fatherland, come in for their share of awakened emotions ; *esprit de corps* and patriotism have their birth. Here the development often ceases ; sometimes even before this point is reached. It is only the few whose real sympathies extend to the universal brotherhood of man, and eventually to everything that hath breath ; who have risen to a sympathy that is universal.

It has before been pointed out that practically the chief end of sensation is action. The point must here be further insisted on and developed. And this in especial must be noticed, that as long as self is the sole emotional centre, so long will the actions which personal pleasures and pains call forth be entirely self-interested. The little child is, to use the modern expression, a thorough-going egoist. But as soon as a widened sympathy has arisen, conduct which is purely self-centred will give place to conduct which is more or less sympathetic. And when a yet wider sympathy is reached, self-regarding and sympathetic actions will pass into those which are moral— moral, that is, if I may define the moral action as that which is done consciously for the universal good. This morality casts out selfishness. But though it is thus the very antithesis of selfishness, it is at the same time in most cases the highest self-interest. I say in most cases because it is only so long as such morality is reciprocal that

this is so.   In a truth-loving community, it is not only my
highest duty but to my own self-interest to speak the
truth ; but in a nation of liars and sharpers, though it
would still be my duty morally, it would not be to my
self-interest.   It is to my advantage to be as moral as my
neighbours ; it is not to my self-interest to be more moral
than they.   There seems to be a bitter cynicism in this
fact, but it is true ; and the finger of history points grimly
to the sufferings of moral reformers.   This other fact, however, is equally true, that it is to *our* self-interest (as a
nation) to cultivate individually perfect morality ; that
national morality and national well-being go hand in hand.
Shall we not all, then, do our best ?

One more point is closely connected with this widening
of the sympathies.   It involves, and is perhaps invariably
accompanied by, an extension of the reasoning powers.
So long as the gratification of pleasure or the avoidance
of pain is immediate, there is no need for much knowledge
or the rational application of it.   There is more need for
the application of such knowledge, when the personal
gratification is not *immediate* but needs *intermediate* steps.
Still greater is the need for reason when the pleasure
aimed at is not personal but sympathetic ; and the widest,
not necessarily the deepest, but the widest and most comprehensive, grasp of the intellectual powers is required
when the action performed is a consciously moral one, in
the sense above defined—that is, one performed, not for
personal pleasure, not for the sake of those near and dear
to us, but for the bettering of humanity.

In what has gone before the word sympathy may,
perhaps, have been used in a more extended sense
than usual.   Mr. Darwin, for example, writes : " The all-
important emotion of sympathy is distinct from that of
love.   A mother may passionately love her sleeping and

passive infant, but she can hardly be said to feel sympathy for it." I should, however, class this love as a sympathetic emotion ; and I must, therefore, define more definitely what I mean by this word sympathetic. I cannot do so better perhaps than by connecting these sympathetic emotions with personal ejects. I have already drawn attention to the distinction between objects and ejects. My neighbour's mind, feelings, emotions are ejects to me ; they can never be objects. Now, all my emotions which cluster, not only around my own mind and feelings, but round the ejected minds, feelings, and emotions of those who live with me, I call here sympathetic.

Sympathy in this sense is more wide-spread than would at first sight appear. Even the individual study of inanimate objects is influenced by it. "If a scientific man looks at the stars, and considers their motions, it seems to him as if he is in the presence of an intelligence and is talking to somebody, and it is the thought of Plato, and of Aristotle, and of Hipparchus, and of Ptolemy, and subsequent astronomers which is bound up in his notion of the heavens, so that all these great men seem to be actually talking to him whenever he looks at the stars. In the same way, too, the poet, when he looks round upon a beautiful scene in Nature, feels as if he were looking upon the face of a friend. All the sensations of beauty that have been in the minds of previous poets are embedded in language in the general conception by means of which he thinks of this scene, and it is they who are looking out with their dead eyes upon the scene which he sees around him " (Clifford). Here, then, sympathy comes in ; for the scientific man and the artist are influenced not only by the inanimate objects, but by the mind-play of generations of their predecessors. Here we have the generalized sympathetic influence of what may be called the social mind. In other cases we may have the special influence of an individual mind. When, for example, a congenial friend is by my side, my pleasure in the woods and flowers is largely increased. And why? Because I know he too feels a pleasure, a delight like my own. Here, then, individual sympathy comes in. My emotion becomes partly sympathetic, because I am not only dealing with inanimate objects, but with a mind and feeling with which I have a fellow-feeling. And I should class the love of a mother for her sleeping infant as a sympathetic emotion, because it deals not only with the object but with the life and feelings of her babe. Nay, more, I should consider such love as typically sympathetic, because as she gazes on her sleeping child all self is for the moment merged in her little other-self.

Let us now proceed to consider briefly some concrete examples which may illustrate some of the foregoing remarks. And first, let us take that which ordinarily goes by the name of *appetite*. This is an apparently continuous sensation which is directly accompanied by a feeling of pleasure or, if the appetite passes into pressing hunger, by one of pain. It is also entirely personal. But this sensation gives rise also to cognitions, tells us an important fact that the system is in want of nourishment, and suggests the somewhat complicated actions involved in the process of taking food. Here, again, we have a simple example of a sensation, which gives rise both to feeling and know-ledge, and also prompts to action, the feeling suggesting and the knowledge directing.

This, like the analogous feelings of cold and of fatigue, would be called, in ordinary speech, a sensation. The feeling of terror, on the other hand, would be called an emotion. Terror is, indeed, a *consolidated group of feelings* called into being by some perception such as, for example, the sight of a snow avalanche which may overwhelm us. The essence of the feeling is helplessness and inability to escape ; its physical accompaniment is the cessation of the normal contraction of the muscles and the stoppage of the vital functions. It is entirely personal. What, then, is this feeling or emotion of terror? It is a mental anticipation of those feelings which will, not improbably, be ere long occasioned by that which inspires the terror. It is, indeed, an actual experience of those feelings in a subdued form. The same is true of other emotions of like kind, such as that of anger, which is an anticipation of those feelings which may ere long accompany the carrying of the anger into action. For passion in this sense is action barely suppressed. And so we see that the man who is fairly overcome by this emotion knits his brow, clenches his teeth, doubles his fist, or carries his hand to his sword hilt, breathes hard, and assumes a defiant attitude—all this, though he may be fifty miles away from the man whose insults have called up this paroxysm of emotion. And it would seem that such an emotion may have arisen somewhat in this way. In our savage and pre-human ancestors sensation was promptly followed by action. Certain sensations, for example, were followed by fighting with all its concomitant feelings. As we have advanced, however, from the savage state the interval between sensation and action has become greater ; and now the sensation is not followed by action fully carried out. But it is still followed by nascent action carrying with it the appropriate group of feelings in the form of an emotion.

We may here, perhaps, with advantage revert for a moment to that *determination* or *wish* which, as we have seen, forms part of an ordinary act of volition so called. A determination is an anticipation of the feelings which normally accompany the action which we are determined to carry out.   A wish is an anticipation of the feelings which normally accompany the gratification of the wish.   If I determine to stretch out my hand, the action determined on at once becomes nascent, and carries with it the appropriate group of feelings, or rather, *is itself the nascent action and accompanying feelings.*   So, too, if I wish to eat, that wish is a subdued experience of the feelings which accompany eating ; and if my wish is strong, my mouth may water for the good things imagined.

Both in these cases, however, and in that of anger, and other like emotions, the group of feelings is highly generalized.   An emotion, like a generic idea, resembles a composite photograph of several individuals, in which the corresponding features, being often repeated, strengthen each other, while the unlike features tend to neutralize each other ; so that the final portrait exactly resembles no one individual but somewhat resembles all.   So is it with these emotions.   They are generalized groups of feeling. Each emotion, such as terror, anger, desire, hope, is generalized from the feelings accompanying a number of more or less similar actions, so that the emotion itself exactly resembles no one of these groups of feelings but somewhat resembles all.   There is, indeed, much to be said for the view that pleasure and its opposite, as *we* feel them, are the most highly generalized of all our emotions.   But as the emotion becomes more and more generic it becomes more and more consolidated and more and more separate ; so that when this has been carried far the emotion stands out clearly as a distinct and individual mental state.   It becomes somewhat abstracted from the determining sensations, and becomes, too, quite separate and clearly distinct from any one set of actions, though it is in itself nascent action.   And this has given rise to the idea, commonly entertained by those who have not considered these questions, that an emotion is a simple and undecomposable element of the mind, the dissociation point of which cannot be attained by any amount of mental fervour. If there be any truth in what has gone before, this is an altogether erroneous view, the emotions being highly complex in their character.

If now we pass from such emotions as those we have hitherto glanced at, to such an one as *hate*, we find this difference,—that we are no longer dealing with those which are personal only, but have reached one which is also sympathetic. In this, as in so many cases, it is well to take together opposites. With *hate*, then, we must take *love;* and the sympathetic nature of the emotion at once becomes obvious. For love is proverbially unselfish. What can be more absolutely unselfish, for example, than the love of a mother for her child? She is ready to undergo any amount of personal pain for the love she bears her child. Not because it is right that she should do so, but simply because she loves him. Love is therefore a sympathetic emotion. Of this love, hate is the antithesis. It is not unsympathetic; it is anti-sympathetic. The man who loves a friend rejoices in his joys, and sorrows with his sorrow. The man who hates a neighbour is miserable at his joys, and is heartily glad at his sorrows; grieves at his success, and rejoices over his failures. This also, then, must be placed· in the sympathetic class. And how, we may now ask, may these sympathetic emotions have originated? From what may they have sprung? There can be little doubt, I think, that they have sprung from personal emotions; in other words, that they were originally selfish in their nature. First, we may notice how much more selfish hate now is than love. If we hate a man he has, in nine cases out of ten, given us some personal cause for that feeling, and in the tenth case the hate generally arises indirectly out of love. Some one we love has been injured, and we hate the injurer. In fact, disinterested hate (unless its origin be moral) would seem as worthy of condemnation as disinterested love is worthy of commendation. For love is very often disinterested, purely sympathetic, entirely unselfish, as the mother's love for her child. And yet, at any rate in the mammalia, it is easy to see how even this, now utterly unselfish, emotion may have arisen out of feelings of personal pleasure. It is indeed difficult to say how early in the scale of development personal emotions, connected merely with objects as such, gave place to sympathetic emotions, dealing with objects endowed with *feelings ;* very early in the evolution of the mammalia, as I imagine. However this may be, the contented purr of a cat seems to show that, in suckling her kittens, she is gaining a proportional amount of pleasure. And puppies come in for more than their usual share of caresses and licking, expressive of maternal love, during their frequent meals. This, then, and the pairing love, both of them in the first instance selfish in their nature, may have been the source from which has sprung that disinterested and sympathetic emotion, so much higher and nobler as to be worthy of a separate name, could a sweeter word than love be found. And we must not forget that, if there be any truth in evolution, children who have had the advantage of loving protection during their tender years would be more likely to survive than those who had not this advantage ; that they, therefore, would be the ones to perpetuate the race, and to transmit an increasing emotion of love ; and that the emotion thus transmitted and becoming more grafted in the nature, would partake more and more of an instinctive, and hence unselfish, character.

So far we have only considered love or hate as applying

to individuals. But when there come to exist together a group of individuals having close bonds of blood-relationship, there come into play emotions which have for their object the family or group as a whole. When the proud father hears that his son has done a scoundrel's deed, he grieves for his boy, but he grieves still more at the shame of the family honour dragged in the mire. Mrs. Poyser felt more keenly the disgrace to her house than the misery of Hetty Sorrel. On the other hand, the justifiable pride in the lustre thrown on the family name, has softened the grief of many a mother for her son, slain in rescuing a comrade on the field of battle. And many a man has been helped to do the right, and shun the wrong, by the love he bears to his father's untarnished name.

Other groups beside the family call forth their appropriate emotions. Among these in especial the school, the college, the town, the fatherland. Listen to the schoolboy speaking of what "one of our men" has done on the river, in the cricket-field, or elsewhere; hear the tone in which the 'Varsity man claims some one of the leaders of English thought as a Magdalen man, or a Fellow of Trinity; notice the look of a Lancaster man, when Dr. Whewell, or Professor Owen is mentioned, and he claims them as his fellow-townsmen; or once more, listen to any weather-beaten old sailor, as he speaks to a chosen few upon what England has done and could do again at a pinch. Do they not all tell the same tale—that with these several groups there are bound up very definite and heart-stirring emotions?

These emotions, which take their origin in the family, school, college, town, fatherland, are, it must be noticed, generalized sympathetic emotions. They are sympathetic, because they cluster round ejects, and are not only called into play by objects. They are generalized because they

deal not only with single ejects, but with a group of ejects regarded as an unit. Their importance, however, is very great. For they lie at the foundation of all social action, all comradeship, all band-work. Without them, in fact, a *moral* being could not have been evolved.

Let us, in conclusion, consider one of these feelings, *patriotism*, a little more fully. I have often heard it said, that this is an emotion which cannot be accounted for, which is directly God-given, mysterious, like the love of a mother for her child. A hint has been already given as to how this last emotion may have arisen; and it seems to me that, on the evolution hypothesis, patriotism may just as readily be accounted for; nay, it seems that the general absence of all patriotic feelings in any leading nation would be surprising to a degree. For how have nationalities come into existence, and how have they become predominant? The evolutionist will probably answer, that just as, in the animal world, war is the great fact, and the survivors are they who have conquered, so too, in the world of tribes, war has been the great fact, and the survivors are they who have conquered; that as evolution progresses, the struggle for existence tends to cease among the members of a group, which then unite to struggle for the existence of the group as a whole; that, during this process, tribes have combined with tribes for mutual defence or united aggression, and out of combined tribes have eventually grown nationalities, which have kept up the fierce struggle for existence; that when families united with other like groups into tribes, the individuals widened the sphere of their emotions, and felt that pride in the tribe which had previously been restricted to the family. And in the prolonged life and death struggle, we may ask, which tribe is likely to prevail; that in which the members are knit together in strong bonds of love for, and pride in, their tribe, or that in which the members are indifferent to the tribal welfare? And when the tribes have united into nationalities, which nation will rise to a proud position of pre-eminence; that, the members of which are united each to each against all enemies by a burning feeling of patriotism, or that, the members of which care little for their country's honour? There can surely be no doubt about the answers to these questions? It is surely self-evident that the noble feeling of patriotism has been one of the traits, the possession of which has enabled a nation to prevail, just as power in fight and speed in flight have enabled certain animals to survive. And if we wonder at the existence of patriotism in civilized peoples, we must wonder at the claws and teeth of the lion, and the agility of the African antelope.

There can, however, be little doubt that there is some truth in the oft-repeated saying, that English patriotism is, at any rate in some quarters, on the wane; that there is even growing up in some centres a bias of anti-patriotism. This would seem to be due to two opposite tendencies; the tendency of some, on the one hand, to restrict the sympathies to the narrowed sphere of party; the tendency of others, on the other hand, to extend the range of the sympathies beyond the limits of our island and its dependencies. For we must remember that the units which compose the social organism are distinct; that they are to some extent independent, and to that extent capable of individual evolution. During the quiescence of the organism as a whole, therefore, that is during times of peace, the units undergo differentiation. Here is a group in which the sympathies are narrowed down to this or that theological party, political faction, or social clique. There is a group in which the sympathies are so inverted that rabbits and monkeys are reckoned before suffering humanity.

Here again is a group who weep for the benighted South Sea Islanders, but are deaf to the cry of distress in their own parish. And there, once more, is a group whose sympathies embrace all men, and all in something like their due degrees. Such differentiations go on within the social organism during peace, the period of quiescence. But when war comes, and the organism as a whole has to struggle for very existence, then factions tend to cease, and the units tend to co-operate for a common end, the safety of the fatherland. Then that struggle which was going on among the factors subsides, and all unite for the common good. The tendency towards disintegration in the social organism ceases, and is replaced by the integrating bonds of patriotism.

But, it may be said, there is a higher integration than this. And those whose sympathies embrace all men, who maintain that universalism is higher than patriotism, look forward to that higher integration. Even so. It is an ideal to be steadily kept in view. The seed sown by Christ nearly nineteen hundred years ago is bearing fruit in our own time ; and never has a deep feeling with and for the universal brotherhood of man been so general as it is now. That it will continue to spread and to strike its roots deeper into "the general heart of man," we may be sure. But we may be equally sure that, as the world is now, it will be checked from time to time by war, and that at these times patriotism will resume some of its old force. How the balance is to be kept between the integrating bonds of universalism and the isolating claims of patriotism, is a question to be solved by the evolution of the future.

NOTE.—I remind the reader that no attempt has been made to analyze a single emotion. From my point of view, an adequate analysis of love in my breast would involve nothing less than an adequate analysis of my whole character.

CHAPTER III.

CONDUCT.

"The end of our study is not knowledge but conduct."—ARISTOTLE.

I. *Conduct and Determinism.*

"Necessity simply says that whatever is is, and will vary with the varying conditions. Fatalism says that something must be ; and this something cannot be modified by modification of the conditions."—G. H. LEWES.

WE have already seen, in the chapter on *Choice*, that intelligence involves delay ; that the intelligent act is one performed with a sense of choice ; and that this sense of choice is generated by the mental hesitation, due to the equilibrium of motives. And we have also seen, in the chapter on *Feeling*, how large a part the emotions play as incentives to action. We must now, fusing these results together, notice that the conscious determination of conduct is, in all cases, partly emotional and partly rational. Emotional, inasmuch as it is our object to embrace pleasure and shun its opposite, to do the right and leave the wrong undone ; rational, in as far as we have deliberately to select one course of action among many. Knowledge, choice, and feeling, must converge upon conduct. To act aright we must use both heart and head.

"But if free-will be a myth, if all our actions are ruled by a stern determinism, then," some one may ask, "in what

sense can a man be said to be responsible for his actions ?
That every man should be responsible for his actions, this
surely is at the very foundation of all right social conduct.
In striking away this, determinism cuts the tap-root of the
tree of morality.   If determinism be true, what is morality
but a system of dull, inert mechanism ?   What are virtue
and vice but the interesting resultants of a complex paral-
lelogram of forces ?   The murderer, and the adulterer, the
unselfish, and the pure—these are most instructive examples
of the effects of inevitable causes, and worthy of our most
attentive and critical study ; but as for horror at the one,
or admiration of the other, these are surely altogether out
of place, and the relics of a barbarous pre-scientific age.
And if the determinist be himself impelled to sin and crime,
why should he feel remorse?   Was it not inevitable, as
inevitable, in his case, as the fall of a stone to the earth ?
And why should he strive to reach a higher moral ideal,
when he is assured that all is determined by strict necessity, and that after all he only fancies that he strives ?"

Let us briefly consider this question, for it is obviously
a vital one.   Let us first ask : Is a man responsible for his
character ?   We are sometimes told that he is not responsible for its intellectual side, but that he is responsible
for its moral side.   It is often said that only those who
have the brains can be clever, but all of us may at least be
good.   Would that it were so!   I fear that it is too true
that just as there are stern limits set to the intellectual
progress of the individual, so, too, there are stern limits set
to his moral progress.   But even if this be granted, as it
will be granted by those who are observers of men, still
it will be said that, within these limits, he is free to act.
If a man is not responsible for his intellectual capacity, he
is at least responsible for the use that he makes of such
talents as he possesses ; and if he is not responsible for his

moral character, he is at least responsible for his deeds within the limits of his moral capacity. In a word, if he be not responsible for his character, he is at least free to act within the limits of that character. Most certainly. And this is just what the determinist not only admits but contends for. He maintains that every individual has a predetermined character; and that every act of his life is the result of the play of determining motives on determining character. As Mr. Ruskin somewhere says: " If you give a man half-a-crown, it depends on his disposition whether he is rich or poor with it—whether he will buy disease, ruin, and hatred, or buy health, advancement, and domestic love." If free-will mean no more than this, there is no question at issue.

But with this the believer in free-will will not be satisfied. He is very probably, although he little knows it, already nine-tenths a determinist. He believes that his acts are the outcome of his character, and he knows that his character is, to a great extent, inherited, and to a great extent, the result of his education. But still he maintains that he is free within limits to improve his character; he is free to choose the right and to avoid the evil; he is free at any rate to avoid temptation. Most certainly he is—under one condition; that there be in his character the germ of improvement, that he already possesses or is possessed by a *desire* to do right and to avoid temptation. It is just the presence or absence of such a desire, or earnest wish, that determines the future conduct of the man. It is just this, that differences those who are working their way painfully upwards towards the higher life, from those who are descending in the moral scale. But the desire *must* be there. A man can no more create the desire in himself than he can alter the shape of his skull. And do we not all practically know this? Does not the Christian Church endorse it, in teaching that man of himself, in his own strength, is powerless, but must earnestly pray for help from above? And in constantly insisting on the paramount importance of prayer, which is to the Christian the outward expression of the inward desire, does she not endorse the view that the earnest wish to do the right is the really essential thing? The Christian who is not "instant in prayer" has no real living desire for the higher Christ-like life.

But how can we regard a man as responsible for his actions, if they are simply the outcome of his character or disposition, over the formation of which he had no control? Let us note clearly what the real question here is. It is not whether a man is to be held responsible for his acts; for, as a matter of practical fact, on this head we are all agreed. The question is, whether it is *just* that he should have this responsibility forced upon him. It is really a question of abstract justice. Is it just that I should suffer for that which I cannot help? To this question I can give no answer; for I hold it to be an illegitimate one. Nature is neither just nor unjust. But, whether just or not, it is an inexorable fact. The moth which loves the light is urged by a dominant instinct to self-destruction in the candle-flame. Is this just? Whether just or not the moth dies. And throughout the whole process of evolution thousands and millions of creatures have been impelled to their own destruction through no fault of theirs. Is this just? Just or unjust it is stern fact. It is Nature's way of evolving a healthy, active, clever, and powerful race. Only the fittest survive; the rest are doomed.

The determinist accepts this fact. He sees around him men weak and sinful, and he hates the weakness and the sin; but he lovingly helps the sinner, and he does all that he can so to alter his vicious character and disposition that

Conduct and Determinism.

the sin may be avoided in the future. He knows that all
his actions are rigidly determined, that he is only free to
yield to the strongest motive. But he feels within him the
earnest desire so to live as to improve himself and do the
greatest possible amount of good to his fellow-creatures.
And he not only agrees to accept the responsibility of his
actions, but he earnestly entreats that such responsibility
shall, in every possible way, be forced upon him, and that,
if he sin against his fellow-man, he shall be made so to
suffer that his sinful character may be thereby altered, and
that he may go and sin no more. It is in the interests
of humanity that man should bear this burden of
responsibility.

It will thus be seen that the determinist, in fully and
freely accepting responsibility, does *not* strike away the
foundations of all right social conduct ; that morality is as
real and living for him as for the most strenuous supporter
of the doctrine of free-will. And he can afford to smile—
though the smile have a tinge of pity in it—at the ignorance
or wrong-headedness of those who ask him why he continues to strive to reach a higher moral ideal, when he is
assured that all is determined by strict necessity, and that,
after all, he only fancies that he strives. When will people
learn that determinism is not fatalism ? Why does he feel
horror at murder and adultery! Why has he a loving
admiration of virtue and purity! Why does he feel
remorse! Why does he strive after the higher life, so
difficult of attainment, but so full of grace and beauty!
Why! Because all this is in him, as we characteristically
say. Because it is innate in or instilled into his disposition. Because to do so is the outcome of his character.

Oh, my brother, who believes in free-will, do not force
into the mouth of your determinist brother conclusions
which only betray your own complete inability to com-

prehend his position. Depend upon it a doctrine which is accepted by many of our wisest and greatest is not sheer nonsense, and does not lead to conclusions palpably at variance with the results of all experience. Determinism may be true or false; but it is not nonsense; it is not fatalistic; and it does not paralyze conduct.

2. *Ethics and Evolution.*

"These mental forms, like the so-called laws of Nature, are not to be conceived as antecedent and independent realities ruling mental and cosmical phenomena."—G. H. LEWES.

Can there be an evolution of ethics? On two grounds it is sometimes argued that there cannot. First, on the ground that the truths of ethics are, like the truths of mathematics, absolute, and as such cannot result from any process of evolution. Secondly, on the ground that, though our knowledge of ethical truth, like our knowledge of mathematics, may exhibit a progressive advance, the truths of ethics, like the truths of mathematics, exist whether we know them or not, and are by their very nature eternal and immutable, and incapable of such change as is implied in evolution. Both of these arguments have been answered by implication in the section on *The facts of Nature and the laws of science.* It will therefore only be necessary here to apply the principles there laid down.

Let us take the latter objection first. It has recently been urged by Mr. Wilson, of Clifton College, in a lecture on "Evolution; physical and biological," at the Bristol Museum. He drew attention to the distinction between facts and our knowledge of facts. An organism is a biological fact: the solar system or the contour of a continent is a physical fact: they are things which exist altogether apart from our knowledge of them. And to them the term evolution can be strictly applied. Now carry this distinction into mathematics. That the three angles of a triangle are equal to two right angles is a mathematical fact. It is a truth which exists whether we know it or not. But it is not a fact which could by any conceivable process be evolved. It is a fact for all time, eternal and immutable. Worlds and animals have no existence till they are evolved. But the truths of mathematics are not evolved. Now in which category, he asked, are we to place ethics? Do the laws of right and wrong exist before our knowledge of them, like the properties of an ellipse ; or are they growing like a valley or a plant by an automatic process? Are we making them or discovering them? Clearly the latter. Our *knowledge* of them may advance towards completeness by a process bearing a superficial resemblance to evolution. But the truths themselves are, like the truths of mathematics, eternal and immutable. By no conceivable process could such truths, regarded as facts, be evolved. Such in brief was Mr. Wilson's argument.

And now it may be asked, in what conceivable sense it can be said that the truths of mathematics exist whether we know them or not? In the first place they are abstract truths : facts that are only true in the abstract, not in the concrete. But waiving this ; granting that the three angles of a concrete triangle are practically equal to two right angles ; in what conceivable sense can this truth be said to exist whether it be known or not? What we perceive is a certain relation ; this relation is essentially a perception ; and apart from the percipient there can be no perceived relation. All that we have any right to say is, that the facts are such that, if there be a percipient mind, they will be seen to exhibit this relationship. Of mathematical principles it is essentially true that their *esse* is *percipi.* They are laws. And it has already been pointed out that Nature presents us with facts not laws. It is we who make the laws out of the facts.

The facts of mathematics differ in no wise from the facts of physics and biologics. There exist, let us say, three stars. And these three stars exist whether we know their existence or not. We perceive that, if they be joined by the shortest possible lines, a triangle will be formed, of which the three angles are equal to two right angles. But this truth is a human product, a bit of human knowledge. Whether it be the product of an evolution or not depends upon whether human knowledge has, or has not, been evolved. But in this case there are no facts to be evolved, beyond the bare fact of the existence of the three stars. In this case, in a word, the knowledge and the fact are one and indivisible.

So, too, with ethical laws. They are human products. The only sense in which we can say that the laws of right and wrong exist, before our knowledge of them, is the sense in which we can say that the properties of an ellipse exist, before we know them as such and such. Just as the course of a planet is such that the mathematician is led to perceive, in the figure approximately described, the laws of the ellipse, so is the course of human action such that the moralist is led to educe therefrom the laws of right and wrong. The facts are there. And the facts, in each case, are such that man can construct out of them an ideal world of scientific laws. But the truths so elaborated are a joint product of the given facts and the perceptive mind of man. And to say that the truths exist whether we know them or not, is tantamount to saying, that the product would be the same in the absence of one of the factors. Assuredly we are making the laws. But assuredly also we are discovering them in exactly the same sense as we make other discoveries in scientific principles, generalizations, and laws. Just as the truths of mathematics presuppose a mathematician, so do the laws of ethics presuppose a human soul capable of moral perception.

We may now pass on to the objection raised on the ground that the distinction between right and wrong and the laws of right and wrong are absolute. If this be so, if we know them to be absolutely true in the realm of Nature, then clearly this knowledge cannot be the product of any process of evolution. For evolution is by steps ; and the step to the absolute, no matter from what degree of practical certainty, is an infinite one, and therefore no step at all.

Now here again the analogy of mathematics is helpful. It is frequently asserted that the laws of geometry are absolutely true ; that the three angles of a triangle are absolutely, immutably, and for ever, equal to two right angles. If so, if we know that they also are absolutely true in the realm of Nature, then clearly this knowledge cannot be the product of any process of evolution. But we have already argued that we do not and cannot know that the laws of geometry are absolutely true in the realm of Nature. We know them to be practically more exact than our most exact experiments. But this is an altogether different thing. In the realm of Nature we only know them to be practically true ; but in the abstract realm of geometry, a realm which we can limit and rigidly define by our axioms and definitions, we construct them absolutely true. In this sense, as limited to the abstract realm of geometry, the equivalence of the three angles of any triangle to two right angles is absolutely exact, and is, in fact, already implied in our definitions and axioms. So, too, in ethics. In the realm of human action there is no absolute right, no absolute wrong, but only the practically right and the practically wrong. But in the abstract realm of ethics we construct, and are wise in constructing, an absolute distinction between right and wrong. We, so to speak, polarize our moral conceptions, just as our forefathers polarized their ideal conceptions of the Infinite Spirit, whence grew up the Christian conception of God on the one hand and the devil on the other.

It is to the ideal realm of ethics, then, and not to the practical realm of human conduct, that absolute maxims of morality rightly belong. And it is almost impossible to over-estimate their value. They stand in the same relation to practical conduct that ideal standards do to practical measurement. But their true nature should not be lost sight of. They are human products, made and discovered by man for man, right worthy results of the all-embracing process of evolution.

3. *Self-regard.*

" Every thing, in so far as in it lies, endeavours to persist in its own being."—SPINOZA.

If we pay but a slight attention to our ordinary every-day actions we cannot fail to see that they are determined by various motives. In the first place, many of our actions are undoubtedly performed in pursuit of our own pleasure, happiness, well-being, call it what we will. Then, again, much of our conduct is determined by considerations of the happiness and well-being of others, our relations, our intimate friends, the community at large. Other actions are the outcome of religious influences ; yet others are performed in obedience to social customs and the bondage of etiquette; and others, once more, are prescribed for us by the legislature. Some, therefore, are performed because they are pleasant, some because they are right, some because they are expedient, and some from coercion actual or possible. And the moral status of a man is in the main determined by the relative strength of these various incentives to action.

Now it is clear that these motives fall under two heads— self-regard and other-regard; egoism and altruism. But well-defined as this distinction seems, it is by no means easy to disentangle the one set of motives from the other. Self-improvement may be, and very often is, striven after for social ends; since "whoever improves his own nature improves the universe of which he is a part." On the other hand, when we do good to our neighbours, and find therein our highest pleasure, there will always be found cynics to maintain that this is, after all, but the subtlest form of self-gratification. Still, hard or even impossible as it may be to keep the two factors entirely separate, it will, I think, be well by a preliminary consideration of self-regard to pave the way for the far higher and nobler other-regard.

Without further preface, therefore, let us devote our first attention to the individual or egoistic factor—the natural and inevitable tendency to self-maintenance and self-improvement. Self-preservation is obviously a necessary condition of our continued existence : were it otherwise, were self-abasement instead of self-preservation the aim of each, the result would clearly be the rapid deterioration and ultimate disappearance of the individual and the race. Nor is self-preservation enough : each of us naturally aims also at self-improvement. He desires to make the stream of his individual life as full, and broad, and deep, as possible. And in what way full, and broad, and deep? In mere pleasurable enjoyment? No. Not only in happiness, but also, as a means to this end, in efficiency.

And now let us see whether these aims can be explained and justified on evolution principles. It will be remembered that, in the chapter on *Feeling*, the fact that pleasure results from the healthy and normal exercise of the bodily functions and intellectual faculties, was pointed out. And this fact was further shown to be readily explicable on the evolution hypothesis ; for those whose pleasure was bound up with self-maintenance and self-improvement would inevitably have a better chance of survival than those whose pleasure was bound up with self-deterioration and excess. In these facts, then, we have at once an explanation and a rational justification of the determination of conduct by the promptings of pleasure. Nor is the aim at efficiency less easily justified. For it is clearly on this view but another aspect of the aim at pleasure. To attain our maximum efficiency and thus get on in the world, we must exercise fully our functions and faculties. But such exercise is essentially pleasurable, since it is only under-exercise or over-exercise which is unpleasant or painful. In aiming at efficiency, therefore, we are taking our best course to obtain pleasure.

This point is of sufficient importance to warrant our dwelling on it. In aiming at efficiency we are taking our best course to obtain pleasure. Pleasures and pains are not the things on which we normally fix our attention. Not the enjoyment itself, but the means by which happiness may be secured ; this is what we set before our minds. The means to the end itself becomes an end, beyond which we do not look. The aim of the man of business is, not happiness, but success. The sculptor loves, not pleasure, but his art. The man of science directs his efforts, not to the increase of his happiness, but to the discovery of new truths. Still, when we come to ask why these various men chose their various pursuits, we shall see that ultimately their choice was determined by considerations of happiness. The man of science left the counting-house, where he was wretched, to carry out the experiments in which he delighted. The sculptor was from a child fond of modelling in clay or carving in wood. And the man of business, though when he began work he found it irksome, yet even-he also chose his profession because he saw that it gave him the best chance of eventually settling down comfortably and living at ease. In each case the ultimate consideration is pleasure to be gained. But it is gained, not directly, but indirectly. In each case success depends upon the concentration of energy, not upon the pleasure, but the work. And it had often been remarked before Mr. Sidgwick described it (in his valuable " Methods of Ethics ") as the fundamental paradox of Hedonism, that " the impulse towards pleasure if too predominant defeats its own aim." The mind must be fixed, not on the pleasure to be ultimately gained, but on the efficient carrying out of the means which have been chosen to that end.

Accompanying this concentration of the attention on the means rather than on the end—a process which accompanies that widening of the intellectual horizon which marks the progress of the individual and the race—accompanying this advance in the complexity and efficiency of conduct, is a progressive increase in the remoteness of the end in view ; an increase which necessitates increasing powers of prevision, and heightened imagination by which remote results may be vividly pictured in the mind.

This may be seen in the individual and in the race. Little children, in whom neither memory nor its inversion, prevision, is strong, are guided in their actions by the promptings of immediate pleasures and pains. Even when

U

the children have grown up to be lower schoolboys, few of them would fail to choose a half-holiday to-day before a whole holiday at the end of next week. And there are but too many grown men who revel in to-night's pleasure and elation, heedless of to-morrow's pain and depression. But as the little children grow older, pleasures and pains more remote begin to influence their conduct. As the schoolboy develops, thoughts of the future steady him to his work. And wise men avoid to-night's intoxication, not only because of to-morrow's headache and discomfort, but because the idea of a ruined constitution in the future is sufficiently strong to influence their conduct. But in these cases, while increase of the power of prevision makes conduct better, it also makes it more difficult.

Turning from the individual to the race, we see the same fact. That savages are influenced mainly by immediate desires is shown by their impulsiveness and their want of self-restraint. Like children they live in and for the present, whereas the civilized man lives to a great extent in and for the future. It is a common, but, I presume, exaggerated remark, that the freed slaves of the Southern States of America cannot be induced to provide in any way for the future. And if it be objected that this, if true, is one of the evil results of slavery, we have only to turn to accounts of the lower races, to see how little they are influenced by the idea of such pleasure or pain as is in any degree remote. Instance the Dogrib Indians, of whom Richardson says, " that however high the reward they expected to receive on reaching their destination, they could not be depended on to carry letters. A slight difficulty, the prospect of a banquet on venison, or a sudden impulse to visit some friend, were sufficient to turn them aside for an indefinite length of time." Even in our own times and in our civilized community, do we not commonly accuse the lower orders of improvidence? and, on the other hand, do we not constantly observe that the ablest statesmen, the keenest men of business, the most successful merchants, are they who can " see well ahead " ? In these cases, again, we may notice that, while increase of the power of prevision makes conduct more perfectly adjusted to the conditions of existence, it at the same time renders the needful adjustment more difficult.

The growth of intelligence, then, brings with it this difficulty, that we have to conform our actions to future events, more or less accurately foreseen. If we may say that a man's individual conduct is mainly influenced by an environment of possible pleasures and pains, then we may say, further, that, during the growth of intelligence, this environment is extended in all directions. For as we shall see presently, the pleasures and pains of others become a more and more definite portion of the ever-widening environment. Confining ourselves for the present, however, to self-regard, looking at the individual merely as an isolated unit, we may infer that the result of this extension is, that the wise man denies himself an immediate pleasure when he sees that his enjoyment will either shut him out from a greater, though, perhaps, more remote, pleasure, or that it will lead to subsequent pain. His acts will be guided, in fact, by some such set of rules, unconsciously acted on, as the four Canons of Epicurus, which Mr. Lecky thus formulates : (1) The pleasure which produces no pain is to be embraced. (2) The pain which produces no pleasure is to be avoided. (3) The pleasure is to be avoided which prevents a greater pleasure or produces a greater pain. (4) The pain is to be endured which averts a greater pain or secures a greater pleasure.

But now we must pass on to notice, as a fact of fundamental importance, that no such set of rules, regarded merely as so much knowledge, has much practical influence on conduct. *Knowledge has to be converted into feeling* before it deeply influences our actions. As long as a man sits quietly in his armchair, and muses on the past and on the future, it is not difficult for him to lay down, in broad yet fairly definite lines, a rational and sensible course of action. But all this is forgotten at the moment of action. For unfortunately many of those immediate pleasures, which a rational man wisely eschews or tastes in moderation, have a way of presenting themselves to the mind with extreme vividness ; while on the other hand, at such moments, those future pleasures, such as a perfectly clear head on the morrow and undimmed faculties a dozen years hence, which in our quiet hours we know to be most valuable, retire into the dim background of consciousness. We are not at such moments in a position fairly to balance the pleasures and pains near and remote. We act irrationally.

Fortunately, however, we have not to await the arrival of the remote pains to assure us of our foolishness. For suppose that we yield, irrationally and impulsively, to the prompting of the immediate pleasurable appetite ; then it cannot fail that, the next time we sit musing in our armchair, we have not only a perception that we have acted unwisely, but a keen *sense of dissatisfaction*, due to the fact that the normal desire to act rationally has been baulked by the temporary predominance of an abnormal irrational impulse. As Wordsworth says—

"That which we have been weak enough to do
Is misery in remembrance."

Knowledge is converted into feeling, and conduct is influenced. And, I suppose, there are few of us who have not often, in our quiet moments, experienced this sense of self-dissatisfaction. At such moments we see clearly what the wise and sensible course of action would have been ; and at the same time we find it hard—nay, it is almost impossible—to represent to the mind the immediate desires which prompted the silly action. Hence the well-known fact that it is easy enough to *say*, " Ah, if I had been in such a position I should have acted in such a way," but much more difficult to act " in such a way " when we *are* in such a position.

For in these quiet and rational moments the perception that a given course of action is for our eventual good, is sufficiently strong to determine us to follow that course ; but in our impulsive and irrational moments, pressing and immediate desires drown this perception ; and it is only when the moment of impulse is past, and the deed is actually done, that we perceive that, after all, we too have been as foolish as our neighbours, and are overcome by a keen sense of dissatisfaction. We feel that, after all, we have acted unwisely. We trusted ourselves ; and we have to undergo the pain of a disappointed faith in self. We did not fulfil, as we say, our own ideals. And this I imagine we feel the more, the more developed our powers of reflection—the greater the ratio of our quiet and rational periods to our periods of unreason and impulse. In the lower individuals of our race, indeed, it is doubtful whether the rational sense of dissatisfaction would, at any time, be strong enough to overcome the idea of the immediate dissatisfaction consequent upon the non-gratification of appetite. And as, during the evolution of the race, this rational sense of dissatisfaction becomes a more and more important factor in our mental life, and grows, by inheritance, a more and more ingrained part of our nature, we may hope that the irrational pursuit of immediate pleasure will become less and less a characteristic of average man. Nay, further, we may hope that eventually pleasures ultimate and immediate may so interfuse, that the promptings of immediate pleasure shall inevitably lead to ultimate good.

But the voluptuary may, not improbably, argue thus : "I am perfectly aware that I am ruining my health. I know that I shall suffer for my intemperance. But I deliberately choose my present course. I am ready to knock off ten years of my life for one hour of this exquisite enjoyment." How are we to answer such an one ? From the point of mere self-regard, apart from other regard, that is to say looking at him as an isolated unit, we have nothing to say; we must leave him to choose for himself. But from the other-regarding point of view we shall have somewhat to say to him presently.

To unalloyed self-regard we need devote but a few more words. We have only to note, that there are other impulses than those prompting to the gratification of the appetites, over which reason has to keep guard. Here we find a man of quick temper and strong physique, whose tendency to summarily thrash a mean scoundrel or two has to be kept under. There we have one who has acquired or inherited a trick of distorting the truth and who, spite of previous determination, cannot help adding somewhat to the account of what he has done, or giving a little extra piquancy to the good story he has heard against his neighbour. There again is one who is aware of his indolence, and fully intends to overcome it, but allows his energetic intentions to sleep. The one confesses that his hot temper is always getting him into trouble. The other sees that his neighbours smile sceptically while he talks. The third confesses that his indolence prevents his getting on in the world. Each in his rational moments sees how his conduct may be improved. Each when the time comes acts irrationally. And since, in most of these cases, the after-sense of dissatisfaction is not always of the keenest, they are more difficult of cure.

With respect to self-regard, then, we may I think say, that the ultimate aim of the individual, merely regarded as an isolated unit (so far as it is possible to regard him as such), is to compass his own individual happiness ; but that to do so effectually he must concentrate his attention, not on his own pleasures and pains, but on the special work he has to do in the world, and must do that work as efficiently as in him lies ; that he must aim, not at the immediate pleasurable gratification of the senses, but at the prolonged happiness of a lifetime ; that the mere perception of the wisest course of action is of little avail, but that he must be made to *feel* what is for the best ; and that, if a man chooses to say, " I am willing to chance the happiness of a lifetime that may be cut short in a week, and shall yield myself up to the enjoyment of the passing hour," from the point of view of pure self-regard we can have nothing to say to him ; we must let him choose for himself, though we may do our best to prove to him that his conduct is irrational, and below the dignity of humanity.

Finally, let us remember that in every act of our lives, no matter how trivial, we are laying the foundations of the actions (who can tell how momentous ?) of our future. " Does it seem a trifling thing to say that in hours of passionate trial or temptation a man can have no better help than his own past ? Every generous feeling that has not been crushed, every wholesome impulse that has been followed, every just perception, every habit of unselfish action, will be present in the background to guide or to restrain. It is too late when the storm has burst, to provide our craft with rigging fit to weather it ; but we may find a purpose for the years that oppress us by their dull calm, if we elect to spend them in laying up stores of strength and wisdom and emotional prejudices of a goodly human kind, whereby, if need arises, we may be able to resist hereafter the gusts of passion that might else bear us out of the straightforward chosen course " (*Edith Simcox*).

4. *Other-regard.*

" The thing to be lamented is, not that men have so great regard to their own good or interest in the present world,—for they have not enough; but that they have so little to the good of others. . . . That mankind is a community— that we all stand in a relation to each other—is the *sum of morals*."—BISHOP BUTLER.

So far our considerations have been entirely connected with the individual self. No question of morality in conduct has been touched upon ; for the individual has been regarded as altogether isolated. And neither morality nor immorality is possible in a state of complete isolation. But with the progress involved in evolution there goes, as we have seen, a progressive widening of the mental horizon, emotional and intellectual. The sympathies extend, in ever-widening circles, until they embrace the whole of humanity. Beginning with the family they spread out over the school, the college, the fatherland, and at last reach the dwellers in the uttermost parts of the earth. And as this process goes on, there develops in the individual, alongside the idea of his own good as a thing to be aimed at, the idea of his neighbour's good as a thing to be aimed at, and also the idea of his family's, township's, country's good, and the wider good of humanity. Of these the idea of his neighbour's welfare is the specialized conception, answering to which the ideas of the welfare of family, township, country, humanity, are successively more generalized conceptions. In the person of every several

human being, we individualize our general conception of humanity.

It will be seen that, in entering thus upon the sphere of other-regard, we come to conduct, the nature of which is moral. We enter upon the consideration of a man's duty to his neighbour. And we do so, be it noticed, through sympathy, a matter of the heart rather than of the head. From what has before been said, however, it will be seen that both feeling and knowledge must be brought to bear upon conduct in all its phases. Prompted by the emotions, our conduct must still be guided by reason. Even in the case of a mother's love for her child, she does not merely persist in that act which she sees is giving her little one momentary pleasure ; but she anxiously strives to do that which will be for her child's permanent good. She chooses the wisest course of action. And if, in a moment of impulsive love, she acts unwisely, she experiences a bitter after-sense of dissatisfaction. " Blinded by my love, I acted foolishly," she says, and makes resolves for the future. And if in this case, where the emotions are direct and well-defined, reason has to be exercised, much more must it be exercised in those cases where the emotions are less direct and not so well-defined. In a word, we have all of us determinately to choose the right and avoid the wrong.

During the widening of the sympathies, then, there grows up a conception of other-selves, individual and corporate, for whose good we are to work. And during the evolution of the race this conception grows in depth and strength. I have before stated my belief that the sympathetic emotions have grown up out of the self-regarding emotions. The question *how* they have been developed may, indeed, be still awaiting a satisfactory answer ; but there can be no doubt, I think, that, once developed, they would be strengthened by use and natural selection. It must be clear that such sympathy, such fellow-feeling (for I use the word here in this sense) would be, as we say, the making of any community, the members of which possessed them, to an unusually large extent. It is by such feelings that a group is bound together and converted into a consistent whole. The existencé of some sympathetic fellow-feeling is, indeed, a pre-requisite of all social development; for without it there could be no division of labour, or, at any rate, without it division of labour could not proceed very rapidly nor be carried very far. In fact, the possession of some bonds of sympathy, rational or instinctive, makes just the difference between a mere aggregation of similar units and an integrated group of mutually dependent parts. Fellow-feeling is the essential condition of the social state. In the struggle for supremacy, then, which has been carried on for generations between tribes and nations, there can be no shadow of doubt that success would fall to the lot of those whom a developed fellow-feeling within the group had closely united, and that failure would be the fate of those in whom a developed selfishness had given a tendency to dissolution.

It must not be imagined, however, that fellow-feeling is the only cement which binds a nation together during the process of its evolution. As soon as a certain amount of consistency is acquired, chieftainship becomes possible, and with it a certain amount of subordination to the chieftain's will. Hence arises coercion. For though the chief cannot make the members of his tribe feel sympathy, he can prevent overt acts of aggression. Eventually the chief's will is replaced by more or less codified law, enforcing a body of rules to maintain the social state and repressing anarchy. Apart, too, from the chief's will, and in later times established law, the fear of transgressing which becomes a motive for action, there is a further motive in the fear of offending the community who may execute that summary justice known as lynch law. Add to this, again, a religious sanction bearing in the same direction; and finally remember, that social action is eventually regarded as wise on rational grounds.

There thus grow up together several sets of rules of conduct more or léss convergent. There is the right and wrong which is in the individual intuitive; there is the right and wrong enforced by his law-courts; there is the right and wrong propounded by his community (*e.g.* in the so-called code of honour or in matters of etiquette); there is the right and wrong which he is taught as revealed truth; there is the right and wrong dictated by his reason. All of these influence a man's conduct. And inextricably bound up with them all, and arising in their midst, is the moral right and wrong which has its roots in sympathy.

During the development of the integrating bonds of sympathy, then, the germs of the moral sentiments are sown, the foundations of morality are laid. And it is not improbable that, as Mr. Darwin was, I believe, the first to suggest, those foundations are laid somewhat in the following manner. During the double process of selection —the selection of those tribes in which social feeling and action are best developed, and the selection in that tribe of those individuals in whom social feeling and action are best developed—during this double process, I say, the performance of social actions becomes instinctive. But the social instincts thus developed, powerful as they may eventually become, are always liable to be overridden by the passionate, self-regarding impulse of a moment of strong excitement. So that the actions of the individual are subject to two forces—the constant and persistent tension of the social instincts, and the intermittent jerks of passionate desire. "At the moment of action"—I quote from Mr. Darwin—"at the moment of action, man will no doubt be apt to follow the stronger impulse ; and though this may occasionally prompt him to the noblest deeds, it will far more commonly lead him to gratify his own desires at the expense of other men. But after their gratification, when past and weaker impressions are contrasted with the ever-enduring social instincts, retribution will surely come. Man will then feel dissatisfied with himself, and will resolve with more or less force to act differently for the future. This is conscience ; for conscience looks forward and judges past actions, inducing that kind of dissatisfaction which, if weak, we call regret, and if severe, remorse."

It is, perhaps, a point worth noting in this connection, that among our own Teutonic ancestors the conditions seem to have been especially favourable for the development of such a sense of dissatisfaction ; for the consequences of the commission of a crime fell not only on the head of the criminal, but on the whole community of his relations in blood. The criminal must, therefore, have felt in his calmer moments, not only that he had injured the whole community in the person of one of its members, but that he had involved the whole of his own house and all his kinsfolk, and made them participators in the consequences of his crime. Out of this joint suretyship of members, united by ties of kindred, grew, in somewhat later times, a similar joint suretyship of members united by voluntary ties. And every freeman in the land was bound to become a member of a frith-borh, as it was termed. In still later times, as is well known, Henry II. made this system of frith-borh, or frank-pledge, as the Anglo-Normans termed it, the basis of his assize of Clarendon. Thus the principle of mutual responsibility must have become ingrained in the very natures of our forefathers. And every facility was afforded for the growth of those sympathetic and social instincts which form the foundation upon which the moral structure may be raised.

It must be noticed, however, that on this view of the origin of the "moral sense" the formation of the social instincts was not a process necessarily guided by reason. Primitive man does not say to himself, "I clearly perceive that my interests are bound up with that of the community in which I live, therefore I will act in such and such a manner." On the contrary, without any reasoning at all, he acts. If the action is a social action, well and good ; but if not, then the unsatisfied social instincts within him speak to him with the voice of conscience. Secondly, it must be noticed that, on this view, the moral sense is not developed by the individual, but is inherited. Mr. Mill, in this and in other points, seems to have failed to grasp the importance of inheritance ; that is, if we accept his statement, that "the moral feelings are not innate but acquired," in the sense that they are individually not ancestrally acquired. From Mr. Darwin's point of view, however, these feelings are essentially innate, for they are gradually developed in the individuals of a community for the sake of the community as such. But they are innate in the same sense as intuitions of space and time are innate ; that is, they are like space and time, "organized and consolidated experiences of all antecedent (social) individuals." And this is why conscience, when it warns us, seems like a voice from another world.

Thirdly, we must remember—and it is a point to be steadily borne in mind—that, under existing circumstances, conduct is *variously* influenced from within and from without. From within we have, first, egoistic promptings having their roots in individual desires ; secondly, religious promptings having their roots, not in the form of faith we profess, but in our real and living beliefs ; thirdly, rational promptings having their roots in the intellectual powers ; and, fourthly, moral promptings having their roots in sympathy. On the other hand, from without we have, first, social incentives and restraints, now exercised mainly through the medium of approbation and disapprobation ; secondly, religious incentives and restraints ; and, thirdly, legal restraints, imposed by the powers that be. Of course, these influences, internal and external, merge the one into the other. For just as the internal promptings, egoistic, religious, rational, and moral, are not wholly from within, but are excited by and answer to things without us, so are the external influences, social, religious, and legal, not wholly external ; for, at any rate in the case of the social incentives and restraints, corresponding to the influences without us there is developed individually, and in the race, an answering inner sense, a reverence for custom. Of what avail else would be the expression of approbation or disapprobation ?

Having now made the important passage from the promptings of the self-regarding instinct to the promptings of the sympathetic instincts, we may forthwith proceed to consider, in order, (1) the influence of social custom, (2) legal influences, and (3) religious influences. This will lead us to a consideration of conscience, and that, again, to the problem of the rational aim in conduct.

I. First, then, as to social custom. No one can doubt the immense influence that this has had in the evolution of our race. As Mr. Bagehot has pointed out, the first pre-requisite of a successful group, in the struggle of nations, is that it shall have a polity, a set of customs, a law which may bind the group into a mass with some consistency, some power of hanging together. "A polity first," he says—"what sort of polity is immaterial ; a law first—what kind of law is secondary ; a person or set of persons to pay deference to—though who he is or they are by comparison scarcely signifies." The first step, then, is to get a binding law; but the next step is to break through that rigid law and reach something better.

Now there can be no doubt, I think, that the evolution of such a law-bound nation would be accompanied by a constant growth of the belief, that simply to obey such custom is really the only thing to do, and is, besides, an act of the highest wisdom. This belief having grown up, strengthened, and crystallized, the breach of any point of such law would be accompanied by a subsequent sense of dissatisfaction in self. And to see the breach of any point of such law by a neighbour would be accompanied by a sense of disapprobation. Presently, however, it would be seen that this or that rule, obeyed for so long, was in reality a more or less irrational one ; and even more, that the blind obedience to such a rule was an irrational act. Still, from the force of the old habits of thought, from the massive nature of the general belief, the rational breach of a customary rule would be accompanied by a large share of the old sense of dissatisfaction or disapprobation. And not unnaturally; since though the breach of a customary rule, regarded as an isolated rule, may be perhaps rational, the breach of custom in general would be most irrational.

In some such way as this we may account, I think, for much of our bondage to etiquette, and for the pain felt at occasional breaches of the rules of so-called society. This pain is caused, not so much, I imagine, by the consciousness of having broken a rule in particular as by the shame of having sinned against the social etiquette in general. Thus, though the particular form of social etiquette may change—though our so-called betters may introduce, from time to time, novelties, which we must ere long consciously or unconsciously imitate—still to this changing etiquette we pay an unchanging homage. We do not pause to think whether the homage is rational. The prestige of social custom overawes us. But to be under a law regulating our manners is good for us; it has helped to raise us to the status of civilized beings. Whereas, therefore, it is irrational to obey this or that rule of etiquette, regarded as an isolated rule, it is perfectly rational to obey it as a part of our allegiance to civilization. The dissatisfaction that we feel when we break, perhaps in a moment of abstraction, a rule that we know to be irrational is due to the fact, that we have been untrue to civilization; in a word, we have been bearish. And those breaches of etiquette which, when performed by ourselves, give rise to dissatisfaction, seen in others give rise to disapprobation.

II. This leads us to the legal restraints, about which a few words must suffice. The enforcement of legal penalties is simply an emphatic way which the corporate disapprobation has of expressing itself. Society finds, as it seems, that there are some who can do wrong, moral and social, and suffer neither a sense of personal dissatisfaction nor distress at the disapprobation shown by others. These she regards as abnormal developments. After first ascertaining that the transgressor is a responsible being—for in the insane it is impossible to calculate the strength of motives—she adds to her disapprobation a sting which shall enter into the calculations of the intending criminal, which shall take the place of the personal dissatisfaction that would follow the criminal act in the normal individual, and which shall act as an artificial deterrent from vice, since the natural deterrents are not strong enough. We may thus regard punishments as artificial spikes placed on either side of the unsteady criminal's course, to keep

him, as far as may be, in that narrow path which a more
steady head would enable him to keep.

III. In addition to these social and legal incentives
and restraints, there are those which spring out of the
religious system under which a man lives ; and with regard
to this point also we must be brief. In three ways, I
imagine, is a Christian's conduct influenced by his religion.
In the first place, it is influenced by his love of a personal
ever-present God. And the satisfaction or dissatisfaction
which he feels, according as his actions are in accordance
with or contrary to God's will—constituting his religious
conscience—is, if his faith be real, for him the dominating
guide of life. Given, in any individual, the sincere love
of God, and this sense of dissatisfaction on disobeying the
God Whom he worships, must be a prime factor in the
determination of his conduct. And it is as natural as
the sorrow of a little child at the pain she has thought-
lessly given her mother. In the second place, a Christian's
conduct is more or less influenced by hopes and fears of
everlasting rewards on the one hand, and eternal punishment on the other. This influence, however, lessens with
increasing righteousness, and, even as man now is, in the
higher natures becomes a vanishing quantity. For the just
man is just, neither for hope of reward nor from fear of
punishment. We may say, then, that just as in legal
punishments we have temporal spikes, so placed as to
prevent the lower natures among us from leaving the right
path, so too we have, in future punishments, spiritual spikes
to guide lower natures aright. And, as a further aid, to
these deterrents is added the promise of rich rewards for
those who keep the narrow way. In the third place, a
Christian's conduct is influenced by what I may perhaps
be allowed to term the social pressure of his religion ; that
is to say, by the rules which the religious community of

X

which he is a member have laid down for their mutual guidance. This influence, however, so closely resembles the purely social influence considered above that, concerning it, nothing more need here be said.

We have now considered, or briefly adverted to, what seem to be the most important influences which are normally at work in the determination of conduct. And we have seen that a sense of emotional pleasure or pain, arising in more ways than one, accompanies the satisfaction or non-satisfaction of certain emotional instincts within the individual, which instincts are the outcome of his relations to his fellows or the central object of his religion. This sense we may regard as the basis of conscience. But conscience is—at any rate in civilized man—something more than this; for, in addition to the sense of dissatisfaction at some evil done, there is, in conscience, a perception of some good left undone which *ought* to have been done. This perception is the so-called "sense of duty." It is, however, in all probability, later in its development than the sense of dissatisfaction. It is, indeed, questionable whether it exists at all among the lower races; for it has been remarked that "the lower races of men may be said to be deficient in any idea of right, though quite familiar with that of law" (Lubbock). We may at least presume that the word *ought* is not of supreme importance in the savage vocabulary. And this is surely precisely what we should expect; for, whereas the *sense* of dissatisfaction or its opposite is indefinite and emotional, the *perception* of right or its opposite is comparatively definite and rational. It may be, indeed, that just as we have, in the lower races, curiosity, the germ from which love of knowledge shall spring, so too we may find in them a germ from which the moral sense may arise. The fact remains, however, that, in the early periods of social evolution, the conduct of the majority is mainly influenced by external restraints—legal, social, religious. It is only in later times that a man becomes a restraint unto himself, that he acts from a sense of duty; and only then are his actions performed from a truly moral motive. An act determined by fear of eternal punishment, temporal punishment, the disapprobation of the community, is not determined by a moral motive. But when these external restraints have given place to restraint from within, when the act is determined by a sense that it is right or wrong, then the motive is moral. In this way, I imagine, the coerciveness of the sense of duty may be explained; for the restraint from within partakes of the coercion that belonged to those external restraints which it has gradually and insensibly replaced.

Among civilized people conscience is innate. Intuitions of right and wrong are a part of that moral nature which we have inherited from our forefathers. Just as we inherit common sense, an instinctive judgment in intellectual matters, so too do we inherit that instinctive judgment in matters of right and wrong which forms an important element in conscience. But it is a distinguishing feature of man, that he is a rational agent in his own evolution. The question, therefore, arises, What is the rational right? If I am to be a conscious instrument in my own evolution and that of my race, I must seek an answer to this question. In my relations to my fellows, what does reason point out as the ultimate aim? Is it to be the greatest happiness of the greatest number? or the greatest efficiency of the community at large, and of the individual as a unit of the community? Let us hear the advocate of the latter view first. "Man," he will remind us, "is a being placed in a complex, social environment. By evolution beings become more and more perfectly fitted to their environing con-ditions; and when such beings most perfectly harmonize with their environment, all their functions, bodily and mental, are performed most efficiently and at least cost. But the performance of these functions in such a way produces happiness. In striving, therefore, after the most perfect state of harmony, with all the conditions of life in a social community, both as one who is under the influence of the environment of his neighbours and as one who is to his neighbours part of their environment, the individual is going the right way to get happiness himself and to secure it for his fellow men. But if he puts the cart before the horse, and seeks for the greatest happiness of the greatest number, it may be that, by aiming directly at that which should be reached indirectly, he may run some chance of missing his mark. In evolution feelings are a by-product, a means to an end. Pleasure is not the end of eating, delight is not the end of seeing, enjoyment is not the end of hearing ; nor is the greatest happiness of the greatest number the end of rational morality. Perfection, not happiness, is the end to be striven for. To make the world better, not happier, is that for which the moral reformer yearns. And as Solomon of old asked, not for riches, but for wisdom, and in and through that wisdom received also riches in abundance, so does the man who seeks, in singleness of heart, to do the right gain, in and through his righteousness, the highest happiness."

With much of this the Hedonist will, without hesitation, agree. But he will, perhaps, say, " I grant you that, by aiming directly at the greatest happiness, we may sometimes miss the mark ; but pray do not fail to observe that, by aiming directly at the greatest good, you may also sometimes miss the mark. Nay, be honest and confess that, in striving after the greatest good, you are forced to take happiness and misery as your guide. And, after all, in this aiming at greatest efficiency, do not you do so because efficiency brings with it happiness? And in endeavouring to make men better, do you not do this because you believe that thus they will find a higher and a purer happiness? But to come to a yet more vital matter. Are you not putting a conception, apprehended by the rational faculties—maximum efficiency—in place of an emotion · which touches men's hearts—perfect happiness? Remember, too, I beg, that perception of right must pass into love of right before it is operative on conduct. It must become an emotion. And the emotion must bring more happiness than misery, or else it will act rather as a deterrent than an incentive. Were it possible to place before mankind this alternative—maximum efficiency accompanied by the minimum of happiness, or maximum happiness with the minimum of efficiency—can we doubt which of these both churl and philosopher would choose? Surely, then, for the practical reason, greatest happiness is the ultimate end, lying behind maximum efficiency or highest perfection."

Which is it to be, then, we repeat—greatest perfection or greatest happiness? May we not answer, Both. For that which, under its purely rational aspect, is greatest perfection is, under its emotional aspect, greatest happiness. Greatest happiness and greatest perfection are, in fact, the different faces which the ultimate object of social and moral conduct presents to us. Evolution being as it is, the fact is undeniable, that increased efficiency, greater perfection, fuller harmony with the conditions of life, are inseparably connected with increased happiness. Goodness and happiness go hand in hand. And since this is so, why should we hesitate to say that "pleasure is as much a necessary form of moral intuition as space is a necessary form of intellectual intuition?" (H. Spencer.)

But some may say, quoting Seneca, "We know that virtue brings with it pleasure, but for all that 'we do not love virtue because it gives us pleasure, but it gives us pleasure because we love it.' " And this old saying has a vital core of truth. But before noting what it is, let us pause for a moment to consider how so complex an emotion as the love of virtue may have had its origin.

We must, first, note then, that virtue, like colour or symmetry, is an abstract idea ; and just as it is impossible to detach colour or symmetry from coloured or symmetrical objects, so is it impossible to detach virtue from virtuous actions. There are, in fact, no separable things which we can label colour, symmetry, or virtue. Still we have certain general and abstract ideas which are symbolized by these words. The moment, however, we begin to think clearly and precisely on these subjects the general and abstract idea fades, and gives place to a concrete example, or a rapid succession of concrete examples. It is quite impossible to get a clear-cut, well-defined mental picture of an abstract idea. And yet abstract ideas are perfectly real mental conceptions. How, then, have these abstract ideas been generated ? By the super-position and blending of concrete ideas ancestrally and individually acquired. The conception thus formed has considerable body from the frequent super-position, and at the same time it has an indefinite outline from the frequent overlap. The same is true of the emotions. For just as virtue, like symmetry, is an abstract idea, so is the love of virtue, like the love of symmetry, an abstract emotion. But the abstract emotions have still less definiteness than the abstract ideas. And this is what we should expect, since emotions are always less definite than cognitions. The love of virtue or that of symmetry, then, is an abstract emotion answering to the abstract idea. And it grows up with and alongside of the abstract idea ; for we have seen that knowing and feeling emerge from the same sensations. Parallel, then, to the process of abstraction, in the realm of cognition, runs the process of abstraction, in the realm of feeling. Along with the *conception* of virtue, vaguely separable in thought from this or that virtuous action, there grows up the *love* of virtue, vaguely separable in thought from the love of this or that virtuous deed.

Let us now return to Seneca's dictum, "We do not love virtue because it gives us pleasure, but it gives us pleasure because we love it." If we place beside it another dictum, equally true, we shall the better see its meaning. "The painter does not love his art because it gives him pleasure, but it gives him pleasure because he loves it." And why? Because, as we have already seen, the surest way to attain an end is to devote yourself heart and soul to the means for procuring that end. The means thus itself becomes an end, and eventually comes to occupy so large a space in the mental horizon as to throw the true end into the background, and make it seem subsidiary. The true end of knowledge is conduct. But we are wont to lose sight of this end and love knowledge for its own sake. And we must do so if we are to advance either knowledge or conduct. So, too, the end of virtue is, from one point of view, the bettering of humanity, from another obedience to the will of God. But virtue must be loved for its own sake, or we shall never better humanity or truly obey God's will.

Before proceeding further, it will be well here to summarize what has been said since leaving the subject of pure self-regard. First, the fact was pointed out that as the sympathies widen, to the idea of his own good as a thing aimed at, a man adds the ideas of his neighbour's good and that of his race. Secondly, it was shown that the development of bonds of sympathy help to knit together an evolving community; but not only bonds of sympathy, for there are other bonds—political, legal, religious. Hence several sets of rules of conduct, in the midst of which there arises the moral rule. Thirdly, the origin of the "moral sense" in a feeling of dissatisfaction following the non-gratification of social instincts was dwelt upon. Fourthly, certain other factors—social, legal, and religious—in the determination of conduct, were considered at some length; it was pointed out that conscience arises in more ways than one, and the coerciveness of the sense of duty was explained. Fifthly, we arrived at the conclusion that to the question, Is it to be greatest happiness or greatest good? the answer *both* was to be given; greatest happiness and greatest good, or efficiency, being different aspects of the same ultimate aim. Sixthly, the mode of origin of the abstract emotion love of virtue has been indicated, and it has been pointed out, that though virtue is, in truth, a means to an end, yet must we, if we would attain that end, love it for its own sake.

Still the ultimate end, lying behind even the love of virtue as such, is the greatest happiness of the greatest number, together with the greatest efficiency of the community and of its units. And the question here inevitably arises, How can I, as an individual, best aid in the attainment of this ultimate end?

The community is an aggregate built up of units, and there is one unit whose efficiency—let us here look chiefly at that—I can increase, and whose happiness I can thereby promote. My first duty is to make *myself*, as far as may be, a healthy centre of efficiency and of happiness. My first *duty*, I repeat. For since I am a social being, born into a community as one of its members, such talents as I may possess are not my own to do as I please withal, and such enjoyment as I am capable of I may not waste in selfish indulgence. My very health is not my own to squander as I see fit. Since I may become a father, it is my duty so to live as to pass on to my children the inheritance of as sound a constitution as may be ; and, in any case, decreased health brings decreased efficiency, decreased efficiency unhappiness. So that, by failing to maintain my own health, I am making myself a centre of comparative inefficiency and unhappiness. Here, then, we have the moral and social answer to the voluptuary, who imagines his health is his own to ruin if he likes. It is nothing of the sort. No man is an isolated unit. We are all members of a larger or smaller social group, and the efficiency of a group depends on the efficiency of its members. Since, then, there can be no doubt which is the most efficient unit, the diligent, chaste, temperate, well-informed man, or the idle, unchaste, intemperate, and ignorant man, we may unhesitatingly regard idleness, unchastity, intemperance, ignorance, as sins ; and, in general, we may regard as sin everything which diminishes our personal efficiency or lessens our power of spreading around us a healthy atmosphere of happiness.

Our first duty, then, is to aim at personal efficiency and happiness, that we may thereby raise the level of the general efficiency and happiness of the community. But while we are thus to aim at our own happiness as units, we must be careful that we do not trench on the happiness of our neighbours ; nay, more, we must anxiously endeavour to *promote* the happiness of our neighbours. First, in natural order, we must endeavour to promote the happiness of the family circle in which we live, and then that of the society of which our family is an integral part, and finally that of society in general or humanity. Our aim should be, in fact, personal happiness, *plus* family happiness, *plus* social happiness, *plus* universal happiness. And so too with efficiency. And when we do this, when we endeavour to promote the happiness and efficiency of others, we find that we have thereby increased our own individual happiness and efficiency. The happier and better my family, the happier and better am I as a member. The happier and better my country, the happier and better am I as an Englishman. "The well-being of each individual," writes Mr. Herbert Spencer, "is involved in the well-being of all. Whatever conduces to their vigour concerns him; for it diminishes the cost of everything he buys. Whatever conduces to their freedom from disease concerns him; for it diminishes his own liability to disease. Whatever raises their intelligence concerns him; for inconveniences are daily entailed on him by others' ignorance or folly. Whatever raises their moral character concerns him; for at every turn he suffers from the average unconscientiousness."

"This, then, turns out to be," some one may exclaim, "a system of pure selfishness. First, we are to aim at our own happiness for the sake of the community; but the happiness and efficiency of the community is to increase our own well-being, so that we come back to self as the centre of conduct." Nothing could be more erroneous, however, than to call this selfishness. Self-interest it may be; selfishness it undoubtedly is *not;* for selfishness is self-gratification *at the avoidable expense of others.* But on this system, not only is this expressly forbidden, but the promotion of the happiness of others is directly enjoined. It may even be doubted whether the highest social conduct is always to our own self-interest, though this doctrine is widely preached. "Honesty is the best policy," runs the old maxim; but to this there is the somewhat cynical gloss, that this depends on the efficiency of the police force. As the world is now constituted, it *pays* best to be about as honest as, perhaps a little more honest than, our neighbours. It does not pay to be much worse, it does not pay to be very much better. But since our aim is the increased efficiency and increased happiness of the community, and since no one can doubt that perfect honesty is for the universal happiness, it is our bounden duty to be honest and true, if need be, against our own interests. Our moral ideal must ever be in advance of the existing standard of conduct; and we must endeavour to act up to that ideal.

There is, I suppose, no thoroughly earnest man who is contented with his own moral conduct. There is always an interval between duty and conduct. And if at any moment conduct attains the standard of duty, a higher ideal is forthwith conceived and the interval is again reconstituted. "There is something truly infinite in duty," says Dr. Martineau; "it is a region which can never be enclosed." "The objection to ideals," writes Mr. G. H. Lewes, "on the ground of their surpassing human nature, is a misconception of their function. They are not the laws by which we live or can live, but the types by which we measure all deviations from a perfect life."

The pity of it is that there is not—there cannot be, as the world is now constituted—a rule of absolute right. It is the conflict of right that constitutes our main difficulty in conduct. In five cases out of six there is no right course, but only a less wrong. To a man who is forced to hesitate between telling a lie and betraying a friend, there is no right course. He can only choose the less wrong. Shakespeare has made his Hamlet see this. For him there was no right. Circumstances forced upon him the duty of revenge. And Shakespeare clearly indicates that, for Hamlet, this revenge was a duty. But the prince hesitates from conscientiousness. He cannot bring himself to do the lesser wrong, which was for him the only right. And his failure in duty involves the ruin and destruction of Ophelia whom he loved, of Polonius his beloved's father, of his friends Guildenstern and Rosencrantz, of Laertes, and of his mother. Every day the conflict of duties presses on all of us. Our religious duty is in conflict with our duty to the state; our home duties are at variance with duties more widely social; our patriotic duties are at issue with the claims of universalism. In each case the individual has individually to choose the relative right or lesser wrong.

If we look forward to the future, however, we may perhaps dimly (alas, how dimly!) foresee a time when this conflict of duties shall have vanished, or, at least, shall have become less perplexing. Even now for us the conflict is less severe than it was for our forefathers. Day by day, in fact, conduct becomes easier; and yet day by day it becomes more difficult. Easier to attain a given moderate standard; more difficult to reach the higher standard we at once conceive. Day by day the performance of right actions becomes more habitual; and yet day by day fresh habits of right living have to be acquired. Still, throughout this constantly progressive modification of conduct, there is a tendency for stern duty to pass into pleasure, and, as it does so, for the coercive sense of obligation to become evanescent. We have before seen that the coercion which was originally exercised from without becomes, in moral man, a part of conscience, and is exercised from within. We now see that as conduct more nearly approaches perfection, the coercion becomes a less and less important element, and eventually vanishes when duty and pleasure become one. We see the process in the individual just as we see it in the race. The child must be firmly guided in his actions by *external coercion;* as boyhood passes into manhood, irksome tasks are performed under the *internal coercion* of a sense of duty. Eventually these tasks are no longer irksome; their performance has become one of the highest *pleasures* of adult life. The critical moment of life is that in which the external coercion is partially withdrawn and the lad is master of his own actions. Then it is that he has consciously to struggle upwards towards the right, in spite of temptations many and great. He drills himself, puts pressure upon himself, and strives to keep the narrow way. And gradually as he does so, and, in the similar development of the race, as his fellows do so, his right actions and those of his fellows become instinctive. The actions which were painfully performed from a sense of right are now performed at once, naturally, without sense of effort, almost without thought. And eventually the perfect man shall be he who does right instinctively, in whom there is no thought even of wrong. For him shall perfect right be perfect happiness. Many good men see this evanescence of the sternness of duty, and it gives them pain. They look round them and see that the world is better, purer, truer, than it has ever been before ; and yet something is wanting ; the old types of men, great and good in spite of a wicked world around, in spite of warring passions within, these have well-nigh passed away. Mr. Lecky points this out, and seems to mourn that "as civilization advances, the heroic type will become more and more rare, and a kind of self-indulgent goodness more common." Nor is this mourning unnatural. In times of perfect peace some are always to be found to look back with longing eyes on the .pomp and circumstance of war. But others love the times of peace, and look forward with longing eyes to the time when perfect right shall have become one with perfect happiness.

THE END.

PRINTED BY WILLIAM CLOWES AND SONS, LIMITED, LONDON AND BECCLES.